The Red Velvet Turnshoe

Also by Cassandra Clark

Hangman Blind

The Red Velvet Turnshoe

CASSANDRA CLARK

Minotaur Books ⚏ New York

THE RED VELVET TURNSHOE. Copyright © 2009 by Cassandra
Clark. All rights reserved. Printed in the United States of America.
For information, address St. Martin's Press, 175 Fifth Avenue,
New York, N.Y. 10010.

www.minotaurbooks.com

Library of Congress Cataloging-in-Publication Data

Clark, Cassandra.
    The red velvet turnshoe / Cassandra Clark. — 1st U.S. ed.
        p. cm.
    ISBN 978-0-312-53736-4
    1. Nuns—England—Fiction. 2. Relics—Fiction.
3. Great Britain—History—Richard II, 1377–1399—Fiction.
4. Europe—History—1492–1648—Fiction. I. Title.
PR6103.L3724R43 2009
823'.92—dc22

                                                    2009028474

First published in Great Britain by John Murray (Publishers),
an Hachette UK Company

First U.S. Edition: December 2009

10   9   8   7   6   5   4   3   2   1

To Kingsford

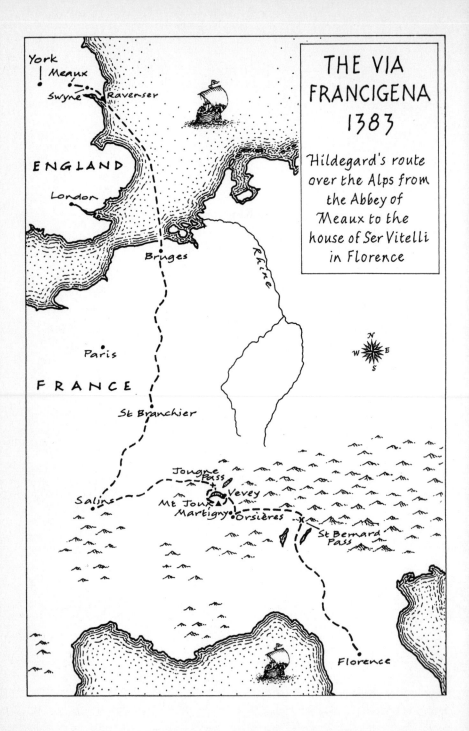

I

Black February in the year 1383: the rains started before Martinmas and swept throughout Europe, bringing floods, murrain and the plague. They did not cease until St Lucy's Day when a brief respite lasted until the new year. After Epiphany they returned with greater force and had not stopped since.

Floods bring famine. Famine brings disease. The Black Death bestowed its grace from town to town. When the buboes appeared the end came swiftly. Bodies were piled in open pits. The lime was spread. Panic flew from Avignon to Stockholm. Paris shut its gates. Cologne and Florence followed suit. In the crowded streets within the city walls, the chanting of the doomed continued night and day while barefoot flagellants scourged themselves and walked through blood.

Prologue

The sound of rain falling in the garth and the gurgling of the sluices became a constant accompaniment to the holy offices of the day at the English abbey of Meaux. Water brimmed over the margins of the dykes, the canal burst its banks, and the land reclaimed by the monks over six generations returned to marsh. Drowned sheep with bloated bodies wallowed in the brackish waters. The abbey itself, pinnacled and serene, was reflected in the standing pools, like a palace in a magic lake.

In another part of the county, two men were talking secretly within the upper chamber of a castle by the sea. The younger of the two listed allies and enemies and gazed through the lancet at the grey surge of the northern ocean where it reached to the rain-bellied sky. Breakers crashing on the rocks two hundred feet below sounded like a siege-ram battering the castle's foundations. The guest, shrouded in an expensive velvet cloak, with fur at his neck and a ring on his first finger, inched his goblet towards his host, indicating that he wanted it refilling.

The younger man reached for the wine flagon with an ill grace. 'So can we count on your brother or not?' he demanded. 'After all, he is admiral of the northern fleet.'

'Leave my brother to me,' advised his guest evenly. 'More important is this question of sedition.'

'My bloodhound has been dispatched. He'll finish the job.'

The man in the velvet cloak raised his brows.

'I was sent north with a task to do and I'm doing it,' snarled the younger man.

The guest sipped his wine and made no comment.

*　　*　　*

At this same time shortly after Candlemas when darkness came early, a lone figure appeared out of the gauzy air not far from the abbey of Meaux. He was wading through the puddles on a ribbon of track that wound through the marsh, travelling from an easterly direction, from the iron-bound coast across the moors. It meant the wind was at his back so that his tattered cloak flew before him and hurled his hood over his face.

As he approached the abbey his progress slowed. Before risking each step he began to prod the pools before him with a stave of hazelwood and only when he was convinced that he was not going to plunge in up to his neck did he go forward. In this way he reached the drier ground of the foregate and came to a halt. There was no one about. Pulling his hood more securely over his face, he turned onto a narrow path that ran along beside the abbey wall. Still testing the ground like a man who trusts nothing, he proceeded until he came to a back gate set under a small, stone arch. He slipped through like a shadow. The gate creaked as he closed it, the sound instantly lost in the roar of water gushing between the banks of the canal.

Hastening into the shadow between two buildings, the traveller peered across the garth towards the gatehouse. A few flurries of snow were beginning to fall from out of the freezing fog that crawled over the slant rooves.

He had been walking across country for five days. His boots were encrusted with mud to the knees. His nails were black-rimmed. The hand-bindings worn as protection from the pinching frost were torn and caked with dirt.

A guttering flare was brought out of the gatehouse, lighting up the scene and gilding each separate snowflake, as if gold coin fell from heaven. The traveller watched them turning and tumbling out of the void.

A group of pilgrims had preceded him. They were jostling in a cheerful bunch within the lambent glow of the flare while a ruddy-faced porter took down their names and destinations. By the sound of their voices they relished the imminent prospect of food and bed.

A bell began a summons to the next office. Compline, he thought with satisfaction. He had timed it perfectly.

★   ★   ★

Joining the tail-end of the group, he soon found himself sitting in the warmth of the refectory, holding out a trencher for some thin gruel. No one questioned him. He bit into the bread. It was sour. As soon as he had taken his fill he would get a horse from some unsuspecting fellow traveller and be on his way. He glanced round at the other guests. They were living in a dream of angels and incense; the real world was a different place.

Living rough, dodging the law all winter, he had hatched a plan in the long hours of darkness. An old Welsh astrologer in Scarborough market place had set his seal on it. 'The time is nigh!' he had told him and a lot more besides that didn't make sense. But holding back until the time was at its most auspicious made it sweet.

It had been November when the nun had nearly done for him. He could be dead now but for his brute will to survive.

His fingers touched the scar that ran crookedly down the side of his face. She had disfigured him as surely as if she had hurled the rocks at him herself. God's bollocks, the mare had all but drowned him.

Wiping his mouth, he got up and left the pilgrims cackling among themselves.

He had business here. It meant gold in his pocket. But after that he would be off, first to the nun in the priory at Swyne, then on the road to the killing fields. He would go by way of Ravenser, taking ship to Flanders, then over the mountains and down into Lombardy. There he would join one of the free companies, maybe the one commanded by John Hawkwood, the greatest mercenary of them all.

His grandmother, the heartless old crone, had told him one thing: shift or starve. But he had had enough of starving. And he had had enough of being treated like a dog in his own country. He would get clear of the place and make his fortune. It was sure, neither God nor man would do it for him.

But first, and maybe best, to Swyne.

Chapter One

N ARROW FLEW through the air with a hiss. There was a thump as it hit the target. Hildegard, clad in her white habit of unbleached stamyn and high knee-boots, went to withdraw it.

The orchard where she was practising was covered in mist. It was a bitter February morning and the bare branches of the apple trees were rimed with frost. But at least it had stopped raining and the snow had not settled.

From over by the wattle fence separating the orchards from the priory kitchen garden, a voice called a greeting. It was Lord Roger de Hutton's steward, Sir Ulf. Lanky and good-natured, he wore a smile behind his clipped blond beard as he asked, 'Expecting trouble, Sister?'

Hildegard watched him wade through the wet grass towards her. Her spirits lifted. 'What brings you over here, sir? Life at Castle Hutton too dull for you?'

'Never! Not with Lord Roger around!' His glance fell to the bow she was holding. 'Are you sisters planning on becoming archers as well?'

'In time, maybe. It's just a precaution.'

Ulf towered over Hildegard although she was a tall woman and when he looked down into her face, flushed now with the cold and the exercise, his eyes took on a serious cast. 'You've no need to worry. The grange you'll lease from Roger has never been attacked. Not even when the Scots were raiding every summer. It's too remote.'

'I know that. But there's no point in trusting to luck. Not in these times.'

She didn't need to explain. The people's rising in London during the feast of Corpus Christi when young King Richard was still only fourteen had been the culmination of years of unrest. The leaders and their most prominent followers had been exterminated under the orders of John of Gaunt, the king's uncle, and those who had survived the bloodbath had fled to the woods. Now, two years later, they still had no choice but to live outside the law in poverty and desperation. The threat that worried Hildegard, however, was not from the brotherhoods and companies of the outlawed. It was the threat of invasion by the French with the Duke of Burgundy at their head.

'Whatever happens we'll be prepared,' she repeated.

'You should stay here at Swyne where you'd have the protection of my men-at-arms and the stout men of Beverley,' Ulf advised.

'But if there is an invasion, Roger's going to call on you to muster to the king's aid. You won't be here to defend us. And if intelligence brought from France is correct, it's likely to be at Ravenser where they'll try to breach our defences, not in the south where they know they'll meet with opposition.'

Ulf frowned. She was right. Once married to a knight killed some years ago in the wars in France, she had no illusions about the dangers they might face if the rumours turned out to be true.

If it came to open battle, the northern landowners like his own lord, Roger de Hutton, feared that the abbots of Rievaulx, Jervaulx, Fountains and Meaux would place their allegiance with their mother house in France. As Cistercians they were allied with Clement, the false pope in Avignon. England supported Pope Urban in Rome. With rival popes throwing in their support it could become a bloody contest for power with nothing less than the Crown of England at stake.

He took her bow and ran his hands over it. 'What's this?' he asked, trying to keep his tone light. 'Spanish yew?'

'Nothing but the best for us.' Hildegard smiled, knowing what was on his mind.

'Your prioress must have money to burn.' Without appearing to check the distance or the target he loosed off an arrow. It hit the bull squarely with a thump.

Hildegard took back her bow.

'I doubt whether I can match that,' she said. Taking careful aim, she loosed an arrow. To her satisfaction it split Ulf's arrow firmly down the middle.

After vespers later that same day a servant found Hildegard in the cloisters and informed her that the prioress wished to speak to her. She made her way across the garth to the prioress's lodging.

It was bleak inside. The stone antechamber had nothing in it but a chest bound in iron standing on the cold flags. The prioress herself was nowhere to be seen but candlelight glowed from within her private chapel deep inside the building. Hildegard stepped over the threshold. As if formed from the frosty air itself, the prioress appeared in the distant doorway. She gestured for the nun to approach, then closed the door behind her.

It felt even colder inside the chapel. The massive slabs of York stone from which it was constructed trapped the air and made it dank. Several guttering candles stood on a small altar. Between them a panel painting depicted the virgin and child. It was the only ornament. Blue and gold, it glowed in the flames' light, bringing the incandescence of magic to the vault.

The prioress's face was framed in a tight wimple of spotless linen. She had a raw, unprotected look, her narrow nose somewhat red at the tip, that made her seem more frail, more human. As usual, however, she conducted the conversation while standing.

'I have an errand for you, Sister. One I believe you may relish. But first, tell me if anything interesting passed between you and Lord Roger's steward this morning.'

'I understand he was here to discuss that matter of litigation over the grange at Frismersk,' replied Hildegard.

'Oh that, yes, that's Roger's excuse for sending him. Did he mention where his lord was?'

'He told me he was on his way to Meaux. Ulf was sent on ahead and that's why he decided to take the opportunity to come over here to settle things with us.'

'Good. And it is settled – and not at all to our disadvantage.' The prioress smiled with pleasure. 'So Lord Roger's descending on

Meaux, eh? Now why would he want to do that? Is it only to see the dispatch of the staple he's sending to Flanders?'

'Ulf said something else, about using it as a base for meeting an armourer from York.'

'He did, did he?' This piece of information evidently interested the prioress very much but Hildegard could tell her nothing more.

The prioress, however, hadn't finished. 'He brought Roger's clerk with him, I understand?' For someone who rarely seemed to leave her cell she was remarkably well informed.

'He did.'

Hildegard had met the clerk, briefly, and thought him a gaudy fellow, dressed in a most unclerical green hood with a long liripipe of purple and red, which he wore twisted round his head in the manner of a sultan.

'Something's afoot,' murmured the prioress as if forgetting for a moment that one of her nuns was present.

Hildegard paid careful heed. Perhaps she was being asked to find out why Roger suddenly needed the services of an armourer. Maybe she would even be ordered to Meaux to see what was going on. The thought of the abbot, Hubert de Courcy, distracted her for a moment until she brought her attention back to what the prioress was saying.

When she realised what she was being asked to do, Hildegard gazed at her in astonishment.

Back in the cloister she paced the stones, scarcely aware of the deafening roar of rainwater jetting from the overflowing gutters.

It began with Alexander Neville, the Archbishop of York. He had asked the prioress a most extraordinary favour. He wanted her to send a nun secretly to Rome to bring back the legendary cross of Constantine.

When Hildegard had looked sceptical the prioress had taken time to explain. Everyone knew that Constantine had been converted in York where he had been a mere consul – although some still claimed it was a deathbed conversion. Be that as it may, his father, the Roman emperor, had named him as his successor. There were six other claimants. But when Constantine faced the army of Maxentius at the Milvian Bridge near Rome a cross of flame had appeared in the sky. It was seen as a sign from God that he was the chosen emperor. The story went that living fire inscribed the words: 'In this I will conquer.'

The archbishop had decided he wanted the small wooden cross Constantine had carried into battle. 'Bring it home to York – and at any price,' his grace told the prioress, hinting that the reason he wanted it so badly was so he could compete with the Talking Crucifix of Meaux. Famous in its own small way for its prophetic powers, it attracted pilgrims to the abbey in their hundreds, bringing money there instead of taking it to the shrine of St William at York.

The prioress had given Hildegard a thin smile. 'That's his avowed reason for wanting it back,' she had said, 'but we can assume there's more to it. I don't need to tell you how well his grace will reward us should we accomplish this small errand.'

Small errand? The long and dangerous journey to Rome was no small errand. And Hildegard's alarm had increased when she heard that the cross, its whereabouts kept secret for centuries, was believed to confer almost supernatural powers on those who possessed it. With Gaunt's opposition to King Richard mounting by the day, it was clear the cross would be a valuable asset for Gaunt, or even a talisman to be used by the king himself against his enemy.

They had been alone and unobserved in the private chapel. The walls were thick and the candles on the altar shed only a weak light. Whatever was said here would disappear like smoke into the shadows and yet Hildegard had nerved herself to query the archbishop's allegiance.

The prioress held her glance, her eyes unexpectedly luminous, and withheld a direct answer. 'Tread carefully, Hildegard,' she warned. 'Remain unnoticed. There will be spies from Avignon, Burgundy, Flanders and from England too. No one, not your confessor, your closest confidante, nor any priest or monk – and certainly not the lord abbot of Meaux – must know that you are on the trail of something with such importance for the safety of our king.'

Hildegard shuddered. A feeling of dread had swept over her but she had risked an objection. 'I was promised that when I found a suitable grange I could set up my own religious house with seven nuns to help heal the sick and teach the children of the villeins to read and write. Yet now—'

The prioress had nodded. 'That promise will be kept.'

'But—'

'When you return from Rome you will find no further obstacle to your desire. Indeed,' she added significantly, 'you will find help from the highest quarters.'

The usual forthright manner of the prioress had softened as she shifted one of the candles as if its guttering flame were a distraction.

When she had repositioned it she said, 'I suggest you take one of these new bills of exchange instead of gold. Easier to carry. But don't mention it unless absolutely necessary. I also suggest a pilgrimage as a suitable cover for you. And of course it will be prudent to approach the lord abbot for permission. Be warned,' she fixed her with a stern glance, 'we do not know where his loyalties lie. He must know nothing of your true purpose!'

Hildegard had one further objection, even though she knew it was useless. 'The abbot will be surprised to find I wish to go on pilgrimage at such a time—'

'On the contrary,' the prioress had countered, 'he will think it perfectly natural to seek confirmation of your faith before embarking on the toil of setting up a house of your own.'

There was no refuting her. Hubert de Courcy might be astonished by the abruptness of her decision but he would not be surprised by her alleged purpose.

Chapter Two

IT WAS EARLY the next morning when, well girded against the weather, Hildegard was preparing to set out for the abbey of Meaux.

The prioress searched her out where she was busy gathering a few vegetables in the kitchen garden to take to the abbey cooks. 'Ah, Sister!' she exclaimed with a quick glance round to see whether they were being overheard. 'I just want to stress how important it is that we satisfy the archbishop in this errand. The existence of our little priory depends on it.' She lowered her voice. 'He could have us closed down like that!' She snapped her fingers. 'What would our sisters do then? Where would they go? What refuge would our labourers and their families have? Not to mention the destitute and the dying who come to us in their final hours?'

Hildegard rose to her feet and thrust some leeks into a basket on her arm. 'I'll do whatever I can to fulfil our purpose,' she vowed. 'I will not fail.'

Later, as Hildegard rode the track to Meaux, she imagined the hazards that lay ahead. Meaux was only an hour's ride. Multiply that by the many hours it would take to travel one thousand miles to Rome when every step led deeper into danger, the weeks and months stretching ahead. It would be summer before she would see home once more.

Her horse plodded to the end of the lane that led to the abbey and her fears suddenly vanished as Meaux appeared in all its grace and beauty. She looked with love on its silvery walls, the bell-tower, the stone arches of its many buildings, the way the light slanted across the great court, and within the quiet halls, as she knew, the silent, serious, kindly monks would be going about their tasks in the peaceful order of their days.

Even the dull light of February and the devastation of the floods could not detract from its harmony.

And, of course, it owed its perfection to the will of one man, Hubert de Courcy.

Peace was in poor evidence, however, when she rode the mud-spattered palfrey through the gatehouse and onto the garth. The abbot kept some fine horses but now these were augmented by a dozen more. Lord Roger and his retinue had arrived before her.

The de Hutton men in their distinctive livery of scarlet and gold were all over the place, shouting orders, making sure their mounts were being sufficiently well attended, joshing and jostling each other in their usual boisterous manner. Not that they should have any doubts about the care taken with their animals. The abbey lay servants, the conversi, cheerfully dealt with every shouted command, treating the animals like royalty.

When a stable lad hurried forward to take the reins of her own horse, Hildegard handed them over with thanks. Now to business. It would be best to seek audience with the abbot before Lord Roger had chance to come bustling between them. She sent a boy pell-mell with her request then made her way over to the guest lodge for a warming glass of wine while she waited for his response.

'Pilgrimage?' The abbot looked stunned. His handsome features froze. 'You have need of such?' he demanded in an accusing tone.

Hildegard made an all-purpose dip of her head. He had been standing by the casement in his parlour with a book in his hand when she entered. Gratified that he had so quickly agreed to see her, she was chilled by his manner. He remained at a distance, staring at her with unfathomable dark eyes down the long length of the chamber.

There had been no welcoming smile on his face when she went in. Indeed, he had seemed put out by her appearance as if there were more pressing matters on his time and he wished to get rid of her as quickly as possible. In consequence she had announced her petition simply and clearly if somewhat briskly. Indeed, if he had been so inclined, he might have read her own manner as cold too. Now he seemed to take great care to match it.

'Why Rome?' he snapped.

This was a question she had not expected, for surely it was obvious? Swallowing, she managed to stutter, 'It is the great mother of the Church.'

'Not Avignon then?' he flashed back with the air of having scored a point.

She remained silent. Rumours about his allegiance flooded in. The atmosphere chilled by several degrees and she felt as if she were standing in a blizzard.

The last time they had met – in the garden beneath this very window last autumn – the mutual warmth that had been kindled then had been stoked over the intervening winter months by the exchange of gifts: a small leather-bound book containing the writings of a German nun he thought she might find interesting, a silk stole to add to his collection from the priory at Swyne, not made entirely by my own hand, she had hastened to tell the go-between, not wishing for compliments where none were deserved. Then there had been produce from the gardens at Meaux: choice cabbages, a fat peach, a trivet of rose stems covered in small buds, the season so late that they never opened.

She should have seen the symbolism of that. In happy ignorance she had replied by sending several trusses of dried lavender and rosemary and three kinds of mint to sweeten the masculine atmosphere at the abbey.

Now it was all as nothing. He was looking at her with an expression bordering on distaste. What had she done? Had he heard some rumour and made the mistake of believing it? She was confident her reputation was unsmirched.

His eyes were cold as they swept her face and she noticed how sunken they were. It gave him a haunted look. His skin was taut over the sharp bones of his face. He was as pale as death.

Putting his book down, he made a rough gesture with his free hand. His jaw clenched. 'Go then. Go to Rome! Have my permission! Do you imagine I'll stop you?'

He picked the book up again, opened it, pretended to read. It was a dismissal as definite as a slap across the face.

She faltered. Then, fumbling towards the door, she went out with an expression as coldly indifferent as his own.

Only when she reached the solitude of her guest chamber did she allow herself to rage – silent, furious, hurt.

She threw herself onto her bed.

Had she expected him to deny her this opportunity to visit Rome? She would, she knew, have had to resist. It wasn't that. No, what she had wanted – what little she had wanted – was some show of concern for her safety. The horror of the journey filled her mind but it was as nothing to the feeling that the thing she valued – his concern, his regard? – had for some inexplicable reason been withdrawn.

She sat up, set her mouth in a firm line and brushed a hand across her eyes.

To Rome then.

And as soon as possible.

Lord Roger's steward, Ulf, came storming into the guest-house kitchen like a tornado. The cook, master in his own domain, stepped forward grasping a knife. 'My lord?' He held the knife at chest level but, eyes wary, forced himself to make a bow.

Ulf elbowed him to one side. His gaze alighted on Hildegard sitting quietly at a bench with a basket of onions on her lap. She raised her head.

'Is it true you're going on pilgrimage to Rome?'

'Why yes, I—'

'Are you mad?'

Before she could protest he went on, 'Do you know what that route is like? You'll have to go through Flanders! Have you forgotten the battle of Roosebeeke already? Have you any idea how desperate the survivors from that bloody episode are by now? They're starving, they'll stop at nothing to rape a nun for no better reason than hatred. They see all Church folk siding with the Count of Mâle. And that's not all. The companies of mercenaries are on the rampage. If you escape one you'll not escape the other. How do they earn a living? By slitting the throat of anybody with anything they might happen to want. If not gold, then flesh. And there's more. What about the swindlers and cheats that frequent the inns along the way, outlaws, pardoners, fake friars lying in wait to rip the cloak from the back of any innocent that passes by? And then there's the journey itself. Have you given a thought to that? The snow? The Alps? Have you ever seen a mountain? A real mountain? Have you seen one in winter? Have you ever tried to cross a ravine on a rope bridge? And then there's the Black Death, rife in every town and vill from Bruges to the gates of Rome itself. Hildegard, please. Think again!'

His glance held hers.

'Please,' he said more quietly.

She was conscious of the faces agog at everything they had just heard. 'I'm not ignorant of the dangers,' she managed as calmly as she could. 'I'm also aware that many pilgrims make this passage without hap or harm. Why should I not be one of them?'

Ulf's scowl deepened. 'I can't believe the abbot gave his permission. Is the man mad? Does he not give one single jot for your safety?'

Hildegard flinched.

Suddenly the steward swivelled on his heel. 'I'll confront him. And if he doesn't change his view I'll see him in hell!'

With that he strode violently from the kitchen. Everyone stood open-mouthed. Hildegard came to her senses first. She picked up the hem of her robe and ran after him.

'Ulf! Stop!'

He was already halfway across the great court, heading with long strides towards the abbot's lodging.

She increased her pace and by the time he was at the door she had almost caught up with him. She was just in time to see the prior, frail and silvery and standing on his dignity, put out a restraining hand. 'Sire, you cannot enter the abbot's private chambers—' But Ulf swept on and disappeared inside. There was the sound of raised voices. A door slammed.

After a brief pause the abbot's scribe appeared, wringing his hands. To the prior he said, 'I couldn't stop him! He's gone straight in!' The prior answered by fluttering his fingers and raising his eyes to heaven.

An alarming silence followed.

Before anybody could summon the nerve to go in to see who was being murdered, Ulf reappeared. He was looking somewhat shame-faced. The abbot followed. He stood in the doorway looking out at the crowd in the great court, taking in his fluttering prior, his worried scribe, and Hildegard.

Their eyes met with arctic brevity. He turned back inside.

Biting his lip, Ulf set off towards the guest lodging without another word. With a sigh, Hildegard returned to her task in the kitchen.

'Sounds as if you made a bloody fool of yourself.' Lord Roger didn't mince words. 'What the devil did Hubert say to you when you burst into his private chamber?'

'He said Hildegard was free to do as her conscience told her and we should all be humbled by her piety,' Ulf mumbled.

'I heard there was a bit of a scuffle though.'

Lady Melisen stepped forward, sliding her fingers inside Roger's tunic. 'Oh, sweetkin, do let be. You need a steward with a fiery nature, otherwise everybody would trample all over you.'

Momentarily distracted, he kissed her fingers one by one. 'My little martlet,' he murmured then jerked his head up and rumbled something incomprehensible before guiding Melisen, his young fifth wife – no more than a year older than Philippa, his eldest child – to a chair heaped with stitched fox pelts.

He swivelled to face his steward. 'Don't let it happen again, that's all. I've got plans and I don't want you upsetting them. Is that clear?'

'It is, my lord. However – ' Ulf leaned forward urgently, 'I was thinking, as you're about to send a cargo of staple to Bruges with Ser Ludovico in exchange for the—'

'What of it?' Roger interrupted with odd-seeming haste.

'Well, in view of the fact that Sister Hildegard is determined to set out on this foolhardy pilgrimage, might I suggest, sire, that the sister at least has the protection of the armed baggage train as far as Bruges?' He turned to her. 'From there you can find a merchant with an armed escort to take you over the Alps.' He turned back. 'I know how fond of the sister you are, sire, and would only blame yourself if, through the abbot's cold disregard for her safety, she should come to harm.' He eyed Roger expectantly.

Roger pulled at his beard and after a moment looked at Hildegard. 'I won't ask why you're intent on going to Rome but of course I won't let you travel all that way without protection. Let's have some music while we plot and plan this venture. Minstrel?'

A sulky youth appeared, carrying a lute.

'Play something quiet and thoughtful, Pierrekyn, while we talk.' With a glance at his wife he added, 'I heard you murmur something about a new pair of sleeves, my lady. Why don't you give Sister Hildegard your list of desires? While she's in Flanders she can make a few costly purchases for us if she will.' He glanced round the chamber. 'Where's that mincing clerk of mine to write up the list?' Everyone shrugged. 'God's teeth! Reynard?' he bellowed. 'Where the devil are you?'

When the clerk failed to respond Roger snorted with impatience. 'Ever since he came back from Kent he's been as elusive as a bevy of ghosts. Somebody fetch the losel. He'll be in his bed, no doubt.'

He turned to Hildegard with a majestic smile. 'You can keep my men out of fights and taverns for me, Sister. And you might cast an eye over Ser Ludovico's activities as well. Ulf will explain. You leave the day after tomorrow!' With that he swept out, shouting, 'Reynard? Work to do! Come forth!'

Hildegard gazed after him in astonishment. Ludovico? Sleeves? And so soon? She shrugged helplessly. 'I'll need new boots!' she told the nearest person standing by.

Chapter Three

AS IT HAPPENED she had no need to return to Swyne for final orders or, indeed, for anything else. The prioress dispatched her personal servant as soon as she was informed of Hildegard's imminent departure.

In addition, a new pair of buskins suitable for all terrain were cut and stitched in short order. The pattern-cutter, who had come to Meaux to measure Lord Roger for a suit of armour, thought nothing of dashing off a pattern for some boots. It was handed to a shoemaker in Beverley as the armourer rode through on his return to York and the finished boots appeared late the next day. Hildegard pulled them on, then stamped about in them to soften the leather and tried to imagine the many miles they would have to last before she eventually returned to Yorkshire.

Up in her cell she ticked things off. Boots: made. She wriggled her toes. Knife: sharpened. She slipped it into the sheath on her belt. Scrip: packed. It was stuffed with foot balm, stomach powders, linen bandages, and had taken most of the day to find and prepare. With these necessities she rolled up in a small bundle a spare undershift, a light summer habit and a pair of much darned woollen leggings. On top of all that came her missal in its leather pouch.

There was one more thing.

The prioress's servant had met her discreetly in an empty chamber off the cloister.

He drew something from his sleeve and handed it over. 'The bill of exchange,' he whispered. 'She says to guard it with your life!'

It was now tucked inside a secret pocket in her belt. She ran her fingers round and felt the slight bulge of the folded sheet of vellum. It was the price of the cross of Constantine.

Shadows were lengthening across the inner court as she made her way down to the wool-sheds with everyone else to witness the final stages of the packing of the staple. The high-roofed timber shed was a fog of wool fibres. Cressets were lit, casting a misty glow over everyone and making the shadows leap along the bales.

Wool was sold in two ways, as clip or skins, and graded as either good, middle or young. After that it had to be weighed and corded up into sarples for ease of taxation. After the St Martinmas slaughter the skins with wool still on them, the fells, had been snapped up by Ser Ludovico, an envoy sent by the Vitelli company in Florence. He had also made an offer for the clip that Lord Roger, after much negotiation, had accepted.

The skins were now being sacked up, two hundred and forty to a sack, and by tomorrow the entire consignment would have been loaded onto packhorses for departure at dawn. The clip was also ready to go and formed a soft wall deep inside the shed

Roger had already made his entrance when Hildegard slipped in through the doors. He was accompanied by Ludovico and a large and gossiping retinue of household servants.

Ludovico was the darkly handsome Florentine banker betrothed to Roger's daughter, Philippa, and was accompanied by his own retinue as befitted his status. He stood by, smiling and silent, while Roger strode about the sheds, getting in everybody's way, seeing, no doubt, not wool but gold ingots stacked up. He was due to make a handsome profit even though there was a tax of thirty-three per cent on exports. The northern lords, including the abbots, had been given a special dispensation from the king to send their staple through Ravenser to Flanders instead of from London to Calais where the rest of the wool export was sent. Well pleased with this arrangement, Roger was saying, 'Think of the saving we're making on carriers' costs, let alone insurance against pirates in the Bay of Biscay!'

'Top-quality wool is this,' said his foreman, equally pleased. He went to stand beside the cellarer from Meaux. Both men were covered in fibres but were grinning with satisfaction just like Lord

Roger. It was the crowning achievement of a year of hard labour for the floods had meant many sheep had been lost on the more vulnerable pastures. The bad weather had hit Meaux harder than de Hutton where the chalk uphills were well drained. But now both domains were content. The harvest of wool was gathered home.

The packers were still cording the fells as the light waned, stacking them in great soft bales, to leave narrow passageways between. The shed was full of shadows by the time they called a temporary halt to have a bite to eat and drink before finishing the job.

Everybody lingered. The bales and the skins inside the sacks were being marked with the owner's stamp: 'de H' for Roger de Hutton above a small image of a castle on a hill, and the initials 'Mls' indicating the abbey of Meaux, over the sign of the cross to show its monastic origin. Mls stood for Melsa, the Latin name by which the abbey was referred to in its charters and legal documents. It meant honey, a place of sweetness and delight, Hildegard remembered, her heart heavy.

Despite the bustling of the final preparations, she felt sharply aware of time fleeting by. She stood apart from the others, unable to share their excitement at the prospect of the great convoy about to set off into the unknown. Soon, she thought miserably, the sheds would be empty, the labourers gone, and nothing would remain. Even Roger's liveried servants in their scarlet and gold would be forgotten, the monks and their saintly toil gone as if they had never existed. All things pass like time and glass.

She avoided the feast Lord Roger laid on later and instead walked slowly back along the lane towards the guest house.

The decision to leave had been too sudden, she decided as she reached the gate. There had been no chance to say farewell to anyone at Swyne – and who knew whether she would survive the dangers of the journey.

All day the bell had been calling the monks to the various offices. The prior had conducted one set of prayers at tierce, the sacristan had seen to sext and nones. At vespers the abbot was still nowhere to be seen and the prior had appeared again.

Now the purplish light of evening increased her sense of the end of things. Soon, she thought, even our names will be unremembered in the fall of days.

Angry with herself for being unable to join in the general merriment, she lingered on the garth for a final breath of air before turning in and scarcely noticed the steward as he came striding down the lane from the direction of the packing sheds until he planted himself in front of her. At his heels was one of the abbot's young clerks.

'I'm still looking for Reynard,' he stated in a harassed tone. 'You haven't clapped eyes on him, have you, Sister?'

She shook her head.

'We've searched every nook and cranny and nobody's seen him since he went down to check on the staple yesterday.'

'I thought he was supposed to be travelling with the convoy to Bruges?'

'So he is. That's what's so enraging. It's the worst time to go missing, damn his eyes. Even young Pierrekyn knows nothing.'

'Who's that? Roger's new minstrel?'

'That one.' Ulf gave a sort of grimace. 'Reynard met him in Kent and got permission for the lad to travel back with him. Roger was overjoyed to have sent a clerk and got a minstrel and a contract in return. Good business, says he. Losing the clerk somewhat spoils the deal!'

'Is this contract you mention the trading agreement Roger was making with Melisen's father, the Earl of—?'

'You know about that, do you?'

'I suppose somebody must have mentioned it,' she replied, carefully.

Ulf was watching her closely. 'Are you worried about something?'

She nodded. 'I don't know what's the matter with me. I feel sick and confused. Maybe it's something I've eaten. I'll take an infusion of St John's Wort when I get back to my chamber.' She felt tears begin to prick her eyes.

'I've never seen you like this before.' He put a hand on her arm and, touching her sleeve, added, 'And this is thin stuff. I hope you've got a good, thick cloak to go over it for when you're in the Alps?'

'I'll be fine.'

'You won't be fine with frostbite or the rheum. Come and see Lady Melisen. She's got more cloaks than she knows what to do with.'

'I'm a Cistercian, not a mendicant—' she began but he was already escorting her along the lane towards the guest lodge, the young clerk running eagerly behind.

Melisen was more than happy to offer Hildegard a travelling cloak. First she had her maids bring out a scarlet one lined with squirrel. It was a heavy woollen fabric dyed in a sumptuous, eye-catching shade and was quite unsuitable for someone who wanted to travel unnoticed. Hildegard ran her fingers over it but said it was a colour her prioress would not allow.

'These sumptuary laws,' scoffed Melisen. 'Never mind, I've got lots more. Bring forth the green one with the cat-fur lining,' she told her maid. 'Oh, and there's that dark one of camlet with purple taffeta inside. And I do believe there's a blue wool with a sheepskin lining. Now that will suit you, Sister. Try it on. You're very fair. I would think blue is very much your colour. What do you think?' She hauled it out herself from the pile being strewn on the bed.

Feeling a little overwhelmed by Melisen's generosity and enthusiasm, Hildegard took up the cloak. She remembered liking blue in the past. It had been her husband Hugh's favourite colour.

At Melisen's insistence Hildegard was forced to try on several other cloaks until they decided on the blue one after all.

'That's just right, isn't it, Pierrekyn?' Melisen turned to the minstrel.

He stepped from out of the shadows. He had been so quiet Hildegard had not realised he was there.

'For a youth he has remarkably good taste,' said Melisen giving him a dig in the ribs. 'Go on, tell us your verdict.'

Tall, and as broad-shouldered as a ploughman, the boy still wore a sulky expression but despite that he was surprisingly good-looking, with full lips, a mop of dark copper-coloured curls and green eyes veiled by thick, dark lashes.

He eyed Hildegard consideringly and then cast his glance over the pile of cloaks. 'The blue, definitely,' he agreed before returning at once to his dark corner with his lute.

His fingers floated over the strings in a phrase from a *chanson* Hildegard recognised. It was a lament by a lover for his mistress: '*So fast the fetters of her love have bound me …*'

She glanced swiftly across at him but he was gazing innocently into space.

Hildegard was pleased with the cloak and thanked Melisen sincerely. It was a good blue but dark enough to allow her to pass unnoticed and warm enough for the worst the weather could unleash. The prioress would probably have expected her to wear a long white pilgrim's cloak but there was no time for that if she was to leave straight away. There was no time for anything.

She thought of the abbot again in a flood of confusion.

'This is so kind of you, my lady,' she repeated when a few other garments had been thrown onto the pile, a couple of fine wool shifts and a pair of red woollen hosen among them.

'It won't matter about your hose being red,' Melisen said, 'because nobody's likely to see and if they do then they're the ones at fault, not you.'

She also brought out a pair of mittens made of fur and to top it all a rather fine beaver hat.

'Now you hardly look like a nun at all!' she exclaimed when Hildegard tried on all the outer garments together. 'You're very good-looking for a nun. Roger never stops wondering why you didn't remarry. Anyway, I'm so immensely grateful you're going to bring me those sleeves. I've longed and longed for some ever since I saw the Duchess of Derby wearing a pair at court. They had little pearls sewn all over them. If you can manage to find some I'll be your friend for ever. And the brooches too,' she added. 'You won't forget those, will you?'

Hildegard made her way back to her chamber with her parcel of clothes. She wanted to get a good night's sleep in preparation for their early start. The brooches Melisen had described interested her. They were intended for her personal retinue and were to depict a white hart wearing a gold crown and chain.

It was the symbol used by King Richard as his own emblem. It had also been adopted by the rebels after they had been routed at Smithfield and their leader, Wat Tyler, had been done to death by the Mayor and his men.

The general view was that the promises made by the fourteen-year-old king were broken only under pressure from his ambitious uncles, the barons. It was Gaunt, above all, who had made the king renege.

Now men and women wore his symbol to show whose side they were on. Some of them let themselves be known as the Company of the White Hart as if they had formed a guild of rebels. Their enemies claimed they were bent on bloodshed and destruction, while their supporters claimed they would be the saviours of the common people and of the king himself. Gaunt had brought in draconian measures to forbid all kinds of associations and societies, making himself many enemies among the guildsmen in the process.

It was strange that Melisen should want brooches modelled on such a symbol, thought Hildegard as she got into bed. Maybe it was just a whim, a pretty device that had caught her eye. Her father's lands were down in Kent, of course, where the insurrection had been fomented. It might be worth remembering that.

They were due to leave in the pitch dark of early morning, but Ulf came banging on her door with an urgent request as soon as the household started to wake up.

'Reynard's still missing. It looks as if I'm going to have to leave without him. Before I go will you come along to surprise Pierrekyn from his slumbers? You're good at getting things out of folk and we might be able to startle the truth from him.'

'Surely.' Hildegard took her bag with her. There was nothing to come back here for. She took a last bleak look round the cell.

As they made their way out into the bitter cold she said, 'What's this Reynard like? Is he the type to go off without a word to anybody?'

'I wouldn't have thought so. He's a gregarious fellow. Always spouting off about something or other. Must be around thirty and old enough not to throw it all in for no good reason. He helped the notary draw up this contract I've mentioned, then he went down to Kent to get the earl to sign it. Roger was about to give him a handsome reward for his services.'

'And why should the minstrel know anything?'

Ulf did not answer but he was grim-faced as their feet crunched over the ice-filmed puddles in the garth.

There was no moon. Across the great court the monks were already filing into prime, cressets set along the passage revealing their hooded shapes as they moved between the stone pillars.

The steward led her to a part of the abbey she had never visited before – living quarters for the servants and lay brothers built on two storeys, located between the kitchens, the food stores and the packing sheds.

Puzzled, she asked, 'Won't the minstrel be staying in the guest house with the rest of the retinue from Castle Hutton?'

'Reynard keeps a chamber over here as his work often brings him to Meaux.' Again Ulf said little but merely set his lips in a tight line and Hildegard took it as a sign not to ask him to explain further.

Making little sound, they hurried up the narrow steps to the first floor. Ulf reached one of the doors and without bothering to knock hurled it open. A candle was burning in a niche and by its light they saw a figure stumble back from a high desk. Something fell to the floor and in the dim light they saw the minstrel back away against the wall, one hand reaching for his dagger.

'Take one step closer and you're dead!' he announced in a shaking voice.

'Shut up, you sot-wit. It's me, Lord Roger's steward. We're still looking for Reynard. Where is he?'

The youth slowly put the dagger back in his belt. 'Forgive me, my lord steward. You entered like an assassin.'

Ulf ignored the undercurrent in the youth's tone. 'Explain what you're doing.'

The abruptness of the command confused him. His glance flew to Hildegard for help. When she said nothing he shrugged and dropped his glance.

'So where is he?' Ulf demanded again

The boy's fear was replaced by anger. 'How in hell should I know where he is, steward? He's gone! Vanished! He dragged me all the way up here from Kent, with promises and fine words, and now what? I'm left with no master, nothing.' He gave a bitter laugh.

Ulf ignored it. 'Get your cloak and lute. You're coming with us to Bruges. Lord Roger's orders.'

The minstrel went very still and his anger seemed to vanish as quickly as it had arisen. In the flickering candlelight his eyes glinted but their expression was ambiguous. 'You mean I'm to be one of de Hutton's men and not just a follower?' he whispered.

'That's what I'm told,' said Ulf. He clearly had an opinion contrary to his lord's on the decision.

'Is this another lie?'

'Are you with us or not?'

Pierrekyn went over to the desk, he picked up one or two things from it and stowed them inside his bag. Then he fell to his knees and groped around on the floor to find what had fallen when they came in. He palmed it into a pouch on his belt and straightened up.

'Ready, my lord – when you are.'

Ulf gestured for him to go out, then followed closely at his heels as if half expecting him to make his escape.

'Are we really taking young Pierrekyn with us?' Hildegard whispered when the group assembled for departure. They were standing in the guest hall and wassail was being brought out.

'Why not? Don't you like music?'

'It depends what sort,' she replied. It was strange to be setting out with a secular party with all the vanities that would ensue. She touched her beaver hat with her fingertips.

By no means was she the only one dressed for the cold.

Lady Philippa, Roger's seventeen-year-old daughter, was garbed in a fetching set of mixed furs. Although she was not travelling with them, her betrothed was, and she had come down from her chamber to wish Ser Ludovico Godspeed. He had to return to the branch in Bruges to oversee the smooth exchange of goods and the onward passage of the wool purchase to the cloth-makers in Tuscany. He and Philippa held hands with eyes for no one else.

Next to them stood Lord Roger, a massive bearskin thrown over his nightshirt, one arm round his wife's girlish shoulders, his eyes quick and observant as he checked everything off on some mental list in his head. He looked pleased, thought Hildegard, like a card-player with a winning hand.

Lady Melisen too wore furs. They must have been snow marten or something else light and silvery, for the flares carried by the linksmen passing in and out of the hall made them glitter and turned her into a figure of shimmering light.

Roger and the abbot were sharing the carriers' costs. The staple from Meaux was placed at the beginning and end of the convoy with the de Hutton staple well protected in the middle.

'Not that he's afraid of brigands this side of the water,' said Ulf in an undertone when Hildegard remarked on this. They exchanged smiles. Then he cast a lugubrious glance at the two couples. 'It's like living in a *chanson*, what with Roger so besotted and Philippa and Ludovico acting like a pair of turtle-doves. I'll be glad to get out on the road with my men.'

'They surely have good cause to feel themselves in love, being so young and foolish,' replied Hildegard, gazing over at the younger pair. 'They'll soon learn that *amour* and love are two different things.'

'Maybe I'm just jealous.' Ulf looked into her face. She dropped her glance! 'Hildegard,' he said, lowering his voice, 'take care for your safety when I leave you in Bruges. I'm told there's going to be a knight engaged to escort you after we leave you there.'

'There's really no need for that. I can—'

He interrupted. 'It's already arranged.'

'By Roger?' she asked, surprised.

Ulf shook his head. 'I don't know who's footing the bill.'

Was it the prioress using her influence? she wondered. Both she and the archbishop had a vested interest in her safety.

A mass was said for the convoy by one of the abbot's priests and soon the wagons began to move off as the restless string of packhorses came to life.

With scores of cressets flickering against a mottled, pre-dawn sky, the convoy stretched ahead like a winding ribbon of light between the standing pools of the marshes. The entire retinue from Castle Hutton came to see them off. With the abbey brethren and the conversi, it was a large crowd. Hildegard's glance swept the faces of the well-wishers. There was one absentee: the abbot himself.

Ahead lay the sea port of Ravenser and the crossing to Flanders. In a little time the abbey at Meaux and all its inhabitants would be no more substantial than a shroud of turrets rising from the marsh.

Chapter Four

ORD ROGER HAD chosen Ravenser in preference to any of the other ports on the Humber for the good reason that his brother-in-law, Sir William of Holderness, had been responsible on behalf of the exchequer for collecting import and export taxes there. To have someone in the family in charge sometimes made life easier. Lately banished, however, William would by now be well on the road to Jerusalem as penance for his crimes. Meanwhile, Roger himself had taken over the lucrative role of tax collector. This trade was what kept the folk of Ravenser alive.

But it was a wild place.

Continually inundated by the sea on one side and the mighty tides of the Humber estuary on the other, the port lay at the end of a long, narrow spit of shingle that was slowly being squeezed out of existence. Some claimed this was a punishment from God for the many crimes of incest and piracy that prevailed in the small town. Others knew it was the combined forces of tide and storm that were pressing it to the point of annihilation.

Nowadays it could be approached only by a mile-long track, clamorous with sea birds and the constant rustle of the salt-water grasses that fringed the remains of a Roman road. They said a beacon had been built on the point as part of the great chain of communication that kept marauders from this far edge of the Roman Empire, but if so, it too, like many buildings in recent years, had disappeared beneath the waves. Despite its harshness it was a beautiful if remote part of the county.

When Hildegard saw it she became aware of the elemental power of its desolation. The sky seemed huge, the land small. She could die here, she felt, surrendering to its presiding spirits. She mentally shook herself. This was no way to approach the adventure of voyaging abroad.

The town itself, grim and vigorous, and rife with the stench of herring, clearly hung between heaven and hell. When the cavalcade drew near, the sea was petrel blue in the waning light. It appeared in stabs of colour between the sagging, dun-coloured rooves of the wattle-and-daub dwellings. Despite the imminence of the curfew, folk bustled in the few narrow streets around the quay, reluctant to miss the grand spectacle of the carts laden with staple passing by. The men-at-arms observed the spectators with a mixture of disdain and wariness. They were massively outnumbered by the denizens of the town but the latter were a weak, half-starved bunch, armed with no more than cudgels and gutting knives. Even so, there was dignity in their stares, blank looks concealing what might be the defiance of their thoughts.

The dock was fully protected against entry by any but the officers of the customs. Those with documents of passage to Flanders were held at the checkpoint. The toll-master and his bailiffs were slow and methodical. Even though they had already been informed of the embarkation of the contingent, they still took their time, conscious that they had the power to prevent anybody from leaving the country should they so wish and they were not ashamed to display their importance. The first wagons had already gone through, however, nothing at fault with the documents produced by the abbey scribes.

Then the de Hutton wagons began to pass one by one between the line of guards. Hildegard was sitting beside Ulf with a group of his men, the minstrel, and an abbey clerk, all of them crammed together in the third cart. The Florentines were delayed in the port office to drill home to them the fact that they were foreigners. The five henchmen stood in an impassive group while Ludovico argued their case.

Pierrekyn began to fret about the stowing of his lute. During the pitching of the wagon over the churned mud on the track, he had had to relinquish his hold on it, agreeing to being parted from it only when Ulf found a niche where, he said, it wouldn't be rattled into a heap of sawdust and broken strings. Now Pierrekyn began to rummage around for it, making a great fuss, much to the amusement of the serjeant-at-arms who had stopped their wagon with one foot planted on the running board.

Briefly glancing down the list of passengers, he began to smile when he heard what the commotion was about. Addressing Ulf, whom he knew well, he said, 'Tell your singing lad, my lord steward, he's not the first minstrel we've had taking ship down here. We're not barbarians, you know.' He handed back the dockets with a genial flourish. 'As long as it's not made of wool he's free to take it anywhere he likes. Does he think we're mad enough to put a tax on music?'

He and Ulf exchanged glances. 'These musicians!' he replied affably. The bailiff removed his foot. They were through.

'We go on board now and leave the men to load the cargo,' Ulf told Hildegard. 'I'll find you a place to sleep on deck under the awning. Your hounds should have been sent on from Swyne by now and will be loaded on in their wicker cage. It's probably best to let them stay in that if they will, so they don't get under everybody's feet – or swept overboard,' he added with a teasing grin. He paused and asked awkwardly, 'I hope you don't mind travelling with my men?'

'Their humour is more ribald than that usually heard around the priory,' she said, unable to keep a twinkle out of her eyes, 'but I expect I'll survive.'

Smiling, Ulf went away to attend to his duties and Hildegard climbed the ladder onto the deck to find her hounds.

It was dawn again by the time everything was stowed to the shipmaster's satisfaction. Hildegard had just stepped ashore to stretch her legs when she felt a tug on her sleeve and, looking down, she saw a small boy holding something out to her.

Recognising him as one of the oblates from Meaux who had come along to fetch and carry, and who would be going back in the wagons with the imported merchandise, she bent down to see what he wanted. He was holding out a small bundle of cloth. As soon as she took it he scampered off into the crowd.

'Wait! What is it?' she called but he was already lost to sight.

Cautiously, she opened the bundle. There was nothing in it. All she held in her hand was a piece of cloth. It felt like silk. When she looked closer she saw it was yellowed with age. She held it up. It was a neckerchief like the sort of thing a knight might wear under his mail, or fasten to his lance. It had the softness of long use and was clearly no ordinary piece of fabric. There was a motif in one corner. Looking closer she saw it was an embroidered pattern of leaves dotted with several small blue flowers. Borage, she realised at once.

What did they say? *Borage for courage.* It was the emblem knights carried into battle or, in earlier times, wore close to their hearts when they went on crusade. Templars had carried such talismans. Puzzled, she put it safely into her scrip and climbed back on board.

Everyone was leaning against the rail to get a last look at England.

Three ships were due to leave but the third was still being loaded and would probably miss the tide. Its passengers, pilgrims and their servants, as well as several delayed members of their own party, were milling around on the quay. One traveller, his hood up against the wind, was standing apart from the commotion, watching their ship as its lines were cast off. His stillness amid all the activity attracted Hildegard's attention and thinking about the surprise gift of the silk neckerchief, she wondered for a moment whether it was he who had sent it. But she could think of no reason why he should do so.

Above their heads a cloud of gulls shrieked like drowning sailors. The pennants on the masthead snapped in the wind.

When she looked back towards the quickly receding shore the hooded man was a still point in all the activity on the quay. He was turned to watch them as the laden cog slipped faster into the stream. The shouts from the shore were folded away.

Hildegard glanced back.

The stranger was still watching. Even as the ship slid at last into the rushing flood mid-river he was watching it, and it was only when the sails bellied up, and the ship ran close-hauled past the fort at the river mouth, that he became too small to make out.

'Are you sorry to leave?' Hildegard glanced along the rail to where the minstrel was staring back at the shore with tight lips.

35

He gave a start. 'Glad to shake the dust of the treacherous place from my boots,' he muttered, turning as if to go.

She put out a hand. 'A moment. I understand you met Master Reynard in Kent when he went down there with Lord Roger's mission from Yorkshire.'

'What if I did?'

She ignored his scowl and said, 'I was wondering what sort of fellow he was.'

'The usual.' His lower lip jutted.

She waited to see whether he would add anything but when he appeared to have nothing more to say she was about to leave when he suddenly muttered, 'He was an artist, I'll give him that. His saving grace was his skill with pen and ink.' He threw her a challenging glance. 'What he couldn't depict couldn't be drawn by any man on earth.'

'I understood he was a clerk, assisting the notary in the drawing up of contracts.'

'A man has to eat. You don't see Lord Roger having any use for an illuminator, do you?' He gave a harsh laugh. 'If you can't kill it, eat it or buy it, de Hutton has no use for it. Unless it's a woman, of course.'

His disrespectful reference to Roger prompted her to say, 'If you feel like that I'm surprised you've decided to don his livery.'

'As I said, a man has to eat.'

Man, she thought, with an unexpected feeling of compassion. He could be no more than seventeen. Only his pride and his look of having seen the world ten times over and been unimpressed by it made him seem older.

'I hope your lute came to no harm on that rough journey.'

'It's well enough.' As always he had it beside him in its leather bag. He drew it forth and ran his hands over the walnut case. It was a beautiful instrument, worn to a patina with use and age.

'Where did you learn to play?'

'Kent.'

'Canterbury?'

'Did I say so?' He turned to her. His green eyes were like chips of ice.

As if irritated by the conversation he plucked at the strings but before he could coax them into a tune she said, 'That was the lament to Bel Veger you played yesterday in Lady Melisen's chamber, wasn't it?'

He raised his eyebrows. 'Indeed, Sister. Surely not heard in your cloister?'

It was her turn to ignore the question.

He gave her a considering glance. 'Well, well,' he said, coming to some conclusion. He began to play then, very fast, with great skill and dexterity, but it was not the lament for the adulterous wife of a duke but a different tune, a jig, something he punctuated with ironic chords that offered a ribald double meaning.

Soon a group of people formed round him and, half suspecting that this had been his intention so he could put an end to her questions, she edged away. There was something dangerous about Pierrekyn, she felt. Rage or some other powerful emotion seemed to simmer beneath the surface of everything he said.

There had been little opportunity to talk to Ser Ludovico on the way over, with the pitching of the wagon and the tumult of the horsemen in their armour. Now she made her way along the canted deck in search of him. She found him playing dice with his men in the stern.

From here they could see the entire length of the deck if they wanted: the merchandise that would not fit in the hold lashed to the stanchions fitted for the purpose, the group of admirers round the minstrel, the wicker cage with her two hounds sleeping in safety, Ulf amidships in conversation with the master, the sailors spidering about in the rigging.

Ludovico rose to his feet at her approach. 'After thirty hours of this, Sister, how do you feel?' His English had become fluent after nearly a year of Philippa's tuition.

'I feel good,' she replied. She swayed with the tilt and lift of the deck. 'I believe my ancestors were seafarers.'

'I'm better on dry land,' he told her, and indeed his olive skin was already beginning to acquire a greenish tinge.

'I have a concoction in my scrip that's supposed to help if you need it,' she told him.

'I'll brazen it out for the while. Why don't you join us?' He set aside the dice and made a space in the nest of ropes where they were sitting. 'They tell me you're off on pilgrimage to Rome.'

'That's so. But I'm also charged with making a few purchases for Lady Melisen on the way. I was wondering whether I could ask your advice.'

When she explained what she wanted to buy, he was helpful. 'I can take you to a goldsmith in Bruges who'll make these brooches she wants and as for the pearl-embroidered sleeves I know just the man. You must let me come with you and make sure you get a good price.'

She mentioned the silk the nuns produced at Swyne. 'Do you think there'd be a market for it in Flanders?' The prioress would be delighted if she could manage to find a way of bringing in more revenue.

Ludovico smiled. 'There's a market for everything in the world if you know where to look but I'm afraid your sisters would find themselves in competition with the silk-spinners of Lucca. Still, as I say, there's a market for everything. I'll ask my contacts if you like. It's English wool everybody wants at present.'

They talked for a little while in general and when he mentioned Tuscany she said, 'I don't think Lord Roger knows the difference between Lombardy and Tuscany.'

He laughed. 'He knows full well I'm no Lombard moneylender. I'm attached to the bank of Vitelli in Florence. Philippa's always taking him to task for calling me a Lombard. She's so loyal—' With a sudden soft smile that lit up his usually sombre features he added, 'As well as beautiful and clever.'

'I'm fond of Philippa. I remember her when she was a ten-year-old with two long, flaxen plaits and a book in her hands.'

'I'm more than fond of her.' A shadow crossed his face. 'I thought her father had agreed to our betrothal and that our marriage would take place within the year once my *capo* had given permission. But now,' he frowned, 'Lord Roger seems to have other plans. And it's all my own fault.'

'What do you mean?'

Apparently pleased to be able to unburden himself while his hench-men resumed their game of dice, he explained. 'Lord Roger asked me to tell him about the different contracts we use to raise capital.'

'I expect he was interested in that!'

Ludovico smiled ruefully. 'So interested he thinks he's an expert now.'

'And it's a problem?'

'It wouldn't be if it didn't encourage him to act in a way which—' He bit his lip. 'I'm being indiscreet, Sister, forgive me.'

'I've known Roger all my life. I'm familiar with his ways. And I receive many confidences, which I guard well. But I gather you were both happy with the agreement you reached over the staple?' She tilted her head.

'That was no problem. It was a pleasure doing business with him. A most convivial experience, in fact!' He gave a short laugh that quickly turned into another sigh. The horizon lifted and fell and he seemed hypnotised by it for a moment before saying, 'I fear he's about to do something perilous. He brushed my advice aside so what can I do? The problem is this. There are some ventures unaffordable except by kings and princes and these are subject to a *commenda* contract.'

Hildegard's glance sharpened.

'For instance it takes about twenty-four shares to finance a vessel on a long-term voyage, say to the East, to bring back spices and such-like. This vessel, being so small,' he gave the cog an assessing glance, 'is owned outright by just three owners who hire her to men like Lord Roger and the abbot. For bigger trade it's necessary to buy a large, well-armed ship, a Venetian galley for instance, and to make sure she's well insured. I sell shares in that sort of enterprise. The capital,' he said, 'is at risk for the finite term of a single voyage.'

Hildegard listened patiently, not sure where this was leading or what it had to do with Roger.

'Sometimes,' he continued, 'the more speculative contracts can last up to twenty years. They can be used to finance mines and mills and other big enterprises like that. They can also provide the finance for ongoing loans for whatever the company concerned thinks is a good risk.'

'I see,' said Hildegard carefully.

'To offset the greater risk they obviously carry a higher rate of interest. A city like Florence sometimes consolidates all its debts into one big debt, what we call the *monte*.'

'So if the money is loaned for as long as twenty years, it can carry a bigger risk and there's no guarantee that the lender will get back their capital?'

'Exactly,' he said in a sombre tone.

'And are you saying that Roger intends to put his capital into something like that so he'll get a high rate of interest?'

His eyes gleamed. 'He's a gambler at heart.'

Hildegard could scarcely disagree. It was one of his failings. Moreover, he had a firm belief in luck, which made his decisions alarming to anyone of a more cautious nature. It was Ulf's constant worry that his lord would bankrupt himself.

'The dangers of trading in the East are obvious,' Ludovico continued. 'Bad weather, shipwreck, dishonest sea-captains, and the constant attacks of pirates to name a few. But that's what I do, that's my task – I set these things up. Sadly for me I pricked Lord Roger's imagination and now he wants to place Philippa's dowry in a long-term venture. He's enticed by the interest rate. The trouble is, the risk is also enticing – if you're a gambler like Roger. I almost believe that if there was no risk he wouldn't be so interested. He loves the thrill of it. All he can see is the glory of winning and the massive profit he'll make if everything turns out right. If it doesn't, of course, he'll lose everything—'

'Philippa's dowry, you mean?' Hildegard was aghast.

Ludovico's usual enigmatic expression was clouded with worry.

'Surely he hasn't put that at risk?' she asked.

'I mean no disrespect to Lord Roger but it's becoming most difficult. Philippa doesn't yet know the extent of the risk he's taking.'

'I'm sure Roger is happy to have you as his son-in-law,' she tried to reassure him, 'and as for the dowry, surely he doesn't expect Philippa to wait twenty years for the loan to mature before she marries! There must be some misunderstanding.'

'No, he imagines he'll get his money back within a year or two.'

The way he uttered these words showed just how long even that seemed to him.

'But if it's a long-term loan how can he expect—?' Hildegard frowned.

There was something else on Ludovico's mind. She waited to see whether he would say more but he merely gave another worried shrug.

'I'm sure things will be arranged to everyone's satisfaction,' she said gently.

'He's sending his steward to open the discussions with my manager in Bruges who'll act as marriage broker. The details will be passed on to my *capo* in Florence. My father died of the plague when I was a boy,' he explained. 'The man who became my guardian is head of both the company and the family. He has the final say in everything I do. He's my lord and protector.'

'And do you think he's going to refuse Roger's stake when he learns it's part of the dowry?'

'If he does and Roger looks elsewhere he may also look for another husband for Philippa. '

'My dear Ludovico, is it likely your *capo* will refuse Roger's offer?'

Ludovico's laugh was hollow. 'Ser Vitelli's no fool. He runs one of the largest banks in the known world—' He broke off.

'I had no idea you carried such a burden.'

Ludovico's look was bleak. 'Neither does my lady. She has no idea that our betrothal is in jeopardy. She guesses something's afoot but doesn't yet know the full risk her father is taking with her future. With our future,' he corrected.

'There must be a way to bring it to a happy conclusion.'

'If I can persuade my *capo* to accept the terms of the dowry and if I can bring Lord Roger the good fortune he assumes is his by right, then yes, everything will end well. But if I cannot … '

Ludovico's exotic, dark looks had attracted many a glance at Castle Hutton. It would be easy for him to catch the eye of another marriageable girl should the match with Philippa fail, especially with the sort of business connections he had with the house of Vitelli. What father wouldn't relish the opportunity of allying his family with one of the major banks in Florence? Roger must be mad to gamble with Philippa's prospects. He must have been swept along by a vision of the massive fortune he could make.

'I know how much you mean to Philippa.' She put a hand on his sleeve. 'Thank you for telling me about this. We cannot let it rest.'

She would have a word with Ulf. She would make sure he knew what was in the marriage contract and advise him to ask Ludovico to prime him before he met the broker in Bruges. How could Roger dream of jeopardising the future of two young people who were so clearly meant for each other?

For a moment she imagined what Hubert de Courcy would have to say about the sin of usury – before thrusting aside any thought of him.

The night passed in fitful sleep under the awning spread out above the afterdeck. The rolling of the small ship increased, and now and then a wall of water would surge through the gunwales to come sluicing down the foredeck. Hildegard had bedded down among her few belongings. For comfort she released her hounds from their wicker cage and let them lie beside her. Bermonda, the little kennet, snuggled in the crook of her arms but the lymer, Duchess, spread herself full length, warming her from top to toe.

As the stars faded and the sun rose next morning, the heaving back of the sea was riddled with gold and scarlet flecks. The ship's cook sent up beakers of wine from the galley followed by flat, hot cakes baked on a griddle and dripping with butter. It was a lull, calm and pleasant, as they ate and drank on deck, suspended between one country and the next.

Ludovico and his men were nowhere to be seen. They could be heard, though, as they had been heard most of the night, throwing up over the side. A couple of Ulf's men-at-arms suffered the same sickness and there were ribald jokes about their manhood. Ulf kept apologising to her for their language.

Pierrekyn sat by himself staring at the horizon. She had seen him brushing his velvet doublet with fresh water from a pail. His garments had once been of the best, she noticed, but were now frayed and stained with wear. His livery, amounting to no more than a tunic in the de Hutton colours, was almost new and if you didn't look too closely the boy seemed passably well turned out. Not good enough for his own standards, by the look on his face, however, as he again started to dab at the nap of his velvet doublet. He wore a silver ring, she noticed, with an emblem on it, but it was too far away to make out.

Just then he lifted his head and caught her watching him. He turned away. That he didn't appear to like her was no puzzle. They inhabited different worlds.

As the day progressed a rumble of complaint rose from the ship's crew. 'These bales stink!' exclaimed one of the sailors as he swung down onto the deck. He held his nose. 'What in hell's in them? Rotten cheese?'

It couldn't be denied. They stank to high heaven and what little wind there was didn't dispel the rank odour that came from them.

'The skins were cured,' Ulf remarked, poking at them with his stave. 'But he's right. Well,' he amended, sniffing along the row, 'this batch has a fair old smell.' He looked at the mark. 'From Meaux as well. I am surprised. I thought they looked after their exports better than that.'

Later, when the wind came up again, the cog began to fly more swiftly over the waves and any lingering odour was eventually dispersed. Soon the port of Bruges appeared as a smudge on the horizon.

Chapter Five

HE GOLDSMITH HAD a narrow pencil-line of finely trimmed brown hair that ran vertically up his chin to his bottom lip, matching similar pencil-thin stripes along the top of each cheekbone. His upper lip was clean shaven. Hildegard observed these three ink-strokes with a steady glance. His eyes were sharp though near-sighted. They narrowed when they fell on gold or jewels. About forty, expensively dressed in dark brown velvet, he was said to be the greatest master of his craft in Bruges.

Now he put to one side the drawing of the white hart enchained and nodded.

'Very pretty. Good drawing.'

He touched the piece of paper Hildegard had handed him with the tip of one finger. She now knew the drawing to be an example of Reynard's work. It confirmed what the minstrel had told her. The clerk had been an artist just as much as this wealthy member of the guild of goldsmiths, though less honoured and rewarded.

In a desire to impress Ludovico, knowing well whom he represented, the master had conducted them into a private chamber where he kept catalogues of the drawings of all the pieces commissioned by the chivalry of Europe. Most impressive was a coronet in the process of being made for a princess of Bohemia. The worked gold was outdone only by the stones being set into the design. Those jewels alone must be worth a king's ransom, thought Hildegard, striving to maintain a look both interested and unimpressed.

She left to Ludovico the negotiations over her small order for the brooches. He spoke Flemish to the goldsmith, whose few words of English seemed already to be exhausted, and only now and then did they break into the sort of Norman French she could understand.

When the deal was done and they had shaken hands and taken a cup of Burgundy together, they were ushered out and after more hand-shakes and flourishes found themselves once more in the square. Like five shadows, Ludovico's henchmen rejoined them.

'Lady Melisen is going to be delighted,' she told Ludovico.

'I hope her husband realises how much his wife is costing him,' was his wry comment. 'Now for her sleeves.'

Bruges was a most extraordinary place to anyone used only to the desolate marshland of Holderness and small, out-of-the-way towns like Beverley. It was true that York perhaps might measure up in some way because of its great minster and the palace of the arch-bishop, but set in the north of the country it couldn't hope to win the variety of international trade that made Bruges one of the richest cities in Christendom.

Its wealth and power derived from its location at the crossroads of all the major routes of Europe: north to Germany and the Hanseatic ports in the Baltic, east to Bohemia, west to France with its traffic over the Pyrenees to Spain and Portugal, and south over the Alps to the rich markets of the Italian city states and the seat of the papal empire. From there communications stretched, almost unbroken, by land and sea to Byzantium and beyond.

The advantages were everywhere, the streets full of bankers and money changers, merchants and traders of every description, carriers and muleteers, a panoply of servants, attendants and hangers-on.

Business was mostly carried out in the portico of the square named after the banking family who had made themselves seigneurs of the city, the van der Beurse. There churchmen, bent on trade like every-one else, processed formally, and with immense grandeur at the head of their lavishly attired retinues, on their way from one transaction to another. Smaller merchants, guildsmen in distinctive cloaks, arti-sans, scribes, scriveners, wandering friars, pardoners, white-robed pilgrims by the score, as well as anyone connected to the ordinary day-to-day business of a large town, market traders selling produce brought in from outlying farms, bakers, butchers, cheesemongers, wine-sellers, basket-makers, suppliers of ribbons and fabric – all were there, shouting their wares, and in among them itinerant vendors selling piping-hot food to eat in the street, and everybody busy turning a profit.

Yet, observed Hildegard, like any town it is not without its beggars. She could not get used to the violent contrast in personal fortune she saw everywhere. The beggar-children did not deserve to live like this. Barefoot and ragged, unwashed, uncared-for, they swarmed about the streets, squabbling over scraps fallen from the mouths of the rich, the smallest children trailing piteously behind the bigger ones, hungry and forlorn. Their plight made her heart bleed. The extravagance of the wealthy was flaunted without shame.

In addition to the poor, there were the wounded, just as Ulf had warned her, survivors, though scarcely that, from the recent battle against the French when the army of artisans captained by Van Artevelde had been thoroughly destroyed at Roosebeeke. They said that afterwards the nearby river ran with blood for ten days and nights, and the conditions of the rebels became worse than before.

Now, as she stood watching the square, one of these battle-ruined survivors came towards her, holding out two bloody, bandaged stumps where his hands had been. Another groped his way through the hurrying crowds as best he could, the sockets of his eyes red and raw and sightless.

She helped a man whose legs had been severed at the knees lever himself to a vantage point under the portico where he could beg alms from the customers at the money changers' in order to support him for the short time he had left in the world, and she took water from the public fountain to another with a terrible, weeping wound across his chest. There was so little she could do in the midst of such extremity. Eventually, exhausted and close to despair, she set about finding her way back to the inn where she was to spend a second night.

Just as she reached the alley where the inn lay, a beggar appeared from nowhere, blocking her path and thrusting out two bandaged hands to detain her. He was a tall fellow with a rough, grey hood pulled well down as if to conceal a head wound. Otherwise he seemed hale enough.

'Alms, Sister?' he demanded in English. 'For the love of Mary, mother of God!'

He looked well able to find work to feed himself. But she felt inside the purse at her belt and took out the last of her coins.

He snatched them without a word and made off towards a nearby alehouse. She sighed and moved on.

There was another row of money changers in booths along this side of the square and she paused to watch. They were making calculations by using a board divided into squares. When she looked closer she realised one of the changers was a woman, her arithmetical skill as dazzling as the swiftness of her fingers as she shuffled the coloured counters around the board. Unsurprisingly, she had a constant stream of customers changing money of every denomination. Currencies were slipped into secret pouches or concealed in bags, chained and locked to the wrists of the merchants making the transactions, or carried from one dealer to another by bands of armed servants.

Everywhere, profit and loss overran any other kind of transaction. Hildegard felt faint with it, both dazzled and repelled.

But it was no good being blind to what was going on. She would have to negotiate a good rate for the bill of exchange when she reached Rome. What sum the guardians of the cross of Constantine might demand was an open question. Her instructions were to pay whatever it cost.

The de Hutton contingent was lodged at an inn close to the main square with large stables where her hounds were kennelled. Ulf took it for granted she would stay under his protection until he had to leave. The half-dozen conversi, sent to keep an eye on the goods exported from Meaux, were staying with a cell of brothers on the other side of town. They were to return to England on the next passage. Ludovico was lodged at the Florentine Consular House off the Place de la Bourse. Soon she would be alone.

'We leave tomorrow at first light,' Ulf told her.

'You look worried,' she remarked.

'I've just had a meeting with Ser Ubriacchi, Ludovico's manager, to pass on Roger's suggestions for Philippa's dowry,' he explained. 'I don't understand the half of it. It seems to depend on the trading contract he's making. Ludovico told me the gist but it still doesn't make sense. They can run rings me, these money-men. Anyway, I'm just the messenger.' He looked ruffled. 'She loves Ludovico and to the best of my belief he loves her, yet it seems to come down to the skill of the clerk who penned the contract.'

'A pity he's not here to put the case.'

'Damn his eyes! Anyway, I've done what I can.'

'I'm sure Ludovico will do the rest.' She looked at him kindly. 'I'm sorry you're having to leave tomorrow. I'll miss you. And I'll miss your men's rough language,' she added. 'Where are you going next?'

'Down the Rhine.' He gave her an apologetic glance and although he didn't put a name to his destination, she guessed at once it was something to do with Roger's need for armour so she held her tongue. It was not difficult to see that the steward was prepared to return with more than just one suit of armour for Roger. Why else would he be taking twenty men along? If Roger was re-equipping his men it could mean only one thing. He expected war.

'We'll be back as soon as possible,' he told her. 'We go straight to our contact, do the business, then return. Three weeks at most. We might even meet up here again. What do you think?'

'I doubt it. I'll have left long before then and I certainly won't be back within three weeks. Rome is somewhat further than your destination, I imagine.' It must be Cologne, she thought, they made armour there. These days it was said to equal that from Milan.

Before she turned to go to the cubbyhole of a chamber where she was to sleep, Ulf said, 'I have something to tell you. A messenger from England came in while you were out to say your escort is on his way. He's a knight called Sir Talbot, earned his spurs a couple of seasons ago and is just beginning to make a name for himself on the tournament circuit in France.'

'You mean he's a tourney knight?' Hildegard threw him a derisory glance.

'Don't mock. He built up quite a following last summer. The new season doesn't start until after Easter so he's probably delighted to be given something useful to do.'

'Do you know who hired him?'

He shook his head. 'I'd tell you if I did. I know no more than I did before. My instructions come through Lord Roger and I know he's not footing the bill. Not, of course,' he added, loyally, 'that he would object if it was a question of your safety. Sir Talbot has been instructed to find you here at the inn.'

She pulled a face. 'I don't need a knight with a sword. I've got my hounds for protection.'

'You'll be glad of his company, all that way.'

'Not if he talks about tourneying all the time!'

Just as they were about to part, Ulf to join his men in the ale-house and Hildegard to her prayers, there was a commotion at the door and one of the conversi from Meaux burst in. He pushed his way through the crowd hanging round the door and hurried over to Ulf.

'My lord. We have a problem. It's urgent. Will you come with me?'

'What is it?' Ulf was reluctant to give up his recreation after the busyness of the last few days.

'I'd rather not say, my lord.'

'Is it something they want you to read?' The conversi were not allowed to learn to read, their sphere being crops and animals, and obeying orders.

'It's not that, sire, no.'

Ulf turned to Hildegard. 'Would you like to come along? Who better than you to solve any problems?'

She pulled on her cloak again at once. Any excursion into this strange town by night was more enticing than her solitary bed.

The servant, who complained that he had expected to be back on board ship by now and on the way home to the safety of Meaux, led them to the loading sheds where the staple was being held until it could be inspected and repacked for carriage onwards to Tuscany.

There were one or two anxious-looking port officials standing on the quay with a couple of conversi from Meaux. When Ulf strode up they all came to meet him.

'There's a problem with the consignment,' explained one of the abbey men. 'It has some defect and we want you as witness that it was in saleable condition when it was put on board ship.'

'I'll vouch for that,' agreed Ulf.

One of the local officials stepped forward. He spoke English. 'We need to open it and inspect the contents,' he explained. 'It's probably nothing much. But there is something wrong with it.'

'What the devil do you mean?' With a sigh, Ulf followed the men into the shed.

Some light came in through the open doors but more was needed to dispel the crawl of shadows across the stacked bales.

Flares were lighted. The bales shone in their brilliant flood and at first glance everything seemed to be as it should be but then, somewhat overpowered by the rank smell that filled the shed, the foreman came to the fore to point out some dark mass that lay within one of the bales.

'Unfasten it,' Ulf ordered.

Two men worked knives through the cords that bound it. After a few moments the fibres snapped and the pack sprang open. The smell was stronger now. With one hand over his nose Ulf reached into the soft mass of uncarded wool. A strange, dark shadow could be seen within. He began to pull the wool to one side. Then he jerked his hand away with an oath. A servant gasped in horror.

Inside the cocoon was a shape.

It was a man.

Contorted in the rigor of death, he was standing upright, both hands pressed to his throat.

The shadow they had seen before the pack was opened was blood. Now dried to a black crust, it had spouted from a gash in the man's neck. His hands were covered in it as if he had tried to hold it in.

The smell, which none of them had identified, was due to the heat, generated within the bales, rotting the dead flesh. Mixed with the natural oils of the wool, the corpse exuded a sickly emanation, at first unrecognisable to any of them as the odour of death.

'God's teeth!' exclaimed Ulf after he had forced himself to take a closer look. 'Better call the constables.'

'If I may suggest, messire, this is a consignment that has yet to be passed through customs. It is subject to maritime law. The corpse belongs neither to England nor to Flanders. We shall have to take legal advice before we proceed.'

'Is that so?'

As he spoke Ulf was pulling the wool aside so he could look more closely at the putrefying head of the corpse. Although discoloured and puffy with fluid its features were identifiable.

Ulf turned to Hildegard in dismay. 'Now we know why we couldn't find him. This is the missing clerk, Reynard of Risingholme.'

Chapter Six

‘WHERE'S THE ENGLISH minstrel?’ The steward's tone was abrupt and it cut through the hubbub like a knife. The drinkers in the alehouse, de Hutton men-at-arms, some travellers, merchants, a few burghers and body servants, stopped talking and looked up.

Ulf bulked in the doorway. Two of his men rose to their feet, swords swinging at their hips, and went to stand at his side. A voice asked, ‘Is it that lad Pierrekyn he's after?’

‘What's he done?’ Somebody translated into Flemish. It became obvious when Ulf didn't budge that something serious was afoot. The ale-master pushed his way forward and in broken English asked, ‘Am I at fault, messire?’

Ulf shook his head. ‘Not that I know of, master. I seek a compatriot on a matter not your concern.’ He swept the crowd with a look of menace.

‘He was playing in here earlier,’ somebody admitted.

There was a rumble of agreement.

‘And then?’ Ulf raised his brow.

There was a general shifting as glances were exchanged.

In a friendlier tone, he asked, ‘Did he leave with anyone?’ His eyes checked for absentees among his own men and, satisfied, he subjected those present to a hard look.

‘Didn't he leave with that pardoner?’ somebody muttered. Another remark followed in Flemish, its coarseness guessed by the kind of laughter it aroused.

‘You might try round the back of the market,’ the ale-master suggested. ‘It's nothing to do with me.’

Ulf spoke to his men-at-arms. ‘Let's bring him in.’

They left.

Hildegard slipped unobtrusively into a space on one of the benches set up between the trestles. She was wearing the blue cloak with the hood up and nobody gave her a second glance. Her grasp of Flemish was not sufficient to allow her to follow the conversations that broke out after Ulf left but a French speaker at the next table began translating for his companion. She blushed at the obscenities. She was starting to feel sorry for Pierrekyn.

He would surely be top of Ulf's list of suspects in the murder of the clerk, and now these folk had condemned him out of hand. She wondered whether their own sins were so negligible they had room to judge a fellow soul so harshly. The boy has no chance, she thought. The Church decreed that sodomites should burn. If he was ever brought to court he would be condemned to the pyre whether he was guilty of murder or not.

And if Ulf is wrong? She didn't know whether Pierrekyn was capable of killing a man nor why he would kill his benefactor. He had seemed genuinely angry at Reynard's disappearance when they burst in on him in Reynard's chamber at Meaux. Angry, not guilty.

There was nothing she could do at present. Meanwhile, news of the murder had reached the alehouse and was soon out of control. One or two were calling to raise the hue and cry. Swords were being drawn, the blades of daggers examined, cudgels found for those lacking weapons. The alehouse rapidly emptied once the idea caught hold that it was a hunt for a murderer – and a sodomite at that.

The ale-master watched his customers leave with a look of exasperation. 'Profit down the hole,' he growled, slapping a cloth over his shoulder and hobbling back into his kitchens.

Hildegard went out into the street. The pursuers were coursing back and forth across the square like an undisciplined pack of hounds. When they saw Ulf and his men returning from the back of the market without their quarry, they started a thorough search for Pierrekyn themselves, upending carts, creating mayhem. Every shadow was attacked, every doorway searched. Soon they started knocking on people's shutters, forcing their way into their houses. The whole town was in uproar. The word murder linked with sexual depravity had roused every faction against him.

Hildegard decided to retire to her chamber and watch from the window where she would have a view of what was happening. The lust for blood shocked her. But there was nothing she could do yet. Ulf and his men could be out half the night. She prayed that if Pierrekyn was found it was by the de Hutton men and not by the shrieking rabble.

She went up the narrow stairs to the top floor. Fortunately the wife of the ale-master had a warren of small rooms to let out to travellers such as herself. 'We get many single women pilgrims with the wealth to pay for privacy,' she had explained in French when she grasped that Hildegard could speak it well enough.

Now Hildegard made her way to a door at the far end of a corridor above the kitchens. It was warm though it reeked of garlic and fried onions.

Pushing open the door she was surprised to find a candle burning in the room. Then she gasped as a hand clamped itself firmly over her mouth and she was propelled inside. She heard the door kicked shut. She was released. When she jerked round she found herself standing face to face with Pierrekyn. He held a knife.

'Don't scream!' he warned.

Hildegard threw him a look of contempt. 'If you put that ridiculous knife away I might do as you ask.'

The knife slid warily back inside its sheath but the boy remained firmly with his broad shoulders against the door, preventing escape.

She turned her back and went to sit on the bed. 'I hardly think it wise to add a second murder to the first,' she said.

'Murder? What murder? I thought they were after me for something else.'

He genuinely doesn't know why he's being pursued, she realised.

'What murder?' he demanded impatiently. 'I'm always the first to be blamed for anything. I thought it might be different here.'

'It'll only be different when you're different,' she said. 'But you must have heard what they were shouting in the square just now?' The continuing search was faintly audible below the window despite its height above the square.

'I don't understand their barbarous dialect. What are they baying about?' he asked dismissively.

'Sit down, Pierrekyn. I've something to tell you.' She indicated a wooden chair by the wall.

Reluctantly, he left his position against the door and sat down.

'It's about Reynard,' she said. 'His body has been found.'

'His body?' The confusion on the boy's face looked genuine. 'How can his body have been found? It doesn't make sense. How can—?'

'His body was discovered at the docks. The suspicion is he was murdered in England.'

Pierrekyn rose to his feet. 'It doesn't make sense,' he said again. 'Why would anybody murder him? Why would they bring him here?'

Swaying, he put out one hand as if to steady himself then rushed abruptly to the clay pot in the corner and began to retch. He emptied the entire contents of his stomach, resting one hand against the wall afterwards, his face ashen.

'Forgive me,' he muttered, wiping his mouth on the back of his sleeve. Sweat glistened on his forehead. He came to sit on a chair beside the bed. He was breathing heavily as if there was not enough air in the room. His eyes were blank until he managed to say, 'So this is why those dogs are hallooing the fox. Let's have done with it then. Hand me over. I'm ready.'

'Am I to hand you over?'

His head jerked. 'Why wouldn't you?'

'Did you murder him?'

'I did not.'

'Then a little breathing space might be of benefit to everybody,' she told him, thinking quickly. 'No decisions should ever be made in the heat of the moment. It's late now. I suggest you prop the chair against the door to prevent anyone coming in unexpectedly. I shall take the bed and you'll sleep on the floor. It would be a bad idea to try to leave tonight. You'd get no further than the alehouse door,' she warned. 'We'll decide what to do tomorrow when our minds are clear.'

She knew she was taking a great leap of faith. He could murder her in the night as she slept.

He was staring at her with a blank expression and it was difficult to tell what he was thinking. He dashed the back of one hand over his eyes and asked gruffly, 'How did they do it?'

'They cut his throat.'

He turned away and, with a small, strained laugh, said, 'Tonight will be a first for Pierrekyn Haverel, sharing a sleeping chamber with a nun.'

Then he bedded down on the blanket she threw to him. As soon as she saw him burrow down she blew out the stub of candle the guest-mistress had allowed, stretched out on the pallet and pulled her cloak over her head.

When Hildegard woke up around four to the sounds of the kitchener and his staff three floors below, she poked her head from under her cloak and was relieved to see Pierrekyn, one arm outflung, lying in the tangled heap of blanket. His eyes were wide open. It was clear he had not slept. The rustle as she stretched her limbs on the straw mattress made him sit up. There were prints of dark shadow under his eyes.

'So that was no nightmare. He really is dead?'

'You'd better lie low. I'm going to find out what's happening. When I come back we'll determine what's best.'

'I don't know what you want from this,' he said when she had retied her coif and pulled on her cloak. He was sitting cross-legged on the folded blanket.

'Why should I want anything?'

'Everybody wants something.'

'There is another view.'

'I've never observed it.'

She pulled up her hood and opened the door. 'Put the chair back. Don't answer if anyone knocks to come in.'

She knew Ulf was lodged in the general quarters with his men. As she approached there was a deal of activity going on, his men, fully armed, milling back and forth with an air of busyness.

'No sign of him,' Ulf announced in greeting. 'He's vanished into thin air. Nothing could be a surer sign of guilt. But why the devil did he kill the clerk?'

Hildegard took him by the arm. 'Ulf, come with me. You need to break your fast. You look like—' She had been about to say 'death' but thought better of it.

'I really haven't time—' he began but when he saw the expression on her face he checked himself. Snarling some order over his shoulder to the men, he allowed her to propel him towards the stairs.

'What the devil's going on?' he demanded as they rushed down them, two at a time, and marched along the passage to the refectory.

'Eat,' she said. They were sitting in a quiet corner, with hardly anybody else about just yet, and no chance of being overheard. Even so she spoke in a low voice.

'I know where Pierrekyn is but before you send your men to fetch him in, let me explain.'

She told him exactly what had happened during the night, detailing the minstrel's reaction to news of Reynard's murder. 'To my mind that's not the response of a guilty man,' she concluded.

He looked unconvinced. 'Is this just you seeing the best in the lad?'

'At least let's give him the benefit of the doubt before the town gets hold of him. The mob was terrifying last night. If they'd found him they'd have torn him apart.'

'That's what it's like these days. Folk are hardened to cruelty after what they've suffered at the hands of the Count of Mâle and the Duke of bloody Burgundy. Their own blood has been drawn. Innocent blood. Now they want to make the guilty shed theirs.'

'But we don't know that Pierrekyn is guilty, do we? And an armed mob isn't going to listen to the evidence. In fact, we don't have any evidence against Pierrekyn.'

She gave him a searching glance and he reluctantly admitted that they had nothing beyond the known connection between the two of them and Pierrekyn's presence near the wool-sheds along with everybody else.

'What I want to know is, Ulf, do you agree to give him a breathing space until the real murderer is found?'

He glanced up as a serving woman entered from the kitchens with a couple of bowls of pottage and two steins of the pale, straw-coloured ale made locally. When she left Ulf took a deep drink and replaced his stein with a frown.

'What if he absconds?' he objected. 'I could walk upstairs into your chamber right now, clap him in irons and have him whisked back home to await due process of law. What's to stop me doing that?'

'Nothing at all,' she agreed. 'But wouldn't it be on your conscience if he was innocent? Once back in England he'd be judged guilty by the mob at once due to the simple fact that you'd taken him back as a prisoner. But look at the facts, Ulf, why would he murder his benefactor? It doesn't make sense.'

'I can think of a multitude of reasons. A lovers' tiff for one,' he growled. 'A hope to make away back to Kent with Reynard's possessions for another.'

'But if neither of those is true?'

'Some other reason then. Consider, Hildegard. Who else could want the clerk out of the way?'

'Maybe it was a simple argument with somebody down in the packing sheds,' she suggested. 'A drunken brawl?'

'In the abbey precincts?'

'Someone at the abbey with a grudge?'

'What, one of the monks?' He gave a derisive laugh. 'And it can't be one of the conversi either. They're devout lads and never cause a moment's trouble.'

'At this stage I really have no ideas,' she admitted. 'All I have is a feeling that the boy should be given a chance. There's something wrong – it makes him difficult to trust – and I don't mean his love of men. There's something else: sorrow, betrayal – something. It has destroyed his faith in people. He must be given a chance.'

He narrowed his eyes. 'So what do you propose?'

Chapter Seven

ILDEGARD WAS SHOWING signs of exasperation. 'I know it's irksome, Pierrekyn! But think about it. When we get you safely out of the town and into another jurisdiction we'll think again. But maybe you have a better plan?'

Pierrekyn threw her a baleful look from his chair by the window. 'An esquire? Me?' His lip curled. 'So who is this knight who's going to rescue me?'

'He's a tournament knight, resting until the season starts. He's been hired as my escort on the road to Rome.'

'I hope he doesn't expect me to fetch and carry his armour about the place. And I suppose I'll have to dress and undress him?'

'That's something for the two of you to decide,' she replied tartly. 'All I ask is that you remain within this chamber until we can get you safely away.'

'I can't see why the lord steward is taking such pains to keep me alive. What's in it for him?'

'There's nothing in it for him. Just be thankful he's agreeable. Do you have any further objections to what we propose?'

He shook his head.

'Well, then, do as you're told.' Couldn't he see how much they were risking in order to save him from an ugly death at the hands of the mob?

'I'm going out,' she told him. 'I'll bring you something to eat when I return.' She didn't say when that would be. Let him learn patience and humility, she thought. It was a lesson long overdue.

To her surprise when she turned at the door to give him one last warning, she saw tears streaming silently down his cheeks. She hurriedly closed the door and went over. 'My dear child, what is it?'

He turned his chair so she couldn't see his face and appeared to be studying the window-blind. His dark russet hair curled boyishly in the nape of his neck. It had the unexpectedly tender appearance of a child's downy locks. The sight moved her. It reminded her of her own son, now an esquire in the Bishop of Norwich's army.

'How old are you, Pierrekyn?' she asked softly.

'What's that got to do with it?' he muttered, unmoving.

'I was just wondering how long you've had to fend for yourself.'

'Long enough,' he said. Then he turned his young, world-weary face towards her. 'I can't believe he's dead.' He tried to blink away his tears but they stood on his lashes like drops of crystal. His voice became gruff. 'They'll torture me when they get me, won't they?'

'They won't get you. Not if you do as the steward and I suggest. Answer my question,' she prompted gently.

'I'm sixteen.'

She gave him a long look. Fourteen or fifteen then. 'And—?'

'And what?' he asked, staring at the floor.

'And the more you tell me the easier it's going to be to defend you.'

'Why should you bother?'

'God knows!' she replied, 'But I'm your only chance. Think on it.'

Wiping his eyes on the back of his hand he offered a ghost of a smile. 'You're the strangest nun I've ever met.'

'Have you met many?'

'I've met enough churchmen to last a lifetime.' He bit his lip as if he'd said enough.

'Go on.' She came to sit beside him.

He didn't look at her. 'I know you people. Say one thing and do another. Power is what you want. Gold. Not after you're dead – but now, in this world. How strange is that when you're supposed to believe in an afterlife in which everyone gets their just deserts?'

'That's human nature. I don't condone it.' She paused to invite him to continue.

Eventually he said, 'I was introduced to the secret life of the Church when I was seven years old. I'd had precious little kindness till then. And there it was – for a price, of course.'

Hildegard was silent but when he didn't elaborate she asked, 'And is that when you were taught to play the lute?'

He shook his head. 'That came afterwards. It was my singing they wanted me for, as well as—' His mouth twisted and he shrugged. 'When my voice broke, I wasn't much use as a chorister. And especially not with the sort of voice I learned on the streets. I was taught to play this,' he ran a finger over the curve of the lute, 'by a minstrel from Provence. Then he moved on, as they do, and I was taken up by another master. A tavern-keeper. Big as a barn. A real brute. He certainly knew a golden goose when he saw one.' He flexed his fingers and stared at them as if they reminded him of something. 'At least I can still play,' he said almost to himself.

'You play and sing wonderfully. You could have a glittering future. Talented minstrels are always wanted.'

'That's what I've been thinking,' he said with a sudden lift in his voice and although his expression was still bleak, he added, 'Reynard said I should find a way to join the guild and be taken up by some rich lord and become a court musician.' His eyes flashed before clouding over again. 'It's a pity Lord Roger is tone deaf.'

'I'm sure you can make a good life for yourself somewhere.' She rested a hand on his sleeve. 'Just lie low until we can get you out of here. Be patient, Pierrekyn. Let's see what fortune has in store.'

'Fortune? Don't you mean the blessed Mary and all her saints?'

'Have I your word?'

He nodded, then the light in his eyes went out. 'What choice do I have? I'm finished.'

Ulf eventually agreed with Hildegard. He would not arrest Pierrekyn at this stage. There was nothing substantial to link the boy to the death of the clerk. They would need evidence if they were to bring him to court. Ulf was also relieved not to have to delay his journey down the Rhine. He told her he would leave a man in Bruges while the lawyers made up their minds what to do with the body.

'I'll keep an eye on Pierrekyn,' Hildegard promised. 'If I discover anything linking him to the murder I'll inform the authorities at once. And then it'll be up to you.'

Together they had hit on the ruse for getting Pierrekyn safely out of the city. Hildegard had countered Ulf's initial idea of trying to pass him off as her servant and then they remembered that as yet no one knew anything about Sir Talbot. Nothing could be more natural than for him to be accompanied by an esquire to attend to his armour.

'We'll have to make sure Pierrekyn hides that hair of his inside a cap,' Hildegard observed.

Fortunately none of the travellers at the inn was going south and if a description of the hunted boy ever got out she would warn him to go well disguised until he was safely outside the jurisdiction of the Count of Mâle.

'I hope my escort is agreeable,' she added, 'and can invent a story to explain two esquires.'

'He won't need to,' Ulf replied. 'Whoever gave him instructions made it clear he should travel alone.'

Shortly before supper that evening Hildegard was sitting in the refectory with a group of Suffolk pilgrims who were staying there for a few days before returning north. When they discovered she was travelling in that direction they were eager to tell her about their recent visit to Rome, but although she was avid for information, she could not prevent her gaze from continually straying towards the door.

Eventually a crop-haired stranger came in and after a brief scrutiny of the rows of diners he noticed Hildegard. His eyes narrowed. A moment later the ale-master's boy came over and, in a miasma of raw onion, whispered a message into her ear, 'The square before vespers, Sister.'

After a moment or two Hildegard offered her excuses to the pilgrims and went outside.

The square resounded to the tolling of bells summoning worshippers to church while the ungodly loitered by the dozen round the fortune-tellers and other entertaining tricksters. Hildegard paced thoughtfully under the portico where she had an unobstructed view.

In a moment the stranger materialised at her side. 'Sister Hildegard?'

She nodded.

'Sir Talbot at your service.'

'We'd have more privacy to discuss this matter in my chamber.' Explaining where to find it she moved away.

If she had wondered how he would make contact when he arrived she was amply reassured now. But why the secrecy? She supposed it was because less attention would be drawn to her – and to the secret purpose of her journey – if she was seen to be nothing more than a lowly nun travelling alone. There could be no doubt he was a tournament knight.

It was a fact, observed Hildegard, that his rough wool cloak concealed everything about him but his athletic physique.

On returning to the inn and going up to her chamber, she found the door jammed. 'Pierrekyn, open up,' she whispered. There was a rustle from within but the door remained shut. 'Open it!' she urged. Eventually it inched open to reveal Pierrekyn's frightened face in the gap. When he saw Hildegard he drew it ajar enough to allow her to slip inside and then shut it quickly behind her. Evidently he had imagined a dozen armed constables standing in the passage.

'I shall be glad to get away from this festering town,' he whispered. 'How far is it out of the court's jurisdiction into safe territory?'

'Some way.'

With the chair wedged against the door again, she said, 'My escort has arrived. I've asked him to come up here as it's the only place we can meet without people prying into our business.'

'This won't work!' Pierrekyn flung himself down on the bed and put his hands over his eyes. 'I'm done for, Sister. I may as well go out and face the mob. Let them hack me to pieces!'

Hildegard tutted as she removed her cloak and hung it on a hook. When Sir Talbot approached the chamber a moment or two later he did so with such stealth she was unaware of his presence until she saw the chair legs bend with the pressure of someone trying to force their way in. Wedging a foot behind the door she opened it a crack.

'No one saw me come up, Sister.' He entered instantly and strode about with his head bent to avoid the beams. Close up, he was as striking as when she had first noticed him.

Ruddy-cheeked, with a square, handsome face and dancing blue eyes, he seemed to glow with vitality. His nose had been broken several times but it only added to his cheerful good looks. Light-brown hair cropped short to fit under the helmet he carried under one arm gave him a clean-cut, military look. His shoulders were broad and his neck corded with muscle. He moved in a poised, contained manner suggesting strength and speed beyond the usual. His sheer physical exuberance filled the chamber. Hildegard at once felt safe.

After giving the place a thorough inspection he turned to her. 'So who's this fellow?'

'I'll explain the situation about the minstrel here in a moment,' she began. 'But first, can you tell me who retains you?'

He shook his head. 'No idea. Somebody powerful. My instructions came through a third party.' He glanced at Pierrekyn. 'We can only surmise who instructed them,' he added meaningfully.

She would get to the bottom of this later, she decided. Meanwhile she selected the barest details about the previous night's events, telling him that for reasons there was no time to reveal, the boy had to be smuggled out of the town in the guise of the knight's squire.

When she finished Sir Talbot chuckled. 'I'm game for that. It's going to be more fun than I imagined. There might even be chance for a bit of a scrap after all!' He gave Pierrekyn an assessing glance. 'Know anything about the code of chivalry, lad?'

Pierrekyn snorted in derision.

They decided to leave as soon as the town gates opened just after prime next morning. Ulf and his men had left for the Rhine. Ludovico was lodged with the consul according to instructions from his patron. Their own bags were packed. Now all they could do was wait out the rest of the day.

Hildegard went down later to look to her hounds and Sir Talbot tracked her to the kennels. After admiring the animals and lamenting the fact that he had been instructed to leave his own hounds behind, he said, 'Sister, I have something to give you in private.'

With a covert glance over his shoulder, he drew a sealed letter from inside his tunic and handed it over.

He said, 'I'm told your cover is that you're on pilgrimage. But I deduce from the fee they're paying me that you're on Church business of some magnitude and,' he lowered his voice, 'some danger?'

'It seems so,' she agreed.

He stood to attention. 'You can trust me, Sister. My word is my bond.' With a nod towards the letter he had just given her, he tactfully withdrew.

When he left, Hildegard's immediate feeling was to trust him but, remembering he was a hired man, she decided she would remain watchful until she found out who maintained him.

Bermonda pushed her wet nose into the parchment as Hildegard prised open the wax seal. It was one she recognised as belonging to her priory at Swyne. Holding the letter out of reach of the inquisitive kennet hound, she began to read. The message was in the angular hand of her prioress. When she finished she could only stare at the words in astonishment.

After the usual greetings it baldly stated:

Go not to Rome but to Florence. We are told that you will find what we seek in the possession of the sacristan of the church they call Santi Apostoli. God be with you.

There was the familiar flourish of the prioress's signature.

Florence? After her initial shock she reminded herself that at least the journey would be shorter. She would be back at Swyne – back at Meaux – the sooner.

When she returned indoors she found Sir Talbot at once. 'Were you informed of our destination?' she asked.

He shook his head. 'I go where you command, Sister. Those are the terms of my employment.'

'We go to Florence then.'

He nodded, unperturbed, his ruddy features cheerful, and after a quick calculation he said, 'It's a journey of under twenty-five days in the height of summer. I reckon it'll take forty days at this time of year. And as I'm to conduct you back over the Alps as well, forty days to return.' He nodded with satisfaction. 'By the time we're back on this side of the mountains, the tournament season will be about to start. The journey should keep me in trim,' he added. 'Are you well prepared for the rigours ahead, Sister?'

'As well as I ever will be.'

She went up to tell Pierrekyn to be ready to leave at first light and found him fingering the strings of his lute in silence. Seeing him occupied, she took the opportunity to check over her own belongings again.

At the bottom of her scrip she found the piece of embroidered silk that had been handed to her on the quayside at Ravenser.

It was a puzzle. There was no doubting what it was. Sir Talbot himself was wearing something similar round his own neck under his gambeson although his was new looking and lacked embroidery in the corner. Long ago the Templars wore similar tokens to the one she held. Borage held the same meaning among all the chivalry.

Courage.

Was it a token from someone who wished her well? The person who had hired Sir Talbot maybe? Or was it a warning? She tucked it back inside her scrip and glanced up to find Pierrekyn watching her.

'A love token, Sister?' he asked in mock reproof.

'*Amor vincit*, Master, as I'm sure you agree.'

He laughed aloud and, remembering just in time to keep his voice down, whispered, 'I don't think you're a nun. I think you're a spy.'

When she replied it was in a whisper but the warning was clear. 'Don't ever let anyone hear you hint such a thing, not even in jest. Have you any idea what could happen if such a rumour got about?'

'Why should I care – if you're spying for the wrong side?'

'And which one is that?'

'Ha! You think I'm going to fall into your trap, do you?' He shut his mouth and ran his fingers over his lips to show they were sealed. Then he began to play his silent tune again.

Hildegard rose to her feet. 'I'm going out. I'll bring you back something to eat.'

There was one visit she had to make before they left. With the change of destination it had become important. She had to see Ludovico. His *famiglia* had their headquarters in Florence. One of the twelve priors who ran the city was his *capo*, Ser Vitelli. His help might be vital.

Chapter Eight

THERE WAS A sharp wind from the east. It snagged the pennants on the lances of the militia, pulled at the hoods of the travellers milling at the south gate, and made the tarpaulins on the goods wagons billow and crack as they began to trundle down the hill away from the town.

As Hildegard had expected, dawn was the best time to leave. The constable was yawning his head off and paid little attention to what in his eyes must have looked like the usual trail of folk leaving the town – merchants, always merchants, their baggage trains a source of revenue, the drivers and their guards too numerous to count properly, and among them the white-cloaked pilgrims and the riff-raff who followed them, pardoners and friars and others leaving Bruges on personal business.

The constable reeked of ale. All the better she thought, as they jostled past him. Pierrekyn's face was concealed by a parti-coloured hood purchased, with some forethought, by Sir Talbot in the market yesterday. Now, knight and squire were already through the inner ring of guards. Hildegard had suggested they go on ahead and rejoin her as soon as the convoy was on the move. That way they would draw less attention to themselves. Her hounds remained close at her heels.

Sir Talbot had hired a horse. It had been skittish when it was brought out from the stable, too full of oats and proud of its power over the unskilled riders who usually sat him, but the moment Sir Talbot threw his leg over his back he surrendered at once to a master. Pierrekyn, too, was walking obediently by Sir Talbot's side as if bewitched into good behaviour.

Holding her breath she saw them start out under the portcullis. They reached the outer gate with its gathering of militia. Then, with a sigh of relief, she saw them pass through. Soon only the erect figure of Sir Talbot was visible as the milling foot-travellers closed in behind.

Her own turn came. The constable barely glanced at a nun in a blue cloak. She followed the stream of foot passengers through the gate and was soon safely on the road to the south.

As she walked with the other pilgrims, always keeping Sir Talbot and Pierrekyn in sight, Hildegard thought about Reynard's murder and how she might question the boy further. She wondered how much she could confide in the knight when she did not know who had hired him. But she could not help but notice how kind he was to the horse, leading him some of the way, allowing Pierrekyn to ride beside the wagon while keeping an eye on him, now and then gently reproving him for pulling at the horse's mouth, and giving praise whenever he could, all with the greatest good humour.

Later that morning a wagon drove alongside her and as it drew level the driver called down, inviting her to climb up if she wanted. 'Always room for a Cistercian, Sister! Make the most of it. Your feet are going to be sore blistered if you're planning on walking all the way to Rome!'

Thanking him, she climbed aboard. He didn't waste time in conversation. There were too many pilgrims following the road to make them interesting any more. Instead he chatted to his lad and whistled now and then between his teeth with satisfaction at his lot.

Sir Talbot and his squire continued to make good progress. They managed to get further ahead when the wagon she was on was held up because somebody decided to unload their belongings and travel with friends they'd spotted in the crowd. With much cheerful shouting the wagoner heaved down their luggage, to be grasped by eager hands and hauled up onto another wagon following theirs.

As they started to move off again Hildegard was startled to find a man clambering up beside her.

She recognised him at once, even with the hood half over his face. It was the beggar from the market place, the one who had made off to the alehouse with her alms as soon as he had the coins in his hands. Now he pushed back his hood to reveal his face completely. She drew in a sharp breath.

'Aye, you remember me all right, don't you?'

Her heart began to hammer and one hand slid to her knife.

He gave a sneering laugh. 'You won't be needing that yet, lady. Do you think me stupid enough to try anything with this mob so close at hand? Not to mention those bloody brutes of yours.'

He scowled at the two hounds. Duchess and Bermonda were trotting beside the wagon, all their attention on the stranger with his head so close to that of their mistress.

'Escrick Fitzjohn, what do you want of me?'

'I remember you posed the same question last time we met.'

'You mean when you broke into my chamber at Castle Hutton in the middle of the night with a blade in your hand?' She faced him squarely.

'The answer's still the same,' he said. 'Just a little matter of redress.'

He lifted his left hand and ran a finger down the side of his jaw, tracking the scar that deformed his features. Pricks of blood seeped from an unhealed sore. Reaching out, he ran the same finger across her cheek to the corner of her mouth.

As she dashed his hand away he jumped down from the wagon. There was the same smile on his face she had seen before. She shivered. The wagon carried on. Soon his ragged shape mingled with those of the other foot-travellers and even when she craned her neck he was nowhere to be seen.

She scrubbed at her cheek with her sleeve. He had been outlawed for murder and must have fled to the low countries as many did. Surely it was chance that he had caught sight of her leaving Bruges. She shivered again at the thought that he might have followed her, remembering the hooded figure on the quay at Ravenser, waiting for the third ship to leave. The idea was too fanciful to entertain for more than a moment.

Oblivious to what had happened, Sir Talbot and Pierrekyn rode on ahead.

Eventually they reached their first night's halt, a sprawling inn, purpose built for the trade to and from the south. They were offered a straw pallet each and as much pottage as they could eat, rough fare but welcome. The main highway from Flanders and Paris converged on the town and many merchants joined the convoy while others saw their merchandise sent onwards along the Seine before returning home. In all the traffic along the route there was no sign of Escrick Fitzjohn.

Hildegard didn't mention her encounter to Sir Talbot. It would involve telling the knight what had happened last autumn between Lord Roger, his ambitious sister-in-law Sibilla and her husband, Roger's brother Sir Ralph. Their plotting to dupe Roger's eldest son of his inheritance by passing off a servant's child as their own had been revealed and the couple had retired to their stronghold near Scarborough Castle and were lying low to give Roger time to forgive and forget.

Now, it seemed, their outlawed house-servant, Escrick Fitzjohn, was on the loose. He had murdered one of Roger's maids and one of the brothers at Meaux, in addition to many other heinous acts for which he deserved to be punished, but instead of showing remorse and asking for his sins to be forgiven, it seemed all he wanted was revenge on the person he held responsible for revealing his crimes: Hildegard herself.

It was like a bad dream to discover him travelling the same road. The fact that he had vanished only added to her sense of danger.

She slept badly throughout that first week. Sharing a dormitory with other religious travellers, one of whom snored lustily every night, left her yawning and exhausted. Even so she made sure she kept up with Sir Talbot and Pierrekyn on the road and that her hounds were always to heel. Unaware of her fear but with the code of chivalry never far from his mind, Sir Talbot insisted she ride the hireling as often as she wished but she often chose to walk instead, feeling less conspicuous with her feet on the ground than sitting high up above the heads of the other travellers.

And so the days unfolded. Bruges, Troyes, Dijon. There was a rhythm to the journey that soon took over and seemed to obliterate any other thought beyond the next destination. If the limbs of the travellers ached during the first few days, as the weeks unfolded they became hardened to the continual exercise.

Sir Talbot in particular relished the opportunity to stride out on foot at the head of the cavalcade, or meander off into the trees on the pretext of scouting for robbers. He was astounding in his physical fitness. His unbounded energy was the envy of many.

So far there had been only rumours about the bands of thieves known to prey on the baggage trains carrying merchandise back and forth to the fairs in Champagne and beyond – their prevalence putting up the cost of insurance – but for safety three mercenaries had been engaged at the last halt to escort them through the notorious tracts of forest separating Champagne from the duchy of Burgundy.

Big, rough, well-armed fellows who clearly despised the merchants and their companions, they rode mettlesome horses fore and aft of the convoy while maintaining a professional distance from everyone.

Pierrekyn trudged along with his lute across his back, saying very little, or sat on the tailgate of one of the wagons and let his fingers pluck a tune from the strings, sometimes singing to himself.

A different person emerged then, one who was vulnerable and full of fun. He was painstaking in learning new tunes, practising the same phrase over and over again when he thought he was out of earshot. Most evenings he would flex his fingers at the fire then entertain the travellers after their repast. The merchants were particularly generous to him and soon he acquired a pouch filled with many different currencies.

One evening he spread them out on the table in front of Hildegard. 'Teach me their value,' he asked. 'I know you talked to Ser Ludovico about such matters. They look like nothing but buttons to me.'

She explained the difference as well as she could between soldi, denarii, fiorentini and gulden. 'The comparative values are difficult to work out as they change almost every day. Each town sets its own values on its coins. This grosso for instance,' she poked one of the coins with a finger, 'had to be launched in Venice recently as a multiple of several smaller silver pieces because they'd become almost worthless. But you can get a cup of burgundy for one of these.' She pushed another coin towards him. 'And this silver farthing will buy you a pie.'

'I'll put you to the test.' He swept up the coins and went to the back of the house where the innkeeper kept his barrels. When he returned he held a flagon of burgundy crooked under one arm, two clay beakers and a couple of steaming rabbit pies. He set them down on the table between them.

'You were right, Sister,' he said with a rare smile. 'And here's your earthly reward. Now tell me, having got me safely out of Flanders for reasons best known to yourself, what are you going to do with me? Am I to come all the way to Florence with you?'

'I insist on it.' By the time they arrived Ulf would surely have sent word that Reynard's murderer had been found and the boy would go free.

'Just so I know you're not going to discard me in some godforsaken mountain hamlet without a farthing to my name.' He poured a generous cup of wine for each of them. 'I almost believe I can survive this hellish journey,' he said after a long drink. 'Here's to you and nuns in general!'

She raised her cup. 'And to you and the brotherhood of minstrels.'

Sir Talbot joined them. 'Aren't you going to give us a song this evening, Master Pierrekyn? Or do I have to order you to pick up your lute?' Full of good nature, he thumped the boy heartily on the back to encourage him.

In response Pierrekyn produced one of his dazzling smiles. 'My pleasure is yours, sir knight.'

Talbot watched him set up with his instrument on a stool by the hearth. 'He's a fresh, perverted sort of lad,' he observed. 'But I suspect there's good in him, somewhere. I've half a mind to take him back to Paris with me. He'd do well there. They don't begrudge paying for their music. I'm just wary about the looks I'd get. My lady might have something to say to me!''

'I wonder about his future,' Hildegard confided. 'He needs a master if he's to join the guild and make his living from his playing.'

There had been no sign that Pierrekyn would harm a man, let alone plunge a dagger into his chest, but who would take him on with a suspicion of murder hanging over him?

A small boy of no more than ten had joined the convoy at the last town and now, clearly a fan of Pierrekyn, was standing close by, watching the minstrel's fingers carefully as if memorising their movements. When Pierrekyn noticed him he gestured for him to come closer.

'Are you going to sing for us then, young princeling?' she heard him ask. The boy nodded as if that was his precise motive for pushing himself to the front. She watched the two heads bend close as they discussed their repertoire. Then they began.

The child had a pure unbroken treble and Pierrekyn let him trill alone to his heart's content for quite a while with only the soft continuo of the lute as support, until he began to add his own husky tenor to the tune, weaving intricate melodies round the piping voice, echoing it in a lower register and reversing the phrases until the audience were spellbound with the magic of two such contrasting voices weaving in harmony.

When they brought the song to an end there was a burst of applause and a few folk banged their mazers on the wooden tables for an encore. Gold and silver coins cascaded at the singers' feet.

'Quite a partnership,' observed Talbot. 'I never could get my head round a song.' He stretched his long legs and flexed his muscles, ready to listen to more.

Pierrekyn glanced across at his two companions. He gave a secret smile and paused with his fingers poised over the strings until there wasn't a sound to be heard. Then he began to play.

It was a plaintive melody, a lament for the death of a knight, which began: 'There were three ravens on a tree ...' It went on to tell the story of a knight killed by a gang of robbers, and how his faithful hawk and his hounds protected his body until the appearance of a magical fallow doe, which carried his body to a lake and buried him, then died there beside him. It told of love and death. And there was scarcely a dry eye when he finished.

Despite the plaudits that followed and the cries for another song, Pierrekyn was suddenly unsmiling. He rose abruptly to his feet as if to break the spell he had created and, thrusting his lute into its bag, grasped the boy by one arm and pulled him towards the taproom where the dice-players gathered.

The three mercenaries, unlikely as it seemed, had been drawn to stand in the doorway to listen to the performance and now they called out to Pierrekyn as he pushed his way past. The smallest of the trio said something to his comrades and peeled off to follow him.

'I hope Pierrekyn isn't going to give that little lad strong ale,' remarked Talbot.

Hildegard fixed her eyes on the door, waiting for them to reappear, but there was just the usual milling of folk in and out, and loud guffaws from within over some game or other. Talbot noticed her expression.

'I'll go and see what he's up to. We don't want him drawing unwelcome attention, do we?'

He was back in a moment. 'He's intent on losing all his earnings in a game of dice. He sent the child back to his guardians with a handful of florins.'

Believing this was a good opportunity to explain a little more, Hildegard bent her head towards the knight and, speaking in a rapid undertone, she told him about the corpse in the wool-shed.

'It was the body of a clerk from England who brought Pierrekyn out of Kent while on business there on behalf of Lord Roger,' she explained. 'The boy's music charmed everyone and Roger decided to let him wear his livery.' She faltered. Until now she hadn't thought to question Roger's decision to send Pierrekyn away. Continuing, she said, 'When Reynard's body was found it was assumed that the boy must know something – because of their intimacy.'

'Do you mean he's seriously suspected of murder?'

'We have no reason to think he's guilty but the mob obviously decided otherwise when they heard the bare outline of the facts. That's why we had to get him quickly out of the duchy of Mâle and into another jurisdiction.'

'Meanwhile, the question remains: guilty – or innocent?'

She nodded. 'He cannot fail to be under suspicion until the real murderer is identified. If no one else is accused the only way that Pierrekyn will return to England will be in chains.'

'But if he is guilty he could well abscond, leaving Lord Roger's steward with his neck at risk?'

She nodded again.

'Trust me,' said Sir Talbot. 'I won't let him out of my sight.'

So saying, he got up and strolled through into the taproom where the game of dice was causing some excitement.

Chapter Nine

PIERREKYN'S FACE WAS flushed and angry. His lower lip jutted. He was making a token attempt to struggle out of Sir Talbot's grasp but the knight gripped him by the scruff of his neck in one capable hand.

Avoiding Pierrekyn's kicking feet he was laughing genially. 'Obey me, you little wildcat, or you'll rue it. You were losing every penny you earned to those fellows. They dice and fight and dice again. They do nothing else. You'll never beat them. And if you do they'll relieve you of your winnings in a most unpleasant manner.'

He forced Pierrekyn down onto the bench next to Hildegard.

'You talk to him, Sister. He's behaving like a numbskull.'

'Numbskull? Me? That's rich coming from somebody who risks having his brains knocked out of his head whenever he goes to work!' Pierrekyn retorted.

Sir Talbot laughed. 'It's me who does the knocking, I can tell you. The other fellows will bear me out if they can still spin two words together through their broken teeth.'

The three mercenaries came up. The more forthright one clapped Sir Talbot on the shoulder. 'You rescued him just in time, sir knight. We were about to step in ourselves. Can't have these Flemings running rings round one of our own.'

They were English, or, at least, two of them were. The third was a Scot, a big, brawny fellow with a wild red beard and an expression that, like those of his companions, showed he would take no truculence from anybody.

'Join us,' invited Sir Talbot. 'I notice the other travellers are somewhat wary of you.'

Indeed, nobody trusted mercenaries. One of the pilgrims had

even been heard to whisper when they were first hired, 'Today – paid to keep us from harm. Tomorrow – paid to slit our throats. It's all the same to them.'

'They're devils from hell,' agreed a friar, as everybody nodded their heads. 'Best to keep away!'

The men, however, seemed affable enough in their rough way and were deferential to Hildegard if not to the other religious Orders. They made frequent sport of a couple of crutched friars in their conspicuous cloaks with the large red crosses sewn to the backs, some obscene joke passing back and forth between them. But they had made no jokes at Hildegard's expense.

'So you're another mercenary just like us?' observed the leader in a provocative tone to Talbot as they took their places at the trestle.

'Just got up more fancy,' added the shorter of the three in a thin voice. His hair was thin too and lay in lank strands across the top of his balding head.

Sir Talbot sprawled at his ease, quite unruffled by the men's tone. 'Certainly I am,' he agreed. 'I bear arms for fame, fortune and my lady's love. What better purpose does life offer?'

They seemed to accept this and lost no time in explaining that they were going down to join Sir John Hawkwood's White Company in Tuscany.

'We've heard it's getting lively,' their leader announced with relish. On the way they had decided that they might as well have the journey paid for by the cowardice of the merchants and the pilgrims as they were all travelling the same road.

'I'm Jack Black,' he told them, 'and these two devils are Harry and Donal.' He glanced at Hildegard as if expecting criticism but she held her tongue. 'Aye,' he said, piercing her with his hard, black gaze as if reading her thoughts, 'but somebody has to do it.'

She grimaced. 'My heart goes out to the peasants who scratch a bare living from the soil then have their crops stolen by Hawkwood's army. I've heard his men are like vultures.'

'The peasants don't suffer. They all run for shelter to the towns. They're safe as houses. And if they don't run it's their own lookout,' grunted Harry, his gaunt face full of bitterness. 'We've got to eat and, if their rulers want us to do their work for them, where's the harm? We deserve the spoils of war since we're the ones who run the risks.'

It wasn't just the theft of crops, it was also rape and the wanton destruction of entire communities that made the mercenaries so hated, as the man well knew. Hildegard saw no point in getting into an argument with him.

The trio worked as a team, specialists in siege warfare. It was their job to dig tunnels under a town's fortifications and set explosives so that the rest of the army could get in through the breach. From the look of their personal equipment they were well paid for such work.

'So you're the fellows who decide where the siege tunnels should lie?' asked Talbot with interest.

'Harry here's the one to decide. Like a rat, he is, underground,' agreed Jack Black.

'It must be a glorious thing to wage single combat under such conditions,' mused Talbot. 'No wonder the combatants in such encounters are honoured by becoming brothers-in-arms.'

'We keep our distance from all that. We're not knights nor never likely to be.'

'We're useful crossbow men if it comes to it,' pointed out Harry. 'And Donal here's a devil with an axe or mace.'

'So where are you fellows from?'

'Ask no questions and you'll be told no lies,' Jack Black replied firmly for all three. 'What about you, sir?' he countered.

'I'm a Sussex man myself.'

'And your squire?' Harry put in.

As one they turned to stare at Pierrekyn and a silence fell. The moment was over in a flash. Pierrekyn merely displayed his tunic with Roger de Hutton's emblem on it, then spent the rest of the evening digging thoughtfully at the table with the tip of a small knife.

The quayside at St Jean-de-Losne was a busy transit point where some of the merchandise was to be transferred from wagons onto river boats.

As they approached, the weather darkened. For days the country-side had been black with rain. They seemed to move in a perpetual night. Daylight lasted for only a few hours, a grey presence filtered through a mass of cloud.

There were vast numbers of barges being loaded for transportation down the Saône. Some of the merchants decided to travel on with their merchandise by boat, rather than attempt the quicker route through the Jura and the Jougne pass and on through the Alps. Others were undecided. The dangers that lay ahead were a constant topic. Some wanted to go on by river rather than hazard the mountains, while others were keen to get to their destination as soon as possible.

'It's a choice of being knee-deep in mud or knee-deep in snow,' said one.

'God's will is clear,' declared another, looking out at the rain and opting to stay.

Others expressed regret that they had made a bad choice in Dijon when they could have continued on through the easier terrain of the Rhône valley instead. Now their fate, it seemed, depended on the snows. Would they come or wouldn't they? Nobody knew what to do for the best. They were in a continual fret.

Hildegard's group decided to push on, regardless of both weather and terrain.

The atmosphere between Sir Talbot and Pierrekyn was another thing that worsened with the weather. Everything about the knight seemed to draw some barbed comment from the boy. When, every morning, Talbot practised swordplay in the yard of wherever they were lodged, robustly impervious to the rain, Pierrekyn would stand and watch from the shelter of the thatched overhang, with a jeering expression that the mercenaries for one would not have tolerated.

Hildegard wondered how long it would be before Talbot struck back. He showed no sign of anger, however, but kept a courteous smile for everyone.

She accidentally came across him one morning while he was exercising in the yard before the rest of the travellers emerged. He pulled on his tunic at once, murmuring apologies. She let out a long breath as she walked away. His lady, the fair Rosamund of whom he often spoke in most reverential terms, was a fortunate woman, she decided. As a knight competing at the highest level in the tournaments he would have to be in magnificent physical shape, she knew. He was an athlete in his prime.

His sincerity towards Rosamund was not in doubt. Before they set out from Bruges he had asked Hildegard to accompany him to a goldsmith's and she had taken him to the one who was making up the brooches for Melisen. From among the stock on display he had purchased an intricately wrought gold buckle and asked for an inscription to be added: *je suy vostre sans de partier.*

During quieter moments of the journey he sometimes took it out to look at it and once or twice had asked for Hildegard's reassurance that it was a good choice.

He was, he told her, the youngest of four sons and had no wealth other than what he could earn himself. The patronage of a wealthy woman, married as Rosamund undoubtedly was, stood as just one of the many prizes he risked his neck for.

Pierrekyn was apparently irked by Talbot's chivalry and envious, too, of his moral certainty. There was safety in being sure of where one stood in the pecking order. Talbot's very confidence must be a thorn in the boy's side. Between himself and starvation lay nothing but a talent for music.

They reached Salins. It was a long, narrow town, with closed shutters, situated at the bottom of a winding, limestone gorge that would eventually take the travellers up into the Jura.

An endless train of wagons passed through the town both night and day, either bringing logs to the boiling houses that stood over the brine wells where the salt was evaporated, or else carrying away salt in the form of crystals packed in great pine barrels. These weighed around a quarter of a ton and the rumble of the loaded carts over the cobblestones was a continual deafening roar.

The darkness and the noise added to the sinister character of the town. Hildegard was made nervous by it, aware that Escrick Fitzjohn might be close. She imagined she saw him in every shadowed alley, down every street, as the carts thundered past.

It didn't help that the inn, the only place that could put them up, was a brawling den full of drunks and beggars. Unfortunately for them the Domus Dei, a hospice run by the Canons Regular, had no room. The town was bursting at the seams as people poured in, only to be stalled by the weather: those from the south fleeing the threat of avalanches, those from the north wondering whether to brave the floods ahead. Meanwhile they hung about the town in ever more rowdy and discontented groups.

The pilgrims in their own party were aghast at the drunken, brawling mobs and stayed in a frightened huddle in the belief there was safety in numbers. Their fear increased when those merchants starting out from Flanders began to leave, taking their retinues and men-at-arms with them. The ones remaining were ill equipped to protect anyone but themselves.

The situation wasn't helped by the attitude of the mercenaries.

There were many more now, swarming south to join the free companies in Tuscany. Wherever Hildegard looked they were swaggering about, demanding the innkeepers fulfil their every whim. They commandeered the cellars, took first pick of the meagre fare in the kitchens and left the crumbs to the weak. There were girls on offer too, as always, a sorry bunch, pock-marked, slatternly, resigned to an existence without hope or respite.

How different it is to the priory at Swyne, Hildegard thought. How different to the abbey of Meaux. Its cloistered tranquillity had never seemed more sweet. It seemed now, above all places on earth, to be the sweetest.

To the credit of the three mining mercenaries they remained aloof. As siege specialists they despised the foot soldiers, the pikemen and their followers, but harboured respect for a couple of newly arrived gunners and treated the longbow men with deference.

Harry, the ferrety little sapper, saw himself as above the rest because of his expert knowledge. He was the one who could tell at a glance how the land lay, what sort of rock they had to deal with, what foundations particular castles were built on. Without him the tunnels would be dug in the wrong place, as he never failed to remind them.

'I can read the terrain the way you read a woman's body,' he boasted to Sir Talbot, making sure Hildegard could overhear.

The Scot seemed to be the jack-of-all-trades, a one-man army in his own right, a tough backstop in any fight that broke out, as they frequently did. He was, not least, a cook. He carried a flat baking stone, which he heated every morning over the fire in the kitchen, then he would take it outside and bake flat cakes of bread on it in order to feed his companions. Eventually he began to share this bounty with Hildegard, her knight and squire.

Soon, every morning was started in the same way and they would break their fast together. It was an unlikely alliance, but Hildegard welcomed it. Escrick Fitzjohn would think twice before trying anything while she was so well protected.

Jack Black was the instigator of this unexpected accord. Hildegard assumed it was because the militia held a superstitious belief that a nun brought good luck. At first she found him affable enough, despite a hint of irony whenever he addressed her, and until she heard him holding forth, she found it hard to imagine he was an expert in the lethal skill of setting explosives. But it was a fact. His comrades vouched for it.

He spoke with a chilling precision when he described the exact amount of explosive needed to destroy specific ramparts of stone. He even claimed to be able to work out, to the ounce, how much was needed to blow a man and a horse limb from limb. His favourite pastime was to cast an eye over the pilgrims, assess their weight, then work out how much explosive he would have to use on a particular man to do what he called 'a good job'.

Wherever he went came the death-scent of saltpetre.

They shook themselves free from the noise and violence of Salins as soon as possible and travelled on along a route that was supplied with a string of unremarkable inns where Pierrekyn was for ever in demand for his singing. A particular favourite was the lament about the knight and the three ravens, which never failed to draw a sentimental sigh from even the most hardened traveller as the last note died away.

One night Hildegard had a strange feeling as soon as Pierrekyn started to sing, causing her to blink back tears before anyone could notice. It took her a few moments to understand the reason.

As the music wove its spell she discovered that she was haunted by the memory of Hubert de Courcy. She seemed to see him standing before the altar in the chapel at Meaux, his austerely handsome features softening as he turned to look at her. Unwillingly she recalled his voice in the pear-tree walk when he had uttered her name for the first time.

Before Pierrekyn finished singing she got up and went out into the yard at the back of the inn. The ribald sound of drunks floated from another tavern across the street but there was a crystalline quality to the air, and the stars, small and frosty, brought a surging sense of the immense emptiness in which the globe of the world turned.

Her hounds were kennelled close by and she went to release them. It's just a cheap song, she told herself as she paced the yard. It's no wonder the Church rails against minstrels.

After a circuit or two she sank down onto one of the benches against the wall. Her husband's death in France had prompted many offers of matrimony but the last thing she had wanted was to be bartered for her inheritance. To live in loveless idleness with some semi-literate magnate from the shires was not to her taste. She had retreated to the priory instead. For seven years she had not regretted this decision. In fact, in an unexpected way, she felt she had found her vocation. The dream that had later inspired her to found a separate cell was on the verge of becoming reality. As soon as she returned to England she would move to the grange Roger de Hutton had promised to lease and set it up to help the poor.

Now, the sorcery of Pierrekyn's playing aroused an unexpected sense of loss. She sat for a long time, thinking things over. Eventually, she rose briskly to her feet.

An abbot? she thought. Am I mad?

Just then, Pierrekyn himself came outside.

'Those pigs!' he raved, storming over to her. 'What do they know about music?' He looked as if he was about to sit down but, apparently regretting his outburst, swivelled on his heel to return indoors.

The way, however, was barred. It was the thin-faced mercenary, Harry, who stood there.

'Bon-jewer, messire,' he began in a needling voice. Then he burst into hoarse laughter. 'You! You're no more a Frenchman than I am!'

Pierrekyn had started to effect a slight accent, being increasingly asked to sing *chansons* now they were journeying south. He didn't reply but simply tried to push past the sapper who pushed him back, harder.

'You're not a frenchie. You, a troubadour?' He jeered. 'You're a Kentish man just like me. And the point is, *master*, I know all about you.'

'Let me past, you pathetic cur,' replied Pierrekyn, incautiously. 'I've nothing to say to you.'

'Well, monsewer, I've plenty to say to you!' The man prodded him in the chest.

Hildegard stepped forward. Bermonda and Duchess pricked their ears.

'Piss off, you piece of dung!' yelled Pierrekyn, losing his temper with astonishing speed.

He quickly propped his lute against the wall, then launched a wild punch at the grinning mercenary. This was not well advised. The man was a professional fighter. He dodged the blow with a mocking laugh and retaliated with a heavy fist to the stomach. Then, before Pierrekyn could get his breath, he smacked him hard in the mouth, grabbed him by the neck and rammed him up against the wall. It was then that Sir Talbot came sauntering into the yard.

'What's all this?' he asked.

By now the mercenary was pounding Pierrekyn's head against the wall. The latter, refusing to fight, had his hands over his face.

Sir Talbot took three strides, dragged the mercenary back by his tunic and smacked the back of his hand across the man's face, making him stagger with the force of the blow. Then he gripped him by one ear, forcing him to his knees in the mud.

'The code of chivalry does not allow me to chastise a commoner, sir, or by God you'd regret this base attack on one of my party.'

With a swinging movement he hurled the man bodily down the length of the yard. The sapper collapsed to the ground and, half scrambling, clawed his way back inside with a hurried glance over his shoulder.

'What was that about?' demanded the knight, rubbing his knuckles.

Pierrekyn refused to answer. His mouth was swollen. He picked up his lute and turned to go back in. Then, clearly bothered by what might lie in wait, he hesitated.

Talbot understood. 'Go through that door with your head high. Don't let them see you're afraid.'

'They'll kill me.'

Talbot gave him a level glance.

Clenching his fists, Pierrekyn turned on his heel and returned indoors.

Hildegard was standing with her hand inside her cloak where it lay secretly on the hilt of her knife. Her hounds were still poised. Talbot shook his head. 'He's something of a loose arrow, our young friend. But not without a certain reckless courage. I'd better stay close to him. I may be needed again.'

Hildegard, her hounds at her heels, followed.

The last of the pilgrims were having a drink before turning in for the night. Talbot had wedged Pierrekyn in among them on one of the benches.

The group looked peaceful enough. The matter was not yet over, however, because, as Hildegard entered, the three mercenaries were swaggering over in a group. She noticed Talbot's hand move to the hilt of his sword.

Jack Black spread his arms. 'That was untoward, sir knight. But I believe this rancour has a history preceding our journey. Ask the lad the truth of the matter. And then we can judge who's right or wrong.'

Pierrekyn, confident in the safety afforded by Sir Talbot, scowled. 'There is no history. I've never clapped eyes on that dog in my life.'

'No,' replied Jack, 'but he's clapped eyes on you.'

Pierrekyn's bruised mouth turned down. Jack shouted for one of the serving women to bring ale all round as if to make up for his companion's roughness towards the boy, but Pierrekyn's expression did not soften, nor would he answer any questions. When the last of the pilgrims went up to bed, he took out his own little dagger and began to hack sulkily at the edge of the table in a black silence.

Talbot had been made restless by the skirmish and clearly wanted some resolution to it. He drank down half the contents of his mazer in one gulp and then looked around for something to excite his interest. Noticing what Pierrekyn was doing, he hooted in amusement and whipped the knife in an instant from between his fingers.

'What's this little toy, young master?' He twirled it like a stick. Pierrekyn tried to grab it back.

Laughing, Sir Talbot leaped to his feet and waved the knife above his head. 'What is it?' he teased. 'You don't expect anybody to be frightened of this, do you? It's no more lethal than a piece of straw. Even a monk couldn't sharpen his quill with it!'

There were a few guffaws at the double meaning. With an explosion of rage, Pierrekyn threw himself bodily on the knight and tried to snatch his knife back but Talbot was as quick as lightning and whenever Pierrekyn tried to make a lunge he lifted it a carefully judged inch out of reach.

The mercenaries cheered every time Pierrekyn failed to snatch his knife back.

'He scraps like a jade,' mocked Harry with a snort of contempt.

Talbot offered the knife, handle first. 'Here, take it. You need something better than that. It wouldn't even gut a rabbit.'

'I know what I can gut and what I can't!' Pierrekyn shouted, unappeased, grabbing the knife by its handle. With all his strength, he rammed the blade straight back towards Talbot's chest. Startled, the knight smoothly disarmed him and the knife flew across the floor.

Harry bent to retrieve it and held it up. 'It's rubbish, is this,' he declared. He stabbed it hard into the table and the blade snapped like a twig.

Pierrekyn gaped in horror. 'That was my only weapon,' he exclaimed, gazing aghast at the broken blade.

Hildegard thought he was about to burst into tears so she said hurriedly, 'I'm sure we can find you something to take its place, Pierrekyn. Let's find you a better one tomorrow.'

As if he had not heard he spun away but as he did so something fell from inside his doublet. It came to rest under the table at Hildegard's feet and she crouched to pick it up.

It was a red velvet slipper no bigger than a hand's span. A child of ten could have worn it. Sewn with hundreds of tiny seed pearls, it was a little turnshoe, stitched inside out then turned right side out. In the lining thus formed was something stiff that rustled as she crumpled it in her palm.

She pushed it into Pierrekyn's hand. 'Yours, I believe?' She stared at him closely. His face was ashen.

Without looking at her, he stuffed the turnshoe inside his doublet and marched out.

Hildegard gazed after him with a feeling of horror. She was astonished at the lack of control the boy had shown. If his knife had been stronger and Sir Talbot less agile, he could have run him through the heart and his victim would now be lying dead at their feet in a pool of blood.

Talbot exchanged a glance with her and without speaking followed the boy out.

Jack Black noticed her expression. 'Harry here knows him from down Kent way, ain't that right, fellow?'

'No doubt of it. He was active in the Rising,' he affirmed. 'As were we all. When they took the leaders and hanged 'em and set up courts on all the manors around to hang the rest, somebody betrayed a heap more names to the Justices. Men were hanged even if they hadn't marched to Smithfield. Next thing was, that lad's master was found dead, his throat slit, and, when the constables showed up, the lad had gone. Make of that what you will.' He spat into the sawdust on the floor but would say nothing more.

Sick of the animosity, and troubled by the alarming thought that Pierrekyn might well have more to hide than she believed, Hildegard made her way up to the dormitory she shared with the other pilgrims.

It hadn't taken long to reveal how uncontrollable Pierrekyn's temper could be. And the sapper's accusation was revealing. Why would the boy flee his master if he was innocent? And if guilty of one murder, why not a second?

Chapter Ten

THE FROST RETURNED and the danger of avalanches receded. It was best to risk going on while they could. The cavalcade entered the Jura.

Talbot pulled rank and found a place for Hildegard on one of the wagons so she wouldn't have to continue on foot. After a few days, when she had been shaken black and blue on the wooden seat, he again showed his consideration and managed to obtain a cushion for her. With her blue cloak pulled well up over her face to keep out the wind, she was as comfortable as she was likely to be on such a tough and tedious journey.

Towns and villages came and went. The linen bales carried on the wagon formed a wall that kept out the worst of the weather, but even so, the constant jolting of the cart made her feel queasy and there was nothing Sir Talbot could do about that. It was thanks to his chivalry she wasn't sitting in the wagon full of herring. The smell wafted strongly in the thin, clear air and it was best to travel upwind whenever possible.

Halfway through the morning Talbot swung up onto the wagon to sit beside her, bringing a couple of hot pies from one of the vendors who swarmed round them like flies at every town and custom post. 'I was unkind to tease poor Pierrekyn so remorselessly over his little knife,' he said. 'I should have realised that it had a value beyond its practical use.'

'Meaning?'

He grimaced. 'I suspect it might have been a memento of some sort. There's no other reason for him being so upset about it.'

'Perhaps he just doesn't like being teased?'

'But it's true I was cruel to him. I'm going to make amends.'

He showed her a dagger with a blade about five inches long, narrow and well sharpened, its handle smartly bound in red leather.

'It's pretty enough to appeal to him, don't you think?'

Hildegard gave it a careful scrutiny. 'I didn't try to find him a replacement because I wasn't confident he wouldn't misuse it. Do you think he's safe with a knife?'

'I believe he lashed out without thought the other evening. At the back of his mind he knew such a thin blade would do no harm against my mail shirt.' He noticed her uncertainty. 'This is wild country, Sister. Everybody needs to be able to defend themselves.'

'I hope your faith in him will be proven. It's a kind gesture, one to be hoped he'll appreciate.'

Pierrekyn was riding the hired mule exchanged for the horse Talbot had obtained earlier. Now the knight sprang down from the wagon and, loping with long strides beside the mule, suddenly flourished the knife in front of Pierrekyn to display its scarlet handle.

The boy's expression changed. He smiled briefly and took the knife. Hildegard found herself praying that he would use it only for good.

Talbot came striding back to the wagon. 'At least I've put things right.' He threw Hildegard a puzzled glance. 'What sort of boyhood has he had to make him take a bit of teasing so amiss?'

Hildegard did not tell him what little she knew. She did, however, mention the sapper's accusation.

'We've only Harry's word. No one should be without a good knife these days. I'm prepared to give the lad the benefit of the doubt,' Talbot added firmly.

The matter of the velvet turnshoe she kept to herself.

They were now somewhere in the Vaud, a territory ruled by the Count of Savoy. After their descent from the Jougne pass, the Jura had been left behind and they soon cleared the toll at Les Clées.

There had been no sign of Escrick Fitzjohn since Bruges if those fleeting shadows in Salins could be discounted.

Once through customs, their road joined several others on a run down to Vévey on the shore of Lake Geneva. It was much frequented by pilgrims travelling to and from Rome. The town was overflowing with travellers, the lake itself a windswept expanse of sharp-fanged waves. There they joined another road that ran along the upper Rhône to Martigny before at last beginning the steep ascent through St Branchier to Orsières.

Ahead were the towering heights of the Alps and the place they all feared, the dreaded Great St Bernard pass.

The last of the merchandise was offloaded at Martigny for shipment along the Rhône where it would again be loaded onto wagons at Brig for its final destination to Milan. Some, however, was put in store until the roads opened again in summer. The innkeepers along the route made a rich profit from offering guarantees to the merchants for the safe storage of what were often goods of high value. In summer the pack animals would continue through the pass and on into Tuscany.

This was the route to be followed by the de Hutton and Meaux woolpacks – except for the one bale that remained in Bruges, despoiled by the presence of a dead body.

By the time they reached Orsières near the entrance to the pass, their party was much depleted. It now consisted of Hildegard, Talbot, Pierrekyn, the three mercenaries, and half a dozen pilgrims who, for reasons of spiritual purity and not a little fear, kept themselves to themselves. Even Pierrekyn's singing partner left.

While they were at the inn in Orsières, a courier arrived from the south. He was shivering despite his hard walking and, before he leaped onto the back of the mule waiting for him, warned them that snow was falling in the mountains. It was expected to get worse over the next few days.

After a brief, worried conference, Hildegard and Talbot decided to go on. If the courier had got through the pass with his leather satchel of mail, then they could do the same with their few belongings. It was, after all, only eight miles.

Pierrekyn looked disgruntled but offered no view of his own. Jack Black and his comrades, hardened to all weathers, were in a hurry to get to the lucrative fields of war and gave no thought to the trivial inconvenience of snow. They were prepared to hire guides to see them over the summit. It was what you did in these parts, they said. They would all keep together. There was no sense in waiting.

So now, with a handful of the more hardy pilgrims, their small group was ready to set out for the worst part of the journey.

Although only eight miles, a distance that could have been covered in a couple of hours' brisk walking on the flat, it was the height of the climb, the roughness of the terrain, and the snakelike meanderings of the route that made it near enough a day's climb.

They had been on the road since dawn. As they discovered, what made it difficult were the frequent slow traverses they had to make from one side of the mountain to the other. Sometimes there was nothing more than a few ropes to help them; at others there were frail cord bridges suspended over the ravines, which they could use only one at a time.

It was frightening. Hildegard felt her breath stop every time she set foot on the cordings set loosely on their net of ropes. From a distance the bridges looked no more substantial than a silken web. Close up they seemed little better. What made them more dangerous was the fact that ice clung to them, adding to their weight, and making them groan under the strain even before anybody set foot on them. A hundred times over, Hildegard imagined the ropes snapping under the strain and the unlucky traveller pitching down in a blitz of ice to the bottom of the chasm.

Apparently oblivious to danger, the mercenaries went doggedly ahead to dislodge the ice with great sweeps of their axes, hooting with glee every time the shards smashed on the rocks below.

When Harry saw Pierrekyn gingerly peering over the precipice after a particularly large block had fallen several hundred feet, shattering into a thousand pieces or more, he yelled, 'Bet you're glad that's not your bloody 'ead!' For once Pierrekyn held his tongue.

Sometimes they had to cross frozen brooks where the ice crackled under their tread. At the last halt they had hired overshoes studded with nails to stop them slipping on the ice and were encouraged to wear horn eye-pieces with narrow slits cut in them through which the world could be seen, elongated and somehow clearer.

Ulf had warned Hildegard what it would be like but no words could match the physical reality. Each step taken was a small victory against the elements. The wind pierced like a knife through every gap in their garments. Hildegard's fingers turned into useless lumps despite her fur mittens. Even the beaver hat did not prevent ice cutting her face and forming a rime over the eye-piece.

By the time they reached the hospice on the summit they were exhausted, but there were smiles of satisfaction all round. They stamped their boots to dislodge the snow and jostled to get inside with a palpable sense of achievement.

What made it bearable for Hildegard was the thought that she would soon be in Florence. The thought had sustained her all day. When the prior came down to greet them she saw it as one more waymark on the long journey to obtain the cross.

The prior and canons of St Bernard had been offering hospitality to pilgrims and other travellers for over three hundred years. Bernard himself was of royal descent, related to the counts of Savoy, and he had built the hospice on the site of a small monastery with endowments from his relatives. Nowadays an increasing number of pilgrims made the journey from the northern countries down to Rome on what was called the via Francigena and as a result a network of similar refuges had been set up. But the Great St Bernard hospice was the first.

Unlike the inns that had sprung up as trade increased, at intervals of a half-day's journey, where travellers were charged as much as the market would bear, the hospices offered free accommodation to everyone. This, together with the fact that the buildings were expensive to maintain at such an altitude, made them perpetually short of money. The prior also offered the free services of *maronniers* whose job was to guide travellers through the pass, act as a rescue service, maintain the fixed ropes and bridges over the steepest part of the route and keep up the *perches,* the signposts without which anyone could become lost. On top of that each traveller was given a portion of bread and a measure of wine before leaving.

In order to do all this the place was run by a number of Augustinians. One of them fell into conversation with Hildegard once he knew she spoke French. He was helping a couple of lay brothers to arrange the implements for the evening meal.

'I am,' he told her, 'a *quêteur*.' When she asked him to explain, he said, 'I'm usually out on a quest, begging, of course, as I'm a mendicant.' He glanced round the hall. 'It takes money to keep this place running. It's a pity we can't charge as the innkeepers do!'

'There are many members of your Order in the towns close to my priory in the North of England,' she told him. 'They do a lot of good among the sick.' They both moved on, he to finish his chores in the kitchens, Hildegard to feed her hounds.

Duchess and Bermonda had worn small leather pouches over their feet with nails to stand in lieu of claws but had not taken kindly to such an indignity. Now when she found them they looked at her with forlorn expressions. She ruffled their ears and spoke kindly to them to cheer them up, and in reply they leaned heavily against her legs as if to plead with her not to put them through such an ordeal again.

'My poor creatures,' she murmured. 'Only one more day and then we'll be over the mountains and you'll be basking in sunshine and walking in marble halls.'

Quêteur, the canon had called himself, a quester. That was her own role too. In her case it was a quest to find the cross of Constantine and bring it home.

There was not much singing from Pierrekyn after supper that evening. Not that he was unwilling but his repertoire had to be tailored to suit the religious nature of their lodging.

Eventually he found a suitable song. It was another *chanson* about a lady in a bower. 'The arrow of love has pierced my heart and now I bleed and die,' he warbled in a mocking falsetto. Apparently he was quite revived from the day's ordeal.

Hildegard closed her eyes. All day she had thrust aside every thought of Hubert de Courcy. Now weariness made the effort too much and he appeared before her, not as she had last seen him, cold and indifferent to her fate, but as he had been on that autumn afternoon in his garden. Banal as love often seems to outsiders, the song expressed her feelings with shaming accuracy: an arrow had pierced her heart, she bled, she died.

Chapter Eleven

WHILE THEY WERE recovering their strength before starting the next and worst leg of the journey, Hildegard came to a decision. It was no good taking risks.

The Augustinians had their own courier service. It was fast and efficient. The Order even had an English house in Beverley and no doubt exchanged correspondence with them but the message she wanted to send was not intended for them.

It would go to Bruges. Ulf would have been and gone by now but the Vitelli company ran their own courier service and would be able to pass a message on to Castle Hutton. It seemed prudent to inform the steward about her misgivings concerning Pierrekyn.

Nothing he had done in the days following his futile attack on Talbot gave her confidence that he wouldn't erupt again. He was smouldering in a black and silent rage that would find its release soon, she was sure. Once Ulf knew what had transpired it would be up to him to determine a course of action. She would ask him what he expected her to do when she reached her destination. So far she had fulfilled his request but it would be the easiest thing in the world for Pierrekyn to vanish into thin air down some busy back street once they arrived. Ulf would have to send his instructions.

Borrowing ink from the friendly canon she had spoken to before supper, she found a quiet place where she could set pen to paper. The ink was frozen in the bottle. She warmed it at the fire until it ran freely and then began to write, finishing in time to be able to hand the letter to the courier before he left at dawn.

★　★　★

Her misgivings about Pierrekyn were justified not much later.

Shortly after the courier left she prepared to join the depleted group of travellers in the courtyard. Three *maronniers* had been provided to guide them down the glass-like precipice.

The air was crisp. Mont Joux stood over them in the blue sky. Sunlight glinted off the snow. Dazzled, they put on the horn eye-pieces again. Their breath issued in puffs of steam whenever anybody spoke. Already noses were pinched and fingers were throbbing with chilblains. They stamped their nailed boots, newly waterproofed with pig fat, throwing up small shards of ice as they waited to set out.

Emerging into this brilliance with her pack of bread and wine and her forlorn-looking hounds, Hildegard squinted round. At once she noticed an absence. 'Where's Pierrekyn, Sir Talbot?'

'I thought he was with you.'

'I haven't seen him since compline yesterday.'

'He told me he was coming to play his new tune to you to see how you liked it,' he explained.

'He didn't do anything of the sort.' Hildegard was puzzled. This was hardly the place from which to make his escape.

Nobody admitted to having seen him until one of the pilgrims, smiling, said, 'Your knight's young squire, Sister? I saw him going out after dining last night as soon as the snow stopped. He was heading for the rocks up yonder.' He pointed back the way they had come. 'I assumed it was a call of nature and thought nothing of it.'

'When was this?' asked Talbot.

'Just after compline. I was called outside for the same reason,' he added.

Grim-faced, Talbot turned to Hildegard. 'He's absconded.' He took her to one side. 'What do you suggest, Sister?'

She was uncertain. 'I can't see him surviving on the mountain by himself.'

'He's tougher than he looks. Nearly beat me at arm-wrestling the other day. And running away surely proves his guilt?'

'It looks like it. Even so I'm worried for him.'

'We certainly can't set off in pursuit. We don't know these mountains and we've no idea where he's likely to be heading. And you have your own journey to consider.'

'We'll ask the prior to send his men after him. If they find him they can hold him until the steward from Castle Hutton instructs someone to take him back to England to face justice.' She stifled her anger. 'This is all my fault. I should have been less trusting.'

'And I should have kept a better eye on him,' replied Talbot gallantly.

She put a hand on his sleeve. 'Let's press on. I've already sent a letter to inform the steward of our doubts. Let him make of it what he will. The prior will send out his men when he knows the boy's wanted. We have to go on. I can't delay any longer.'

The prior was more than willing to send men out in pursuit of Pierrekyn when he heard what had happened. He also told them he would have prevented them going after him themselves if they had tried as they knew nothing about the mountain trails nor which ones they could travel in safety in the present weather conditions.

They found their group of travelling companions had dwindled further by the time they went to rejoin them. Two of the more faint-hearted had decided to stay on in the comfort of the hospice until they were convinced beyond doubt that the good weather would hold.

The descent was said to be more dangerous than the road up to the summit. As they set their faces towards the south they all agreed that it would be the toughest day yet.

It was hard going, there was no doubt of that. The path was all but obliterated by the snow and without the *perches* there would have been no knowing where they were. The guides, with felt hoods wrapped tightly over their heads, led the way with thrusts of their long poles deep into the snow at every step. Everyone followed in single file, first Sir Talbot, then Hildegard, then the three pilgrims, and finally Jack Black and his crew.

Progress was slow. At one point the wind had blown the surface snow off the rock, leaving a carapace of ice. It looked black like rock but this was deceptive as they discovered when an unwary pilgrim put one foot on it and went yelling and tumbling on his backside while everyone in front tried in vain to catch hold of him.

Fortunately for him, he ended up in a drift at the brink of the cliff. There was much amusement as he was hauled out with his hood awry and a fringe of snow on his brow.

Whenever it was safe, the guides helped them slide down the ice on hides. Then they cried out with whoops of joy that were probably heard all over the mountainside.

Thankful for her tough new boots from the shoemaker in Beverley, Hildegard trod in the prints left by Sir Talbot. He was striding out, some way ahead of the others, and she had to walk briskly to keep up with him. She carried her little hound, Bermonda, like a baby as her legs were too short to see her easily through the depth of snow, but Duchess, tall and stately, ran along like all lymers with a high even tread, her nose in the air.

The pass would eventually bring them out on the other side of the mountains at a custom post in a town called St Rhémy. The name was like a beacon that drew them on without regard for pain or danger.

They were only about two thirds of the way, however, when, out of the deceptive clarity of a cloudless sky, a blizzard burst over their heads with sudden and unexpected violence. Even the *maronniers* were taken by surprise.

Almost straight away everybody was separated by driving shards of ice. Hildegard could see Sir Talbot just ahead but he looked like nothing more than a shadow in the white-out. Unable to judge how far back the others were, she made an effort to catch up with him. Her thoughts flew to Pierrekyn.

When she drew level with Talbot she shouted, 'I hope those canons have found the boy. I don't give much hope for him, alone in all this.'

They soon found themselves walking in a world of their own. In the whirling flakes it was impossible to tell whether they were heading towards the precipice or keeping to the track. To make matters worse, darkness fell prematurely, decreasing visibility even further. After a few more paces it became clear that it would be folly to continue.

Sir Talbot decided to call to the others. Putting his head back, he let forth a great war cry. From out of the darkness some way behind came an answering shout. It sounded like one of the mercenaries. Talbot said, 'No doubt they'll catch up with us if we stop here.'

They waited for some time before realising they must have somehow missed the others. The snow had settled into a steady blizzard. Flakes flew into their mouths whenever they opened them to speak.

Talbot risked another shout but this time there was no response. Everything was muffled by the tumbling flakes. Even Duchess whined. Hildegard was shivering with cold. She cuddled Bermonda to share a little warmth.

Sir Talbot was undaunted. He suggested they camp where they were for the night. 'We'll get a better view of where we are in the light of morning.'

Hildegard was horrified at the thought of spending a night on the mountainside. 'You mean here, in the open? We'll surely freeze to death!'

He gave a genial chuckle. 'Trust me, I've done this many times. It's part of a soldier's training to know how to survive in the wilds.'

Stopping just where they were, he started to burrow into the snow and when Hildegard helped they soon dug out a hole big enough for both of them to shelter in, together with the hounds.

Gallantly Talbot spread his cloak and asked whether she would mind tenting her blue cloak over their heads. He explained, 'That way we'll keep within the ice chamber all the warmth our bodies magically give out.'

Seeing the sense in it, she did as he asked. When she began to take off the fur lining she wore underneath the cloak in order to share it between them, he refused adamantly.

'I insist,' she said. 'This is no time for gallantry. It would be most inconvenient if you froze to death!'

Conceding the point he put his arms around her to increase their natural heat and they huddled politely together in the snow house. The hounds added their own body heat, giving off a strong smell of the pennyroyal she rubbed on them to kill fleas. Soon all four drifted into a comfortable and aromatic doze.

It was the sunlight on her face that woke Hildegard. She was amazed when she opened her eyes to find that it was day. The blizzard had abated and the sun was crawling in through the cracks of their makeshift canopy, now sagging under the weight of snow, with the promise of a fair day. Sir Talbot opened his eyes as soon as he felt her disentangle herself from his embrace.

She was already pushing the cloak to one side when he sat up. Bars of gold light fell across his face as he leaned back for a moment with the fur falling away from his shoulders and breathed out a long, contented sigh.

'I've just had the most magnificent dream. It was like something out of a *chanson*.' He sighed again in contentment. 'I was walking through a meadow. It must have been spring because it was filled with the scent of flowers. Ahead of me was a gate and, when I opened it, who was waiting for me in a bower but my Lady Rosamund! She greeted me with the most loving smile. And at that moment I knew I had attained my heart's desire.' He closed his eyes as if to savour the feeling of bliss a little longer. When he opened them he asked, 'Do you think it might be a portent of things to come?'

'It could well be.' She smiled. 'At least she was with you through the night.'

He rose to his feet, carefully shook out her blue cloak so that the snow did not fall on them and then climbed outside.

At once he gave a shout. 'Sister! Come and look! This is like paradise itself!' She heard him whoop with joy as his footsteps crunched over the snow.

Poking her head out she saw what he meant. The snow lay in perfect smoothness in every direction. On one side was a low cliff but over on the other side of the valley the peaks and crags glistened under a gleaming mantle.

He dropped back inside the snow chamber with his breath steaming, careful not to tread on the huddled dogs. 'There's a sharp little breeze eddying about. May I borrow your cloak for a moment?'

She could see he was shivering despite his efforts. She put it over his shoulders. Despite the soft blue fabric, he still had an endearingly military look.

He climbed outside again. His footsteps made crimping sounds on the ice crust as he strode towards the privacy of some rocks.

It must surely be a good day to attempt the last few miles to St Rhémy, Hildegard thought with satisfaction. If they set off now they should soon catch up with the others. They must have passed in the night, or maybe had decided to camp out and would be visible on a different part of the track. Their guides would be as wise in mountain-craft as Sir Talbot.

Stretching her limbs she fondled her hounds behind the ears. Duchess was already pawing at the snow as if wondering whether to scramble into the open and Hildegard was about to follow when there was an unexpected sound.

She couldn't place it. It was a whine like a missile being thrown, followed by a thump. Then silence. Talbot must have heard it, too, for his footsteps stopped.

Curious, she peered outside. Something was heaped in the middle of the field of snow. When she looked more closely she saw it was the confused folds of her blue cloak.

She gave a cry. It was Talbot. He was lying on the ground and in the middle of his back was a bolt from a crossbow.

The edges of the cloak lifted in the breeze but Talbot did not stir.

With no thought other than to reach him, she scrambled out and hurled herself across to where he lay. 'Talbot!' she cried.

He was face down in the snow. She tried to turn him over but as she did so a stream of blood poured from between his lips. The snow was stained with it.

Cradling him in her arms she whispered over and over, 'Talbot, oh my dear Talbot, my dear, my poor Talbot.'

His eyes, only moments ago full of life, were already beginning to film over. Scarcely aware of the tears falling onto the backs of her hands, she wiped a few ice crystals from his brow and after a moment pressed his eyelids shut.

Before she could work out what had happened she heard a sound from the direction of the cliff. She glanced up.

Near the summit was a scattering of rock. Purplish shadows crawled between glittering fingers of snow. In the confusion of ice and shadows nothing seemed to move.

It took a moment for her to realise that what she could hear was the rewinding of the crossbow.

She scrambled to her feet. There were only minutes left before it could be rewound. Thinking quickly, she loosed Talbot's scabbard and dragged the heavy sword over to the shelter. She must take it with her as proof of his death. His bag lay where he had dropped it the previous night. Now she pulled the rough brown cloak they had slept on from underneath it and threw it over her shoulders. Abandoning the rest of their equipment, she shouted to her hounds to follow.

Duchess had already pushed through the snow, chest-deep in the drifts, nose pointing at the cliff, but at the sound of her mistress's command she reluctantly turned and bounded after her. With the heavy sword dragging through the drifts, Hildegard waded over the unmarked snow that stretched to the edge of the ravine. The mountain-wall on one side was her only guide to the descent.

With the remorseless sound of the crossbow being wound to fire another bolt, she hastened away from the scene, leaving behind the body of a most chivalrous knight.

Sir Talbot le Bel.

There was little time to make their escape. Slipping and sliding down the ice slope with her two hounds, Hildegard knew that whoever had fired the bolt would have to hold the bow steady by the foot-stirrup to shoot and a target moving downhill would be difficult to hit. And if the killer followed before fully rewinding it, he could not shoot the bolt.

She risked a glance over her shoulder. There was no sign of a pursuer, which meant that he was intent on firing a second time.

In a panic she battled through the snow as fast as she could. Little Bermonda was struggling to keep up. She kept getting buried in the drifts as she fought a way through the freezing shoals.

It was a choice between Talbot's sword and the hound.

With great reluctance she slithered to a stop, grasped the sword in her right hand and hurled it as far as she could. She saw it disappear into deep snow, hidden as secretly as at the bottom of a lake. And there we will build a shrine, she vowed.

With hands now free she was able to pull Bermonda from the snow and thrust her firmly inside the knight's cloak as she set off again.

Before them the precipitous track opened up, inviting them to their doom. But at their backs was a huntsman bent on death.

There was no real route down the mountain, at least, none she could see, so she simply threw herself headlong across snow-filled gullies where the snow heaped in unguessable depths and over ridges where the wind had scoured the rocks to leave only a treacherous film of ice. Dry-mouthed, she trampled the frozen surface of mountain streams, calling to the lymer, but always going down, ever downwards towards the valley with its belt of pines and its scattering of wooden houses.

When she reached a dip she took a chance and looked back up the mountainside, seeing her trail dwindling away into the distance. There was no sign of a pursuer, not any sign of the rest of their party either. And in the silence of the peaks there was no sound of a crossbow being rewound.

Eventually she came to a rope bridge across a ravine. The cords were weighted with ice. There was no way round it. Tucking Bermonda more firmly under one arm, she told Duchess to stay.

With one hand for the rope and one for the kennet, she set foot on the bridge. After no more than a few steps it began to swing like a pendulum. Chunks of ice broke off and fell into the ravine. She paused a moment to let it settle. The further away from the cliff, the more fiercely the wind howled and tore at her clothes. When she happened to glance down she saw, way below the web of rope, a watercourse with rocks pricking the skin of ice that covered them. She felt she would faint with fear.

Praying that the *maronniers* had kept the bridge in good repair and that her added weight would not sever the ropes, she forced herself across, one slow step following another, until at last, with a gasp of relief, she was able to jump the last cordings and throw herself to safety on the other side. Bermonda slipped from her arms with a yelp.

Now for Duchess, she thought, turning and beckoning to the lymer on the other side of the bridge. 'Come, my beauty. Slowly now!'

With a look of distaste, Duchess set one paw on the iced cordings and then drew back.

The nails on the lymer's foot-covers skittered on the ice when she eventually set her paws on the cordings again. Bravely she began to cross. But for the close weave of the ropes on each side she would have pitched over to her death. Carefully, however, with all the strength of character she possessed, she slithered her way across the bridge towards her mistress.

Hildegard dropped to her knees, wrapping her arms around Duchess's neck. She rubbed her face into the animal's frozen coat. Her tears were not for the hound alone.

'As heaven is my witness, Talbot,' she vowed as she stood up, 'I shall bring your killer to justice!'

She took out her knife. With no sign of the other travellers and with a murderer stalking the mountain on the other side of the bridge, she had only one choice. She must cut the ropes that held it.

With snow beginning to fall again she crouched down to see how it was tied together and when she found the main cord she began to hack through it. As soon as she managed to sever it, the rest was easy. The ropes snaked away and the cordings scattered like cards into the ravine.

In the silence that followed she stood there for a moment with snow settling on her hair where her hood had fallen back. She felt a confusion of emotions. But now, at least, with the bridge gone, she was safe.

Calling the hounds up she turned to face the final stage of the descent.

But then something happened.

From out of the shelter of some rocks lower down a figure appeared. It was a man. He must have been watching as she hacked through the ropes because now he began to take long strides up the slope towards her.

His hood half covered his face but she could see a strip of cloth over his mouth and a horn snow-shield concealing his eyes. His cloak was tied mercenary-style across his chest, allowing the rest of it to billow out behind him as he approached. In his hand was a knife.

Hildegard couldn't move her feet. She stared, transfixed.

Chapter Twelve

HEN THE MAN was almost level, he pushed back his hood and lifted his eye-shield. 'You've cut off all help from the other side,' he said. 'Was that wise?'

It was Pierrekyn. He looked pinched with cold but other than that he was the same as when she had last seen him at supper back in the hospice. It was a lifetime ago.

Bermonda gave a small growl. Duchess, chest-deep in snow, hackles spiked with ice, observed him in silence.

Hildegard saw that the knife Pierrekyn held was the one with the red leather haft given him by Sir Talbot. Voice steady, she gripped her own knife more firmly under her cloak and asked, 'You seemed to be heading back to Orsières so what are you doing here?'

He shrugged but didn't explain. Aware of the hostile reception of the hounds, he was eyeing them with caution. 'Where's your valiant knight?' he countered.

'What do you mean?'

He looked confused. 'What's happened to everybody? Why are you alone?'

'We were separated in the blizzard last night.' She stepped away from the edge of the precipice. How had he managed to get ahead?

'I was lucky to find a cave,' he told her. 'When I get away from here I never want to set foot on a mountain again.'

He still held his knife and she saw that he had bandaged his fingers separately to allow freedom of movement. It was what the crossbow men did, the dexterity of their fingers being vital to them.

Watching carefully, she said, 'Sir Talbot has been shot in the back by a bolt from a crossbow.'

His expression did not change. He merely gazed at her for a long moment, his green eyes veiled. Then he turned abruptly and began to slither away down the side of the cliff, following the slippery indentations of the track.

She followed. It was the only sign of the downward path to safety.

She was aware now that it was just the two of them in all the vast solitude of the Alps.

The *perches* stood out boldly against the glistening drifts and the track was well defined lower down the pass. They reached St Rhémy in good time and got through customs without incident. They found an inn a little way outside the town and decided to stay overnight to dry their boots and then hitch a lift in the morning on one of the wagons carrying local produce between the towns.

Hildegard concluded that the *maronniers* would find Sir Talbot and take his body back to the hospice. The murder had taken place in another jurisdiction and did not need to be reported to the authorities in St Rhémy.

A decision about Pierrekyn was more difficult to make.

She peeled off her buskins in front of the fire as soon as they were settled in. Pierrekyn seemed to assume they were travelling on together as if there had been no break in the arrangement. Now he came up behind her and whistled. 'Red hosen, Sister? How scandalous!'

She jerked round. 'I was told by Lady Melisen when she gave them to me that it would be the person who saw them who would be at fault, not I.'

'Ah, Melisen!' Despite his derisive tone his eyes kindled. 'How can she be so enamoured of that old fellow?'

'Love falls where it will.'

'That's true.' His expression became sombre.

Giving her hounds a wide berth, he came to sit in the inglenook as close to the fire as possible, with a bowl of gruel and some bread in his hands.

He gazed into the flames.

Hildegard watched him.

'I'll miss Talbot with all that cleaning and polishing of his stupid mail shirt,' he muttered eventually. 'Was it an accident?' He lifted his head.

'No. It was deliberate.'

'Why would anybody want him dead?'

'I've no idea.'

He looked back into the flames and made no comment.

She went on, 'I'm amazed you left without telling us. What made you leave like that?'

'A whim,' he replied, barely audible.

He began to hack off pieces of wastel to mop up some gruel in the bowl. Whoever had shot Talbot had clearly mistaken the figure in the blue cloak for herself. She recalled the prioress's warning before she set out. Many forces would want the cross if they knew its power. Then she remembered Escrick Fitzjohn and his threats. Then she looked at the boy sitting opposite with his bandaged fingers.

'Pierrekyn Haverel,' she remarked. 'Is that your real name?'

A sudden wary look came into his face and after some consideration he admitted, 'Not all of it's real.'

She noticed he was dropping slivers of food for the hounds as if trying to befriend them. He would know that they would defend her to the death if need be. As carefully as she could she asked again, 'So – what made you leave so suddenly?'

After a pause he said, 'I was going to go back to that little vill near Orsières, if you really want to know.'

'All that way alone?'

'I'm not alone.' He trailed long fingers over his lute on the stool beside him.

'Why there of all places?' It had been a grim little hamlet with a third-rate inn where the last of the merchants had left.

Eventually, as if she had drawn the confession from him, he muttered, 'You could say I had a penchant for a certain little skylark.' He avoided her glance. 'Then I realised how foolish I was being – not to say sinful – to drag such an innocent into my sort of world.' When she didn't say anything he threw her a defiant glance. 'He'd have come with me like a shot.'

'I expect he would,' she replied. 'So what's in Florence for you?'

'Fame and fortune,' he said at once.

'No fame and even less fortune until you're a member of the guild,' she pointed out. 'You'll have to play in the taverns or the streets, entertaining drunks like the ones you called dogs back up the road.'

There was a long pause. Under Hildegard's steady gaze he ran his fingers round the inside of his collar. 'I might find a new master. As you say, I'll be playing on the streets otherwise.'

She leaned forward. 'And might it also be something to do with a red velvet turnshoe?'

An expression of fear flitted across his face until he recovered with a jaunty smile. 'A little memento from my youth,' he said. 'What's that got to do with anything?'

She could tell he had prepared this answer. It was clearly a lie. The slipper was a costly thing, fit for a prince.

Not wishing to lead him into a skein of untruths that would take time to unravel, she didn't pursue the matter then. Instead she said, 'I think we shall probably make good time to Florence. The weather on this side of the Alps is much better. It'll be easier on the roads. I'd like to try to get a lift as soon as it's light.'

'That's well with me.'

Hildegard rose to her feet. 'I'm to my bed.'

She could not tell him what she longed to admit, that Talbot had probably been murdered in mistake for herself.

If innocent, he would learn the truth soon enough. If guilty, he hid his shock at his mistake well but eventually he would do or say something to reveal his guilt and would then be brought to justice.

Her eyes blurred as she imagined the knight as he should have been, striding down to Tuscany with the wind in his hair.

Chapter Thirteen

ENGLAND HAD BEEN drowning under incessant floods when they left. Tuscany, on the other hand, was burning up under the heat of the sun. It was not only that. The fires of war made the *contado* look like a burned-out wasteland. Hildegard lost count of the gutted farms the convoy passed on the way, the fields of blackened wheat, the scorched groves of olives.

It was a relief when the shout went up as soon as the walls of Florence came into view. After many months of plague when its gates were shut, now the fever had receded they were flung wide again. Rose pink against the azure sky, the city seemed to float in the fiery haze like a vision.

As they rattled under the stone arch of the Porto Rosso – the Red Gate – a couple of hours later, the tumult of a crowded city echoed deafeningly in the narrow streets and on all sides people jostled round the newly arrived convoy to inspect the travellers. Vendors, militia, guildsmen and apprentices, beggars, of course, churchmen, flagellants: all impeded their progress despite the shouts of the drivers to let them pass.

Hildegard got down from the wagon, telling Pierrekyn they would walk the rest of the way. It was cool here within the walls. The palazzo of Ser Vitelli, she was told, was further along the street.

An announcement of their imminent arrival had been sent from the last halt and Ludovico's *capo*, Ser Vitelli, had instructed liveried servants to meet them. Now they conducted the two travellers along the Via Porto Rosso to the palazzo of the Vitelli company. With Pierrekyn at her heels, Hildegard followed them through a pair of iron-studded doors. As soon as they entered the doors clanged shut behind them.

It was strangely quiet inside the small, roofed yard, busy as it was. Here their credentials were checked and Hildegard's well-thumbed letter of introduction from Ludovico was scrutinised. Only afterwards were they allowed through into the inner courtyard.

Hildegard had a vague impression of a tall building with many levels, open to a small patch of distant sky. At ground level was the counting-house and on both sides under a portico were many trestles covered with bright Turkish rugs where rows of accountants worked. Balconies on every floor gave onto the courtyard. The walls of Tuscan brick were relieved by one small window at first-floor level.

It was like an eye.

A servant noticed Hildegard's quizzical expression and explained that it was the private apartment of Ser Vitelli where the strongbox was kept.

She imagined him sitting up there, keeping an eye on his house like a spider in its web.

To the left of the main entrance was a set of wide, shallow stairs, open as far as a night gate with a half-latticed barrier patrolled by armed guards. They were conducted through this to an upper floor, lodgings for Vitelli's closest advisors and his guests. Above that, their guide explained, were living quarters for the trainee traders – the *fattori* – and, above them, the stores and, finally, on the open roof under a wooden shelter, the kitchens.

The street doors were locked and guarded at night.

Hildegard was ushered into the principal chamber overlooking the street while Pierrekyn, as a servant, was taken off to the guest quarters.

She knew as soon as the man entered that it was Vitelli himself.

An aura of power was instantly apparent. A hush descended. He walked towards her on soft-soled leather slippers, wearing a full-length gown of black camlet. Its only decoration was six silk-covered buttons and it fell in stiff pleats as if carved from marble. A plain linen cap concealed his hair. The simplicity of his attire ran counter to his famed wealth.

When he moved closer she noticed that his irises were yellow. With his smooth-shaven olive skin and black pupils fixed unmovingly on her face, he looked like a burnished snake.

He offered one hand with a large ring on the middle finger as if he expected her to kiss it. She inclined her head.

He withdrew his hand inside his sleeve.

'Forgive me, Sister. I did not intend to infringe your vow of chastity.' His yellow eyes glinted, the pale lips lifting briefly. He continued as he began, in Latin. 'Welcome to the house of Vitelli. I congratulate you on your fortitude in undertaking the journey from England. If you would like to come onto the terrace we can better inform ourselves of our respective needs without being overheard.'

He indicated an open door at the far end of the chamber where a breeze blew in, bringing with it a scent of lavender. Hildegard followed him outside. So this was Ser Falduccio Vitelli, *il padre*, head of one of the most powerful banks in Europe. She arranged her thoughts with care.

On the journey to Bruges Ludovico had told her about the company's interests. They stretched from headquarters here in Florence to Aigues Mortes and Avignon, to Barcelona, Paris and London, to Ghent and the low countries, and on into the Baltic, with a reach into the Russian steppes and as far as the Orient by way of Venice, Constantinople and Trebizond. Despite this, Ser Vitelli himself pulled out a chair for her overlooking an immaculate formal garden, surrounded by high walls.

Slippered servants attired in black and gold appeared with bowls of fruit. Dark wine was poured into two goblets. At first the only sound was a mechanical nightingale singing among the sculpted branches of an evergreen close by. When it stopped it left only the clink of Ser Vitelli's silver knife, cutting into the flesh of a fat peach.

'These are from my own gardens,' he told her, sending a servant to her with the slices on a dish. He poked at another one with the tip of the blade. 'They're rather early, I'm afraid. You must taste them later in the year when they reach the peak of maturity when all things are best.'

His eye caught hers and held it.

'I would be honoured,' she replied as she became aware of the continued penetration of his glance. She dipped her head, adding, 'Alas, my permission allows for only a short absence from my priory in England.'

'Ah, England!' He sighed with the air of welcoming the introduction of the topic. But then there was a measured pause.

He struck her as a man who did not move so much as his little finger without first having considered the matter from every possible angle. Now he went on, 'I have never been to England. It is one of the few countries I have never had the pleasure of visiting. My youth was spent almost entirely in Avignon. I did not start out as a banker. It was trade that dominated my life in those days.'

He was referring to his start as an arms dealer. He had become rich from such trade. Later he supplied luxury goods from the East to the international clients at the court of the false pope, Clement VII.

'I never go anywhere but where the market dictates,' he continued. 'It has never ordered me to England.'

'Yet now you are a major importer of English wool?' She smiled.

He bowed his head. 'And I hear that my nephew Ludovico wishes to import something else from your fair shores?'

The yellow gleam might have been a hint of humour. It might have been malice. All Hildegard could do was agree. He had got to the point more quickly than expected.

Having planted the seed for their discussion, he was in no hurry to go on. Instead he told her about the cloth-making industry in Tuscany; how Lucca had taken the lead in silk manufacture; how the despotism of the Visconti brothers in Milan, Bernabo and Giangalleazzo, worked against the peaceful conduct of business; and how merchants like himself might have to go on using Sir John Hawkwood's mercenaries to ensure safe passage of their goods, until, after many graceful digressions, he returned to his starting point; the betrothal of his nephew Ludovico to Philippa de Hutton.

More especially, thought Hildegard, he turned to the topic of the dowry being offered and whether the daughter of Lord Roger de Hutton would prove to be a useful business alliance or not.

Philippa and Ludovico. Their future happiness depended on this man.

She murmured something about them being very much in love.

In reply Ser Vitelli made a sound like laughter at the back of his throat and said, 'Love pays no bills.'

'No doubt the betrothed's dowry will ease matters – if her beloved is poorer than he pretends?' She met his glance without wavering.

'As a manager of one of my *fondaci* – one of my branches – he will earn one hundred florins a year. If he demonstrates talent, then more. Poverty will never be an issue for Ludovico,' he paused, 'although generosity may be one of his failings.'

Hildegard's eyes widened. 'Lady Philippa has had many offers of marriage but has rejected them all. She is set on marrying for love, not riches. Ludovico is the first suitor to touch her heart.'

To her surprise, his glance softened. 'I regret only one thing in my life, Sister. I was always too busy building my company to find a bride. My one regret,' he repeated, briefly closing the lids over his yellow eyes.

'So, then, you might look kindly on the match of true hearts?' she asked gently.

He opened his eyes but she could not read their expression. 'Her father, Lord Roger de Hutton,' he watched her intently, 'is he a prudent man?'

Hildegard concealed a smile. Prudent? Roger? There were many words that would more accurately describe him.

Without waiting for an answer Ser Vitelli raised a finger and a servant materialised with a silver tray bearing two documents. Vitelli picked up one of them, glanced at Hildegard and unfolded it.

'I have this by special courier from my *fattore* – my manager in Bruges, informing me of the damage to the consignment of wool belonging to the abbey of Meaux.' He frowned. 'Unfortunate.' He picked up the second letter. 'And here I have the terms for the dowry. I find,' he went on, with a puzzled frown, 'that it is the same as the price of his wool and am left to wonder whether Lord Roger expects the house of Vitelli to subsidise the dowry?'

'If I may be permitted to point out, Ser, in return for your payment for the staple you will receive a consignment of the very best English wool available.'

A lively gleam entered his eyes. 'I also understand that Lord Roger wishes to purchase shares in one of my ships. He wishes to be included in both the *corpo* and the *supra corpo* contracts. From this I deduce that my nephew has been most persuasive during his sojourn in England. Does your northern lord fully understand what he is being drawn into?'

'I imagine he understands as much as any man of prudence,' Hildegard replied with some spirit. 'He is, I gather, in partnership with someone who will share the cost of the loan.'

Ser Vitelli gave an unexpected chuckle. 'You mean the earl who has agreed to stand the expense of the *supra corpo* while Lord Roger,' he indicated one of the pieces of vellum, 'is to take his profit from the *corpo* contract – only six months after putting up the capital. The earl, poor fellow, will have to wait ten years for a return on his investment. Very good. I wonder how he came to agree to such an arrangement?' Chuckling again, he said, 'I like this Roger already. I think he understands these matters very well indeed.'

He handed the contract to the servant who brought it down the length of the table to Hildegard.

Aghast, she scanned it. She saw at once what Roger was about. He was prepared to risk the equivalent of Philippa's dowry for six months while the ship he bought into traded in the East for spices and other goods, and after the six months were up he would receive a profit on the *corpo* contract – and get back the price of the dowry he had put in. The rest of the shares would not yield any profit until long after the ship returned because the capital would be invested in further ventures until the ten years of the loan were up.

As the contract was made out in both men's names, Roger stood to make a further profit when the final dividend was paid. And yet his own money would not be at risk in this longer deal.

The expense would be borne by the earl, Melisen's father, a man who could not read and entrusted the drawing up of contracts to a clerk.

The devil is in the detail, she thought, handing back the document with no comment.

In her mind's eye she saw the body of Reynard in its woollen tomb.

It would suit Roger if the witness to his deceit was dead.

It would suit him very well indeed.

Before Ser Vitelli was called away to attend to business, he had one more thing to say. 'And now,' he smiled, 'for your own request, Sister. I believe you're here not to further the suit of someone who is not even kin but for a reason of your own?'

She was ready. 'I am sent on an errand by my prioress to fetch home a small relic loaned to one of the churches here by a traveller from our shores some years ago,' she said smoothly. He did not need to know that the traveller was the Emperor Constantine, nor how many centuries the relic had languished in Italy.

'So small that she sends you over many dangerous leagues to retrieve it?'

'It has, I believe, great personal value though in itself worth little.' The cross, she added, was made of oak, available in any English copse, and, as she understood, crudely made.

'And the church where this relic lies?'

'The church of the Apostles.'

'Santi Apostoli. I know it well. A small jewel, easily missed, not far from the river. When you want to set out one of my servants will escort you.' He moved swiftly on. 'And your minstrel?' he asked. 'Is he your only escort?'

She shook her head. 'I had the services of a knight to escort me over the Alps.' She told him what had happened. Her eyes were misty when she finished.

Ser Vitelli looked shocked. 'I can send someone to the pass to make inquiries,' he told her. 'But the minstrel and this other business that despoiled the staple – did the citizens of Bruges have reason to believe him guilty?'

'Only the circumstantial one of being a close companion of the clerk in England.'

He frowned. 'And later he happens to be in the vicinity when your knight was shot.'

He stood up.

'There are two deaths to be explained.' He frowned again. 'It seems we must not take risks over your minstrel. He must remain here under house arrest until Lord Roger's steward sends instructions. That is the least I can do.' He must have read her face for he added, 'His imprisonment will be so discreet he will scarcely be aware of it.'

As he went towards the door he said, 'Later we'll see whether he can play and sing as well as he might wield a knife and a crossbow.'

Chapter Fourteen

ARLY NEXT MORNING Ser Vitelli sent a servant to conduct Hildegard to the church of Santi Apostoli. Silent and deferential, the boy led her down an alley near the palazzo that eventually brought them out onto the bank of the River Arno. After a few yards he glanced over his shoulder to make sure she was following, then slipped through a narrow gap between two buildings into what seemed to be a blind alley.

As she rounded the corner she gasped in astonishment. The building that stood opposite them across a small piazza was beautiful. It must be the church of Santi Apostoli, she realised, the resting place for the cross of Constantine.

The building was faced in green and grey brick. Double doors stood open and from inside came a dazzle of light. Vitelli's servant squatted outside to wait and, leaving her hounds with him, Hildegard stepped over the threshold.

What she noticed first was the sparkle of white marble and the sunlight slanting across the tiled floor of the nave through the plain green glass of the clerestory windows. Next was the wonderful sound of a man singing somewhere high up behind the altar in the small, perfect dome that seemed to concentrate the crystalline light of the sun within it.

Above a splendid gold altar screen was a cat's cradle of ropes and pulleys. A wooden platform with a singer perched on it swung slightly as he dipped a brush into a bucket of paint and applied it in broad sweeps of cerulean blue to the inside of the dome. A second painter was filling in a design of stars and trefoils running the length of the wooden beams supporting the roof.

Lost in wonder she made her way down the nave between thick columns of green marble. '*Buon giorno*, messires!' she called up.

Both men stopped at once and peered down from their perches. She saw two dark faces, two red woollen caps, two flashing smiles. The one painting the dome wore a harness of rope. He stared at her as if she were an apparition, then, calling something to his colleague and with his brush between his teeth, he swung down on the ropes to land at her feet with the aplomb of an acrobat. He swept off his cap and holding it to his chest bowed several times. '*Buon giorno, sorella.*' He obviously recognised her white Cistercian habit.

'*Il sacristo?*' She spread her arms.

The man beckoned. Assuming he was taking her to the sacristan's chamber, she followed but to her surprise he led her to one of the arcades in the nave and with a flourish indicated a niche in the wall.

She stepped closer. Protected by rippled glass was a silver bird. Life size, it was sitting on a painted wooden branch against a blue background. The painter pointed to the sky and made flying movements with his hands. Mystified, Hildegard peered again into the niche.

The bird was the work of a master silversmith, she could see that at a glance, but why the two painters were showing her this treasure she had no idea. Still puzzled, she asked again to see the sacristan, trying Latin and then the little she knew of their own dialect, but both men looked at her with blank faces. Suddenly one of them had an idea and began to make slicing movements with his right hand.

'Away?' asked Hildegard, wishing she had asked Ser Vitelli to send an interpreter.

'*Festa,*' the man said.

She glanced around. She guessed he was reminding her it was Lent. The cross on the altar wasn't the only object draped in purple; all the statues in the niches were covered too.

The second painter made a sign for her to follow and behind the altar he reached up for a small box. Inside was a flint-stone and a mound of untreated wool for making light. He mimed the flying movements again, pointing at the sky, laughing at her inability to understand, then indicated a door set in the wall.

When he opened it she saw a cell containing a table, a chair, a narrow bed against the wall and an aumbry with a key in the lock.

A curtained archway led into another small chamber and beyond that was a further door. He drew aside the curtain to let her see the other side and revealed a kitchen, simple and clean, with a bowl, a jug and a water flagon. He crossed over and pushed open the door into a small yard, enclosed by high walls. A spring trickled into a stone basin. A scent of rosemary came from a pot of herbs beside a wooden bench.

It was clear it was the sacristan's domain. As if to demonstrate his absence the painter gave an elaborate shrug.

As they returned Hildegard noticed a cross above the bed. It looked like a million others. Noticing her interest the man took it down and tapped himself on the chest.

She reached out and ran her fingers over it. Her heart sank. The wood was still green. There was no inscription on the back. 'Did you carve this?' she asked.

Whether or not she was right, he nodded, looking pleased.

When Ser Vitelli heard about her disappointment he dispatched a servant at once to find out what had happened to the sacristan. Meanwhile she mentioned the silver bird.

'That's *la colombina*,' he told her. 'It's part of an ancient custom. They set the sacred fire inside to make the dove fly across the piazza on the morning of Easter Sunday. If she flies, good luck will follow.'

When the servant returned he told them that the sacristan was away in Rome and was expected back shortly before Good Friday.

'Everyone is returning then,' observed Vitelli with an enigmatic smile. 'They all want to be here to witness the entrance of Sir John Hawkwood within our walls.'

Although it was Lent, that evening a magnificent feast was laid on. Pierrekyn had presumably passed muster and was included for his playing. The whole Vitelli *famiglia* was in attendance as well as other personages from the upper echelons of the Florentine Signoria. They dined on innumerable dishes brought in by a constant stream of liveried servants.

The centrepiece was a peacock, baked and stuffed with other smaller birds, its feathers put back in place, the tail fan being spread with magnificent artistry to simulate its living glory. As a final tour de force, jets of flame spouted from its beak. This brought a burst of applause from the diners as sparks showered over the table. Some settled among Pierrekyn's russet hair and he shook his head, making his curls dance. Everyone was delighted. He could become quite a household favourite, Hildegard imagined.

Ser Vitelli leaned forward to brush a few sparks from Hildegard's sleeve with a murmured apology. The gesture drew attention to the sapphire in his ring with its own small fire.

All in all it was a scintillating show.

Despite this, when she lay awake that night, what she saw was not the blue of a sapphire but her blue cloak where it shrouded Talbot's body in the snow.

Next morning she was making her way down to the principal chamber with its small devotional altar when she chanced to glance over the balcony and noticed Pierrekyn crossing the yard. He was carrying his lute as usual and wore a cloak over his shoulders. He was making for the lodge. She leaned over to watch.

When he reached the great doors she saw him attempt to go through into the street but the porter stepped forward with a brisk warning. A brief discussion was followed by a more prolonged argument. After a moment, Pierrekyn, his scowl visible even from this distance, trudged back up the stairs. Immediately the faint sound of his lute could be heard being played savagely in the principal chamber below.

Hildegard went to seek him out.

He was unaware of her approach. Only when she spoke did he realise that he had an audience. He stopped playing in mid-chord and gave her a sidelong look.

'You're well versed in music,' he challenged. 'Do you know what it was?'

'What? That tune?'

He watched her closely.

'Was it a hymn?' she asked.

There was a look of relief on his face. She was not surprised.

Of course she knew what it was. Did he think her stupid?

Going up to him before he could start playing again, she said, 'I wonder whether the steward and his men have managed to apprehend Reynard's murderer yet?'

Pierrekyn plucked at the strings and pretended to adjust the tuning.

'Well?' she demanded.

He played a loud discord but kept his head bent, a tangle of hair covering his face, then looked up with a defiant smile. 'Either they have –' he played a chord, 'or they haven't.' He struck the chord again in a minor mode then began to play, not a lament or a dirge, but a loud, brisk jig.

There was a hospital not far distant called Santa Maria Nuova. It had recently been founded by Folco Portinari, the father of Beatrice, the poet Dante's muse who had died during the last outbreak of plague. Fortunately the wave of deaths had receded over the last few months and Florence had been able to open its gates once more. Even so, the building was dismal with the groans of the sick and those dying from many other diseases for which there was no cure.

Santa Maria Nuova was also where the famed nun, Catherine of Siena, had tended the sick until her own recent death. Her name was spoken in a hushed voice by one of the sisters who now ran the hospital and had offered to show Hildegard round the wards.

'Catherine was so saintly she used to drink the pus from the sores of the wounded,' she told Hildegard admiringly as their tour came to an end. 'She wore nettles between her breasts. Of course she never ate. What she ate she vomited at once. Even water became too gross for her towards the end. Nothing in this mortal world was pure enough for so saintly a being.'

Hildegard shivered involuntarily. 'She was, I understand, an emissary for the pope in his dealings with the Signoria?' she remarked.

'Indeed,' said the nun with an imperturbable smile. 'She begged the pope not to send his armies against the Republic.' But then, looking somewhat unhappy, she added, 'But men, even popes, will be men.'

The pope, Urban VI, was as fierce a warmonger as any man and employed professional men-at-arms to fight his cause, among them Sir John Hawkwood, the Essex mercenary. The Florentine Republic was a thorn in the pope's side and, apart from wishing to defeat the other pope in Avignon, he wanted nothing more than to destroy the Republic and keep the city with all its wealth under his own absolute control.

Sir John Hawkwood, whose army Jack Black intended to join, had sold his services to Urban in the intervals when he wasn't fighting on behalf of the higher-paying Republic or for the even higher-paying Duke of Milan – loyalty for Hawkwood being entirely contingent on the amount of gold on offer.

Whether Catherine was as saintly as was claimed was also open to question. It was rumoured that she had been a spy for both sides, pope and Republic, and no one was quite sure which side had won her final allegiance, although shortly before she died the previous year she was said to have pleaded with the pope for an end to war.

Hildegard would have liked to ask the nun whether any of her sisters followed her example and drank the pus of the wounded but she held her tongue. 'Can you tell me something about the church of Santi Apostoli?'

The nun smiled, her ornate wimple flapping like a pair of swan's wings. 'The church is parochial, neither under the control of the Church nor of the brotherhoods. It belongs to the *popolo* and is run by a college of canons. They're rather mysterious. No one seems to know where they have their headquarters.'

Hildegard rolled up her sleeves. 'Now I'm here, maybe I can be of assistance?' It seemed unreasonable not to offer help in the face of the unending tide of sickness that swamped the city. And besides, it looked as if she was going to remain in Florence until the sacristan reappeared.

It was late in the afternoon on the next day, just before the sun went down and left the church of Santi Apostoli lying in a wedge of shadow, that Hildegard came across one of the brothers from an

Order she did not recognise. He was an old man, shuffling his way down the nave towards one of the confessionals. In answer to her question about the sacristan he shook his head and continued on his way.

There were one or two people inside still, the painters working cheerfully high up among the painted clouds, a hunched shape mumbling a prayer at the foot of the altar, a man with his hood up saying his beads beside one of the pillars, and a quick shape following her in and going straight to a side chapel. Aware that it was Lent, that she had purposely avoided confession for some weeks, she made her way to the grille and knelt down.

'Hear me, oh Father,' she whispered. A shadow appeared on the other side. She began to speak in English.

It could not be helped that the confessor would not understand her; there were secret thoughts that needed to be clarified. Her yearning for a distant cloister, the brief joy she had known there, the shame of her desire, had not diminished. When she finished she should have felt better but the burden remained.

By now the painters had left. Their buckets and ladders were stacked against the walls and the ropes of the scaffolding hung silently in the roof. The figure at the altar had gone too, as had the man standing beside the pillar. Daylight was already fading, reducing the nave to darkness. Her footsteps echoed strangely in the hollow silence.

She stopped suddenly, imagining she heard a footfall. The person in the arcade must still be here, she thought. She started to walk again, and again she heard a slight echo like footsteps matching her own. Something moved behind a pillar. It was no more than a shadow but it lifted the roots of her hair. Fear of being pursued by Escrick Fitzjohn flooded back. With a dash of impatience, she went over to the pillar where she had seen the shadow and looked behind it.

Nothing.

She was about to continue on her way when a sudden draught swept the hem of her robe. It was like the opening of a nearby door. Unable to account for it, she stepped out of the nave into the darker shadow under the arcade where there was a side chapel dedicated to one of the saints, a life-size figure draped in purple with his own severed head lying bloodily at his feet. Behind this was a door. When she went over and pushed it, it did not move.

She hurried outside. The little piazza was deserted. Shuttered buildings on three sides blocked out the sky, giving the church a submerged look. She glanced uneasily back inside. It was dark now. Nothing moved.

'For God and profit' was the slogan at the top of the Vitelli ledgers.

At least Ser Vitelli didn't equivocate.

He ran a strict household and listened without making any comment when his *fattori* started their usual rant about local politics and the forthcoming election of the council. There was no knowing which of the many factions he supported. He seemed prepared for any change of fortune; his stores were well stocked, his teams of horses in good condition, the loyalty of his household, no doubt enforced by the sacredness of the blood-bond, firm. His spies, she was sure, were equally loyal. The question she was forced to ask herself was whether all this was sufficient to discover the identity of Talbot's murderer. It was true the company had couriers travelling constantly along the route to the north, passing close to the scene of the crime, but at this time of year when all clues would be obliterated because of the snows, their chances of finding anything seemed slim.

That evening, after work was finished for the day, a visiting *castrato* came to entertain them with a choir from the guild of musicians. He was a tall, shaven-headed Turk and took his place at the foot of the altar steps with great presence.

Pierrekyn sat beside Hildegard on the wooden bench reserved for guests and when the man began to sing the first antiphon the boy's mouth half opened at the purity of his tone. By the time he reached the fifth and more elaborate ending after the magnificat, Pierrekyn looked dazed and, eventually, after the last amen had faded, he turned to Hildegard.

'I would kill to be able to sing like that.'

Startled at his use of the word kill, she replied, 'No doubt he'd prefer to be free like you.'

His lip curled. 'Free?'

She felt a twinge of alarm. Had the boy been in bond and run away from his master? Was that the mystery of his appearance at Castle Hutton? 'Are you bound?' she whispered in a voice quiet with compassion.

He shook his head vigorously and his green eyes flashed.

She was not convinced. 'Change will come. It must. There are too many crying out for an end to wretchedness and a fair share in earth's bounty. The Rising proved it.'

He swung his head so he could look into her eyes and for a moment a look of complicity flashed between them. Then distrust took over and he gave a short laugh. 'Yes, Sister, in heaven, or so we're told!'

'I do not mean in heaven,' she whispered. 'I mean in this world – as you must know I mean.'

Again he turned to look at her. Then he rose to his feet and made off towards the *castrato* as if in fear of what might be said next.

It was the Thursday before Easter. In England King Richard would be offering Maundy money to the poor. Here in Florence every church in the city was open and believers thronged around the steps in a continual coming and going. Hildegard made her way through the now familiar streets to Santi Apostoli.

The renovations were still going on and the workmen were busy as usual, their arias echoing among the rafters as they painted, but there was something different. She sniffed the air. It was the unexpected scent of beeswax. The door into the sacristy was open.

As she quickened her pace, a figure appeared. It was a monk in the black robes of a Dominican, one she had not seen before. He could have been eighty or ninety, the skin of his face like old leather, eyes sunk deep in a skein of wrinkles. He was leaning on a stick but lifted his head when he heard her footsteps.

'*Salve, Suora.* They told me you were coming.'

'*Salve, Fra.*'

He continued in Latin and she replied likewise.

'What is it you want with me, my child?'

'I have a request, Father.'

'So I understand.'

He beckoned and she followed him into his small cell but, moving with unexpected briskness, he swept the red curtain to one side with a clatter of wooden rings and led her through the kitchen, straight out into the yard.

They were met by a dazzle of light. The bench was pushed against the wall to catch the rays of the spring sunshine. As the old man invited her to sit he ruffled his fingers through the leaves of the pot of rosemary, releasing its sharp scent into the air.

He turned to her. 'And so?'

Taking her time, and suspecting that he already knew what she was going to say, she told him about her priory in England and the request made to her prioress that had brought her to Tuscany. When she mentioned the cross and how it was believed by the archbishop to have its rightful home in York, he nodded. Waiting until she had finished, he fixed her with a thoughtful look.

His eyes were small, dark points, very bright in their nest of wrinkles. He took a breath and his mouth turned down. 'And what do we have in return?'

'You would have the satisfaction of knowing that the cross has been returned to its rightful home.'

'You are not the first to come seeking the cross of Constantine. Or, rather, the power it is said to bestow on the one who owns it.' He threw her a shrewd glance. 'Your prioress is aware of the legend?'

'She is. But she does not seek power for herself.'

'Kings and princes would pay vast amounts of gold for it.'

Hildegard's heart sank. The bill of exchange in her belt suddenly seemed insignificant. 'Maybe we can offer something for your poor,' she replied cautiously, remembering the prioress's warning not to mention gold unless it was absolutely necessary.

The sacristan was shaking his head, however. 'We will not sell the cross. Not for a king's ransom. It is not for sale.'

There was a long silence. A bee buzzed among the flowers of rosemary in an ecstasy of pleasure. Hildegard could not hide her disappointment.

The old monk began to chuckle. 'Let me show you something, my child.'

With a struggle he pulled himself to his feet and, leaning on his stick, hobbled back into the building, calling for her to follow. By the time she stepped back inside he was already taking a key from a chain round his neck and opening the aumbry standing against the wall. It took a moment for her eyes to focus and by then he was pulling something from inside the cupboard.

It was wrapped in a rough linen cloth, which he drew off to reveal an astonishing object. It was a reliquary, about twenty-four inches long, made of beaten gold and studded all over with precious stones. Hildegard recognised rubies, emeralds, garnets and sapphires among others. A small gold key was attached to a chain. Inserting it in the lock, he turned it and lifted the lid, inviting her to peer inside.

She expected to see the cross but there was nothing there except the carved bed where it might have rested.

'Yes, empty!' He laughed. 'Do you believe I would leave so precious an object lying around after having brought it all the way from Rome?'

'But the reliquary itself is worth—' she began.

'Worth only a value in the same currency. Replaceable. Gold and precious gems will continue to be mined. The goldsmiths will go on practising their art. The cross, however, can never be replaced. It is unique, without price. That's why we cannot sell it to you.'

'I understand. But I can't deny I'm not disappointed, Father. It would have been a privilege to behold what I've travelled so far to see.'

He allowed the lid of the reliquary to drop shut, locked it and replaced it in the aumbry. 'The common people believe that to touch this flash of gold and jewels would be to unleash a curse on them. To kings and princes, on the other hand, its provenance is so well known that nobody would want to brand themselves a common thief by taking it. It is as safe here as it can be.'

'But the cross,' she murmured, 'that is what is truly precious—'

'Indeed,' he smiled. 'And I am not so trusting that I would flaunt *that* in the face of thieves. I have hidden it. And of course you shall see it.' He patted her wrist. 'Such a long journey, facing so many dangers. I would not deny you some reward, my dear child. However, I believe it would be prudent to speak first to the guardians of the cross before making any decision. They will not object to your seeing the cross for yourself – but they will object to your archbishop's wish to buy it, believing, as I do, that it is beyond price.'

The old man seemed adamant. His next words, however, took her by surprise and he gave her a quick, mischievous smile before he said, 'I may have a compromise to suggest.'

She lifted her head.

'We will never sell – but why should we not allow you to hold it in stewardship for a time?'

'Stewardship?'

'Take the cross back to York for a fixed period, with the understanding that you will return it at a date to be agreed.'

Hildegard put out a hand. 'Father, will that be possible?'

'I shall argue most strongly on your behalf.' He grasped her hand as in a sacred pact.

Hildegard was overwhelmed. 'To be so trusted deeply honours us. You may believe we shall keep our word.'

'Then I shall ask you to return when I have spoken to the college of canons. I shall give you their formal reply. Return after *la colombina* has flown.'

Chapter Fifteen

A FLUTE BELONGING to one of the kitchener's children lay on a ledge in the yard. The time could not pass quickly enough until *la colombina* took to the air. Hildegard picked up the flute and tried a few notes. It gave out a thin, high-pitched sound. Rustily remembering a few phrases, her fingers awkwardly copied the melody Pierrekyn had been playing when she had walked in on him.

She knew what it was but it was a tune not to be acknowledged unless you knew you were among friends. Now, alone, she began to play.

It was an anthem sung by the Company of the White Hart whenever they assembled. They had sung it at Smithfield on the day of Wat Tyler's murder. It was a song of solidarity and rebellion with a plaintive beauty that suited her mood just now. A sweet though somewhat martial air, it finished with a triumphant top note that always summoned a rousing cheer from the listeners. It did so now and she spun round in astonishment.

It was Pierrekyn. He came across the yard towards her with a white face.

'You are full of surprises,' he exclaimed. 'How do you know that?'

'Many people do.'

He looked at her suspiciously. 'It's a rebel song. You can lose your head for knowing it.'

'I think it should be heard often – for more than its beauty.'

He looked startled then laughed nervously. 'Ironic – a song about freedom when I'm cooped up here in golden chains. Vitelli's guards won't let me out.'

'Don't you have everything you need?'

He flung her a withering glance.

'Show me the music room,' she demanded, taking him by surprise.

When it was clear she was going to insist he grudgingly led the way across a loggia and into a small, high-ceilinged chamber at the back of the building away from the sound of the counting house.

It had a painted wooden ceiling depicting a group of knights and damsels dancing in a meadow, the walls covered in tapestries on similar themes. In one corner stood a gilded chest but apart from that there was little else. It was a place where they would be unlikely to be overheard.

He sat in the window niche and began to tune his lute. 'What would you like me to play?'

'That isn't why I wanted to come up here. I wanted somewhere where we could talk in private.'

'That sounds grim, or are you afraid you'll forget how to speak English?'

She smiled. 'You seem to be learning the language. I often hear you talking to Ser Vitelli's *fattori*.'

'Franco's the best. We have a deal. He teaches me Florentine, I teach him English. He's determined to beat Matteo.'

Without a pause she asked, 'And is this where you hide the velvet turnshoe?'

His mouth opened and closed, but before he could think of an answer she asked, 'Well, is it?' She was determined to get the truth from him.

He looked out of the window without answering. It gave Hildegard a chance to peek quickly round the chamber again. All it contained was the painted chest. There was nowhere to hide even something as small as a velvet slipper. Then she noticed the bag where he kept his lute.

'You told me it was a memento from your childhood,' she insisted. 'That isn't true, is it?'

He seemed to brace himself and she had never seen him look so frightened. She expected another lie but instead he muttered, 'I would have to be a king to wear a shoe like that.'

'That's what I thought when I saw it.'

King Richard's name hovered between them, unspoken, with no necessity for either of them to say more. Everyone knew the portent of his lost coronation slipper.

They held each other's eyes.

'I didn't steal it,' he burst out.

'So where did you get it?'

'I'm not at liberty to say—'

'I felt something inside the lining when I picked it up. Is it a document of some sort?'

He neither confirmed nor denied it.

'It's no use trying to deceive me, Pierrekyn. I knew there was something hidden in it the moment I picked it up off the floor at the inn.'

She could see he was battling with the desire to trust her and an equally strong intention to preserve his secret.

'Pierrekyn, you can trust me. Are you in trouble? Maybe I can help. At least take the risk. Whom did you get the turnshoe from?'

With evident difficulty he pushed aside his doubts and began to speak in a husky, hesitant voice. What he told her appeared to have nothing to do with her question.

'It's like this,' he began. 'My mother died of the plague two years after I was born. I don't remember her. They say she was a good woman—' He stopped, his resolution deserting him.

'Go on,' she encouraged.

Staring hard at the floor he said, 'My father brought me up until I was sent to song school at the age of seven. He was a rough fellow but his heart was in the right place. He did his best. The truth was, he never knew what to make of me. He was a weaver. Singing wasn't something in his world except after a few stoups of ale on feast days. He was hanged in the first year of King Richard's reign because of his opposition to the second poll tax. And my elder brother,' he closed his eyes briefly, 'was also hanged – after they'd tortured him for as long as they could keep him alive.'

He hesitated as if still unsure how much to reveal. Then, finding confidence from somewhere, he began to speak more rapidly in a tone of anger and grief. 'The same men who hunted down my father went after my brother. He didn't stand a chance. They had all the power of the law behind them. I was an oblate living away from home. That's the only reason I missed meeting the same fate.'

His eyes never leaving her face, he continued. 'When I heard what had happened I vowed revenge. But I was only a child, what could I do?' He spread his arms. 'After Smithfield, I was older, and when the dukes took out their hatred on the people again, I knew I had to do something. Their reprisals after the Rising were savage. The Justices connived with the magnates. Even the king himself was trailed around from one hanging to the next as if he condoned them. The rebels became the disappeared, men and apprentices, women and girls, the old and revered, all vanished, fleeing to the woods as outlaws or ending up in a ditch with their throats cut. It wasn't only Wat Tyler, John Ball and Jack Straw. It was ordinary people, Saxons, their deaths unrecorded because no one knew what had happened to them and there was no one left to remember them.'

He clenched his fists. 'This is all because they dared to demand the right to speak freely, to pray in a language they understand and to direct their lives without some lord or abbot keeping them in bondage and taxing them to the point of starvation. How many lives lost?' he demanded. 'Nobody knows. But they deserve justice and remembrance.'

He gave her a fierce glance, tears standing in his eyes. 'I expect I'll go to join them when you hand me over to Gaunt's bully-boys. But I warn you, Sister, I'll die fighting. I'll take as many down with me as I can!'

Illumined by his passion, he looked at her with an expression both fearful and defiant.

'I shan't hand you over to anybody,' Hildegard said gently. 'You have my word.' She leaned closer. Now was the time to get the truth from him when he had nothing more to lose. 'Tell me again. Did you murder Reynard of Risingholme?'

'No, I did not. He was the best of men.' Abruptly Pierrekyn's eyes filled and then, losing the last shred of control, he began to sob in a sudden outpouring of grief and rage.

Without thinking, Hildegard gathered him in her arms just as she would have done with her own son in such straits. 'My dear child,' she whispered, 'my poor dear boy. Have you been harbouring such feelings all this time?'

She waited until his sobs decreased, then gently released him. He scrubbed his face with his knuckles, shamed, blinking his wet lashes. 'Do what you have to,' he muttered. 'I'm living in hell.'

'I'm not about to do anything, least of all betray what has been told me in confidence. And whom should I tell when I've no idea whom to trust and whom to fear? There are as many factions plotting against each other here as in England.'

'Are we in danger?'

'Ser Vitelli appears to support Hawkwood and the latter is ambassador to England in that he undertakes commissions on behalf of King Richard. But we must ask ourselves, who is Hawkwood's maintainer at the English court?'

'The Chancellor—?'

'Exactly. Gaunt himself.'

Pierrekyn looked fearfully towards the door. Then he took a deep breath. 'I have something dangerous in my possession. It's been preying on my mind ever since we left England.'

Going over to his lute case he groped around for something buried at the bottom. All bravado had deserted him by the time he returned to kneel in front of her. He had never looked so touchingly young. Holding out a small bundle, he said, 'My chance of making good use of it fades with every passing day. But I must do something! I have to – for Reynard, at least, or his life will have meant nothing.'

He held out a piece of cloth wound around several times. She knew at once what was inside. She pulled the cloth away to reveal the red velvet turnshoe.

'Inside the lining there's a piece of parchment,' Pierrekyn told her. 'Reynard thought the turnshoe would be a good hiding place. A friend who used to be at court gave the shoe to him. Reynard was copying a certain document shortly before he was murdered. Somebody knew what he was doing. They saw it as dangerous and killed him for it.'

She turned the shoe inside out. The stitches looked new and were roughly executed. 'What is this document?' she asked.

'It's a true account of events at Smithfield. It tells what really happened when Tyler was killed. It's written in English by a monk from the monastery in Guisborough. His name is Walter of Hemingborough. When we were in Kent we found out that another account was in circulation, written in Norman French. It's been rumoured that it's the true story. But of course it's not. It's a pack of lies. It gives a false picture of what happened by changing just a few phrases. They've based it on the English version, that's all you can say for it. The name of the writer has been changed as well. Walter didn't sign the original himself. He made it clear he was writing on behalf of Wyclif and the people, by signing it: *anomenalle*.'

'In the name of all.'

'Yes. The false text changed the name to *anonimalle* – as if to say "anonymous".'

'Whereas *anomenalle* is a pun that everyone would understand.' She frowned. 'What was it Gaunt called Wyclif at his trial at Blackfriars when they tried to indict him on a charge of heresy—?'

'Nomen.'

'Exactly. He said, "Avaunt, Nomen!" The name stuck. He banished Wyclif and his nominalist theory in that one phrase. I can understand why Brother Walter would use it as an alias.'

Pierrekyn was watching her carefully. 'Did you know about the false text?'

She nodded. 'Like all the magnates, Lord Roger was instructed to have it read aloud to his household and in all his vills and manors. Not to comply would have been seen as treason.'

'And he did so?'

'It was either that or lose his head. There were riots in the north as well as in the south. Many knights, caught on the wrong side, had their lands confiscated. Gaunt even had the nerve to summons the men of York to appear in London at the King's Bench, to try to stop the right of assembly.'

Pierrekyn was looking fearful at having said too much, but he nodded. 'I know about that. Reynard was in a fury over it. He went to York to support those who wanted to be tried by a jury of ordinary citizens and not down in London where they'd automatically be found guilty by Gaunt's hireling Justices.' He threw her a sharp glance. 'So what's de Hutton's part in all this?'

'He knew the rumours and suspected that the text was a pack of lies but he had no choice but to ask someone to read it out.'

Roger had asked Ulf but the steward had pleaded some cause to prevent him. It was the Chamberlain who had read it out, his habitual lugubrious tones adding a satirical edge to the words, aptly expressing his own views as well as those of his master.

'When he finished Roger looked around at his attendants. No one spoke. Without saying anything, he simply turned on his heel and left the chamber.'

'Reynard said he was out of the common ruck.' Pierrekyn gave a half-smile. 'There'd be nothing Gaunt's followers could indict him on. He'd done as he'd been ordered.'

The danger, as they both knew, was that the false document, written in Norman French to appeal to the magnates, was believed by those who were not present at Tyler's murder, and ordinary people, wishing only for a quiet life and with only hearsay to go on, believed it too. They did not understand the depths to which the power-hungry would stoop in order to hide the truth and attain their ends.

So many copies of the false account had been made and disseminated by Gaunt that its message had already begun to overtake the original. It bolstered the lie that Tyler's followers had malign intentions towards the king. It was naive to believe that truth would out. Unless something was done to counter it, the truth could lie hidden for decades to come. Maybe for ever.

Hildegard got up and the hem of her robe swept the floor as she paced back and forth. She had heard of Walter of Hemingborough's account but had never seen it. She held out her hand. 'May I read it?'

Pierrekyn fumbled in the lining of the slipper and pulled a thread loose then prised from its hiding place a small piece of much folded parchment. He handed it to Hildegard.

It was written closely in a fine, small script in order to get every detail on the two sides.

She read quickly. At length, she said, 'If I recall what was written in Gaunt's version, Tyler was supposed to have drunk a yard of ale in front of the king in a uncouth manner, as an insult. But here it says he asked for a stoup of ale to pledge the king's health and wish him a long and happy reign.'

'He meant it as a symbol of his loyalty. In fact he raised the stoup and cried, Long live the king!'

'And after that, according to this, his men cheered and raised their lances in support.'

'But then some bastard courtier shouted an insult at Tyler—'

'Yes, you mean Ralph Standish?' She looked at the text again. 'This confirms what we heard from some of those who fled north. Tyler was unarmed and alone—'

'He would have been mad to approach the king's retinue by himself and attack them – they were fully armed militia, thirty or forty of them – so Tyler simply stood his ground and denied the allegations.'

'It clearly says here that Standish pushed his way through the men-at-arms with a drawn sword. Tyler stepped back, pulling out his eating knife, and Standish ran him through. At this point, according to *anomenalle* Tyler's supporters, realising that something was wrong, tried to push forward to see what was happening.'

'Mayor Walworth wouldn't allow them close to the king so they were lined up on the opposite side of the square. Walworth called his men-at-arms forward but instead of defending the king, they fell back like cowards.'

She nodded. 'This confirms the rumours we heard in the North. Maybe it was hoped the king would be killed in the confusion and all Gaunt's problems would be over.'

'King Richard was alone between the two factions,' said Pierrekyn. 'He rode forward on his horse and shouted above the tumult to Tyler's men, "Follow me! I am your captain and your king! I will grant you all your requests." And they did follow him. Meanwhile Tyler was taken to the hospice at St Bartholomew's and there died.'

'And those present at his death made a pact—'

'They dipped their scarves in his blood and swore to avenge him.'

'It says that Walworth had Tyler's body dragged out into the square and beheaded.'

'That's true.' He paused. 'I saw it all. I was there.'

Hildegard looked at him in a new light. She said gently, 'So afterwards did you go back to your manor with the rest of them?'

He nodded. 'We all did. Were we fools?' he asked in a subdued tone. 'Did the king betray us?'

Hildegard sighed. 'Who knows. Some say his uncles threatened that if he didn't obey them, they'd do to him what had been done to his great-grandfather, Edward II.'

'I wonder if we'll ever know the truth.'

'Maybe not. Meanwhile we should give King Richard the benefit of the doubt. What happened when you went home?'

'As soon as my master found out where I'd been, he threatened to break my fingers. He gave the names of all the men who marched on London to the Justices – as well as the names of his personal enemies. I wasn't going to wait around for the same fate as my father and brother. I ran.'

'Did you slit his throat before you left?'

Pierrekyn laughed bitterly. 'I wish I had. Someone did the world a good turn that day though.'

'And Reynard?'

'It was my lucky day when I caught his eye. He got me away to Yorkshire where Wyclif's supporters were hiding out. When Walter wrote his account Reynard was determined to make as many copies as he could so people would know what really happened. He said: we must fight fire with fire. If Gaunt can twist the truth and peddle it around the realm, then we can show them the truth in the English version.'

'There are more copies, then?'

'Yes. All sent out. There's also one he started but never finished, hidden somewhere in his things at Meaux. When you and the steward burst in that night I was still looking for it.' He indicated the one in her hand. 'This is the complete version. I knew it was precious but I didn't know what to do next. Reynard would want me to do something.' He gave her a sidelong glance. 'At least, I wasn't sure what I could do until I heard the mercenaries talking on the journey here.'

'The mercenaries? You mean Jack Black and his men?' she asked in surprise.

'They said they were going to join Sir John Hawkwood and the White Company of Free Lances.' He paused. 'I knew about the fate of the White Hoods in Bruges who rose, like Tyler, against their overlord—'

'The Count of Mâle.' She nodded.

'And that bastard the Duke of Burgundy,' he added. 'I thought, if only they had had mercenaries on their side things would have been different. They wouldn't have been slaughtered at Roosebeeke. And then I thought, if only we had mercenaries on *our* side. And then I decided to come to Florence with you – turning my back on the skylark once and for all – and take the turnshoe to Hawkwood—'

'Hawkwood?'

'Yes, to beg him to send arms to England to support the Company of the White Hart.'

'He won't set foot over there!'

'But he could send troops. He must be on our side.'

'I understand he'll be on anybody's side if they pay him well enough.'

As soon as the words were out, Hildegard had a vision of such burning clarity she could only gasp. Hidden in her belt was something that would help such a cause. It was the bill of exchange. Equivalent to a large sum of gold, it would be enough to entice Hawkwood to send his best battalions.

Pierrekyn stared at her. 'Sister, you've gone quite pale.'

'I have had a most dangerous thought,' she told him. 'It's this.' She hesitated. 'I have access to a small fortune – don't ask me how or why – and I have it in my power to make a choice, to give it or withhold it. And yet—' She frowned. 'I cannot see a clear path.'

She went over to the window and stared outside as if for a solution. Turning, she said, 'Forgive me, Pierrekyn, let me consider the matter more carefully. There are many aspects to take into account.' She didn't want to raise his hopes only to dash them later.

Whether by chance or fate, the sacristan's refusal to take payment for the cross now gave her the opportunity to purchase Hawkwood's services. There could be no better cause than to lend support to the king against the cunning of his adversaries.

Before retiring to her chamber to consider the situation, she asked Pierrekyn one more question. 'Did many people know that it was Reynard who was disseminating the true text?'

He shook his head. 'Only his friend in York. Another musician. Reynard knew when to keep his mouth shut.'

Chapter Sixteen

IT WAS EASTER Sunday. *La colombina* was ready to take to the air. Meanwhile, the whole city was in uproar for another reason. Sir John Hawkwood had condescended to enter the city where he was to receive final payment for his services to the Signoria. He clearly had no intention of sneaking in like a thief.

With all the churches flung open to celebrate the risen Christ, bells pealing in exultation from every tower, and everyone dressed in their most expensive garments, it promised to be a grand celebration of the city's gratitude at being delivered from its enemies by God and his English deputy, John Hawkwood.

From early morning bands had been playing in the streets. Wild boar was roasted on blazing spits, wine flowed from barrels set up in the squares and flowers had been strewn ankle-deep over the cobblestones. Banners representing the many different guilds were strung between the houses and the flags of the merchant princes rippled in the breeze in every thoroughfare. Housewives brought out their best carpets to drape over their balconies in a display of wealth, while inside the Palazzo Vitelli the servants threw open the windows overlooking the via Porta Rossa so that the household could crowd into the principal chamber to watch the passers-by. Everyone wanted to view the notorious Englishman as he arrived at the Signoria to take possession of his gold.

Hildegard had had a sleepless night. Pierrekyn had appeared at her door at midnight, demanding to know what she intended to do.

'England isn't Tuscany,' she told him. 'Hawkwood riding to the rescue strikes me as implausible in the extreme. It's not a country he could control with itinerant bands of militia. Other allies would have to be found to support his troops.'

Pierrekyn's face flushed. 'Isn't that what some of them are waiting for? Aren't the northern lords waiting to come out on Richard's side?'

She nodded. It was true. It was the reason Gaunt had seen fit to reward Standish, the murderer of Wat Tyler, with the constableship of Scarborough Castle. It meant he was able to deploy his spies in the north and have early warning of a rising coming from that direction. That was not all. 'The outcome of any insurrection is impossible to forecast,' she told him. 'Whichever way it goes, there'll be bloodshed. I cannot have a part in that.'

Pierrekyn exploded. 'But it's a just cause! Everybody knows Gaunt wants to depose the king. All the omens say so.'

When the newly crowned ten-year-old lost his slipper as he was carried from the coronation feast on the back of his tutor, Sir Simon Burley, some whispered that it was a sign that he would also lose his crown. Now Hildegard said, 'I believe Richard has lived with malign prophecies ever since the day of his coronation.'

'His enemies play on it.' Pierrekyn curled his lip,

As she agreed with him, it was all the more difficult for Hildegard to deny help. But she could not sanction violence.

'Even if the payment offered was to Hawkwood's liking,' she pointed out, 'we have no guarantee he would keep his word.'

'He's our only hope if we want to match force with force.' Pierrekyn had gripped her sleeve. 'We must act and it must be soon. We'll never have a better chance.'

Hawkwood had obtained a peace treaty between the Florentine Republic and Bernabo Visconti of Milan. After receiving the final payment for this service he would be off to another part of the country and another bloody encounter.

When Pierrekyn left, Hildegard had taken out the bill of exchange and stared at it for a long time by the light of the guttering candle. There would be some explaining to do if she spent it on the purchase of an armed mercenary. Pierrekyn's fears for the king were real, however. Gaunt wanted power, not in the role of advisor to an underage king. He wanted nothing less than the throne of England for himself.

Now, Easter Sunday, a group of Ser Vitelli's *fattori* crossed the loggia in an excited crowd as Hildegard descended the steps. Led by

Matteo they were dressed splendidly in their best velvets and greeted her in high spirits.

Matteo made a deep flourish when he saw her. 'We're off to join the crowds outside the Signoria, Sister, and we'd be honoured if you came with us.'

'Listen, you can already hear the procession!' exclaimed one of his companions. There was the unmistakable racket of bagpipes, sackbuts and cornets blaring above the regular beat of kettledrums from the direction of the river. Just then Pierrekyn came into the courtyard.

He was wearing one of the short tunics the *fattori* so loved. His tights were blue and green, one leg striped, the other plain, and a new belt tightly bound his waist. His doublet, a borrowed one in a shade of vermilion that made Hildegard blink, scarcely reached his thighs. It had trailing sleeves, dagged at the cuffs. To complete his ensemble he wore a pair of newish-looking leather ankle boots, somewhat pointed.

Hildegard covered her surprise with a smile of greeting. 'Just in time, Pierrekyn. We're about to leave.'

His glance was fixed when she lifted her gaze. 'It was Franco's idea,' he said, defensively. 'He thought I'd merge in better with everyone else.'

'And so you do,' she replied evenly.

The rest of the boys were already stepping outside to join the stream when Pierrekyn whispered, 'I'm going to speak to Hawkwood. This may be our only chance. '

'It might be better to try to arrange an audience with him when all the excitement is over,' she cautioned.

'Do you mean you have a plan?'

'I don't know, Pierrekyn. I really don't know.'

Ser Vitelli, *il capo,* had already left to join his fellow priors. Hildegard wasn't sure whether he had given permission for his prisoner to leave the palazzo but thought it unwise to ask. In a bunch they forced their way down the street.

The vendors were doing a roaring trade as were jugglers, musicians and fortune-tellers of every description. There was a man with a dancing bear in one of the squares, and some shaven-headed penitents howling and lashing themselves with metal-tipped scourges in another. A fire-eater distracted her, and Pierrekyn tugged her sleeve. 'We mustn't lose them in this throng or we'll never get near the front.'

Vitelli happened to be one of the priors elected by lots for a period of two months. He also represented his guild, the Arte de Medici e Speziali – a group made up of doctors, apothecaries, dyers, spice merchants and anyone who used powders, including painters and gilders. As he was a merchant, it was the most useful trade association he could join, he had told her, though not the most prestigious; the guild of judges and lawyers had that distinction. A handful of families dominated the life of the city and there were many long-standing feuds. Rival supporters of the pope and the republicans also gave rise to plot and counter-plot. For a man of humble birth like Vitelli, it took skill to survive in such tricky waters.

Today, feuds seemed to have been put aside. On the loggia all the elected members of the council were standing in a group, their brilliant scarlet and blue robes a vivid focus of colour against the grey stone. *La colombina* had already been attached to a string that crossed the piazza. Soon, firecrackers would ignite the fuse and propel the silver dove of peace over the heads of the crowds.

Meanwhile, the rest of Vitelli's household, including Hildegard and Pierrekyn, were pressed tightly in the crowd behind a line of armed men keeping the route clear.

It was not often Hawkwood visited any city other than to attack it and lay it waste. This time, as part of his payment, he had demanded a house in Florence in addition to the chests of gold.

Fearing that he would use it as a base in order to mount an insurrection against the city, the council had reluctantly granted him some property – a safe few miles outside the walls. It was said to consist of a sprawling villa, with farms, gardens, vineyards and stables, all protected by a moat.

The preparations for his entry now, within the walls, matched those made for a conqueror. In the view of many, that's exactly what he was.

The sun blazed down. Hildegard pulled on her straw hat. The boys looked hot in their finery but everyone was in the same state and discounted physical discomfort.

Hawkwood would lead his cavalcade over the River Arno with its reek of dye-stuffs, tannin, dead dogs, butchers' offal, decomposing cabbage and any other rubbish fit to be thrown away, and enter the city by the red gate before marching down the Via Porta Rossa, making a short right turn onto the street of the shoemakers, and entering the piazza from the narrow street facing the Signoria.

The onlookers, cooped up behind the line of pikemen, could judge the minute he rode within the walls because a roar of welcome broke out in the distance from the direction of the city gate. It continued in wave after wave, all along the route, getting louder by the second, until the crowds on the far side of the piazza added their own roar of welcome. It reached a crescendo and by the time he appeared it had become a deafening storm.

Matteo and his friends were shouting themselves hoarse as the entourage emerged from between the buildings. First came the armed and liveried men, marching in close formation. Close on their heels was Hawkwood's personal bodyguard of twenty fully accoutred men-at-arms.

Soon Hawkwood himself was visible. There were cries of 'Acuto! Acuto! Giovanni Acuto!' – the nearest the Florentines could come to the English name. Hildegard mentally translated it as 'Sharp John' and grimly smiled. Even so, she too stood on tiptoe to get a first glimpse of her notorious countryman.

He was astride a glistening black battle horse.

Its rich caparisons gleamed scarlet and silver between the scintillating armour of his guards and as he drew closer the gold escalops, recently adopted as his emblem, were seen a million times over in his own dazzling apparel. Sunlight bounced off his men's armour and there was such a glitter of gold and silver it seemed to scorch the eyeballs. His own breastplate was polished to so fine a lustre it reflected the crowd back to itself like a mirror.

The source of this brilliance was a thick-set man of about sixty.

His reputation had been carved out over nearly three decades, first in the war with France, then in the continual competition between the city states south of the Alps. He had started with straightforward plunder. Latterly he had learned to play one side off against the other and, astute and far-seeing, was eventually able to sell the use of his troops to the highest bidder. Sometimes it was the Duke of Milan, sometimes the pope. For the last five years it had been the *priori* of Florence.

Now, coarsened by decades of bloody warfare, he gazed coldly at the upturned faces of the crowd. They waved their little pennants of white silk to display their allegiance with the anxiety of people hoping to ward off evil. His glance swept them for assassins.

The steel links of his mail shirt were visible under his silver breast-plate and over that he wore a white silk banner tied crossways in a style adopted by the rest of his mercenaries. He rode amid the clash of steel. Despite all this, his hands in their steel gauntlets looked light on the reins of his horse.

Hildegard felt Pierrekyn tense as Hawkwood drew level. The man was surrounded by rows of armed foot soldiers, pikemen bristling with weapons, then mounted militia, swords swinging at their sides.

She gripped Pierrekyn by the sleeve. 'Don't risk it. You'd never get near him. They'd run you through and ask questions afterwards.'

He scowled in frustration. 'I'd no idea there'd be such a turnout.'

A fanfare blared from a row of buglers on the steps of the Signoria as the cavalcade came to a well-drilled halt. The priors, arrayed in their best cloaks and chains of office, stood in a line of welcome.

The crowd was pressed tightly on all sides with a mingling of body odour, armpits, unwashed feet, bad breath, and the sweeter scent of flower-water made by the monks at the Santa Maria Novella apothecary. But suddenly, as the buglers blew one final flourish, Hildegard became aware of a smell that did not fit.

She could scarcely turn her head in the press even when a voice growled in her ear, 'That's a fine piece of horse-flesh he's got under him, Sister.'

A rough beard brushed the nape of her neck, making her flesh crawl. There was no way out. She couldn't even reach her knife. She managed to turn an inch then drew in a sharp breath. Standing behind her was Jack Black. The strange smell was saltpetre. By his side was the Scotsman, Donal. As her glance skimmed over them she saw that they wore no badge in the shape of an escalop. They were not with Hawkwood then.

'Didn't mean to alarm you,' Black said, peering into her face. 'But I see you've managed to find your young minstrel again.'

'He wants to have a word with Hawkwood,' she said, to explain the fact that she was still gripping Pierrekyn's sleeve.

'Aye, so would many.'

'How did you get here after the storm?' she asked, aware that she had cut the bridge on the descending path.

'After many setbacks and much travail,' he said with a strange glint in his eyes. 'And your knight, Sir Talbot?'

His glance was alert as he searched her face.

'Sir Talbot was murdered by a bolt from a crossbow,' she told him.

To her surprise he nodded. 'We know. We found his body. Two of the *maronniers* took him back to the hospice and the three pilgrims went with them, as soon as they'd recovered their wits. He was a good lad. What happened?'

'An unknown assassin.' She was curt. 'I was with him at the time. I didn't even get a glimpse of the bowman.'

'And no suspicions – apart from ourselves?'

'You were the only ones in our group with crossbows,' she pointed out.

'And we might yet have done for the poor fellow for all you know. You only have our word, eh, Donal?' He nudged the Scotsman who roared with laughter and said something in his own dialect that Hildegard did not catch.

'He says he'd suspect himself if he didn't know full well he hadn't done it,' he translated. Both men roared again. Then Black looked serious. 'You'll want to know the culprit.' His glance flickered to Pierrekyn who was staring at Sir John Hawkwood sitting astride his prancing horse while one of the *priori* indulged in a lengthy eulogy of Hawkwood's qualities. Jack Black shifted his glance back to Hildegard. 'Any ideas?'

She shook her head.

'I suppose it was you who cut the bridge?' he asked, narrowing his eyes. 'We followed your tracks down the mountainside until we came to the ravine. You caused us three days more in the snow. Luckily the *maronnier* knew of an alternative route. We were mostly on our backsides except when we were hanging from some thread of rope by our teeth. Surprisingly somebody had gone before us.'

'Who was that?'

He shook his head. 'Somebody who knew the mountain or managed to get hold of some secret knowledge of it. From what we saw of his tracks he'll be your crossbow man. And I warrant I have something that might lead you to him. No doubt your sir knight has a rich family who would be willing to pay a price?'

'He was poor. He had nothing but what he earned, just like you.'

He gave her a long look, judged her to be telling the truth, and replied, 'In that case we'll regard him as one of our brothers and you can have it and avenge him.'

Hawkwood had by now begun to dismount at the steps to the Signoria. Tall enough, Hildegard could see over the tops of the heads in front. A battalion of Florentine militia in their red and white colours faced down towards the square and drew their swords in unison. It was obvious to everyone that Hawkwood's men could have dashed them aside without breaking step but there was a good-natured cheer when Hawkwood himself strode forward and knelt briefly in front of the Florentine standard.

'What a showman,' muttered Black.

From a nearby balcony overlooking the square a woman and her retinue of ladies called down. When Hawkwood rose again he raised his head and the woman let loose a silver veil so that it fluttered in a graceful descent to his feet. He glanced up at the balcony and then with a sardonic lift of his lips he simply tramped over it in his riding boots. To the squeal of cornets, he ascended the steps to meet the line of scarlet- and ermine-clad *priori* and their chief the *gonfaloniere* in his star-spangled cloak.

Hildegard glanced up at the balcony. The woman's face had changed from charm to black fury. It was too late. Hawkwood, if he had cared, had already turned his attention to the flare that was held out to him. The honour of setting *la colombina* in flight was his, and Hildegard saw the firecracker ignite. With a great whoosh of flame and a cheer from the entire crowd, the silver bird flew on its string over their upturned faces to the other side of the square. When it alighted safely there were more cheers and Hawkwood, having performed to everyone's satisfaction, disappeared inside the Signoria.

The crowd jostled and swayed to an anthem and began to turn their attention elsewhere. One or two standing close by gazed up at the balcony and hissed, some even made a sign to protect themselves from witchcraft.

'Who is that?' Hildegard asked Jack Black, tearing her eyes away.

'That, sister, is La Gran Contessa, a most dangerous woman. Have you not met her?'

'I think our host moves in different circles,' she replied.

'She's a beautiful woman, no man could deny that, but her wealth, they say, comes from first poisoning her brother and then her husband. She tries to court the *popolo minuto* against the council but the people are too wise to be swayed.'

Matteo caught the tail-end of Jack's words and followed his gaze. 'Some man will get the better of her one of these days.'

'Unless she poisons him first,' Jack added.

The *fattori* said they were going to push their way further forward so they could get near the loggia. They wanted to loiter there until Ser Vitelli came out with the latest news.

Hildegard turned to Jack Black. 'What is this thing that might identify Sir Talbot's murderer?'

With another glance at Pierrekyn, he whispered, 'Something we found on the way through the pass. I'll bring it to you. Where can I find you?' He was already allowing a swarm of people to carry him off.

'At Vitelli's,' she called over their heads. She saw him raise a hand in acknowledgement before being swept away. Donal was already striding off through the crowd, scattering them like chaff before him.

The celebrations looked set to go on long into the night. Certainly there were expectations that when Hawkwood came out of the Signoria with his gold there would be more singing and dancing in the streets to add to the usual Easter carnival. *La colombina* had flown. As the sun began to go down the light from a million firecrackers would light up the sky.

Hildegard turned to Pierrekyn. 'Let's see if there's a better way of contacting Hawkwood. Surely Ser Vitelli will be in a position to arrange a meeting for us.'

Pierrekyn looked at her in astonishment. 'Us?'

She nodded. 'Maybe if we can persuade Hawkwood to announce his support for King Richard it will be enough to deter his enemies and there'll be no need for bloodshed.'

They made their way back in a drift of revellers towards the palazzo. They had no sooner reached the gatehouse, however, than something unexpected happened. Four men-at-arms with the black and white slashes of the Count of Mâle on their sleeves appeared out of nowhere. Swords drawn, they circled them both.

'Is this him?' demanded the captain.

Ser Vitelli's porter, standing at the gate wringing his hands, gave a reluctant nod, at which the men seized Pierrekyn by both arms and tried to snap irons on his wrists.

He struggled but was helpless against four. Hildegard stepped forward, demanding to know what was going on.

The captain's answer was curt. 'Pierrekyn Haverel. Wanted for the murder of a man in Bruges. Now, get out of my way!'

Chapter Seventeen

IERREKYN DID HIS best to resist arrest but was no match for the men-at-arms. 'It wasn't me!' he yelled. 'I didn't kill him! Ask the Sister! He was my friend!'

Hildegard regretted that her hounds were in their kennels. 'You can't seize him. Where are you taking him? On whose authority are you doing this?'

The captain said, 'We act on the authority of the Justices of Bruges with instructions from Lord Roger de Hutton. He commands us to arrest this man and return him to England. If he's innocent he can prove it under English law.'

Pierrekyn was still raging. 'I didn't do it! I won't go!'

It was useless to protest. Hildegard tried to remonstrate with him and only when the men man-handled him and punched him on the jaw did he quieten down.

'Let the Sister get my lute for me,' he managed to ask, his eyes still darting as if to find an escape.

'Yes, let me get his lute. He's a minstrel. It's his livelihood. You can't stop him taking the tools of his trade with him.'

With a show of reluctance, they agreed to wait while she fetched it. She sped up to Pierrekyn's music room, the place that had been his haven in recent days, quickly found the bag with the lute inside it, reached down into the bottom of it until she found the turnshoe and, slipping it inside her sleeve, returned to the group outside. She handed Pierrekyn the bag. Already one of his eyes was beginning to swell.

Turning to the captain, she gave him a hard look. 'Should I discover any harm has befallen Master Pierrekyn on the journey you will feel the full force of the law in whatever country you try to find sanctuary. My Order has power in every country in Europe. Not only that, the boy's master is a great lord in England with the command of many forces. He will take it as a personal insult should one of his people come to harm.'

The captain agreed that if the prisoner would come quietly no more harm would befall him but that, for safety's sake, he would have to travel in irons.

Knowing this was the best they could hope for, Hildegard reached out impulsively to take Pierrekyn by the arm. 'I've got the turnshoe,' she whispered. 'Be strong!' The look that passed between them was confirmation that she would do what she could.

Pierrekyn was dragged away with a last beseeching glance that wrung her heart.

The silence was chilling after the wild noise of the carnival-goers in the streets. She felt uneasy as soon as she opened the great doors of Santi Apostoli and stepped inside.

She glanced up. The scaffold was empty. The ropes hung motionless to the ground.

The singing painters would be raising their voices in the streets with the rest of the town. They had finished painting the rafters. Gold and silver stars glittered in the shadows. The fresco was almost finished too, washes of sky blue, the gold of a coronet, angels' wings touched with pink, a vision of heaven. And yet she had a sensation of impending evil.

She began to make her way down the nave between the pillars, her footsteps echoing softly on the tiles. The confession box was closed but there was no sound of a penitent within. She sniffed the air. It was not saltpetre. Rather it reminded her of a butcher's stall. Slabs of dripping meat.

She was down the nave in a trice and swept open the door of the confessional. Inside was the old monk who had uncomprehendingly heard her confession the other day. His eyes stared ahead as unseeing as glass. When she put out a hand he did not flinch. Then she noticed the thin cord round his neck, the bulge of his eyes and, in the semi-darkness, the protruding tongue.

'Jesus!' she exclaimed, backing away.

But this was not where the smell of blood came from.

Something sent her running deeper into the church, past the altar, towards the sacristy. Thrusting open the door, she burst inside but stopped on the threshold.

It was empty. But instead of its previous neatness everything was upside down, the bed overturned, the pallet slashed open, spilling straw, the chair smashed into pieces, and the olive-wood cross had been torn from the wall and lay broken underfoot. The most damage had been done to the aumbry. Its doors had been wrenched off their hinges as if the key could not be found. When she looked inside, the reliquary had gone.

Fearfully, she went on into the kitchen to find the same scene of destruction, the sacristan's few poor cooking utensils in shards on the floor.

Outside in the yard was a worse sight. The old sacristan himself was lying on his back near the broken pot of rosemary. His face was bruised, his eyes gaping, a gash in his stomach revealing his entrails. There was blood everywhere.

She forced herself closer.

The blood she had smelled as she came in was hot and fresh like that of a recently slaughtered animal. It pooled in a flood over the paving stones. Flies were already buzzing round beginning to sup.

A sound made her turn. Her breath stopped.

After weeks of false sightings: Escrick Fitzjohn.

He was smiling. His hands were as red as a slaughterman's.

He began to tread towards her, taking his time, relishing the moment of his triumph, with the air of a man who had caught his prey at last.

She stood her ground. She would not plead. He would descend into his own hell when the time came.

He approached within a pace of where she stood.

'You're a brazen one. Aren't you going to try to run for it?' Her stillness seemed to puzzle him. He glanced over his shoulder, the movement too sly to give her time to react. He put out a hand and, as he had done once before, ran it over her face with a puzzled expression. 'Flinch, damn you!'

Her eyes flashed. 'Why should I flinch from you? Am I supposed to be afraid of you?'

'With no hounds to protect you, Sister, you should be very afraid.'

'Why kill the two old monks?'

'They were near death anyway,' he said with contempt. 'The old devil here,' he put out a boot to kick the sacristan on the shin, 'had the audacity to swallow the key to the aumbry! Would you believe the cunning of the fellow? I had to wrench the door off. The key must be down his gullet but I couldn't find it.'

She saw now that the sacristan's throat had been ripped open. 'You're a monster.'

'No doubt. But now you're going to do something for me.'

Her flesh went cold.

He reached out, gripping her by one arm. 'Come with me.'

Without another word, he dragged her out of the yard, back through the kitchen, through the living quarters and out into the nave of the church, then, spurs clattering on the tiles, he marched her towards the main door.

For a moment she thought she might be able to escape once outside but to her dismay two armed men emerged from a side chapel and, grasping her by both arms, hustled her into the alley where night was already falling.

When they reached the turning onto the river bank she felt the point of a knife digging into her back. Escrick murmured in her ear, 'Make one move and you're dead. We're going to a celebration. That's what the poor sots of this town do at Easter – especially when they've delivered themselves into the hands of that devil Hawkwood and imagine they've bought peace!'

'If you call him a devil then what does—' A mailed fist smashed into her face and she felt blood in her mouth.

'Shut up, bitch. Speak when I say you can. Let's go!'

He dragged her hood over her face and, with the men on both sides locking her by the arms, she was hurried in among the crowds celebrating with music and fireworks. If she screamed she knew she would not be heard in the hubbub and the only result would be a knife through her ribs. When a passer-by made some comment, one of her captors laughed and said, 'Can't hold her liquor, the drunken mare!' They hurried her on.

She found herself being dragged through the streets, over a wooden bridge, up some steps and across smooth stones. From under her hood she glimpsed a blur of black and white tiles, then colours, red, green, white, then black again as the hood was pulled more firmly over her face. There was a roaring sound louder than the ringing in her ears from the blow Escrick had delivered. She was in a hall full of people. Her spirits rose a little.

When her hood was pulled off, she could only blink under the glare from a hundred glittering cressets.

Not until the men-at-arms standing in front of her opened up to make a passageway for someone did she see a face she recognised. It had been earlier that day on the balcony outside the Signoria. It was La Gran Contessa.

'So what's she? A Cistercian?' The contessa looked her up and down with contempt.

'She must know where the contents of the reliquary are hidden, my lady.' Escrick's tone was servile.

Hildegard glanced at him but her attention returned at once to the contessa. She was beautiful to look at, with fine features framed by an elaborate headdress of velvet and gold filigree that allowed her black hair to cascade in glistening undulations over her shoulders. She wore a gown of gold brocade, the waist tightly pinched, her bosom high and barely concealed under a silk veil.

The hand that reached out to Hildegard was covered in rings, large gold bosses, rubies like drops of blood, and a diamond that caught Hildegard with sudden viciousness across the cheek. The flame of it forced a cry from her before she could stop herself.

Strangely, when the contessa smiled, as she did now, her beauty was dazzling, but it was illuminated by such hatred no surface brilliance could conceal it. Hildegard watched the woman's small, neat teeth bite down on her lower lip as she considered something. It appeared to amuse her.

'Sir Fitzjohn, to whom do you owe your allegiance?' She fixed her brilliant eyes on him.

'To you, madam.' He bent his knee.

'And it is your duty, is it not, to fulfil my desires to my entire satisfaction?'

There were guffaws of amusement from the rest of the men and Fitzjohn, not knowing what was coming next, agreed.

'And I asked you, did I not, to bring me the cross this nun has been sent from England to buy?'

'You did, my lady, and—'

Two thin lines of annoyance forked down her forehead and her red lips tightened. 'You did not bring me the cross, sir. You've brought me this gaudy coffin with nothing in it.'

One of Escrick's henchmen still held the reliquary just as he had brought it through the streets under his cloak. Escrick didn't move a muscle. There was no smile on his face now.

'If I had wanted a gold reliquary flashing with jewels I would have asked for one. Instead I asked for an ancient wooden cross said to bestow unlimited power on whomsoever possesses it. Why do you imagine its whereabouts have been kept secret for over six hundred years? Because, dolt, it's worth more than a king's ransom! I asked you to procure it for me. You said you could do so. But you failed, Sir Fitzjohn, you failed miserably!'

The contessa said something in Florentine to two of her body-guards and they swooped on Escrick before he could move. There was a gilded table near by bearing dishes of nuts, fruit and other delicacies. The contessa dashed one of the bowls to the floor where it shattered, oranges flying out of it, to roll one by one between the boots of the men-at-arms standing next to it.

'Put his hand on the table!' she snarled.

Escrick had no choice. Looking bewildered, he was forced to let them spread his right hand on the table. He wore a ring on his little finger. Hildegard stared at it in surprise.

The contessa pointed as if choosing a morsel from the board. 'That one,' she said.

One of the guards took out his knife and in one swift movement sliced off Escrick's little finger together with the ring. He must have been in agony but apart from the colour leaching from his face, he betrayed no flicker of emotion.

'Who wants a talisman?' his tormentor shouted. She picked up the bloodied finger and threw it, the way a bride might throw a bouquet among her wedding guests, and there was a brief scuffle as the men fought for it. The ring fell onto the floor but in the mêlée over the trophy of the finger no one noticed it. Hildegard picked it up.

'Hold your hand in the air, Sir Fitzjohn.' He did so. 'That's to show everyone to whom you belong.' The contessa's voice rose. 'Maybe now they'll show you more respect than you've managed to inspire in this nun here. When I ask you to get something for me I won't have you bringing me a worthless box with nothing in it!' she screamed. 'I want its contents. Maybe now you know I'm serious?'

'I swear,' said Escrick, dropping to his knees, 'I searched every nook and cranny of that church, everywhere, and there is no cross apart from the one above the sacristan's bed and the brass one on the altar.'

'The cross of Constantine is wood!' she shouted. 'Are you stupid? Do you know what wood is? The cross is made of English oak! The sacristan brought it back from Rome on instructions from the highest source. My informants tell me everything except this one thing – where is it now?"

'Madam, my lady—' He gazed up at her with a look she might have read as devotion, for her mood changed and she moved forward in her rustling skirts and reached out to stroke his head.

'Stand up, sir. You will have your reward as soon as this nun reveals the whereabouts of the cross. Until she does, you'll have to wait for your pleasure. You have several fingers left at present. That should encourage you to show us how quickly you can get her to talk.'

Hildegard turned a scornful glance on Escrick and stepped forward. 'I shall have to put your other fingers in jeopardy, *Sir* Fitzjohn,' she said. 'I know nothing of the contents of the reliquary. I have seen no cross.'

The contessa's laugh was harsh. 'Do better. You do not amuse me.' She turned to gaze at her army of men with a fond smile and asked, 'How shall we help Sir Fitzjohn persuade this nun to speak to us?'

One or two ideas were thrown in from different parts of the hall. Hildegard felt sick.

Then someone stepped forward. 'We're mercenaries, paid to fight.' One or two murmurs of agreement followed. 'Even now Sir John Hawkwood is feasting in the Signoria, unarmed no doubt, his men drunk and less watchful. We're wasting time here with this matter of the cross. It's only a story. It's the power of steel that can deliver booty, not wooden crosses.'

Someone growled in agreement but there was an immediate objection. 'It might be only a story to you, brother, but if folk believe it, it might as well be true.'

The mercenaries being an international crowd, began talking in a mixture of Florentine, English and a few other languages besides, but a good number of the men were English and now there were further objections to this on grounds of logic.

Another man stepped forward. 'Be that as it may, let's have a bit of fun first. These nuns can take a deal of pain. Let's see how far she'll go before she squeals.'

Then Hildegard had a shock. This advocate for torture had pushed his way to the front and stood right in front of her but now, even from behind, she recognised him. It was Jack Black.

'It's a dispute as subtle as that concerning *fine amour*,' he was saying. 'Too much pain and they die before you can extract what you want from them, too little and they laugh in your face.'

One of the Florentines strode forward to stab his stiletto into the table still bloodied by Escrick's wound. 'I disagree with my esteemed English brother,' he declared, turning to Jack Black. Hildegard braced herself for the worst as the men began to elaborate their arguments for and against the different forms of torture that could be inflicted, until she felt someone tugging at her sleeve. When she glanced down she was surprised to see Jack Black's mines expert, Harry, grinning up at her.

A shadow fell across them as the Scot, Donal, positioned himself in front of them, blocking them from view. He launched into an excited tirade while Harry whispered, 'I hope you're fleet of foot, Sister?' Then he pushed her between two men-at-arms who obligingly parted to let them through, then stood like a wall while they made their escape through a door behind them.

In a moment Harry had hustled her outside into a courtyard. The air was cool and fresh after the fetid heat of the contessa's palazzo. Gripping her tightly by the elbow, he marched her past the gatehouse guards as if she were under escort and hurried her onto a busy thoroughfare.

Buildings on both sides of the narrow street forced the traffic into a tumult of carts, mules, celebrants, knights, friars, beggars and street vendors, and in moments Hildegard and her rescuer looked just like any other hooded citizens seeking amusement as they wove their way through the crowds.

Harry kept glancing back over his shoulder as he hurried her along and when they reached the bridge leading back over the river he said, 'I'm going to leave you here. Business afoot.' He chuckled with secret relish. 'But take this with you.' He fumbled around in his belt. 'Jack said you might find it helpful.'

He pushed something into her hand and was instantly swallowed up by the crowd. She glanced down. By the light of the street flares she saw he had given her a piece of cloth.

It had been torn from the hem of a cloak.

Chapter Eighteen

ILDEGARD'S IMPULSE WAS to retreat to the safety of Vitelli's palazzo at once but there was something she had to do first.

Checking her direction, she set off through the crowds of revellers, back over the old bridge towards the church of the Apostles. The alley leading into it was unlit and she had to grit her teeth before setting foot in it again.

With the sounds of the carnival fading in the distance, she felt her way along the wall until she came to the church door. It was still open just as it had been left. It was a well of darkness. She steeled herself to step through and make her way between the pillars towards the pale glint of the altar.

She needed light for what she had to do.

The flint the painter had shown her, used to ignite the taper sending the peace dove on its Easter flight, was kept behind the altar screen. Alert for the slightest sound, her fingers fumbled along the shelf in the darkness until she found the box of flints.

She ran the steel down the side until a spark flared, then she buried it in the tinder, coaxing a flame that she held quickly to the wick of one of the altar candles. It flared as brightly as a cresset. Shadows leaped along the walls. The arcades seemed suddenly crowded with living beings, the undraped effigies of the martyrs displaying their bloodied wounds, their painted eyes glittering from out of the darkness.

Having to remind herself that Escrick could not be lying in wait this time, she edged past the yawning recesses of the side chapels and approached the sacristy.

The horror of the poor sacristan lying out in the yard in a pool of his own blood made her falter but she forced herself as far as his cell.

The cross had to be here. He had promised to bring it out of its hiding place. He had been ready to hand it over.

She tried to imagine where he would keep such a valuable talisman. Escrick claimed to have searched the entire building and she did not doubt he had been thorough. It would be hidden in a place where nobody would think of looking.

At a loss she lifted her candle higher to shed a better light. The curtain between the cell and the kitchen was half open. When she tried to drag it back along its runner in order to see more clearly, it snagged on something and at the same time the light from the candle made the shadows swoop. Her knees began to buckle with fear. She steadied herself against the wall. They were empty shadows, that was all. About to nerve herself to go inside, she happened to glance upwards.

The ceiling was alive, first with a shape like a devil, then with a crook-backed monster. It's nothing but the shadow of the crossbeam holding the curtain, she told herself. But then something made her stare.

It was impossible.

Reaching up, she ran her fingers over the beam and found a second piece of wood on top. No more than three inches thick, it was enough to cast a distorted shadow.

Standing on tiptoe, she managed to get her fingernails underneath it until she could lift it down. She found she was holding a single piece of wood, three handspans in length with a crosspiece no more than six inches wide at the top. A feeling of awe swept over her. She had no doubt what it was.

For a moment the world, with all its cruelty, betrayals and ambition, fell away. It was the cross and what it represented that were real.

She trailed her fingers over it, seeking the indentations that would suggest an inscription, until eventually she found some markings that could be words incised into the ancient wood. Holding the candle closer, she was able to make something out. It was Latin. *In this I conquer*, she translated. It was the inscription that had inspired Constantine to victory at the Milvian Bridge.

Now, suddenly terrified that Escrick or someone else in the contessa's pay might appear to continue the search, she doused the candle and, with the cross held tightly inside her cloak, hurried back into the church. She made no sound as she plunged through pools of darkness between the pillars but by the time she reached the main door she was breathless with fear. She peered outside.

The sky glimmered above the rooves, leaving the square in front of the church in darkness. Trusting that no one was lying in wait, she guided herself along the wall towards the light at the top of the passage. Then with her hood pulled well down over her face, she stepped into the street to join the revellers.

A cloud of smoke drifted from across the river. People were pointing and pushing in excitement towards the bridge. Now and then spurts of flame lit up the towers on the opposite bank. Domes and steeples sprang luridly into being.

Now, she thought, they're even lighting fires in honour of Hawkwood.

Preparations for the journey back to England were almost complete. There was only one more thing she had to do before she left. It was something she dreaded but she had given her word.

Early next morning, she put on a fresh habit, and with her belt girded tightly round her waist, and her knife and her two hounds with her, she set off for the palazzo of the *gonfaloniere* where Sir John Hawkwood was still making the most of his current good fortune.

Smoke still hung in a pall over the houses on the other side of the Arno. What she had seen the previous night as celebratory fires had, in fact, been a building aflame. Knots of interested spectators were standing around discussing the matter with a certain glee.

When Hildegard approached they were quick to tell her that the palazzo of La Gran Contessa had spontaneously burst into flames in the middle of the night. Unfortunately the contessa herself had escaped but there had been many deaths among her followers.

Someone shook their head, saying, 'She has the luck of the devil, that one.'

Even now, they told her, men were sifting through the charred bodies and trying to understand how it had happened.

'They say it was an explosion beneath the building but there are no cellars over that side,' her informant told her. 'It's set on marshland, though the contessa's palazzo is on a little dry knoll of its own.'

'It'll be dry now all right,' came the rejoinder.

Hildegard moved on and eventually reached the residence where Hawkwood was staying. Some of his guards were on duty with several men of the Florentine militia. One or two glances were exchanged when she said she had something to say to Hawkwood but at the mention of Ser Vitelli a guard was reluctantly dispatched to put her request to the man himself.

She was called in after a few minutes' wait. The guard tried to make her leave her hounds outside but she told him they would be more trouble than they were worth. At the sight of their teeth, he allowed them to pass. He led her down a corridor of echoing marble into a splendid chamber blazing with gilt and mirrors.

Hawkwood himself was standing at the far end in front of a window looking on to a garden. She could see the tops of the trees swaying back and forth behind his head. His bodyguards stared suspiciously when she walked in with her hounds but when she stood mildly by the door they relaxed.

Hawkwood had the air of someone coiled to pounce. Staying where he was, he beckoned her to approach with a peremptory flicking of his wrist.

She took one step and then halted. It was near enough.

He was a subtle reader of such things and a weary smile lifted the corners of his mouth. 'So, nun,' he began. 'I'm in the mood for sport. I expect you want gold on behalf of the bastards my men have begotten on those sisters of yours who survived the unpleasantness after Cesena?'

Stifling her revulsion, Hildegard said, 'I'm here on a different matter.' She paused. 'This is to do with injustice in your homeland.'

'Homeland?'

'England.'

'What have I to do with that godforsaken hell-hole?'

'You are still an Englishman. I believe you came here because of the injustice of being abandoned by the old king after the French wars. Now many of your countrymen are suffering injustice but are unable to run. They can only stay and fight.'

It was more than she had intended to say. His glance narrowed and she quickly held out the turnshoe. 'Here is something that may persuade you of the gravity of the cause.'

He trod towards her, spurs jangling with importance, his scabbard swinging from his belt, glittering with jewels. He came to a stop in front of her. His eyes were grey, she noticed, bright, long-sighted. A fold of flesh under his chin and the grooved lines on his face were all that told his age.

'Do you know what they're calling me, Sister? '

'I have heard. Who hasn't?' She didn't flinch.

'Solomon!' He gave a thin smile. 'And you are not afraid?'

They eyed each other. He was an inch or so smaller than she was but made up for it in the force of his presence. A virile man, he was at his peak in many ways, and very conscious of it.

'They call me Solomon because of a judgment I'm supposed to have made on the field of battle. Do you believe the story?'

'I find life itself a test of my belief.'

The story he referred to was one of hideous cruelty. After the final battle at Cesena when his men had been sharing the spoils, two of them came to blows over a nun. To settle the matter Hawkwood was said to have split the nun in two with one sweep of his sword. 'Now take your share,' he had told them.

He was inspecting the turnshoe with some interest now but, as if he suspected it might be poisoned, he did not touch it.

'Inside the shoe is a document I would like you to read. It tells the true story of Wat Tyler's murder at Smithfield,' she told him. 'After he was cut down his followers were outmanoeuvred by men who are more politically astute. Now they need a leader.'

He raised his brows.

She added, 'A leader like you could have saved them from defeat.'

'And am I supposed to feel guilty because I wasn't there?'

'I don't intend to make you feel anything. Right actions should not be coerced by feelings of guilt. They should spring from the free choice to do right for its own sake.'

His eyes sparkled with amusement. 'We have something in common, then, Sister, for I believe my men's loyalty is nothing if bullied into being. I'd rather have the support of men who are fighting by my side from their own choice.'

'And do you believe their choice is free and not bought?'

His eyes narrowed again and the corners of his mouth turned down. Two deep furrows appeared between his brows. Hildegard could have bitten off her tongue. She watched him, alert for what would happen next. But he was beginning to laugh. The furrows became more marked.

'You're right,' he said. 'They're dogs, each with his own price. As are we all. I wonder what yours is, Sister?' He was chuckling. 'I admire your audacity in coming here! Daring to plead with me to defend English peasants! Who sent you?'

'No one. I came of my own accord.'

'Vitelli is not involved then?' His glance sharpened.

'Only in so far as it can affect trade.'

His lips puckered. 'How much are you offering for this adventure?'

Carefully, Hildegard replied, 'I hope you might consider volunteering your services out of regard for your countrymen. They are daily giving their lives in the fight against the injustices of Gaunt and his allies.'

'You mean you're offering nothing?' He roared with laughter. 'I admire your courage even more! Let me put forward an opinion about my so-called countrymen. I believe they're giving their lives because they're a weak force pitted against a stronger. But the aim of both, Gaunt and the people, is the same – to take power and hold it by any means. At the moment Gaunt is the stronger. Sometime, maybe in the distant future, the weaker side will become strong. Their tyranny will match that of their oppressor. This is the law of life. The lust for power is the same in all men. Some hide it. Some do not. The king is a mere boy and is therefore weak, and the weak, recognising someone they think is like themselves, flock to his cause and call themselves the Company of the White Hart. But Richard will become a man and then the balance of power will shift. He will become strong and will disappoint them. The people will desert him to seek another lost cause. Now tell me why I should feel anything for either winners or losers. What is it to do with me?'

'Because there are women and children involved who have no

choice in what their men fight over,' she said levelly. 'They are always the losers. They are worthy of protection but no one protects them.'

He looked astonished. 'And you think I might?'

'I pray you might.'

With an oath he swung away from her and strode back towards the window where he jerked to a halt to gaze out for some moments into the garden. Hildegard held her breath. The guards had moved closer and she sensed one of them standing behind her. Duchess bristled and Bermonda made a small growl in the back of her throat.

Hawkwood half turned. He did not look round. 'Tell her to leave this document. Let's see what it says. Then tell her to get out.' He again gazed out of the window and did not turn back.

Hildegard fumbled with the shoe, took Reynard's copy from inside the lining and handed it to one of the guards. With only the sound of her hounds' claws clicking over the tiles to break the silence, she left.

The bill of exchange would not have been enough, she thought later as she prepared to leave Florence. Nothing would have been enough to negate the dishonour of running from England's shores and living a life based on wanton destruction. Every glittering jewel he possessed represented the death of a fellow being.

She wrote a final letter to Ulf and sent it by means of the Vitelli company courier. It would take about twenty-five days to reach Bruges and from there it would be taken on to Castle Hutton. Given the usual speed of the *scarselle* it would reach him before its subject did, for it concerned Pierrekyn. What he had confessed burned in her mind. She wrote:

The boy is innocent but for fear of this letter falling into the wrong hands I cannot say more. Protect him, I beg of you. I leave Florence within the day.

She was handing over the letter at the couriers' office in the main court when Matteo approached, walking at his usual brisk clip. He was fanning himself with a scented cloth, the smell of smoke still hanging in the air.

'Sister,' he called, 'you have a visitor. I've shown him into the small chamber under the portico where you may talk in privacy.'

'A visitor? But I know no one here. Did he give a name?'

'It's difficult for me to pronounce,' he looked apologetic, 'but he had black hair, smart, with an elaborate capuchon.'

Black hair suggested Jack Black but smart did not. 'And did he have a scar?' she asked, holding her breath.

Matteo blinked. 'Not that I noticed.'

'Or an emblem of some kind?'

Matteo shook his head. 'He's not a Florentine either. He tried to explain himself with touching difficulty!'

Matteo was clearly in a hurry so she thanked him and made her way to the chamber. Her visitor would no doubt solve the mystery.

When she pushed open the door, however, she was puzzled to find the room empty. Before she could go back outside someone stepped from behind the door and slammed it shut.

'As neat as netting a lamprey.' It was Escrick Fitzjohn.

Chapter Nineteen

'**H**OW DARE YOU come here!' she ground out. 'How did you talk your way in? What lies did you tell? Get out, before I call the guards and have you thrown into prison!'

He ignored her words. 'No hounds again, Sister. When will you ever learn?'

He strode confidently towards her until they were almost touching. She was forced to take a step back. He stank of sweat and staleness and smoke despite the outward finery he wore. Matteo was right about the capuchon. Escrick had wound it in a Turkish knot so that it concealed his scar.

He withdrew his right hand from his sleeve and held it up to show a filthy bandage wrapped round the wound from his severed finger. 'You did this to me.' He seemed to expect her to say something but for once she decided to hold her tongue.

Outside she could hear the busy sounds in the courtyard, the click of bone counters, the occasional burst of laughter where the *fattori* and the accountants were at work under the portico. It was close, yet as far from help as a mountain top. The moment she cried out he would use his knife.

Escrick must have seen this realisation in her face because he gave a sneering laugh and drew a broadsword with taunting slowness from its scabbard.

'I am unarmed,' she pointed out. 'If you strike me down your soul will go straight to hell.'

'It might, if I believed in all that, but I don't.'

He came closer, circling her like a wolf, forcing her into a corner. The chamber was empty except for a chest, a dark wood table with ornate legs, and a couple of heavy wooden chairs. They looked too weighty to be moved, let alone lifted and thrown. For once her knife was in her chamber where she had been using it to sharpen a quill.

In addition to the capuchon Escrick was wearing a short cloak. It had been cut from a larger piece of cloth. It was blue.

She said, 'You shot Sir Talbot.'

'Did I?' He laughed.

'Then you stole anything of value, including my cloak, and, presumably having mistaken him for me, you set off down the mountainside in pursuit of your real victim.'

'Pity about the knight. He shouldn't have put your cloak on in that dazzle of snow. The sun was shining straight into my eyes. You cut the rope bridge later, you bitch. Caused me a heap of trouble getting down to St Rhémy. By the time I arrived you'd already left. Where did you pick up that minstrel again? He wasn't with you when you left the hospice.'

'You were watching?'

He laughed again. 'Of course I was watching. I've been watching you for some time. All the way, in fact. I slept out. It was no hardship.' He began to walk to and fro in front of her, backing her further into the corner.

'Why do you hate me so much?' she asked, curious, despite her danger. 'Anybody could have revealed you as the murderer of that poor maid at Castle Hutton last autumn. Would you have hunted them down the way you're hunting me?'

He considered her words and then he said, 'I have instructions. That's why I'm here. You're not the only one after that cross. I want to know where you've hidden it.'

'What makes you think I've got it?'

'If you haven't, who has? The old monk was told to go and fetch it back from Rome. The contessa's spies found out that much. You must have bought it from him. God knows how much you paid but the contessa would have paid double. So where is it? You must have it or you wouldn't be leaving tomorrow.'

He even knew that. Perhaps the contessa had spies in every household. She lifted a hand. The gesture made her sleeve touch his wrist and he jerked away as if stung, bringing up his sword.

'Don't move,' he snarled.

Fighting the desire to scream, she said quickly, 'If you kill me you'll never find the cross and your lady will have your fingers, one by one, and your toes, and much else you value before you can even exit the gates of Florence.'

'And for that reason, Sister, you still live. But your hours are numbered. Now where is it?'

'You'll never know whether I've got it or not—'

'Then you may as well die,' he growled. 'But I think you will tell me – when you know what lies in store for you. We know the sacristan hid it in his church. He must have told you where it was and you went back last night before the fire. Yet it's not in your sleeping chamber. I've already looked.'

'How did you know where I was sleeping?'

He pulled his right ear. 'Same way as I know a lot of things.' His eyes narrowed and he added, 'Things you might not wish your abbot to know.'

She remembered the only time she had spoken her most secret thoughts out loud. Escrick must have been listening in some dark corner near the confessional. Deciding to bluff it out, she said, 'I can't tell you what you want to know. You seem to have silenced the only person who could help.'

'The old monk, you mean? He was just a dithering old fool.'

He regarded her with cold calculation while she thought how badly he had misjudged the sacristan. He had been fully aware of the importance of the cross and had kept silent to the end. He had even swallowed the key to the aumbry to put Escrick off the scent.

'The contessa was upset when you left without permission. She thought you must have been burned in the fire and it was only when I heard you'd been to see Hawkwood that I could tell her the glad tidings.'

'She won't be glad when she knows you've run your sword through me without getting what you want.'

'She's not the only one who wants something. I want something myself—'

He moved closer.

'Hildegard,' he said. His tone thickened. 'I think you know what I want – and I think you want it just as much as me. A woman like you, in her prime, wearing that—' He reached out and touched her head-covering and then, holding one end, he started to pull her towards him.

For a moment she was reminded of the time in the undercroft at Hutton when he had mistaken her for a serving woman and had torn off her cloak to find she was a nun. A sickening memory of the chase that followed came back to her with terrifying clarity.

With her eyes fixed on his, she waited until he had pulled her against him and his surcoat of chain mail was pressing into her bosom, and his mouth, his bad breath making her want to vomit, was approaching her own mouth and then, at the last moment, she butted her forehead hard into his face. As he jerked back with blood pouring from his nose, she ripped off her kerchief, leaving it dangling between his fingers and fled towards the door.

With a roar he was after her but she managed to get her fingers through the door-pull and hold on. His wounded hand was no use to him and she was able to jerk the door ajar. It was no more than a few inches but she wedged her foot in it, then elbowed him in the face and, in the brief pause that followed, dragged the door wider, screaming with all her might, before he managed to clamp one hand over her mouth and drag her back inside the room.

Duchess and Bermonda had been exercising out in the yard with a kennel lad. As Escrick was grappling with her, blood pouring from his nose, the two hounds must have heard her voice because now they came bounding down the corridor.

Duchess hurled herself against the door, forcing it open, and then leaped straight at Escrick's throat. His sword slashed down, missing her by inches. He staggered back with the full force of the deerhound on top of him. As he fell Bermonda snapped her two rows of deadly teeth round his wrist and shook his arm from side to side like a piece of straw until the sword dropped from his grasp. Between them they could bring down a stag at full speed. Escrick was nothing to them.

The commotion brought servants running from all parts of the building. Ser Vitelli himself emerged from the reception chamber at the far end of the corridor. Hearing Escrick raging at Hildegard to call off her hounds, everyone swarmed into the chamber and quickly surrounded him.

Ser Vitelli entered the chamber last and the servants parted to let him through. His glance alighted on Hildegard, her garments in disarray, her hair, grown long in the previous weeks, fully revealed and falling in disorder round her shoulders. Then he noticed Escrick, pinned to the floor by the hounds, his sword unsheathed beside him.

His yellow eyes flashed with rage. Stepping forward, he asked, 'Who is this villain?'

Briefly, Hildegard explained but, remembering the prioress's warning to reveal nothing about the cross, mentioned only that Escrick had been outlawed in England last autumn and blamed her for it.

'He followed you here seeking revenge?' Vitelli asked in astonishment.

Escrick groaned as Bermonda sank her teeth more firmly into his wrist. Duchess had planted herself four-square across his chest with her great front paws on both sides of his head, her jaw only an inch away from his face, awaiting orders. The capuchon lay on the tiles beside him.

'I believe he serves La Gran Contessa and was coerced into coming here,' she said.

Vitelli threw her a searching glance.

'She thinks I have something she wants,' she added.

Ser Vitelli gave Escrick a cold glance. 'Search him, disarm him, then throw him back on the contessa's doorstep. She'll devise a worse punishment than anything the law can allow.'

An attendant whispered something and Ser Vitelli gave a thin smile. 'All right then, throw him in the river. See if he floats. Just get him out of here and fumigate the place afterwards.'

He turned and without a sound padded back to his interrupted meeting.

When Hildegard returned to her sleeping chamber she felt a shiver of revulsion. Even if Escrick had not told her he had searched it she would have guessed someone had been inside. It smelled unpleasant, with a lingering odour, sickly sweet. It made her wonder at the roughness of Escrick's life, the hardships, living from hand to mouth, his choice to be a professional killer and what had brought him to this pitch of degradation.

She opened the window to let in the fresh air from outside. Ser Vitelli had invited her to dine with him on this, her last night in his beautiful and terrible city. Carefully she changed her habit and her hosen, both torn in the scuffle with Escrick.

When she went down later to join Ser Vitelli in the main chamber there were candles everywhere. They gave off a honeyed scent, arousing feelings of luxury and ease. Their light danced over the gilt mouldings on the walls and were reflected many times over in the Venetian mirrors and in the silver and gold of the elaborate tableware. They even stood in clusters on an enormous bracket suspended from the ceiling among a serpentine wealth of blown glass and they were fixed in holders down the length of the black marble table.

There were gold urns fashioned in Milan and filled with flowers, dishes of Bohemian crystal containing strange fruits from the kingdom of Naples, platters of viands from the forests of the Apennines. Maybe Ser Vitelli dined in such private splendour every day, she thought. Or maybe he had commanded his servants to make a special effort for some purpose of his own.

She remembered her first impression of him.

Tonight the burnished snake looked no less splendid than his surroundings. He was wearing a long purple *lucco* of some lustrous fabric and a single ruby on his finger that flashed like fire every time he lifted his gold goblet.

For once his head was bare and his hair, she saw for the first time, was silver, clipped short like that of a Roman emperor. When he leaned towards her she discovered it was perfumed with some exotic oil suggesting great expense in its procurement. The style emphasised the harsh lines of his features.

Once they were seated and the servants had brought in a supply of delicacies, the subject of his nephew's betrothal came up after the familiar graceful foreplay.

174

'I wish to send further suggestions to Lord Roger de Hutton,' he told her. 'My *scarselle* are totally trustworthy, of course, but I wonder if I may presume on your friendship with Lord Roger to—?' He let the question trail away.

'I will take a letter to him in confidence if you wish. I would deem it an honour.'

He offered a glimpse of a smile and bowed his head.

That negotiations were to continue seemed to be a good sign.

Next he mentioned the shipment of staple from Hutton that was still on its way to Florence to supply the cloth manufacturers and how the price had already risen while in transit. He referred to trade from the East too and how lucrative it was and how anyone wishing to make a good profit could rest in the conviction that it would remain so.

Hildegard took this as a hint that Roger's share in the trading ship had been approved and arrangements for the voyage were under way.

He did not question her about Escrick's reason for entering the palazzo uninvited. She felt he suspected there was more than personal revenge at stake. He said only how detrimental to trade between the two countries was the continual warfare of the Tuscan city states, and how it would be worse if England, too, recommended her wars with France or, worse still, fell into civil disarray.

'War is detrimental to good business,' he observed, 'and to be abhorred by all except those who supply arms.'

He left that topic abruptly and went on to tell her of his contrition at allowing a villain like Escrick to assault her. 'A guest in my own house. There is no way of making amends for such a failing, no act of reparation that could assuage my feeling of shame.'

Then he again mentioned his lack of a wife. Hildegard replied by praising the beauty of the local women and adding that she could quite understand why so many English mercenaries decided to make Tuscany their home.

Vitelli laughed and nodded his agreement but his eyes still held a gleam of some other thought that he had decided to keep to himself.

It was a bright morning, the sunlight warm and scented, a day heralding summer and lifting the heart at the prospect of an end to a long and unpleasant winter. Hildegard was ready to depart and head north again, yet she felt a twinge of anxiety as the wagons prepared to leave. News from England was not good. The Bishop of Norwich, Despenser, was preparing to attack France, pre-empting rumours of a French invasion. Her son was part of his army and she dreaded the thought of battle.

Ser Vitelli had arranged for her to travel to Bruges in the company of a group of cloth merchants he knew who were going up to do business there. She told him she had to go through the St Bernard pass as there were things to be dealt with concerning the death of Sir Talbot.

'No matter,' he told her, 'they are going through the same pass themselves as it is quicker than the others and they are always in a hurry to get to their profit before anybody else.' She was to travel in the comfort of a well-padded and opulent char with the Vitelli company coat of arms on its banner.

Standing around, impatient to be off, were her travelling companions, four merchants, all very well dressed, with their own bodyguards, and several hired men to guard their baggage. The three *fattori*, together with most of the household, came to see the convoy depart. There was no sign of Ser Vitelli.

Hildegard was leaving with four objects in her possession: one, a ring from a severed finger; two, a piece of blue cloth; three, the cross of Constantine; and four, a copy of a seditious document hurriedly written out in her own hand.

There was also the embroidered kerchief the child had given her on the quayside at Ravenser.

When she packed she had wrapped the ring in the fragment of cloth, and placed the cloth and the ring in the kerchief. Then she had placed the entire parcel inside her scrip. The document she had pressed between the pages of her breviary where it joined the rest of the things in her hand luggage. The cross was concealed in much the same way as the sacristan himself had done, on open display, sticking out of her bag wrapped in a cloth, a souvenir of her travels.

She strolled over to the char to make sure everything was being stowed properly. The servants, who had dealt with Escrick yesterday and had stripped him of his arms, had not hesitated to hand the rest of his belongings to the porter as instructed. Hildegard had asked not only for his cloak but also for the pouch he had worn on his belt, one she recognised as Sir Talbot's.

Just as she began to climb on board Ser Vitelli came out into the courtyard. He carried a small package in one hand. With an abrupt, self-conscious bow, he held it out. When she took it he did not attempt to detain her but stepped back at once. Then, with much shouting and cracking of whips and with the good wishes of the *fattori* and their colleagues ringing in her ears, they began to move out into the street.

Curious to find out what was inside the package, Hildegard opened it as soon as the char was on its way. The contents fell into her lap like a scarlet mist. She blushed. It was a pair of red hosen. They were of the very finest silk from Lucca. Hastily rewrapping them she found a note:

Forgive me, I could not help but notice. I am eternally at fault. Forever your servant, F.V.

It was Melisen who had said that whoever saw her red hose would be to blame. Ser Falduccio Vitelli seemed to agree.

They were crossing the plain some hours later when there were anxious cries from a man on lookout. Everyone turned to see where he was pointing. On the horizon, approaching at a fast gallop, was a band of horsemen. Their arms glinted harshly in the sunlight and as they streamed closer the banners of Sir John Hawkwood's White Company could be seen on top of their lances.

One of the guards cursed and drew his sword. The men scrambled to face the marauders and the merchants drew their weapons with varying degrees of dexterity, their faces pale. Hildegard rested her hands on the heads of her two hounds to steady them.

The leader of the troop drew to a skidding halt. He waved his sword. 'Put down your arms, friends. We're here to escort you through an army of Pisans camped on the plain ahead.'

He rode alongside the char.

'Is that you in there, Sister?' It was Jack Black.

'I didn't expect to see you,' she greeted him, warily tightening her grip on her hounds as she recalled the last time she had seen him.

'Hawkwood owes Vitelli a favour. There was some dispute about the pay the council promised him. Only Vitelli's eloquence on the virtues of settling one's debts in full allowed Hawkwood to get his payment for services rendered.'

'So you're working for Hawkwood now, are you?'

'We always were. That's why we came south, remember?'

'I remember you saying that but what was your discussion at the palazzo of La Gran Contessa about, then? *Fine amour* you said. It didn't sound very *fine* to me.'

He chuckled. 'I hope it didn't alarm you. No more than a mummer's play. The lads were convincing, I thought. Even the Florentines joined in – not that they wouldn't always rather talk than fight. Even so, they were good. One of them was a sacked cardinal and knew all the ins and outs of rhetoric. Kept us busy almost until we blew the place up.'

'I hope they got out alive in that case.'

'Most of 'em did.'

'So none of them planned on harming me?' She shivered to think of some of their suggestions.

Jack Black looked surprised. 'Just because they like to talk doesn't mean they're lily-livered. They do as they're paid to do. Lucky we got you out in time.'

She noticed Donal and the sapper in his contingent, grinning at her from beneath their helmets.

'My gratitude, masters,' she replied with a dry smile. 'And also for the piece of cloth. It was from the blue cloak Sir Talbot was wearing when he was shot.'

'That's what I thought. It was yours, wasn't it? Escrick Fitzjohn was wearing something similar later on.'

'Can you vouch for that?'

'Anywhere but in a court of law.'

'Sir Talbot borrowed it after the ice storm,' she explained. 'Something less bright might have spoiled Escrick's aim.'

'Not him. He's a dead shot. Famous for it.'

'Unfortunately, by God's grace, not dead yet. He came to my lodging at Vitelli's headquarters yesterday.'

'He survived the fire? The devil looks after his own!'

They travelled on across the plain with their escorts for some leagues. Hawkwood's men enjoyed a brief skirmish with outlying troops from Pisa and afterwards accompanied the convoy through the forest as far as the foothills to the north. Once they had got them safely out of reach of immediate danger they rode alongside the wagons to say goodbye.

Jack Black, teeth flashing in the thicket of his wild black beard, yelled and lifted his big, mailed fist. His men followed his example, raising their own fists in a valedictory salute, before kicking their horses into a gallop and streaming off after their captain.

Soon they were no more than a cloud of dust on the horizon. Hildegard watched until it faded. They were riding off to their deaths without a care. Maybe fortune would smile on them, she thought, and they would survive long enough to enjoy the spoils of war.

III

The land lay under a pall of fog as the ship breasted the overfalls at the mouth of the Humber. It looked like a brushstroke, with only a strip of pale sand visible through the mist as they approached. It was Hildegard's first sight of England for three months. On the muddy dockside at Ravenser, armed men were waiting for the ship to make fast. Not Hutton men, they wore the blue marsh dragon of Roger's banished brother-in-law, Sir William of Holderness.

The captain was the first to be allowed ashore. He was summoned before the serjeant to give a full inventory of his cargo.

'Nothing but tinplate, trays, dinanderie. Look for yourselves.' He was brusque, adding that he wanted nothing more than to get home to his brats, his wife and her cooking. Nevertheless, the ship was inspected from bow to stern, the import duty unhurriedly assessed.

Then the foot passengers, Hildegard and her hounds, a merchant – in truth no more than a pedlar – and a pair of pilgrims were allowed to follow the captain ashore. One of the pilgrims fell to his knees as soon as his feet touched the ground, uttering rhapsodic thanks for his safe return. The rest of them passed quickly through the ranks of militia clutching their personal baggage and drawing no attention to themselves. An escort waited for Hildegard with hired horses. They set out for the priory of Swyne.

Chapter Twenty

ILDEGARD WENT STRAIGHT to an audience with the prioress as soon as she arrived. She found her in her private chapel. Its plain clean lines were pleasing after the opulence of Florence.

The prioress stepped forward as soon as she appeared. 'Welcome home, child. You've done well. Is that it in your bag?'

Hildegard reached into the leather bag that had scarcely left her side on the long journey from Florence. She withdrew the cross. 'The inscription on the back proves its authenticity,' she said.

The prioress unwrapped it and held it in both hands. Her eyes glittered. 'The price?'

Silently Hildegard took out the bill of exchange from inside her belt and handed it over.

'What's this?'

'The custodian would accept no payment. He claimed it would sully the meaning of the cross to use it in a commercial transaction.'

'You mean he gave it to us?'

'Not exactly. Before I left the canons agreed that we are to be its guardians for a fixed period and when it expires we must return it. It was the sacristan's idea.'

'This is most generous. A rare thing these days. I must send my deepest thanks to this monk and—'

'It will not be possible, Mother.'

Hildegard's eyes filled with tears. And then she told her prioress the whole story of her journey, leaving nothing out.

'The sacristan was an old man,' she told her in conclusion. 'He had a pure unwavering vision of good. He believed his life was not worth much now as it was nearly over – he had spent it, he said – but spiritual capital accrues from the value of our deeds and cannot be bought and sold. He believed that whoever held guardianship of the cross must understand this and use its power for the benefit of everyone.'

Deep in thought, the prioress placed the cross next to her own small, hand-hewn one on the altar and looked at it in silence.

Outside the window the branch of a tree tapped now and again against the new glass as if to remind them of the passage of time.

'I confess I am truly sick at heart, Mother,' Hildegard was forced to admit. 'The cross has cost so much bloodshed. If it should not bring peace then it will have been in vain.'

'We are players in a game of chance,' reproved the prioress, coming out of her reverie. 'We must all submit to the game or weary ourselves like birds dashing themselves against the bars of a cage. We can only do what we must, in ignorance of the greater plan.'

'That may be true but it does little to assuage my sorrow at the death of Sir Talbot. Unlike the monk, he had all his life before him.'

The prioress bowed her head. 'I feel his death more than you can know. But,' she said, 'what's done is done.' Her tone became deliberately matter-of-fact. 'There were great changes while you were away. For one thing – you must have noticed this at Ravenser – Sir William has been reinstated.'

'By Lord Roger?' Hildegard asked. There was no understanding Roger's caprices.

'No. He was brought back by Gaunt. Roger was overruled by our great lord of Lancaster. Can you imagine it? Roger hasn't stopped ranting since.'

'But why should Gaunt interfere?'

'Because he's frightened. He doesn't know whom to trust. Many who escaped retribution in Kent and Essex fled north. The people of York and Beverley are in a violent mood. The archbishop made things worse by imposing petty restrictions on the canons at St John's and has had to flee to Scarborough Castle for safety.'

'To Scarborough?" she exclaimed. 'But that's where Sir Ralph Standish has been made steward.'

'Yes – as a reward for killing Tyler. Everyone's in a foment over it.'

'So the archbishop and Standish are allies?'

'Who said anything about allies?' The prioress looked amused. 'And do you really imagine the canons can frighten Archbishop Neville? There's more behind it than we know.'

Leaving the cross on the altar the prioress walked towards the door, the audience over. 'By the way,' she said, 'there have been changes at Meaux as well, all of them sanctioned by the lord abbot.' She fixed a careful glance on Hildegard to observe her response.

'Changes for the better, then?' she suggested.

'Some might say so, although I understand that most of the brothers have a different view.'

'Why, what's been happening?'

'They're being sent out to the fields to do the work usually done by the conversi, for one thing. Even the prior is not exempt!'

Hildegard tried to imagine the delicate-looking prior and his fastidious regard for cleanliness with mud under his nails.

'And they're allowed only one habit and one cloak,' the prioress continued, 'no undergarments of course, unless it's a hair shirt, and only one meal a day, and then only two courses. No meat, naturally, and ale, not wine.'

'The lord abbot does have an austere side,' Hildegard remarked. 'In the snow last winter he wore sandals all the time. The brothers followed suit, though out of reverence, I believe, and not at his insistence.'

'You think there's nothing wrong in bringing simplicity into daily life. I agree with you but Hubert de Courcy goes further than that. In fact, many are saying he goes further than the devil himself.' The prioress looked grim for a moment. 'Of course, he may be forced to it against his will at the behest of Avignon. The change in him seems to have taken place soon after that visit of the papal envoy last November. But, from what I hear, the pope doesn't go without luxuries so why should he expect his monastics to do so?'

'I thought the abbot seemed much the same after the envoy's visit,' Hildegard ventured.

'I thought so at first but I can't think of any other reason why he should go to—' She frowned. 'To such extremes of self-punishment.'

'Self-punishment?'

'Beyond the norm.'

As the prioress opened the door she said, 'I expect you'll want to get over to the guest house and have a word with Lord Roger's steward about the minstrel you told me about.'

Hildegard turned. 'Is Ulf here?'

'He is indeed.'

Hildegard hurried over to the guest quarters. They were small, no more than a couple of bedchambers, a hall and a kitchen, as there were few visitors in this backwater of the Riding and those who did brave the marshes tended to stay in the more lavish house at Meaux.

Ulf was leaning over a stable door when she found him, admiring a fine-looking mare in the stall.

'Hildegard!' He turned with a smile of delight when he saw her and without thinking swept her up into his arms. She disengaged herself and said, 'I'm pleased to see you, Ulf. I'm glad you got back safely.'

He stepped away, aware of his impropriety. 'Likewise,' he mumbled. 'I was just looking at this mare here. It's a present for Lady Melisen from Lord Roger.'

'I've got her pearl sleeves and some trinkets she ordered,' she told him. 'Maybe you'll take them back to Hutton for me?'

'No need. She and Roger are already on their way over to Meaux. They're to stay at the abbey so they can be on hand to attend the court when it sits.'

'The court?'

'The hearing for Reynard's murderer. The authorities are determined to punish somebody for it and—'

'And Pierrekyn?'

'I got your letter.' He looked uncomfortable. 'Things didn't go well in Flanders. They had to render the body down before they'd allow us to bring the remains back home.' He looked wretchedly into her face. 'I swear, Hildegard, I examined the body with a fine-tooth comb, together with a leech who was well thought of in Bruges. We found nothing. One stab wound. Lots of blood. Nothing to show who wielded the knife. Embalming the body and trying to get it back through customs was not an option. It would have told us nothing more to have him lying in the mortuary at Meaux. We did everything we could.'

'So what about Pierrekyn? Why is he being held?'

'He's the only suspect. Lord Roger's bound by the monastic court because the body was found on abbey land. The abbot has to preside at the first hearing and if they think they've got enough evidence it'll go on to the secular court.' He paused. 'Unluckily for Pierrekyn, the coroner only cares about getting a result. It's out of my hands.'

'But surely somebody knows who really murdered Reynard. There were a lot of people in and out of the wool-sheds that day. Somebody must have seen something.'

He shook his head. 'If they have, they're keeping quiet.'

'Surely Roger can't allow Pierrekyn to stand trial?'

'He says his hands are tied.'

Hildegard remembered her conversation with Ser Vitelli when he explained the details of the contract Roger had made with the earl and again she thought how useful it would be for Roger if the man who drew it up was out of the way. It was not a suspicion she could share with Ulf.

'Pierrekyn must be beside himself with fear,' she said.

'He's being held on the basis of hearsay. People are letting their imaginations run riot. I said as much to Roger and got bawled out for it.'

'But what if I have evidence that proves it could not have been Pierrekyn?'

'Then you must attend as witness for the defence.' He gave her a close look. 'Have you such evidence?'

'I may have. I need to check something first.'

'You hinted at something in your letter—'

'I can't say anything just yet. I don't want to raise false hopes. I'm astonished no word has filtered through to identify the real culprit.'

'So am I,' he said with feeling. 'I believe it was an act committed by a professional.' He frowned. 'But enough of that for the moment.' His voice took on a more personal tone. 'It is good to see you back safe and sound, you know. We heard about Sir Talbot from Vitelli's courier. It must have been even harder after that.'

'Talbot was without fault. It's an outrage that he should have been killed and in such a cowardly way too.'

'They're going to miss him in France this summer. He was a hero of the tournaments.'

'On the way back I spoke to the prior of the hospice where the body was taken by the *maronniers*. They'd already built a small shrine where he was killed and they're going to keep it stocked with provisions for anyone caught on the mountains in a storm. I told them I'd had to leave his sword in the snow but that his lady would probably like to have it. They told me it would come to light in the spring melt and they would send it to her.'

She told him about Escrick, and Ulf reminded her that he would escape punishment so long as he remained overseas. She told him as much about the rest of her journey as she could without mentioning the cross of Constantine. It would soon be in the hands of the archbishop and it would be for him to decide how he unveiled it to the world at large. For the time being it was safely in the keeping of the prioress.

'Let Pierrekyn know I'm back and not to give up hope,' she said as they parted.

Ulf raised a hand in acknowledgement but then hesitated. 'Hildegard ... they've told you about Hubert de Courcy, have they?'

'He's the lord abbot, Ulf. It's his duty to purify the Rule!' Smiling, she went on her way.

In her cell Hildegard unpacked her bags and tried to bring some order to the resulting disarray as if it might also help order her thoughts.

Opening out the embroidered kerchief, she took out the piece of blue cloth and the ring. The cloth she had accounted for. Soon everyone would know what it meant. The ring was another matter.

It was in the shape of a silver wyvern with something black like Whitby jet in its mouth. She turned it over. After a while she placed it back inside the kerchief, which itself was a mystery, and turned to the parcel she had picked up on her way through Flanders.

Melisen's pearl sleeves were heavy with the tiny pearls and other jewels sewn on laboriously over many hours of painstaking work and she held them up to admire them. Rewrapping them, she turned to the twelve brooches, white harts fashioned in gold and white enamel with pearls in the harts' antlers and, as the goldsmith had observed, forming a most pretty design.

They too were another small mystery and perhaps it was merely Melisen's frivolity that had led her to choose such a potent symbol. She put them with the rest of the things to be taken to Meaux.

Finally she opened her missal. The document was safe inside where she had hidden it. More copies would have to be made and disseminated if its purpose was to be fulfilled. The idea was a dangerous one. She considered the perils of engaging with the Rising. Civil war was to be abhorred and yet the truth must be told.

Chapter Twenty-one

AFTER NONES NEXT day Hildegard set out for the abbey. She went on foot across the marsh, picking her way by means of a narrow path linking the priory at Swyne with Meaux. The water bubbling along the brimming ditches was the only sound to break the silence.

Soon she noticed a figure in the flat landscape. It was a monk, wearing a habit that had once been white but was now covered in mud. He seemed to be trying to rescue a ewe from where it lay in the marsh. Up to his knees in muddy water, his habit flapping round his knees, he was intent on his task as she approached.

'Hail, Brother!' She began to wade over to give him a hand but when he looked up she gasped in alarm. 'Thomas! Is it you?'

Instead of the jaunty, bright-eyed novitiate she remembered from last November, a pale, hollowed-eyed man looked back.

'Sister Hildegard! What a pleasure to see you. So you're back from pilgrimage?'

'Indeed. But first let me give you a hand. What ails the ewe?'

He sighed. 'Best keep away. We brought a flock over from the North Riding. They didn't seem to like the different herbage and many of them have died but now I'm beginning to wonder if it isn't the murrain that afflicts them. God defend us if it is.'

He succeeded in rolling the sheep over but it was too feeble to rise unaided.

'We've lost so many of our flock last winter. First in the snows, then in the floods, and now this. It seems it'll never end.'

'My poor dear brother, is there no one here to help you?'

'This is my penance, according to the lord abbot. It's my duty to work alone in this,' he stretched out his arms to encompass the bleak circle of the horizon, 'and only then shall I know the true meaning of humility.' He gave a wry smile.

Hildegard noticed that his hands were shaking. 'Have you eaten today?' she asked.

'I have had my allotted rations, yes, thank you.'

'But were they enough?'

'Enough?' His laugh was hollow. 'I stand. I speak. Were they not enough?'

She stepped closer. 'Thomas, you know me well. Tell me, what ails you?'

'In truth, Sister, I know not. I suffer an affliction of the soul. Nothing we brothers do is good enough for the lord abbot. His new regimen is harsh beyond measure. But no doubt we think so because we've become soft with corruption and know nothing of true piety.' His glance was pained. 'I can do nothing right in his eyes. I am truly a most miserable sinner. I have no hope of redemption.'

'That cannot be true. I know you as a forthright and vigorous upholder of right action. What brings you to such straits?'

'I'm at fault even for speaking to you, a woman, even though a sister of the Order.' He bit his lip. 'I fear I shall not survive long enough to achieve my desire to become a monk. I am at my end. My will is weak. I am unworthy.' He turned away. His spoke in such defeated tones she put out a hand.

'Wait, Thomas, let me help you lift this poor creature onto the bank. I'm sure the lord abbot would not despise my help.'

The young brother's hands were blue with cold, the knuckles shining with chilblains. Their usual inkstains had been replaced by the cuts and weals of physical labour. His hair, which usually stuck up where he had raked his fingers through it as he worked on his parchments in the scriptorium, was cut brutally short and lay flat and lifeless against his skull.

As they hauled the heavy body of the sheep onto drier ground, Thomas's words aroused a feeling of foreboding. Ever since she had arrived back at Swyne people had mentioned Hubert's changed manner, his adoption of a harsher regimen. Now she was seeing its effect. Thomas was the best of men. Yet he had been brought to depths of despair she could not have imagined.

They dragged the sheep out of the water. Its yellow eyes were half closed, its wool thick, at its winter weight. The thin legs stuck out touchingly like spindles as it lay on its side, panting for breath.

'Murrain,' she confirmed. 'Have others suffered in the same way?'

'This is the first I've found. Let's hope the watercourses that separate the flocks will protect the rest of them.'

They watched in silence until the ewe gave one last grunt and then lay still. Thomas put a hand to his forehead to hide his face. Hildegard noticed that he was almost barefoot, his rope sandals offering no protection at all from the bitterly cold water in which he stood. Mud caked his legs up to the knees and the hem of his robe was heavy with yellowish loam.

'Come back to Meaux and warm yourself,' she suggested.

He shook his head. 'I cannot. I have to stay here until the light goes. I cannot shirk my duty.'

'Does the lord abbot also suffer from this new regimen?' she asked.

'He suffers worse than any of us,' said Thomas.

Hildegard wanted to probe further but the light was waning. She would discover the truth soon enough when she reached the abbey itself. 'I didn't leave Swyne until after nones,' she explained. 'I must go on. But promise me you'll come on soon? Don't leave it so late you have to make your way across the marsh in darkness.'

'I shall come on soon, Sister. Thank you for your concern. I am quite unworthy of it.'

'Nonsense, Thomas. You are as worthy as any man alive.'

There was no breath of wind to ripple the pools surrounding the abbey. It seemed to rest on the surface of the water as on a reflecting glass. Everything was doubled. Two abbeys, she thought, the one I left, full of the joy of good work, and the one to which I return, a crucible of punishing reform.

She went into the guest-master's office.

'Cell vacant on the first floor,' he told her abruptly, avoiding her glance. 'Second one along.' Surprised by his unfriendly manner, she set off to find it.

The whole place was full. Servants wearing Lord Roger's red and gold livery were hurrying about with long faces instead of their usual good humour. Other retinues were represented by the blue marsh dragon of Sir William and the green and silver lozenge of Lady Sibilla and Sir Richard – but there was one livery she had not expected to see, the silver and azure bands worn by Gaunt's men.

Our great lord of the North, as the prioress ironically referred to him. She shivered with what it might portend.

The new bell, recently cast, was calling everyone to the next office. Files of monks shuffled along the cloisters towards the church. Servants and conversi followed. Hildegard hurried up to the cell the guest-master had allotted her, dropped her bag on the bed, threw her cloak over it, and hurried out again.

Hubert de Courcy would have to be faced. It would be better to meet him now in the harmony of the penultimate office of the day rather than later when he would be taken up with his duties as host to the visitors.

She recalled his coldness the last time they had met and the sorrow with which she had left Meaux for Tuscany. As she crossed the garth towards the church she felt a rising dread at the prospect of meeting him again.

The church doors were already closed. The thin sound of a small choir came from inside. Hildegard turned the heavy iron door-pull as carefully as she could and opened the door a crack. The place was full to the walls. Dipping her head, she slid inside, pressed the door shut, and glanced swiftly around.

The choir were singing a very plain unadorned *ave*, not at all in their usual ornate style, and there were so few of them she wondered whether Hubert had sent the choristers out into the fields as well.

In the stalls where the choir usually stood were the guests, those from Castle Hutton, Scarborough and Holderness, and one or two she did not recognise. The prior was holding forth in his mellifluous tones, directing his words entirely to them as if the rest of the church was empty. With a mass of servants from the different households crowding at the back, Hildegard had to edge to one side to get a better view between their heads.

Melisen stood out as usual. She wore a fur-trimmed gown of crimson velvet and a jewelled fillet, her hair caught up in a crispinette of filigree silver. One of Gaunt's men stood beside her. Lord Roger was nowhere to be seen.

Giving Melisen black looks was Lady Sibilla, her hair pulled elegantly back under a beaded headband, with her husband, Sir Ralph, by her side in a hat with a tall crown and a feather held by a large enamel brooch. Hildegard was surprised to see them here. It would be difficult for Roger to forgive their treachery – Sir Ralph had claimed to be heir to the de Hutton estates on behalf of a baby who turned out to be neither their child nor, in fact, a boy – and Lord Roger was not a forgiving man.

Hildegard was further astonished to see Roger's brother-in-law, William of Holderness, master of the port at Ravenser by virtue of his marriage to Roger's sister Avice, and of many other lands besides. But, surprisingly, his wife was not with him although she rarely let William out of her sight. After the debacle last November when William had tried to take Castle Hutton, he and Avice had been banished. Yet here was William, as large as life. No wonder Roger had kept away.

There was another familiar face among those at the front. Ulf was sitting somewhat aloof from the rest of the de Hutton party and appeared to be lost in thought. When everybody stood for the entrance of the abbot he had to be prodded in the back by one of his servants to jerk him to his feet.

Hildegard felt a shiver run through her as the lord abbot, wearing the traditional white habit of a Cistercian, proceeded down the aisle towards the altar. Instead of his usual splendid silk cope, Hubert wore a plain one of rather threadbare staymyn. He moved differently, too, as if recovering from a long illness, and when he reached the steps of the altar he seemed to stagger slightly. The prior put out a hand.

She watched closely to see whether she could discern from this distance what ailed the abbot. Lifting the chalice in shaking hands, he intoned the Latin in a resolute voice but his face, when he turned to face the congregation, was as pale as parchment. His cheekbones stood out as if the flesh had been dissolved although his eyes flashed as brilliantly as ever as he began to speak.

It was more like a rant than a sermon. Hubert railed against the sin of vanity, enough to make Melisen blush and Gaunt's man fan himself with the edge of one dagged sleeve, although the servants at the back stood stoically enough. Next he railed against venery. There were sidelong looks. Ulf was staring at the floor. Only when Hubert started to declaim against lechery as the greatest of all sins did the servants begin to shuffle and nudge each other. Ulf lifted his head and stared at the abbot with a hard expression as if his thoughts were entirely elsewhere, the seated nobles shifted somewhat shamefaced; and Lady Sibilla and Sir Ralph exchanged secret smiles. Sir William stretched out his legs in their knee-high boots, frowned darkly and looked more like Satan than ever.

Interesting, thought Hildegard. She would have been amused at the different reactions of those she knew if Hubert's rage had not been so alarming. His voice echoed around the pillars like thunder while among the servants there were by now many shifty glances and embarrassed grins as his condemnation rolled on.

No wonder poor Brother Thomas feels unworthy, she thought. Hubert's making me feel guilty too and I know I'm innocent. Then, as if he had read her thoughts, Hubert's voice dropped and in the silence it sounded like a snake's hiss.

'Salaciousness is a sin as much in the mind as in the body,' he said, 'in the thoughts as much as in the act itself, in the soul which it poisons as much as on the lips of the beloved. Man loves and loves what vanishes. Like a sot-witted fool he turns away from the true faith and prefers to wallow in the sink of corruption, calling it love, and we risk our immortal souls in the desire for one night with the sorceress who has bewitched us with her earthly wiles.'

It went on in this vein for some time. When the congregation was finally released Hildegard was carried along by the crowd into the fresh air of the garth.

Night had fallen while they had been targets of the abbot's accusations. Now they stood under a crisp canopy of stars with subdued looks and instead of passing the time in friendly banter began to separate at once to take up their duties again.

Hildegard felt as shaken as if she had been standing beneath a raging storm. There are changes at Meaux you will not believe. The prioress was right. But what on earth had caused such wildness of speech and such wholesale condemnation of guests and brethren alike?

She lingered in the courtyard until Ulf emerged. He had his head bent and did not see her at first.

'Ulf!' She pulled at his sleeve. His eyes lit up at once.

'A flame of sanity in a mad world. Sister, thank heavens you've arrived. Are you coming over to the guest house? We can talk there.'

When they were comfortably ensconced in the small private sanctum reserved for the steward on his frequent visits to Meaux, Ulf poured them both a beaker of wine. Before speaking he took a long drink then refilled his own and topped up the one Hildegard was toying with. He went to sit on the bench opposite, rolling the clay bowl thoughtfully between his palms.

'You first,' he invited.

'How long has he been like this?' she asked without preamble.

'Almost since you left. It started like a whirlwind from nowhere as far as anybody can make out. Maybe he had a vision. The brothers won't say much. Won't or can't. He began by throwing out a couple of corrodians he thought were taking his hospitality for granted and spreading corruption. Then he made the novices start getting up an hour earlier for their lessons.'

'The prioress told me there'd been changes. But why, Ulf? Is it a directive from the mother house in France?'

'Not according to Anselm.' Ulf and the cellarer discussed matters concerning livestock and the harvests but, he told her, Anselm was being driven mad by the abbot's demands.

'It comes from a desire to get back to the original purity of St Bernard's vision, he says. The Order was founded to counteract the corruption of the Benedictines. He says the monastics have grown fat on ill-gotten gains. The result is he's trying to offload a heap of corn on us. Roger's pleased. Anselm's in despair. What can he be thinking of at this time of year? It's not time for the new grain yet. The abbey's going to find itself short and then Anselm will have to pay over the odds in Beverley cornmarket. Everybody's going hungry. He's given half the stuff away already—'

'So what are they living on?' she interrupted, remembering Thomas and his bony wrists.

'Thin gruel. Once a day. It's madness. A man can't work on that.' Ulf took another gulp of his wine. 'It's as if he's trying to expiate some sin. But Hubert has always been so—' He searched for a word. 'Correct, yes, he's always been correct in everything he does. But now? He's following the Rule literally, down to the last letter.'

'I can't see why he would not gain absolution from his confessor for anything he might have done,' Hildegard pointed out.

'Maybe so but he seems to think they can go back to the old ways when the abbey was first founded, living in a log hut through the winter with no heat and eating only what they could shoot or trap themselves. But the world has changed. We're not living in those times any more. There's a proper community here, good granges, a thriving wool trade, the tannery, the mill, their bakehouse, the scriptorium; the monks have tasks, teaching, tending the sick. That's another thing: he's never here any more. He comes in for high mass and that's about it.'

'Where does he go?'

'He spends all his time down at St Giles with the lepers. Eats with them. Practically lives with them. Not many of us would want to do what he's doing, but he's the abbot, for heaven's sake. He's supposed to be in charge, not carrying on like a novice or a penitent. Well,' Ulf couldn't stop, 'that's exactly what he's like, a penitent. But what's he got to be penitent about?'

'Doesn't anybody say anything to him?'

'Who? The prior? He's happy, apart from his dining being curtailed. It means he can throw his weight around. He'll be ousting Hubert next but Hubert doesn't see it. And Anselm tried to say something and nearly had his head bitten off. The sacristan? He's tried. Same thing. That's why the choir's so pathetic. It's breaking his heart. You used to be able to hear some good singing here in the old days but now they're not allowed to sing any of the new stuff, because it's too full of vainglory, done to show off their voices rather than reflect the glory of God etcetera, etcetera, but I tell you, Hildegard, nobody's going to come all the way over here to listen to something they can hear in any parish church in the county. And as for the cross—'

Hildegard pricked up her ears.

'You know he's threatening to get rid of the Talking Crucifix? Then what? Pilgrim trade will be finished. It's serious. When the abbey goes under, de Hutton's in trouble. It's not just going to be the health of the abbot's immortal soul down the sluice. It's going to be the whole Riding.' He stopped, somewhat abruptly. 'I'm sorry, Hildegard. We do need to talk but not about the lord abbot. We need to talk about the murder of Reynard of Risingholme and the proceedings to indict young Pierrekyn.'

'So tell me how that came about.'

'Somebody appealed him.'

'You mean somebody formally accused him of murder? But they must have had evidence to do that.'

'They said they saw him lurking round the wool-shed later that night. They told the constable.'

'Everybody was there at some point. It was a big event, sending the staple to Flanders.'

'Well, the constable got a record of proper accusation so they had to act. The sheriff was brought in. It's got to go to the court of King's Bench because the murder took place outside the realm.'

'Did it?'

'The body was found in Bruges – it's a vague point and the law-men might be able to make something of it. But I tell you what, Hildegard, there's somebody behind it and I don't know who.'

'It's because of the risings they're bringing in draconian measures. Gaunt's lost his grip.'

'If only. He holds power even more tightly now, using the Rising as an excuse to clamp down on everybody.'

They had never talked so frankly about their allegiance. It had always been too dangerous, but now, with this practical concern for Pierrekyn, circumspection was thrust to one side.

'I was astonished when the Count of Mâle sent men to Florence to arrest the boy. I hope they were good to him on the way over?'

Ulf nodded. They both looked at one another in silence.

'So, what next?' she ventured.

Ulf was grim-faced. 'After the formalities here, and if it goes against him, the abbot will have to hand him over. I can't understand why he hasn't done so already. He knows he'll have to in the end. And then Pierrekyn's going to have the joy of being hauled before the Justice of oyer and terminer.'

'Here or in Westminster?'

'Down south, probably. Or at the next assize in York, whenever that's likely to be.'

'So he could be held in York gaol?' She shivered. 'Poor Pierrekyn. Ulf, we've got to do something.'

'You really believe he's innocent, don't you?'

'I do.'

'I suppose you noticed Gaunt's livery everywhere?'

She nodded.

'The Justice is one of his men.'

She went cold. 'So that was the fellow in the dagged turban in the church just now?'

'Protecting their own. And all over the death of a clerk? It doesn't add up.'

'Has it anything to do with the right of assembly?' she asked cautiously.

'You think Reynard was posting notices?'

'That would be an act of sedition. Is that likely? You knew him better than I did.' The text copied from *anomenalle* burned in her sleeve. She wanted to tell him about it, show it to him, discuss with him what to do next. But first she needed to be certain of the situation here in the Riding. It had changed in the three months of her absence.

He gave her a long look. 'What?'

Her lips pursed, and she shook her head. 'I don't understand why they're going to get him tried in the assize, if he's indicted, that is? I really thought this would be a Church matter.'

'They're intending to put him before a presenting jury here, then get him taken to York Castle.'

They were both silent. Hildegard could not imagine why Gaunt was involving himself, unless he knew about Reynard's activities. There must be a spy at work. Somebody must have informed on Reynard. And then his chamber had been searched. But now that the clerk was out of the way, why not just let matters rest?

'About Reynard,' she broached, 'he was a scribe, a simple clerk. He drew up contracts. He'd been with Roger for years. Is there more?'

The mention of contracts had no visible effect on Ulf. He appeared to be unaware of the details of the business between his lord and Vitelli for he said, 'Do you think they might simply want to make an example of Pierrekyn? They know his nature.'

'That would not be just. Look at the court. They can hardly cast stones.'

'Look at Edward II,' he countered. 'If they can do that to their king, what won't they do to a powerless minstrel?'

'Is he so powerless, I wonder?' She was thinking of the velvet turnshoe and its decoration of many pearls.

'No doubt he's told you something to make you believe in his innocence.'

'A little.'

'And you believe him? We know nothing about him,' he warned. 'For instance, what was he doing in Kent before Reynard brought him up here?'

'I'd like to have a word with him. Then let's talk again. Is he here in the abbey prison?'

'I'll take you down there myself in a while.' He filled her cup again. 'I'll also keep you informed if I hear anything more about Gaunt's placeman. He's called John Coppinhall, by the way, and he's a nasty piece of work. He was commissioner for the poll tax and nearly got done in then but for the fact he always travels with a retinue of armed brutes. There's a black rumour attached to him. I'll tell you about it later. Meanwhile, prepare yourself to stand forth as a witness. Pierrkyn's going to need all help he can get.'

Chapter Twenty-two

ILDEGARD HAD AN errand to perform before she went to see Pierrekyn so she had herself announced and was shown into Roger's apartment. He was sitting in a window niche, playing thoughtfully with one of his hawks. He seemed somehow smaller and less powerful than when she had last seen him. It was enough to make her greet him with a jocular, 'Are your rations being kept short as well, my lord?'

He sprang to his feet. 'Short rations! I'll say! Have you dined here yet?' He came towards her, his arms outspread. 'It's good to see you safe and sound.' He stopped short of throwing his arms round her and stepped back, pulling at his beard. 'And I'd like to know what's happening up at Hutton while I'm kicking my heels down here. I think it's a ruse to get at my lands and overrun them.' He scowled. 'You know why we're all called, don't you?'

She nodded. 'Here, look, I have the purchases you wanted.' She offered the parcel with its valuable contents.

'The sleeves? Melisen's going to be cock-a-hoop. By the way, were you at mass just now? Did you notice her?'

'I noticed your absence.'

He saw that she was hedging and said, 'Was she fluttering her eye-lashes at Coppinhall then?' For some reason he looked pleased.

'About your minstrel,' she went on.

'There was nothing I could do to stop them arresting him once they got their teeth into the law books. They've even got bloody William back in charge because I didn't follow due process. I tell you, I'm sick of lawyers. What about the good old days when a man could make up his own mind how to protect himself?'

'I gather some men still do that,' she remarked.

'And they might well go on doing so! And I swear, if I don't get my own way, with a proper show of arms, *then* they can have all the law books in Christendom thrown at 'em! See how they like it then!'

'I was wondering,' she broke in. 'Have they found the knife used to murder Reynard?'

He shook his head. 'Don't think so. But I don't know what they have found. They're keeping quiet. We'll find out soon enough. Pity they had to render the body down to bring his bones back. Anything that might have been a clue will have gone down the sluice.'

'Who gave such an order?'

'Some lickspittle acting for the Count of Mâle. Ulf was furious. At least we gave Reynard a good send-off. Not that there was any family to give a hoot. Just somebody from York dressed like a fancy man, skulking at the back of the chapel. Still,' he frowned unhappily, 'let's forget all that. Tell me how you got on in foreign parts.'

She took Ser Vitelli's letter from her sleeve and handed it to him. 'What's in it?'

'I don't know that, Roger! I didn't open it! I'm simply the messenger. But Ser Vitelli seems quite pleased and called you a sharp fellow. I think you'd get on well should you ever meet.'

'Not much chance of that.' He broke open the seal and read the letter with a beady expression, nodding when he got to the end. 'Right. A thousand thanks.' He stuffed the letter inside the front of his houppeland with a small smile. 'But what about you? We heard what happened to Talbot from the courier but there's no word yet about the bastard that did it. We live in evil times. It's a poor life when you can't go about your daily business without being shot.'

'Did you retain him Roger?' asked Hildegard.

He shook his head. 'Me? No. Wasn't it your prioress?'

She shook her head then told him what she could without betraying the prioress's confidence and finished by mentioning Ser Vitelli's hint of an arms deal in the event of civil war.

Roger was sombre when he heard about Vitelli's offer. Seemingly at a tangent he asked, 'You heard about Despenser's fiasco in France, I take it?'

She nodded. 'My own son wears his livery. I hoped that, as the Bishop of Norwich, Despenser would have been unlikely to go to war. We got through the lines shortly after they marched on Ghent.'

'Nobody got hurt. It was all done to show their muscles rather than use 'em. And anyway, if your boy's anything like his father he'll be well able to take care of himself—' He broke off abruptly, realising how crass this must sound. Hildegard's husband, Sir Hugh, had disappeared in France many years ago, missing presumed dead, whether able to take care of himself or not.

Hildegard had known Roger most of her life and was familiar with his rough ways. Now she merely asked, 'Do you think the bishop's foray served any purpose?'

'It concentrated the minds of the clergy. They had to prove their allegiance by subsidising him. And an army like Despenser's doesn't come cheap. Then it creamed off the rebels in the eastern counties by raising the levies. Some of them don't care whom they fight so long as there's somebody on the end of their pike. Sot-wits. They'll rue their lackadaisical attitude when Gaunt puts the crown on his own head.'

'Will it come to that?'

'Not while there are still good men and true.'

Hildegard had never heard Roger talk so openly. To speak against Gaunt could place him in a dangerous position if his words fell on the wrong ears.

He must have read the alarm in her face because he added, 'I wouldn't say this to just anybody, Hildegard. I got on the wrong side of the duke, damn his eyes, over that reading of his bloody text about the Rising. Lucky for me Northumberland's at my back with the rest of the Percy clan. Might even look to the Scots for help. Reforge the old alliance, eh?'

She remembered how Roger's beloved first wife had been the daughter of an earl of the borders whose shifting alliances had brought him wealth and power. Roger had been able to call on both during times of danger when the Scots were raiding deep into the heart of England and had been given welcome protection. The raids were fewer these days but it was interesting to find that he was thinking of the Scots as possible allies once more.

'That's a dangerous game,' she could not help pointing out. 'If the Scots are allying themselves with the French, as it seemed last year, they could use you and as soon as they've finished with you they could snuff you out like that!' She clicked her fingers.

'I know. I feel beset on all sides, and that's the truth. Why can't these devils stay at home with their hawks and hounds?' He gave his own hawk a fond kiss and it returned it as if kissing a vassal. He ruffled the feathers on top of its head. 'Ambition's the very devil. It sours everything.'

He glanced round as if to summon a servant, then uttered an oath. 'God's teeth! I can't even call on Pierrekyn to give us a tune.' He frowned. 'Tomorrow,' he advised in a lowered tone, 'watch what happens at this court hearing. We're all going to have to tread very carefully.'

The prison was a spartan chamber situated off the cloister garth next to the chapter house. Through an arch at the far end were two small cells, one adjoining the other, entered by a single barred door.

The monk-bailiff greeted them in the outer chamber before showing them in. He knew Ulf well, not only because he was closely connected with disbursements of produce from the granges to the cellarer, but also because they both had the duty of holding customary courts on adjacent manors.

He gestured with his thumb. 'In there.' He nodded an acknowledgement to Hildegard. Ulf took a lighted cresset from the wall and she followed him through to the inner cell.

It had one small, barred window that gave onto the south-west corner of the cloister where the brothers could be heard shuffling back and forth to their various duties. Unfurnished except for a narrow bench to sleep on, it seemed bleak enough to allow free rein to a prisoner's darkest thoughts.

Pierrekyn was sitting on the floor with his head on his knees, looking the picture of despair. There was an uneaten bowl of gruel on the floor beside him.

Ulf went to stand over him. The light fell in a brilliant flood, making the boy's russet hair dance like flame. 'I've brought Sister Hildegard to see you, lad. Get up.'

Pierrekyn didn't stir.

'I'm just back from Tuscany,' Hildegard said, moving towards him. 'Did they treat you properly on the way over?'

Still no response.

'Pierrekyn,' she tried again, 'there are things we need to talk about. I intend to stand as witness for you when this matter comes before the commission.'

He lifted his head. His face was tear-stained and his hair was uncombed. It stuck out wildly from under a little green cap. With both hands thrust inside his sleeves he hugged himself and began to rock back and forth, in and out of the pool of light.

'Pierrekyn.' She knelt beside him. 'I need to ask you one or two things about Reynard.' She glanced up at Ulf. He thrust the cresset in a bracket on the wall and moved away to lounge in the doorway, his face in shadow.

In a lowered voice she said, 'I have the document. I made a copy of it.'

'What document?' Pierrekyn jerked his head up. His green eyes were hostile.

Remembering his treatment as an oblate at his song school and his subsequent hatred for ecclesiastics, she said, 'I'm not trying to trap you. We both know what document. I have told no one else about it, not even the lord steward.' She glanced hurriedly over her shoulder. 'I need to know whether anybody else knew Reynard was making copies of it and disseminating them.'

Pierrekyn stared stonily into space.

'It's really important that I know who else received a copy,'

No answer.

'You said there were others.'

Still no answer. She restrained a sigh.

'I went to see Hawkwood,' she continued in a whisper. 'He laughed in my face as of course we expected, but he took Reynard's text and said he would read it. I don't have much hope that he'll do anything but we cannot know his mind.' She touched him on the arm. 'I have the slipper for you, too, but maybe this isn't the best place to hand it over. Do you want me to keep it safe until they set you free?'

At this he roused himself sufficiently to say in a savage undertone, 'I will never be set free. They want me dead. I may as well hang myself now and be done with it except they've taken away any means of doing so. They've even taken my lute and probably smashed it to pieces. I hate them.'

He took his hands out of his sleeves and wrapped his arms round his knees.

On the little finger of his left hand was a ring.

Rising to her feet she said, 'Trust me, Pierrekyn.'

He lifted his head a fraction but after bestowing on her another despairing glance he buried his face again and did not move.

It was already nearly midnight. The sub-prior could be heard ringing the bell in the dorter to rouse the brethren for the nightly vigil. As Ulf bade her goodnight she saw a junior carrying a lantern, walking at the head of a procession of monks and leading them into the church.

The abbot and the prior stood outside the door as everyone went in. Hildegard pulled up her hood and followed. She took a place at the back and fell to her knees like everyone else, rising only when the abbot processed in. In the distance the bell stopped tolling.

Throughout the prayers that preceded matins she kept a careful eye on Hubert. In the dim light from the candles it was difficult to gauge how sick he was but undoubtedly he was suffering in some way. His voice shook. His steps were uncertain. After the sacristan brought the gospels from the altar he had to be helped to the desk to be vested in his cope while incense and more candles were brought.

Now when he turned she saw his face. It was paler than ever. His eyes were dark in their sockets. By the time he came to read the lesson he could only ascend the lectern steps by gripping the rail as if he would sink to the floor without its aid.

Hildegard felt a flood of rage surge through her. The sacristan continued his duties as if nothing was wrong. The prior and the sub-prior did likewise. Could not any one of these men see that their lord was sick?

Unable to bear it any longer she slipped out into the garth. The service would go on for another two hours. First matins then, without a break, straight on into lauds. She did an entire circuit of the cloister with her hands thrust into her sleeves. The circator was just going in again with a newly trimmed lantern and she watched as the door opened and closed behind him. From inside she heard a snatch of Hubert's frail voice, railing against the sins of his brothers. And no doubt his own.

Last autumn she had had a private interview with the prioress at Swyne. To her consternation and disbelief, the prioress had cast doubts on the abbot's allegiance to the English cause should it come to civil war.

She had drawn a horrifying picture of what might happen if the Cistercian abbeys, like Meaux, Fountains, Rievaulx and the others in the North, obeyed an edict, by way of their mother house in France, from the false pope in Avignon to support another French invasion. The Duke of Burgundy with his allies, acting on behalf of the Dauphin, was arming for war. Everyone knew that. The prioress, and others like her, saw the north-eastern ports as the unguarded back door into England.

Their only defence, should an invasion be launched through Ravenser, would be the landholders, like Roger and his brother barons, and the levies they could raise, but their defence would be as nothing if the abbeys lent practical support to a foreign army. They could withhold supplies from the king while maintaining the invading forces for many months.

Since she had been away in Tuscany the picture had changed somewhat. The Bishop of Norwich and his army had launched an attack against Burgundy and, even though it had come to nothing, attention had been deflected from the North.

'And where,' the prioress had asked, 'does Hubert stand in all this?' His father, she said, had been a French spy at the court of King Edward. Wasn't it likely that Hubert would follow in his father's footsteps?

What this might have to do with his present activities could only be surmised. The clerk, copier of a document deemed subversive by King Richard's opponents, had been murdered within the purlieu of the abbey itself.

His death might have been the outcome of a drunken brawl, but it might equally have a meaning deeper and darker: a deliberate killing to silence a dangerous enemy. It was certainly true that someone had decided to treat Reynard's death not as a simple homicide – for which the punishment might be a fine – but as murder, with hanging as the ultimate penalty.

It was obvious who would gain by silencing him.

Gaunt would gain.

Everything led back to him. To Duke John of Lancaster. Earl of Derby, Lincoln and Leicester. Lord of Beaufort and Bergerac, Roche-sur-Yon, Noyen. Seneschal of England. Constable of Chester. The eldest living son of Edward III. Protector prince of the realm of Albion – and father of young Bolingbroke, cousin of the king, schooled from the age of twelve in the art of war, his heir.

Ambition, as Roger had said, was the devil.

What Gaunt had to do to suppress the true story about what had happened at Smithfield was to get rid of the clerk who had copied the text, then find a scapegoat to accuse of his murder. It would be even better if it could be passed off as a crime of passion.

With the true text suppressed, the alternative story about the killing of Wat Tyler could be fostered. Gaunt and his followers could rip out the heart of the rebellion with lies. They could confuse good, simple folk with a treachery they would never imagine.

More than this: Gaunt's ally was Pope Clement in Avignon, the man who issued orders from the opulence of his palace, orders that echoed down the line of command to the most distant Cistercian cell.

Hildegard waited in the darkness. Eventually the church doors opened and the soft glow of candlelight fell over the even stones of the garth as the brethren emerged. Hubert left the procession and made his way towards his lodge, which stood a little apart from the main buildings. Hildegard followed.

As he reached the door she caught up with him.

'My lord abbot!'

He froze. She watched as he seemed to gather his energy to make the turn necessary to face her. His expression was scarcely discernible in the pale starlight filtering down. He peered at her as if he could not connect her to anyone he knew and to help him she pushed back her hood, stepped closer and said, 'It's Sister Hildegard, your servant in Christ.' She bent her head. When she looked up he was gazing down at her without making a move. She straightened until they were eye to eye.

He lifted a hand in a warding off gesture. 'You?'

'I have just lately returned from pilgrimage,' she managed. Finely attuned to every nuance of his voice, the ice in that one word chilled her to the marrow. Nothing had changed. She was accused and knew nothing of the charge.

'What do you want with me?' he asked in a hoarse voice. He took a step forward.

Her eyes opened wide in astonishment.

A sort of madness seemed to blaze from his face, forcing her to take an involuntary step backwards as if he had threatened to strike her.

'Leave me in peace,' he whispered. 'Leave the precincts of my abbey. Never set foot here again.'

Hildegard drew herself up before her defences could be over-whelmed and said quietly, 'I am not here through choice, my lord. I've been called as a witness in the prosecution of Master Pierrekyn. Tomorrow I register my interest with the sheriff on instructions from the lord steward of Castle Hutton.'

'And what else does he instruct you in?'

'My lord?' She was puzzled.

When he failed to reply, merely giving her a long, piercing scrutiny, she said, 'I'm surprised this is considered to be a matter for the abbey court.'

'A writ will no doubt be issued after they've heard the plea. It'll go to the Justices of the King's Bench. Then the matter will be out of my hands and you can go on taking your instructions from Lord Roger's steward to your heart's content.'

He rested a hand on the door of his chambers as if the conversation had exhausted him. All the fight seemed to have left him. His voice was faint. 'I meant what I said, Hildegard. Get away from me, from here.' He rallied and his tone roughened. 'Leave Meaux and never come back! Remain in your cell at Swyne! I withdraw any permissions I have ever given you. Tell your prioress it's no use battering me with requests to change my mind.'

He finished speaking and in a moment had pushed on into the unlit chamber beyond.

Chapter Twenty-three

THE JUSTICES OF the Peace were elected by the chancellor and treasurer at a meeting of the king's council. It was assumed that magnates like Gaunt and the other barons put pressure on the members to elect someone who would be useful to them. This practice filtered down to all levels of the realm. Knights and esquires were given positions of power through gifts of land or by appointment to official positions within the hierarchy on the basis of their affiliations. Roger himself made no bones about it. 'It's as helpful to have a Justice in your pocket as it is to bribe a jury.'

Hildegard remembered these words now as everyone filed into the chapter house. If Roger hasn't secured the Justice – as he clearly has not – then we are at the mercy of those who have.

Normally the abbey court was held at the vill of Waughen but it was inconvenient for the noble visitors to have to set out on the road yet again. Besides, the hearing was expected to be over within a short time. The boy had no defence. He would hang.

The Justice was a professional lawyer. Roger clearly suspected the man of being maintained by Gaunt. There was nothing to be done about it now.

Hildegard took her place on one of the benches with everyone else. The commission's role today was purely to take down the facts of the case and collate the evidence so that it could be checked by the jurors when it went to the king's court. If matters turned against Pierrekyn, the serjeant-at-law would receive a commission of gaol delivery and hand him over to the Justice of oyer and terminer.

It was then that Pierrekyn would spend time in York gaol, waiting for the next court of the King's Bench to convene. The Chief Justice would decide whether the court should travel or stay in Westminster.

It could be a protracted process unless the boy's enemies took matters into their own hands. Heaven forfend they pre-empt any judgment, she thought.

She worried about how Pierrekyn would withstand imprisonment. His lute had already been taken away but later it would have to be confiscated by the escheator who would assess the value of his possessions. He owned so little: the borrowed attired he had been wearing when he was arrested, his lute, the leather satchel he carried it in. And one other thing.

She had asked the monk-bailiff why he should not have back his lute when the escheator arrived. The monk had gladly agreed.

'Let him keep his belongings for now. He's still innocent in the eyes of the law and I like a tune,' he had argued in deliberately affable tones. The escheator, not wishing to appear uncharitable in the monk's eyes, had agreed, albeit with an ill grace.

The tune Pierrekyn had been practising since early that morning was still in her ears, plaintive but with a defiant chorus that would have had the foot tapping in other circumstances. Whenever anyone walked past his cell window they could hear it. Quite a number of novices had found cause to do their lessons that morning in the south-west corner of the cloister, much to their master's annoyance.

Hildegard's attention was brought abruptly back to the present as everyone rose. Hubert processed in at the head of his chief officials. This morning he looked even paler than before and refused to catch the eye of any of those present. He merely took his seat and indicated that everyone should do likewise. Only the suspect and the serjeant-at-law remained standing.

The latter read out the coroner's deposition, then called the first-finder.

Ulf stepped forward to confirm that he had found the body. The serjeant asked him to confirm when and where he had done so, and to tell the court exactly when the bales of wool had been sealed. Ulf explained that the clip had been packed first, a day before the fells were sacked up. He added that it was around then, a full day before the convoy left, that Reynard's disappearance had first been noticed.

The serjeant asked the man who had appealed the accused to step forth. A frightened-looking servant was thrust from the crowd. When he was asked to confirm his name and rank – he was one of Sir William's grooms – his voice was no more than a whisper. The serjeant demanded to know what he had been doing at the abbey on the day in question and, too terrified to look up, he had come out with the information that he had been sent over with produce for the abbey kitchens from one of Sir William's outlying manors.

The serjeant-at-law then asked him to tell the court what he had seen. Scarcely daring to look up, he claimed that he had seen a young man loitering by the sheds after everyone had gone and, having himself returned briefly to the scene to retrieve a gauntlet, had noticed him slip inside the shed whereupon raised voices had been heard. Thinking nothing of it, he had picked up the gauntlet and returned to the servants' hall.

'And this man you say went into the packing shed, is he here in the court today?' asked the serjeant.

'Yes. He's there.' The groom pointed. 'It was the minstrel, Pierrekyn Haverel.'

The serjeant held up his hand to stem the murmurs that broke out and asked him whether, as was the custom, he would prove the truth of his statement by engaging in armed combat with the accused. Pierrekyn looked startled and was clearly relieved when this convention was waved aside.

The serjeant turned to the young clerk sitting on his left. 'Got all that written down, Will?'

'I have indeed, sir,' he replied, wiping his quill on a piece of rag.

The person appealed had to appear next but to the serjeant's blunt, 'Did you do it?' Pierrekyn answered, equally bluntly, 'No, I did not.'

The serjeant was just about to slam his books together and give orders for Pierrekyn to appear at the county court when Hildegard rose to her feet. She made her way to the front as one of the clerks whispered her name and status to the serjeant. Grimacing at what he clearly thought was a waste of time, he nodded for her to begin.

Conscious of all eyes on her, of Hubert sitting opposite, of John Coppinhall's narrow observation, she opened her scrip and took out the embroidered kerchief. She unknotted it, and spread out its contents on the lectern.

Hubert's eyes were fixed on her fingers as she refolded the kerchief and put it to one side. The first thing she held up was the scrap of blue cloth.

'This is the first piece of evidence I wish to have recorded by the serjeant,' she explained. 'It's a fragment of the cloth they call calimala and it is triple-dyed in woad.' A few glances were exchanged and there was a murmur that stopped abruptly when she turned to Lady Melisen. 'Would you confirm, my lady, that you gave me a blue cloak to wear on my pilgrimage to Tuscany?'

Looking confused, but pleased to be the sudden focus of attention, Melisen rose to her feet. 'I will indeed, Sister. May I see that fragment?'

Hildegard handed it over.

'It's very like the fabric of my own cloak, which I gave you. I had it specially made for me. The dye was my own choice. I have never seen another like it.'

'Thank you, my lady. And is this part of the same cloak, cut down?' She produced a bundle of blue cloth.

Melisen poked it with one finger. 'It certainly is. It's outrageous! They've quite ruined it!'

'Where's this leading?' asked the serjeant.

'This fragment of cloth comes from the cloak Lady Melisen gave me. It was lent to Sir Talbot, my escort in the Alps.'

As briefly as she could she explained the circumstances.

'It was this very cloak,' she continued, 'that Sir Talbot was wearing when he was shot by a bolt from a crossbow.'

'What of it?' demanded the serjeant with the air of a man who fears he might be missing something.

'This small fragment was discovered by fellow travellers coming through the pass a few hours later. Guessing it might be a clue to the identity of the murderer in whose tracks they were following, they handed it to me when we met again. Shortly afterwards I came across a man wearing this cloak cut down to a more fashionable length. I believe he was the murderer of Sir Talbot.'

'One and the same,' cut in the serjeant. 'I still ask, what of it? What's does it have to do with us here? It doesn't prove the wearer of the cloak shot this Sir Talbot you mention. The cloak could have been bought either ready-made or in its damaged state from any pedlar. I assume they're as plagued by pedlars over there as we are?'

There was laughter.

'Indeed they are,' Hildegard agreed. 'However, after taking it from the body, the murderer of Sir Talbot might also have worn the cloak himself or even carried it down the pass, where it snagged on the rock, this fragment being found by the rest of the group scattered in the ice storm the previous day. A blue thing in a waste of white, easily noticed. Further,' she continued before she could be interrupted again, 'the same man who wore the cloak also wore this.' She held up Sir Talbot's leather pouch.

The serjeant-at-arms gave it a sceptical glance. 'So? A pouch is a pouch. What's special about this one?' He seemed to have forgotten Pierrekyn for the moment.

'This pouch is different to many others. Indeed, it is quite distinctive.' She opened it so that everyone could see what she was doing. 'Inside is a secret pocket. The thief failed to realise this. Otherwise he would have found something of far more value than a piece of worked leather.' She took out the brooch and held it up.

'Bear with me,' she said, 'this is relevant to the present hearing.' Everyone craned forward to see what she was holding up.

'This brooch proves that the pouch belonged to Sir Talbot. I myself was with him when he bought it from a goldsmith in Bruges. He had it inscribed: *je suy vostre sans de partier.*'

The brooch was handed from one juror to another. Even Hubert took it although he passed it on to the prior as if it burned his fingers.

'*I am yours for ever,*' he said in dry tones, speaking for the first time. 'Whom did he have that inscribed for?'

'His lady in France,' she replied.

'These facts will be checked.'

It sounded like a warning but she acknowledged it with a lifting of her spirits. 'You will find everything I say is true, my lord.'

His expression was ambivalent.

The serjeant-at-law was looking longingly at his books. He was probably thinking he hadn't studied law for sixteen years only to be unable to have recourse to them now. But procedure had to be followed. Here was a witness who could not be brushed aside. He returned doggedly to the point.

'So this is intended to demonstrate that the fellow stole a pouch from the body of the knight in the wilds of the mountains. What has it to do with us here in England?'

'His guilt will prove the accused's innocence.'

'Guilt of one murder doesn't prove guilt of another. Where's the link?'

'There is a link. It's this.' She held up the ring that had fallen at her feet in the palazzo of La Gran Contessa. Again, outlining events as briefly as possible without mentioning the cross of Constantine, she said, 'It links the murderer of Sir Talbot with the murderer of Reynard of Risingholme. It is the clerk's ring.'

There was a flurry of astonishment, quickly stifled.

'How do we know that?'

'We do know it,' she continued, 'because he had two identical rings made.'

Pierrekyn was standing with his head down, staring at the floor. She turned to him. 'Show us your hands, Pierrekyn.'

Confused and sullen he spread them out. There was a gasp. The ring he wore was identical to the one Hildegard held up.

'Can you confirm that the ring I have here belonged to Reynard of Risingholme?' she asked him.

His face was a picture of bewilderment. He nodded.

'Say it aloud so everyone can hear,' she suggested gently.

'It is.' He swallowed.

'Will you make sure?'

Reaching out, he took it and held it between his fingers. When he raised his head his eyes were glistening. 'It is the very one. He had two matching ones made by a silversmith in Beverley. That's Whitby jet in the mouth of the wyvern. I would know it anywhere. He had them made to his own design. He made the drawings and the silversmith worked from them.'

'No doubt the court will call the silversmith as witness should it be necessary,' Hildegard suggested with a covert glance at Hubert.

'So he had two identical rings made?' began the serjeant-at-arms.

Roger stepped forward. 'Let's be clear—' He stopped, suddenly remembering he was in somebody else's court, and turned to the abbot. 'If I may be so bold, my lord abbot?'

'You may,' replied Hubert tonelessly.

'So the man who shot Sir Talbot, and betrayed himself by stealing his cloak and his pouch, also stabbed my clerk, betraying himself again by stealing the fellow's ring and wearing it? Making him as much a thief as a murderer and, if either, then a blackguard of the first water.'

Hubert roused himself. 'I thank you for your contribution, Roger. That sums up everything so far.' His icy glance fell on Hildegard. 'Pray continue, Sister. I don't doubt you have more to say.'

The serjeant interrupted. 'My lords.' He nodded to the abbot and to Roger, and randomly wherever he felt his deference might be expected. 'The cloak is the weak point. Another weak point is the ring. In short, both are weak points—'

'And *your* point, serjeant?' asked Hubert civilly. There was a quickly suppressed titter.

'Well, the man might have bought the ring at the same time as he bought the cloak.'

'From whom?' asked Hildegard.

'Why, the murderer of course, or maybe from somebody who accidentally came across the body in the wool-shed, picked up the ring and—'

'And then travelled all the way to Tuscany where he sold it and obtained the belongings of another murdered man?'

The serjeant nodded. 'It's not beyond the bounds of possibility—'

'Doesn't it leave rather a lot to chance?' Her tone sharpened.

Before he could answer she went on, 'It is as certain as anything can be in this vale of uncertainty that, just as the murderer stole the ring from the finger of his first victim, he also stole the cloak and the pouch from his second victim. Although it may not prove that

219

the same man wielded either the knife or the crossbow, it strongly suggests he was present close to the time when both murders took place, that is, when Sir Talbot was shot and when Reynard was stabbed and before the latter was interred in the bale of staple.'

The young clerk sitting beside the serjeant interrupted: 'A murderer wouldn't leave a body lying where somebody could find it. And if he did leave it, an accomplice must have come along to hide it and could then have picked up the ring.'

'Did he have an accomplice?' demanded the serjeant-at-law.

'I have no knowledge on that point,' replied Hildegard. She suddenly became aware of Coppinhall. He was watching her like a fox.

The young clerk interrupted again. 'If we accept that it was the murderer who hid the body in the staple, then he must be the one who removed the ring – unless somebody stole it off the dead man's finger on the quayside in Bruges.'

'Impossible,' Ulf broke in. 'It was guarded at all times.'

'Ergo, my lords,' said the young clerk, 'the thief and the murderer are one and the same.'

'I believe the clerk has summed up the situation with precision,' she agreed blandly. 'The murderer stole whatever he could from Sir Talbot. Just as he stole what he could from the clerk.'

'And do we have a name for this thief and murderer?' asked Hubert in a quiet voice.

'We do, my lord. It is Escrick Fitzjohn.'

There was a gasp from those who knew his reputation and muttered questions from those to whom the name was unfamiliar. Hildegard glanced in the direction of Sir Richard and Lady Sibilla. Fitzjohn had once been steward to their household and complicit in their cunning. Sibilla was white-faced. Richard was inspecting his fingernails.

Lord Roger took a step forward. 'My apologies, Hubert, my lord.' He waved an impatient hand to brush away the formalities. 'I thought that blackguard was supposed to be dead?' He turned to Hildegard.

'He lives. I spoke to him in Florence on more than one occasion. I also caught sight of him while travelling through Flanders. It appears he left Ravenser at much the same time as ourselves.' She thought again of the hooded man on the quay.

'Master Fitzjohn is already outlawed for failing five exigents in five different courts, dead or not,' said the serjeant-at-law, pleased to be able to get a word in on the strength of his books.

'The minstrel is innocent,' said a quiet voice from the crowd of servants at the back. 'Give him his lute and let's have a song.' Sounds of general approval came from the back benches. Pierrekyn lifted his head. For the first time that morning there was a spark of hope in his eyes.

'Stay!' Coppinhall stepped forward with his hand raised. 'This matter is not finished. There is this to consider.' He held up a piece of vellum. 'It's an unfinished copy of a document found in the chamber of the murdered clerk.'

'In his chamber? You mean somebody's been poking and prying on my property?' Roger sprang to his feet with a face like thunder.

'No, sire. Not on your property but here in the servants' guest quarters at Meaux. It was handed to me in confidence, having been found by a servant appointed to clear his chamber after the murder.'

Roger had the sense not to ask why the servant hadn't gone straight to the master of the abbot's conversi. He sat down.

The same voice that had asked for the lute to be brought out was heard to mutter, 'A servant who reads, says he. A miracle!' There were a few answering murmurs and an usher told them to shut up or get out.

On Coppinhall's appearance, the serjeant-at-law ceded the floor with a look of relief. It was clear from his expression that they were in collusion. Hildegard waited to hear what would come next. She had already guessed what the text said.

Coppinhall looked round the assembly with a smile on his face. 'It is my considered opinion that this,' he waved the vellum again, 'proves beyond reasonable doubt that the clerk was guilty of sedition.'

The entire chamber fell silent.

'My reading of events is as follows,' he continued. 'This youth, Pierrekyn Haverel, discovered Reynard's true leanings, remonstrated with him and the two came to blows. He's a strong lad and killed the clerk in a fight over the latter's views. Panicking, he ran away. Later, thinking more carefully, he returned to the scene of the crime in order to cover his tracks. Unaware, or uncaring, that the ring had been taken, he hid the gore-stained body within the bale of staple in the belief that it would be miles away by the time it was discovered—'

'That's not true!' Pierrekyn was staring at Coppinhall in blind rage. Two constables moved to restrain him.

'Or,' continued Coppinhall smoothly, 'there is another possibility. It is this: the accused knew all along of the dead man's affiliation to a proscribed society. There was no fight between those two – as he has just so vehemently attested – no fight, because there was nothing to fight over! If this is the case, the minstrel himself, whether guilty of murder or not, is guilty of the far more serious crime of sedition by association.'

He swung on Pierrekyn but before he could extract an admission, Hubert came to life. 'I adjourn this court! We meet again tomorrow morning after tierce.'

There was uproar.

The abbot ignored it and swept from the chapter house with his robes billowing behind him.

He was followed in short order by the prior, the sub-prior and the sacristan. The cellarer, Anselm, drifted through the mêlée towards Ulf who had been sitting with a frown on his face and now stood up, looking round in a dazed sort of fashion.

Pierrekyn was standing aghast with his hands by his sides. The two constables went to take him roughly by the arms and a third was about to clap irons on his wrists when the cellarer nudged Ulf and they went over to the men.

Brother Anselm was firm. 'May I remind you fellows that you are within the purlieu of the abbey of Meaux? We do not have a custom of putting irons on our prisoners until convicted. Nor do you have the power of arrest within our boundaries.' When they hesitated and glanced across at Coppinhall, Anselm added, 'Release him.'

The monk-bailiff, a thick-set, powerful-looking brother, materialised at his side. Ulf stepped forward. 'Do as he says. Be good fellows. You're getting above yourselves.'

Reluctantly the men let go their hold. Pierrekyn glared at them and rubbed his wrists. With the cellarer on one side and the abbey bailiff on the other, he was led out.

Roger paced the floor. 'We have a spy among us. Who is it?'

'God's feet, if I knew I wouldn't be standing here scratching my head, I'd have my hands around his throat,' replied the steward.

'Narrow it down. Which of these sots can read?'

Hildegard spoke up. 'Reading's not necessary. He could have simply looked for anything in Reynard's chamber that seemed unusual.'

'But on whose orders?' Roger thumped a fist into his palm.

'Coppinhall's,' suggested Ulf at once.

'Or Hubert de Courcy's,' growled Roger.

Hildegard went cold.

'Maybe now we know why he's so riddled with guilt that he has to have himself flogged every morning,' Roger went on. 'What do you say, Hildegard?'

Pulling herself together, she said, 'We can't know who the spy is at present. What we do know is that Coppinhall is determined to indict Pierrekyn. I can't see why. It doesn't make sense. What's so important about him?'

Roger pulled at his beard. 'We know nothing about the lad, do we? I let Reynard bring him in and took that as recommendation enough. He needs some hard questioning.'

'Asking him anything is like trying to get exemption from a tax collector,' said Ulf, grimly.

'If he is hiding anything Coppinhall's going to reveal it after tierce tomorrow. Why tierce, anyway? That's a bit late in the day, isn't it?'

Ulf sighed. 'It's because of the abbot, my lord, he's a penitent and the Chapter meets before tierce—'

'Oh.' The light dawned. 'After tierce then. Gives us a chance to talk to Pierrekyn. Maybe it'll give Melisen a chance to work her wiles and get something out of Coppinhall. And Hildegard can find out what Hubert's game is.'

'I see you expect a full complement of cozeners, my lord.'

'You can beguile anybody. Now,' he gave them both a steely look, 'what about this bit of vellum Coppinhall was waving about? Surely he can't go and claim a thing's seditious without it being proven in a court of law first? What's it supposed to say?'

'I believe it's an account of Wat Tyler's death told from a point of view regarded as unofficial,' said Hildegard carefully.

'Anybody found with a copy will hang,' added Ulf.

'Well, they can search me. I haven't got a copy. Have you, steward? If so, now's the time to set a taper to it.'

'I haven't got one, no, my lord.'

Hildegard was silent. Eventually, when they both turned to stare at her, she said, 'They can search my cell if they wish, they won't find one there.' Reynard's text was burning a hole in her sleeve. She reached inside and drew it forth. 'If they searched my person it would be another matter.' She handed the document to Roger.

He read a few lines, then gave it to Ulf. 'It's based on that thing they made us have read out after the Rising.'

'Not based on it, Roger. This is the true version of events. The other one is a false account put together by Gaunt to discredit Tyler and the true commons.'

Hildegard knew she was delivering herself into Roger's hands as she spoke. He could turn his coat to suit his own interests without a qualm. If he decided to support Gaunt and the Lancastrians she was finished.

He said, however, in a lowered tone, 'How many copies have you got?'

'Just that one. I made it from Reynard's version and passed his on.'

'I can tell by your face you're not prepared to say who's got it now. I hope for your sake he's to be trusted.'

'That's a risk I had to take. His help, if he chooses to give it, could be invaluable.'

'I'm in a devilish position here. The commons would get rid of me in a trice, along with Gaunt and his crowd, if they had the power. They don't see the difference between us. Meanwhile—'

'Meanwhile,' said Ulf, 'you're in more danger from Gaunt than from the commons. Besides, Richard demands our support. He's king by right—'

'And the Lord's anointed,' Hildegard pointed out.

'I'm not reneging on my oath of fealty. I just want to keep a hold on my lands – and my head, come to that. It's not going to stop me opposing Gaunt. For that reason I'll do what I can to support the White Hart lads.'

Hildegard remembered Melisen's little hart brooches she had brought back from Flanders and wondered whether Roger knew that his wife had also cast her vote.

Now he smiled. 'Better get a few copies made, Ulf. Anybody left we can trust?'

Chapter Twenty-four

SOMETIME THAT AFTERNOON, shortly after the office of nones, Hildegard went down to the leper house at St Giles. It was a long, low-eaved, wattle-and-daub building beside the bridge on the opposite bank of the canal on the road to Beverley. There were maybe a dozen or so lepers provided for within, all of them in various stages of sickness, young and old, men and women, several bedridden, a couple on the point of death.

Hubert, the sleeves of his white habit rolled up to the elbows, was washing an elderly man's sores when she entered. At first he did not notice her. It was one of the other monks from the abbey, an assistant to the hospitaller, who saw her first.

'Sister, welcome. Have you come to see our work?'

'I thought I might be able to help as I'm staying in the guest house for a day or two,' she replied

Hubert, concentrating on what he was doing, was unaware of her arrival.

'Come with me then,' said Brother Mark. 'We can always find work for useful hands.'

For the next few hours she was kept busy. When Hubert happened to glance up to see who was helping him lift one of the bedridden onto clean straw, he said nothing. They worked silently together, anticipating what was needed, and, to a casual observer, it must have looked as if they were working in harmony, even though they scarcely exchanged a word. After some back-breaking hours it was time to return to the abbey. The bell for vespers could be heard tolling from across the canal.

Giving her only the briefest of glances, Hubert said, 'Come aside, Sister. I have something to say to you.'

They went out into the stores yard at the side of the building. When Hubert was satisfied they could not be overheard, he asked, 'Why are you defending this minstrel?'

Hildegard gathered her thoughts. 'Because it's evident he didn't kill Reynard, as I thought I'd demonstrated. It was Escrick Fitzjohn. He more or less admitted he shot Sir Talbot and he was at Meaux when Reynard was stabbed. You don't doubt this, do you?'

'Let's assume you're right. Is someone protecting Escrick?'

She wondered whether she was being led into a trap. 'I imagine he was maintained by someone.'

'Someone in the locality?'

She was silent. It seemed so obvious. Why was he trying to get her to spell it out?

'And you believe they instructed him to get rid of the clerk?' he pursued. When she didn't answer he said impatiently, 'Well?'

'It looks like that,' she agreed.

'And no doubt you have a view as to their identity?'

She shook her head.

He changed tack. 'This seditious document, so-called, was found in the clerk's temporary lodging in my abbey.'

Believing that she now saw which way his thoughts were tending, she said, 'I don't believe there's any suggestion that you're implicated.' Roger's accusation rang in her ears.

Hubert made an impatient gesture to dismiss the possibility of his own involvement. 'The question we have to ask is how did anyone know the clerk possessed such a document? Was it found accidentally as we are supposed to believe? Or did Escrick point them in the right direction? If so, how did he come to know of it?'

It was back to the same thing by a different route. It had been her very own thought, however, and now she could only shrug. At least it was beginning to look as if Hubert was as puzzled as she was that Reynard's activities had come to a head within the abbey purlieus. With Coppinhall in mind, she said, 'We may guess the name of the master who pulls Escrick's strings, but you're right, we must ask ourselves who told him about Reynard's activities.'

'There's a spy in my abbey,' he replied.

'Not necessarily so. Reynard might have mentioned the document to someone elsewhere who passed the information on. Maybe his master then gave instructions to get rid of Reynard. Maybe they decided it would be easier to do so while he was away from Castle Hutton.'

'But what is gained by his death? Why not just go on betraying his contacts to the authorities and pull them in, one by one?'

'Reynard may have guessed what was happening and revealed his suspicions to someone he thought he could trust.'

Hubert gave her a piercing glance.

'Or maybe the document was discovered by chance,' she suggested.

'In that case why hasn't the servant who found it been called? What are they waiting for? It could only bolster Coppinhall's case.'

'There are a million ways in which its existence could have been discovered.' She couldn't help adding, 'It must be a cause for joy that secrets don't lie hidden for long.'

The look he gave her sharpened and she thought she had either gone too far or been misunderstood, but he returned almost at once to his theme. 'Maybe someone forced the truth of the document's existence from the minstrel himself?'

'I hadn't thought of him as the weak link.'

'Tomorrow we shall see,' he announced grimly. He turned, pulling down his sleeves. 'Time for vespers.'

She watched him leave. He ducked his head under the lintel to make his way back inside through the crowded *hospitium*, many hands reaching out to touch the hem of his garments as he passed. By the time she was at the door herself he was already at the bridge. Unrolling her own sleeves she watched him walk swiftly across and without looking back go under the great arched entrance of Meaux.

Hildegard decided not to go to vespers and returned straight to her cell but when she opened the door she came to a halt on the threshold.

A doughy smell, like the scent of yeast before the bread is proved, made her nostrils twitch. Her glance flew round the small chamber and alighted on her leather travel bag. It was exactly where she had left it on the end of the bed.

She went over to it.

The two laces that held the flap in place were now tied in a slack granny-knot. She always used a fisherman's hitch as it could be unloosed more quickly and never jammed in the rain.

Curious, she opened the bag and looked inside. There was little to attract a thief: a few garments in need of washing, some writing materials, her missal. It was all there. She flicked through the pages of the missal, relieved that she had removed Reynard's document and given it to Roger. Replacing the missal, she looked around for further evidence of the intruder.

Her night boots were arranged slightly differently, aligned rather too precisely side by side under the bed. Her cloak hung on the hook on the back of the door, its folds much as before. Then she noticed her beaver hat was missing. Glancing around, she found it wedged between the bed and the wall, and then she noticed that the bedcover itself must have been moved. Someone had even searched her mattress.

That they had done all this while she was down at St Giles suggested that they knew she would be away for some time. The porter had spoken to her as she went out and any one of a number of people must have seen her leave the abbey.

They had got nothing for their pains, she thought with satisfaction. But then she considered the way Hubert had delayed her with those meaningless questions in the yard. Was that to ensure the intruder had time to get away undetected?

Haunted by such speculations, she went to see Roger at once and told him what had happened.

'Hubert,' he said and looked troubled.

Alarmed at the speed with which he had jumped to that conclusion she asked, 'I hope the copy of *anomenalle* is safe?'

His answer was to pat the opening of his houppeland. 'Nobody but Melisen gets this close.'

He dismissed his servants and turned to her. 'Take a beaker with me, Hildegard. I want to say something in private.' He paused. 'I want to thank you.'

'What for?' she asked.

'That pair of red silk hosen.'

A picture of Ser Vitelli handing her a gift as she prepared to leave Florence came back. 'I was given them,' she explained. 'They do things differently over there. The donor was not to know I wouldn't be allowed to wear them.'

Roger handed her a goblet of wine. 'Melisen sends her thanks as well.' He lifted his wine in a toast and, philanderer that he was, blushed scarlet behind his beard.

From the yard beneath the window the sound of hooves could be heard. He invited her to look. 'That's that Danish mare Ulf brought back for Melisen,' he told her.

They looked down. A groom was putting the mare through its paces. Then, in a most casual-seeming tone, Roger said, 'So you know something about commenda contracts, do you?'

It was late in the day by now and the only light in the chamber other than the one that drizzled in from outside came from the fire flickering in the hearth. Shadows were sent in a dance macabre across the tapestries with their scenes of the hunt. She could make out a stag, arrows piercing its shoulder, the huntsman drawing a knife to complete the kill. It had never appeared at all sinister before now. The absence of servants became suddenly oppressive.

Roger moved up close behind her. She could hear him breathing. He went to the casement and flung it open.

'That's a long drop, ' he observed, gazing down into the yard. He leaned out and shouted down to his groom, 'Take her in now.'

Hildegard saw groom and horse disappear round a corner towards the stables. Roger turned back inside, leaving the window open. She moved away but heard him tread after her.

'You must have talked to Vitelli about contracts,' he continued. 'I expect you know everything there is to know by now.'

'I wouldn't say I knew much,' she replied.

Just then a servant hurried in after a brief announcement, then skidded to a halt.

'What is it?' demanded Roger testily, glaring at him.

'Lady Melisen awaits you, my lord.'

Still clutching his goblet, he turned towards the door. 'Tell her I'm on my way.' He glanced back at Hildegard. 'Can't keep her waiting. We'll talk later.'

Hildegard released the stem of her goblet after he left, her knuckles white.

Roger might well want the witness to his contract with Melisen's father dead. Reynard. And whoever else knew about it. A long drop. She shivered and finished her wine in one nervous gulp.

Hildegard went to visit Pierrekyn in his prison cell. This time he had his lute but it lay beside him while he stared at the flame of a candle. He looked up when she entered. 'Praise heaven. You must help me, Sister—'

'Of course.'

'No, I mean you have to get me something. I cannot stand the idea of torture. I will not be tortured.'

'No one will torture—'

'They'll break my fingers and cut me. I know what they did to a friar down in Kent. They said he'd accused Gaunt of treason, so they cut out his tongue. Then gouged out his eyes and slit him and—' He was shaking with fear, she saw now, his voice coming out in a hoarse whisper. 'Their accusations were based on hearsay as well. Imagine how they'd mutilate *me*.'

She put a hand on his shoulder. 'Pierrekyn—'

'Give me a potion of henbane, anything. Let me die before they rend my flesh, please, I beg of you—'

'Pierrekyn.' Her voice was calm and practical. 'Let's not leap into hell before we've even seen the gates. It's not at all likely that that appealer's accusation will stand. It's his word against yours. I will provide testimony for your character and so will others.'

'The sheriff found no malice in the accusation—'

'We will prove him mistaken. They cannot hold you.'

Pierrekyn was not convinced. 'Coppinhall's charge will stick—'

'Only if they can prove a link between you and the copy of *anomenalle*. They can't charge you with sedition otherwise.'

'They'll try to blacken me and claim I'm of notorious repute. They will not set me free. I know they will not!'

She sat down on the bench. 'Listen to me. I need to know what Coppinhall is going to say next. He seemed very confident that he could indict you on the basis of your association with Reynard. Finding the *anomenalle* document in his chamber was unfortunate, to say the least. But if that's all he has to go on, your denial of conspiracy must stand.'

Pierrekyn threw himself down on the floor and with his head in his hands began to sob his heart out. 'They know about me,' he said between sobs. 'They're going to rake up everything from the past and I won't stand a chance.'

'What do they know about you?' Hildegard insisted.

Pierrekyn shook his head and went on weeping until she stood up.

'If you're not going to tell me then there's nothing I can do.'

She began to walk towards the door and he looked up in alarm. 'Wait!' He wiped away his tears with the backs of both hands and mumbled, 'I was given three exigents before I left Kent. It's probably gone up to five by now.'

'You mean you're outlawed?' She was aghast.

'Why do you imagine I came up here? And then leaped at the chance to get out of the country?'

'I suppose it was out of the question to face trial?'

'And have those lying snakes condemn me anyway?' He seemed calmer now he had told her the worst of it.

'Were you guilty?' she asked.

'Of killing my master? I'm not mad, Sister. I know the penalty for petty treason. It was during the purges after the Rising. Everyone was caught on some invented charge or other. So many disappeared or were being hanged that the wiser ones took to their heels. I thought I was being wise too.'

'Did Reynard know about the exigents?'

'Of course he did. He smuggled me out in his own retinue when he left for Castle Hutton. Without him I'd be dead by now.' He came to kneel in front of her. 'I'm not asking for your respect. I'm a coward. I've tried to be like Talbot. He was afraid of nothing even though they got rid of him anyway. But I just can't take it.'

Hildegard rested a hand on his shoulder. 'Pierrekyn, I promise if it comes to it, I'll give you whatever I can to ease your pain. But give me time to consider this whole matter again. I think we need the help of an expert man of law. Have courage. The game is not yet lost.'

His fear did not abate but he bent his head and kissed the backs of her hands. 'I'll hold out a little longer. I'm beginning to trust you again. If anyone can free me it must be you. Blessings on you.'

She got up to go but he called her back.

'Do you remember asking me about my name?'

She nodded. 'Didn't you say Haverel wasn't your real name?'

He shook his head. 'No. I said, part of my name isn't real. It's the "Pierrekyn" part that's false.' He tried a smile. 'It was Reynard's idea. He thought my own name, John, was too commonplace so he renamed me after a friend of his, once a king's minstrel and now a corrodian at St Mary's in York.' He smiled ruefully. 'He said it was because I was worthy of playing before the king.' He looked shame-faced. 'I've told you everything now. No more lies.'

It was shortly before the end of lauds. Steeling herself for what she had to do next, she waited outside the abbot's lodging. As soon as it was over and Hubert came out of the church, she approached him.

'My lord abbot,' she began, 'I beg audience with you on a matter of life and death.'

He stopped in the process of dismissing her. 'Has something happened?' he demanded.

She inclined her head.

He gave a sigh that seemed to rise from the soles of his feet. 'Then you'd better come inside.'

He glanced once round the garth before admitting her into his private sanctum.

'My lord, I am not intent on trying to reinstate myself,' she said as soon as they were within. 'After the trial of the minstrel is over I shall withdraw to Swyne as you have ordered. However, I am much exercised by the plight of the poor boy. He is innocent of the crime of killing Reynard as I believe even Coppinhall must admit, but he now he has to face this further charge—'

'Sedition by association. We've said all we have to say, haven't we? Has anything new occurred?'

She hesitated. 'I wonder about the legality of bringing someone to court on a charge and then accusing them of something else. Surely this isn't just?'

Hubert frowned. 'Are you suggesting I make an intervention on a point of law?'

She nodded. 'It would delay things until we can find a way round the charge of sedition.'

'And why would we do that – if it's true?'

Her voice was firm. 'Gaunt's attempt to stifle the truth could itself be seen as sedition and it's unjust in essence – unless,' she added, 'we deem freedom of speech a crime.'

'Do you imagine that to be my view?'

'I would be at fault to suggest it.'

Moving to a set of books in the aumbry against the wall, he ran his fingers along their spines until her came to the one he was looking for. He opened it and scanned the pages and after a moment lifted his head.

'It may be possible. I congratulate you, Sister.'

He looked at her in silence for a moment and when at last he spoke his voice had thickened. 'And this is the only reason for your presence in my chamber?'

'I beg of you, represent poor Pierrekyn at the court tomorrow. Introduce this point of law. Allow him justice.'

He gave a short laugh. 'And is that all?'

She bowed her head. 'It is.'

'I can only ensure that due process is followed,' he told her. 'If I suspect that Coppinhall is trying to sway the judgment of the jury, then I shall step in. Have no doubt of that. I imagine you are aware that the men of law will happily argue between themselves for some time about whether it would be appropriate to introduce this point or not. To mention it at all could delay matters for weeks. The boy would have to remain here in the abbey prison.' His eyes gleamed and she knew he had seen through her ruse. 'If I bring it to the attention of the court will that satisfy you, Sister?'

'As long as there is someone who understands the detail and can delay matters until we can unravel the plot against Pierrekyn, then yes,' she replied. 'Otherwise I fear Coppinhall will try to stampede the jury into condemning the minstrel and having him drawn to the gallows, quartered and hanged before any appeal can be lodged.'

'That would not accord with my deepest understanding of justice,' he replied. 'Be assured of that.'

The problem, as she saw it, was that the minstrel was a stranger to the area and was, as he had pointed out himself, what the courts officially termed 'of notorious record'.

With at least three writs ordered against him he would automatically have been outlawed on the fifth. There were several ways he could avoid punishment: he could flee to another country, which he had already tried; or enter the king's service, which was not easy; or he could lie low until he could afford to buy a pardon. This was probably the best course but only if he could remain out of reach of his enemies for long enough.

If Hubert could play for time on the morrow it would give them an opportunity to find the best solution.

The way the abbot conducted matters would reveal his own affiliations too. He might merely go through the motions and yield at once when Coppinhall insisted on taking the matter out of his jurisdiction.

It was obvious someone had leaned on the appealer. He was scared half out of his wits when they asked him to stand forth and in the tumult following the adjournment Coppinhall's guards had kept a close watch on the man. They had left together, allowing nobody a chance to question him.

She smiled grimly. Maybe she could appeal Coppinhall herself on a charge of misprision. If her suspicions were correct it could be claimed he was guilty of concealing treasonable acts against the king himself.

Chapter Twenty-five

I T WAS AFTER prime. The custodian of the cloisters went round checking all the doors of the chapter house to make sure they were locked so that no one could enter. He did it with the bored expression of a man who has done the same thing many times and never found a variation to the chore.

Everyone down below on the floor of the chapter house bowed as the abbot passed through their ranks. Then the prior came forward, kissed the abbot's hand and made a bow of his own. One of the brothers climbed up into the pulpit and read the martyrology for the day, and a priest followed, reading certain psalms and collects in a dull, flat voice. After that he read out the part of the Rule assigned for the day.

Next there was a reading of the tables of names and the duties allotted for the week; after that came a sermon, preached by the abbot in what seemed to Hildegard, from her secret vantage point on the balcony that ran round the building, a subdued manner compared to his rant of recent days.

The whole ritual was carried out in such an orderly and prosaic manner that she began to think the rumours she had heard were nothing more than malicious exaggerations.

Then the novices and conversi processed out. The doors were locked once more and she was suddenly aware of a subtle change of atmosphere. She felt a tingle of fear.

One of the brothers stepped forward to confess some minor faults and ask for forgiveness. One or two others followed. The circator listed the misdemeanours he had observed on his rounds and then the abbot himself stood up.

Making his way to the steps of the altar, he prostrated himself and began to make confession in general formulaic terms, his Latin so rapid and subdued that Hildegard had to strain to catch any of it, and then he pronounced punishment on himself. He rose and shrugged off his habit as far as the waist.

Hildegard stifled a cry of consternation. His back was a mass of bloody welts. As Roger had said, he had been flogged and recently too, for some of his wounds were beginning to bleed again as the flesh opened when his muscles flexed.

Now she watched in mounting horror as the prior and the other senior official produced their scourges. The prior was first. Taking delicate steps to where his abbot knelt, he brought down the leather thong with its metal studs across Hubert's back. At once a scarlet welt sprang up. Beads of blood appeared from reopened wounds. Hubert did not flinch.

One by one the others stepped forward to bring their scourges down.

She could see Hubert tense before each lash but otherwise he did not move. He was silent. There was no sound in the chapter house at all other than the irregular crack of the scourges. When they stopped she leaned forward in time to catch Hubert's broken command. 'More,' he said.

The prior brought one hand up to his face, shook his head, took a deep breath, and stepped forward again. The others followed. She noticed that when the cellarer turned away he had his eyes shut.

Still Hubert did not get up.

The prior said, 'The Rule is we do not cease until the abbot bids us do so.' He looked uncertainly at his fellows but Hubert, overhearing him, croaked, 'Continue.'

Once again the prior brought down his scourge and again the others followed. After the fourth or fifth succession Hubert's back was a mass of bloody meat. Gouts of blood dripped onto the tiles and one or two footprints encrimsoned the floor around him.

The cellarer flung down his scourge. 'Brother Mark, as hospitaller, would you now advise overriding the abbot in this?'

Brother Mark went forward and bending his head said something to Hubert. The abbot shook his head but, turning to face the rest of them, Mark said, 'Enough. He has duties to perform and we need him alive.'

Slumping back in her hiding place Hildegard felt waves of nausea take over. She closed her eyes and fought to steady her urge to cry out.

What crime could lead to the need for such punishment? Surely only murder could be deemed sufficiently heinous to demand it? She tried to recall every incident that had arisen regarding the death of Reynard. Hubert had given no indication of involvement and yet there was no better way of concealing guilt than by pretending concern.

It occurred to her that he might have already been tried by his brothers in chapter after confessing his guilt, and this was how his penance was being meted out. Only the senior obedientiaries would share in the knowledge. Their deliberations would be kept secret from the rest of the brotherhood.

She leaned forward again to peer through the wooden tracery. Below her Hubert was being helped to his feet, the hospitaller on one side, the cellarer on the other. The prior led the remaining members outside while the abbot struggled back into his habit. It must be agonising to have that rough cloth next to such wounds, she thought.

Waiting until everyone had left, she made her way shakily down the narrow steps from the loft and, after a quick look to make sure she was unobserved, let herself out into the garth.

The bell for the next office would start to toll soon. After that Hubert would have to appear in the chapter house again and there, at the scene of his humiliation, he would be forced to conduct the business of the court as if nothing had happened to him. She shuddered and made her way towards the guest house.

A group of servants Hildegard did not recognise were running about in the kitchens as she passed. The tang of baking bread reminded her of the intruder in her cell and she put her head round the door. Two bakers in the colours worn by Coppinhall were squabbling. The clerk of the kitchen came up to greet her and turned to see what had caught her attention.

'Never at peace, those two. I'll be glad when they've gone.'

'Are they here with the Justice?' she asked.

'Yes and he's welcome to them. Is there anything I can get you, Sister?'

'Just water, if you please,' she replied. Her mouth was dry at what she had just witnessed.

He sent a boy to fetch a ewer and she had already set off with it when there was a commotion from the cloisters. A moment later servants appeared, running at the double from all corners of the garth. The clerk came out onto the steps. 'What's the to-do?' he called to her.

'I can't tell.' She handed back the ewer, saying, 'Is it an accident of some sort? I'd better go and see.'

Bunching up the hem of her habit, she set off across the garth. When she arrived there was a lot of shouting going on between Coppinhall and several other men. A few monks and conversi were standing by, saying nothing.

'What's happening?' she asked one of them.

'It's the prisoner,' a monk told her. 'He's escaped.' The monk-bailiff, although roundly abused in the most intemperate language probably ever heard within the precincts of the abbey, was standing silently with a face as expressionless as a piece of York stone.

Soon there was quite a crowd round the door of the prison. When one of the men came stamping out to confirm that the cell was indeed empty, Coppinhall said he was going to raise the hue and cry. His followers went at once to arm themselves. By the time some of them were returning with staves and horses had been brought from the stables, Hildegard had managed to glean a little more.

The monk-bailiff had been in attendance on the prisoner all night but when he came to open the cell just now he had found it empty. No one had seen the prisoner escape.

Coppinhall was in a foaming rage. 'Did you leave your post, Brother?' he barked accusingly at the bailiff again.

'Only once to answer a call of nature,' replied the monk blandly.

'So how in God's name did he get out?' fumed the Justice. 'Can he walk through walls? Or,' he glared around, 'has the little turd got accomplices?' He glowered at the brethren as if expecting one of them to come forward and confess.

When no one answered he grated, 'I expect your abbot to deal with this in the severest possible manner and if he doesn't there's going to be trouble.'

The bailiff inclined his head but to Hildegard, standing quite close by, he looked less contrite than satisfied.

Coppinhall's attention was taken up with organising the men forced by law to join in the hunt. This included everybody except the monks. The conversi were expected to turn to and they stood about in a milling little mob, looking uncomfortably at their staves. Coppinhall had even had the guests roused out of their lodgings. The arrival of the hounds added to the commotion.

Hildegard hurried over to the kennels to release Duchess and Bermonda, calling to one of the grooms to fetch her a suitable hireling as she did so. Accompanied by her own hounds she returned to the stable just as Sir Ralph was riding out.

'Are those bitches of yours astute enough to tell the difference between a stag and a man?' he demanded.

'I expect so,' she replied.

'We'll soon see!'

He was joined by Lady Sibilla on her silver mare. 'Sister,' she called as Ralph kicked his mount forward, 'a word.' She lowered her voice. 'You say you saw Master Escrick alive?'

'I did, my lady.'

'Where and when do you think you saw him?'

'I think I saw him on the quayside at Ravenser and I believe that he travelled on the last ship to leave for Flanders. I very definitely saw him as we left Bruges.'

'Are you sure it was him?' she demanded, suspiciously.

'I am. He jumped up beside me on the wagon in which I was travelling.'

'And you spoke?'

'He did. He threatened me.'

'Why on earth would he threaten you?'

'I believe he was angered by the fact that I had caused him to be accused of murder, with the unfortunate events that followed.'

Sibilla looked askance and had the grace to blush. 'And you saw him after that?'

'Yes, in Florence, and we talked again.'

Without another word Sibilla rode from the yard.

By the time Hildegard joined the hue and cry they were already streaming through the abbey gates. Ulf was roaring orders like a man possessed. She watched in astonishment. He began to discuss Pierrekyn's likely destination with Coppinhall.

'He's as likely to go north towards Hutton as anywhere,' he was saying. 'It's the one place he knows in the county and it's likely he has friends of similar persuasion up there. Failing that, my guess is he'll try to take ship at Ravenser or Hull and flee the country again.'

Coppinhall seemed impressed by this analysis and ordered his men to get moving, sending one posse northwards to comb the woodland that stretched as far as Hutton and another across the marshes towards the river ports and the coast.

Melisen, astride the frisky little Danish mare, said worriedly, 'I hope I don't find him, Roger. I wouldn't know what to do. I could never turn him over to these ruffians.'

'What you'd do is tell me of course,' Roger replied. 'But don't worry, my little martlet, you won't have to make the decision yourself. I'm going to be right beside you.' They both followed at a sedate pace behind those on foot.

Ulf came over to Hildegard as the hunters began to press under the arch and swarm onto the foregate. 'What about you, Hildegard? Which way are you going?'

'I've no idea,' she said, somewhat amazed and confused by his current performance.

He spoke quietly. 'It's my honest guess he'll try to make for York. Brother Mark told me in confidence that he might be wearing a habit that just happened to be lying around next to a helping of wastel and a knife.'

She was shocked. 'You mean—?'

'Don't say it out loud. Walls have ears.' He glanced round. Only Sir William remained behind. He was fondling the hawk on his wrist and appeared indifferent to the excitement.

Ulf strode over to him. 'Not joining the hunt, Sir William?'

'I like a manhunt, nothing better. But my horse is lame. I might follow on foot,' he added. 'What about you, steward? Aren't you going out?'

'I have to let the abbot know what's happening, then I'll follow on.' With a nod to Hildegard, Ulf strode off across the garth. The monks, without permission to leave, stood around in gossiping groups while the bailiff stationed himself at the door of his now empty prison with his arms folded.

Her hounds close beside her, Hildegard led her hireling onto the foregate. There was no one to see her go. The hunters had fanned out over the countryside and were now mere specks of colour in the distance. The road towards Beverley was almost empty, with only one or two followers checking the canal bank in a half-hearted fashion.

The bailiff had claimed that his call of nature was in the early hours, well after lauds, and it was assumed that Pierrekyn must have made his escape after that. If so, he would be well out of the vicinity by now and there was no glory in wasting time looking in places where he would not be.

'He'll not linger round here,' one of the men declared as she passed. She saw them give up and turn back to join the others.

She imagined where Pierrekyn would go to seek safety. He had mentioned Reynard's friend, his namesake, now a corrodian in York. It was likely that he would look for protection there.

Everyone had heard of Pierrekyn Gyles, the king's minstrel.

For a clerk, Reynard had had some unexpected associates.

The ride took her through thick woodland once she had left behind the farmed land belonging to the abbey. Leaves of oak, beech, ash and rowan formed a veil of fragile green over the wet bark. Now and then a blaze of blackthorn stood out, past its best, a reminder that spring was almost over and summer was approaching at last.

The track led deep into the wild wood. A magpie flew through the branches, calling for a mate; a robin pecked viciously at a newly fledged sparrow, the tiny bird too far gone for help. Death defeated life on all sides, she thought, even here in the beguiling beauty of the woods.

She called in the hounds. If she was to reach York by nightfall she needed to increase her pace.

By now the sound of the hue and cry had faded and except for the beat of her horse's hooves and the natural sounds of the countryside she rode on in silence until she came to a division in the path. One lane continued through the woods to join the king's highway in the direction of York while three others went on to different manors. The fifth was the turning onto the road for Beverley. She reined to an indecisive halt.

If Pierrekyn was on foot he could not reach York before her. Calculating the possible speed of his escape she reckoned that he could not be much further on than Beverley. There was a chance that he might have tried to get into the town when the gates were opened that morning, mingling with the suppliers bringing produce to market. There was one other reason for him to choose this route.

She turned her horse's head. There was nothing to be lost. If she drew a blank she would ride on to York. Beverley it was. She set off at a gallop.

After only a quarter of a mile her horse stumbled and one of its shoes came flying off. She gave way to a most un-nunlike curse and pulled up. Sliding out of the saddle, she found the shoe in the long grass not far off. With a good two miles to go there was nothing for it but to walk. Calling the hounds in again she set off, leading the hireling by its reins.

There were few other travellers at this time of day. Most would have been up and about at dawn and would now be busy at their destination before returning to their manors before sunset. She was surprised, then, to hear the drumming of hooves in the distance coming from the direction of Meaux.

She led the horse under the cover of some trees and waited to see who would appear. If it was the hue and cry her fears for Pierrekyn might again be justified and she dreaded to see John Coppinhall in his dagged turban riding at the head of his armed retinue.

It was a relief when a figure in the bleached habit of a Cistercian appeared at the far end of the lane. As he came nearer could she see that it was Hubert de Courcy himself and, astonishingly, he rode alone.

Riding fast, when he caught sight of her he tugged his horse to a rearing halt and called down, 'So, you haven't found him.'

He has followed me.

The suspicions planted by the prioress – that he was a spy in the pay of Avignon and a supporter of Gaunt – and Roger's cryptic remarks all came flooding back. Stifling the fear of finishing up like Reynard, she shook her head. 'As you see. I'm alone.'

Chapter Twenty-six

ULF MUST HAVE told the abbot where she was going. He would not realise that Hubert despite his promise to delay matters could have a vested interest in silencing the boy after all, just as he might have had the clerk silenced. Now, when Hubert asked her what had made her leave the rest of the pursuers and strike out alone, she could offer only a feeble explanation.

'Everyone else is covering the marshes and the Hutton woods. I thought I would try elsewhere.'

'Nothing more?' It was clear he did not believe her. He gave her a piercing stare. 'I wondered whether you thought he might seek sanctuary in Beverley as it's closer than York. He might have heard about the sanctuary stone in the minster, the one they call the fridstool. He might hope to seek the protection it would afford.'

She went cold. 'I believe you can read my mind, my lord abbot. Some would accuse you of necromancy.'

'Let's ride on then,' he said, 'and see if we're right.'

He was about to urge his mount forward when she said, 'My horse has thrown a shoe.'

To her surprise he dismounted, somewhat stiffly, and threw the reins over his horse's back. 'Then I'll walk with you.'

There was no reason for him not to go on ahead. Indeed, it would surely suit his purpose to reach the boy before she did. Apprehensively, she fell into step beside him.

Banks of hawthorn rose on either side of the lane. The buds were just beginning to open and the air was filled with a strong, sweet scent like incense. Every step reminded Hildegard of the bloody wounds the abbot bore but he concealed any sign of pain. She stole a surreptitious glance at his expression. It was as severe as ever, closed over the privacy of his thoughts. They walked on for some time in silence.

All around them birdsong rose from the hawthorn thickets as they passed. The scent of grass was released in a dizzying haze.

Her suspicion that he had followed her to thwart her protection of Pierrekyn did not abate but an air of peace descended. She felt she could walk beside him for ever.

One mile from the town they reached a place called Molescroft, the site of the first of the four sanctuary crosses that marked the graduated boundaries on the way to the safety of the frid-stool. They did not pause but walked on.

'If they got as far as this and his pursuers decided to stop him, as is their right, they would risk a fine if he were later proved innocent,' observed Hubert, breaking the silence. 'His arrest, however, might be deemed cheap at the price.'

'Cheap for some,' she replied.

His dark eyes flashed as if her remark had stung his conscience. 'I was thinking of Coppinhall,' he retorted. 'A fine of four marks for stopping a sanctuary-seeker would be nothing to him. He takes enough in fines and taxes to make him a rich man.'

She had no reply. He was right. As if she had continued her criticism, however, he said, 'I know the abbeys are blamed for their wealth, and justly so. It seems we can't help making money. But in return we use it to improve the lives of the poor. We help the sick. We do what good we can.'

He didn't wait for an answer but went on, 'I intend to restore the purity of the Rule. The novices in particular are up in arms about the new discipline and see any restrictions on their wildness as unfair but if they're to be worthy of the Order they need to submit to the Rule from the beginning. If they don't like it they can leave. As for my brothers, they should welcome the chance to correct their former laxness: gluttony, sloth, backbiting, lack of charity, self-indulgence. Some of them seem to forget why they ever joined the Order. When my eyes were opened to what was happening I was shamed to think I had allowed conduct to decline so far. I will not have monks in my abbey living off the fat of the land, giving nothing in return—' He broke off to give Hildegard a sidelong glance. 'Apologies, Sister, these are problems for me alone to correct. Sermon over.'

They walked on without saying anything more until they came to the line of booths set up outside the town walls. There were people everywhere. Traders shouted their wares. Customers bargained. Banter flew back and forth. The red-brick arch straddling the road was wide enough to allow passage of the wagons bringing produce to market. It was a toll-gate and the site of a further sanctuary stone.

'So he slips through and his worth increases. Now his pursuer would have to pay sixteen marks to stop him,' Hubert observed. 'Still within Coppinhall's pocket.'

He searched the crowds going in and out. Hildegard wondered how many of them were maintained by Coppinhall and whether Hubert recognised anyone.

'These fellows at the toll-booth might remember admitting Pierrekyn,' she suggested as they approached.

They were allowed to go through after a brief inspection of Bermonda's claws, then Hubert addressed the constable on duty. 'Anyone trying to seek sanctuary in the minster?'

The man came forward with an interested expression and several of his companions joined him. 'If you mean a young lad wearing a Cistercian habit several sizes too big for him, the answer's yes,' he told him.

The others joined in describing in detail precisely what time Pierrekyn had appeared out of the mist that morning when the gates were unbarred.

'Right panicked, he was,' the constable continued. 'Spent the night in a ditch by the look of him.'

'What's he accused of?' asked another, pushing his way forward.

'Some petty felony,' replied Hubert vaguely. 'Has he gone on without trouble then?'

They exchanged glances. 'You'll no doubt find him in St John's by the time you've fought your way through the crowd yourselves. It's market day.'

'Let's go,' said Hubert to Hildegard.

They went on into the multitude flocking the streets.

'We'll get rid of our horses,' Hubert decided after a few minutes of trying to force their way through. The stables were around the next corner past the parish church. After leaving them they took a short cut into the market place. The minster, St John's, lay down a lane on the far side. The throng seemed more impenetrable than ever and Hildegard said, 'The mummers must be here as well.'

Hubert, taller than most, stared intently over the heads of the bystanders. He tapped her on the shoulder. 'It's not the mummers. Follow me.'

Annoyed at his peremptory manner she tightened her grip on the leash restraining her hounds and followed, emerging in an open space that had formed in the middle of the crowd.

On one side were four or five men-at-arms wearing a device Hildegard had never seen before. Opposite stood a rough-looking bunch of townsfolk, market traders, a butcher with a cleaver, a carpenter clutching a hammer, and several others wielding weapons of one kind or another. Behind this line, with a face like parchment, was Pierrekyn.

For a moment nobody spoke.

In the silence Hubert walked up to the men-at-arms and planted himself squarely in front of them. 'This boy is seeking sanctuary as is his right. If you stop him now you'll pay a hefty fine. Be aware of that.'

'He might have a right to seek sanctuary but we have a right to stop him – by beheading if necessary.' The leader of the group tapped the hilt of his sword.

'Is that what you would do without knowing the details of the accused's crime?' asked Hubert mildly.

The mob murmured and the man glanced furtively at his three companions.

'Let him go, you bully-boys!' shouted a woman in the crowd. Her neighbours chimed in and took up the chant in an increasing roar of dislike. The tradesmen facing the armed men flexed their muscles. It was clear they were itching for a fight.

Unnoticed, Hildegard hurried to Pierrekyn's side. 'Do you know where the minster is?' she asked.

He shook his head as if too frightened to open his mouth.

'Come with me then. Quick! The abbot will stop them.'

Grasping Pierrekyn by the arm, she pulled him through the crush, bystanders parting to let them through, and she thought they had made good their escape until a mailed fist gripped her by the shoulder and dragged her to a halt. She looked up into the face of one of the armed men.

'Go on, Pierrekyn!' she shouted.

He hesitated. The man released Hildegard as if to pursue the boy but just then Duchess launched herself silently through the air and landed squarely on the man's back, bringing him to the ground in a clash of steel. He wore a breastplate under his tunic and a casque on his head, and the latter rang as it hit the cobblestones. He gasped as he found the muzzle of the lymer hovering inches from his face. The hound opened her jaw and brought it down in a grip that held him by the throat, revealed in all its vulnerability above the neck of his mail shirt.

Bermonda yipped excitedly and threw herself on the fallen man, worrying at his armour until she found a gap of unprotected flesh.

'No!' ordered Hildegard, seeing what she was about to do. The little kennet looked up sadly and uttered a hungry growl. Hildegard went over. 'Hold him, beauties, hold!'

Pierrekyn was standing in a trance. Gripping him tightly by the arm, she pushed him ahead until they could run freely down one of the side streets towards the minster and the sanctuary of the frid-stool.

Behind her she could hear shouting and the thump of wood on steel but without stopping she dragged Pierrekyn towards the church boundary.

'Forty-eight marks!' she exulted, to give him courage as they reached it, and then, when they were at the great studded door of the minster itself, she placed his hand flat on it in triumph. 'Ninety-six marks if they stop you now! Those men-at-arms won't want to risk a fine like that!'

He was panting with fear. 'I thought I was safe once I was inside the town walls.'

'Get in. Go on. You'll be safe then.' She put her shoulder to the doors to heave them open, then pushed him inside. Following, she leaned back to shut them with a grimace of relief.

Two canons looked up from their reading. 'Sanctuary?' asked the quicker of the two, sizing up the situation.

There was uproar outside. The second canon hurried over to the doors and hefted a great beam of wood into place.

'Allow the abbot of Meaux entry,' she suggested.

The man nodded. He dragged a bench to a window near by so he could look out. 'A rabble of townsfolk are coming into the yard. Are they the pursuers?'

Hildegard shook her head. 'Men-at-arms. Whose I know not.'

'I see them. Two of them,' he said. 'And about forty or fifty market traders. They're turning back, the armed ones,' he said. 'Or being turned back.' He chuckled. 'But I see your abbot in his white habit striding through the crowd. He's here now.'

The canon got down off his bench and hurried to lift the beam to allow Hubert to enter.

'Are they safe?' she heard him ask as she hurried Pierrekyn down the long nave.

The sanctuary stool, known locally as the frith- or frid-stool, was made of an uneven lump of strange, dark stone with a curve in it like a seat. It stood next to the altar. When Pierrekyn caught sight of it he threw himself towards it with a cry and as soon as he sat down he burst into sobs, holding his head in his hands like a child.

The first canon clucked around him helplessly. 'Poor young fellow,' he kept saying. 'What can I do for him?' After a moment he disappeared and returned with a brass cup containing water. 'Here, young master, drink this.'

The noise outside increased. It became a triumphant chant broken up by random cheers and Hildegard felt no surprise to hear a hurdy-gurdy start up, followed by some hearty singing.

Hubert reached her side. 'Who were those armed brutes?' he asked.

'I've never seen their colours before.'

His eyes narrowed and he moved away looking thoughtful.

By now several officials of the minster had been summoned and they formed an excited group round Pierrekyn.

'You're outside the king's writ here, boy,' said the dean, a short, chubby fellow with the sharp glance of a schoolmaster. 'But I must ask you some questions before we can accept you,' he began. 'First, have you already been convicted of any felony?'

'Not yet,' muttered Pierrekyn.

'And are you armed?'

He shook his head. 'Just this knife for eating.' He held out the red-handled knife Sir Talbot had given him. One of the dean's clerks took it and made a record of it in a book open on the desk.

Looking at Pierrekyn's dishevelled appearance and the expression on his face, the dean turned to Hildegard. 'You brought him here, Sister. What's his reason for seeking sanctuary?'

'He was arraigned at Meaux after an appeal but the charge was altered and Coppinhall, the Justice, wants him to be indicted by the presenting jury to await a commission of oyer and terminer. The boy doubts he'll get a fair trial. As do I and several others,' she added.

'That's good enough for me,' the dean said. 'Do you know of any reason why he shouldn't seek sanctuary?'

'No, I don't.'

'Come then, young master, there are still a few more formalities. First, you need to make confession and swear to keep the peace.'

'Of course I do,' said Pierrekyn. With his dark russet curls awry and his guileless green eyes, the dean had no difficulty in believing him.

'Then you'll have to be enregistered.'

He quickly went through the details. Hildegard paid the fee to the bailiff and Pierrekyn made the required promise to be faithful and true to the Archbishop of York and promised to carry out a few chores while he was in sanctuary.

'In return we'll lodge, feed and water you for forty days and forty nights. There'll be a watch kept and we'll send a messenger to inform the coroner of your presence as is the law.'

'Is this the coroner from York?' asked Hildegard.

'It is.' The dean threw her a subtle glance and she guessed why. She had already met up with the man on a previous occasion and was reluctant to repeat the experience.

'He's unlikely to show his face unless he's told to do so by some-body higher up,' remarked the dean. 'Likely he'll send that assistant of his.'

Pierrekyn began to imagine the men-at-arms forcing their way in. 'There's nothing to stop them. Just a handful of unarmed churchmen!'

The dean tried to calm him.

'But look what happened at Westminster,' he panicked. 'Two men slain during high mass in front of the prior's stall.' He hung onto the sides of the frid-stool as if he would never let go and it was only when a couple of the vicars-choral came out from their chambers that he was moderately reassured.

A group of them accompanied Pierrekyn into the dean's office to finish his enregistration and while they were doing this Hubert took Hildegard to one side.

'Now he's safe we can leave. Will you have the horse you borrowed reshod and come on later?'

'I would rather not leave Pierrekyn at this point. May I have permission to stay with him?'

Without replying he went off towards the lady chapel. She watched him go inside and kneel before the altar.

Pierrekyn had already gone through the formalities and returned to his place on the frid-stool when Hubert eventually emerged.

He came over to Hildegard. 'Stay. I'll stay as well.' He turned to one of the canons. 'Can you take a message to Meaux? Tell the cellarer he's in charge until I return.'

The canon nodded and sped off.

'Those were not Coppinhall's men in the market place,' he told her, 'although they aroused as much animosity. Are you aware of the rumour attached to him?'

'I heard there was some story,' she replied, careful not to mention that it was Ulf who had related it.

'He is said to have had an opponent murdered and the body thrown into the town ditch,' he told her. 'When he was appealed, the appealer disappeared as well. So much for the king's justice.' He looked thoughtful. 'It appears that Coppinhall exercises his own will in this place but I wonder who his allies are, who keeps him here, and how real his influence is?'

Hildegard had nothing to contribute. She had an opinion but it was nothing more. Coppinhall's unpopularity was not only due to the fact that he could literally get away with murder. It was his allegiance to the Duke of Lancaster that irked the populace of this Yorkshire town. Now that one of his allies, Sir Ralph Standish, was ensconced in Scarborough Castle there was bound to be friction. The role of the archbishop might be questioned also, she felt, despite her prioress's contrary opinion.

The hours passed. Outside in the minster yard the noise from the townsfolk continued although somewhat more sporadically. The hurdy-gurdy stopped and then a little later started up again. Pierrekyn had his hands over his ears to shut out the sound. His lute, which he had somehow managed to carry all this way, had been confiscated by the dean's clerk but there were moves afoot to let him have it back.

'It's a most ungodly instrument,' fretted a thin-faced priest. He looked to the dean for support but, finding none, went away with a look that would curdle milk.

Hubert paced alone down the entire length of the nave and stood at the far end underneath the south window for a considerable time as if deep in meditation. It was getting dark, candles were being lit, and by their glimmer, almost swamped in the soaring height of the building, he was a distant white blur in the shadows, standing motionless, like somebody in another, less brutish world. When he returned to join the group in the light around the altar, he said, 'The yard sounds as if it's still full of Pierrekyn's guards. They seem to have decided to stay and defend their frid-man.'

'He'll be pleased to know that, despite their lack of musical talent.'

Hubert's mouth briefly lifted at the corners. 'These are the townsfolk who were bound over to keep the peace by Gaunt after their civil disorder at the time of Smithfield. I wonder whether they'll find themselves accused of unlawful assembly in the yard.' Despite the hint of humour in his tone his thoughts seemed elsewhere.

The vicars-choral and the one or two canons who were not absent at their other livings, together with a handful of clerks, brought food and drink for their visitors, then sat around the frid-stool trying to cheer Pierrekyn until other duties called. Hubert discussed recent events in the town with the chancellor, himself a vicar-choral but also the legal officer of the abbey and head of the grammar school.

Hildegard went to sit by herself on the steps in the choir. Her hounds had been brought safely in by means of a side door. The clerk who somewhat gingerly accompanied them told her that the man-at-arms they had felled was now in the town prison on a charge of creating an affray.

Hubert came over and she looked up with a start. 'If you'd rather I sat somewhere else—?' he said quickly

She shook her head. 'No, you simply startled me.' He sat down on the step next to her. Her pulse began to race. 'It's going to be a long night,' she began, hurriedly. 'What do you think we should do? Clearly we can't stay here for forty days and nights.'

'I wish to God we could.' His tone was rough. 'I wish it, Hildegard, with all my heart.'

She turned to him in astonishment.

He was gazing off into the nave. 'Here in this sanctuary we're beyond the usual constraints of duty, if only for one night.' He bent his head close to her own. 'I have to speak out. This once only. Then silence. You have my word.'

'Speak out?'

'About my penance. About what is driving me to madness.'

Chapter Twenty-seven

ONCEALED BY THE cloak he reached for her wrist and encircled it with his fingers. 'I can't eat, or think, or pray. I am destroyed.'

'Hubert?'

'When you asked to go on pilgrimage I thought I'd go mad – imagining it might be because of something you felt, which you had the courage to fight – whereas I could only pray and see your face in all my prayers when instead I should have seen the face of God.' He paused. 'The thought of you, on such a journey, Hildegard, with that steward of Roger's—'

'Ulf, you mean? But he's like my brother. We've known each other all our lives—'

He gave her a haunted glance. 'That would not stop a man loving you. It would only make his feelings stronger.'

'Hubert, I—'

'Even though I know you to be a woman of integrity – forgive me, Hildegard, I have to speak – I taunted myself with such—' Again he broke off and again, as if the words were being dragged forth, forced himself to continue. 'When I heard that a knight was to be hired to escort you—'

'Sir Talbot? A tournament knight—'

'But I know these knights with their code of chivalry.' His laugh was strangled. 'None of them is to be trusted around women. Even so, the fault lay with me. I acknowledge that. But it did not stop me torturing myself: why had I given you permission to go? I could have stopped you. I could have—' His eyes were fixed on her lips. 'I could have—' His words trailed away and then, in an undertone he said, 'Instead, all I did was send a pathetic token, secretly, at the last minute.'

'Token?' Hildegard asked.

'You have it. I saw you with it at the hearing when you opened it to reveal your proof of Escrick's guilt. '

'The kerchief?'

'It belonged to my great-uncle, a knight templar, although it was little protection to him in those last violent days.'

'I have it here. It seemed to have a meaning – the embroidered flowers – but it eluded me until—' She faltered. Reaching for her scrip she pulled the kerchief from it. 'I'm honoured you should have entrusted me with such a precious talisman.' When she tried to hand it back he folded his hand over hers.

'Keep it. Take it as a pledge of everything in my heart.'

Aware of the great arching minster about them, the air filled with incense, reminding them of the divine who saw all things, she managed to whisper, 'We cannot admit this, Hubert.'

'I have no choice—'

'Think of the danger.'

'No danger can prevent it.'

'Have you forgotten the punishment meted out to one of your predecessors in France?'

He gave a bitter smile. 'You mean Brother Abelard? Do you imagine I think of anything else? But there is no man like Bernard of Clairvaux to lead the armies of the night against us.'

'Even so,' she replied, her voice husky, 'it would be madness—' She broke off, bound by a sacred oath, unable to voice her desire, not in the night, not in the light of day, not ever.

'I cannot imagine a future after this one night.' His voice was hoarse. His grip tightened.

The thought of Hubert suffering the terrible punishment inflicted on Abelard because of his love for the nun Eloise – castration, solitary confinement, disgrace and humiliation – gave her strength to resist if only for his sake. 'All your vows would be less than straw. Your soul would—'

'My soul be damned, Hildegard. I am only half alive without you.'

There was no time to search for a response because the sound of distant shouting erupted from the black depths of the nave. A cry of protest was cut off followed by the thunderous echo of approaching footsteps.

'Who comes here?' breathed Hildegard with a tremor of fear.

Hubert rose to his feet. His fingers slipped from her wrist and he stepped forward. A crowd of clerks came tumbling dazedly from their quarters. Pierrekyn froze like a rabbit in the light of a huntsman's flare.

A fully accoutred knight emerged from the shadows. Such light as there was flickered over the burnished armour that protected him from head to foot in steel. He wore a round helmet and, low on his hips, a studded belt with a sword swinging from it. He drew to a halt under the full glare of a score of tapers. The sour-faced clerk who had objected to Pierrekyn's lute was hurrying at his heels, saying, 'I could not deny him entry. Heaven forfend! A knight banneret! The very thought!'

With a premonition of what was to come, Hildegard saw that his tunic carried the emblem of the blue marsh dragon. In one corner it had an additional symbol. Horrified, she realised that Sir William himself stood before them. William, the butcher of Holderness.

He drew his sword with a rasp of steel and thundered, 'Hand over that miscreant!'

The army of students, clerks and chantry priests, unarmed, crowded in a confused group in front of the frid-stool. When Sir William made a feint with his sword, they scattered in alarm.

By now Hubert had positioned himself in front of Pierrekyn. Hildegard moved to his side.

'You are liable to a fine of one hundred and forty-four marks should you proceed,' Hubert announced.

Sir William laughed without mirth and rested the point of his sword on the altar steps. 'Cheap at the price, monk. I'd pay ten times that amount to stop this lie-monger in his tracks. Hand him over!'

When Hubert made no move, William reached into his pouch and threw down a fistful of silver pieces. 'Get the treasurer to count it. That should pay the fine and keep you happy.'

Pierrekyn moaned as Sir William raised his sword.

'You would also suffer the penalty of excommunication,' added Hubert, ignoring the coins.

'Out of my way, damn you!'

Sir William began to mount the steps, his sword pointing.

Hubert murmured, 'Stand back, Hildegard.'

She stepped away as Sir William approached. Hubert didn't move.

'If I have to run you through I'll do it without regret, monk. You can't stop me!' William snarled.

Hubert shook his head. He seemed paralysed.

'I admire your nerve,' mocked William, 'but it won't do any good.' He was at the top of the steps by now. 'For the last time—'

'You're wasting your breath, knight. The boy stays here.' Hubert folded his arms.

The tip of William's sword flashed towards Hubert's exposed throat and just as Hildegard shouted his name, he made one small movement that brought him alongside William's outstretched sword arm and, grasping it in both hands, he rammed it down hard over his lifted knee. It didn't break. It was encased in steel and Hubert could do little damage with his bare hands, but the sword shuddered in William's grasp until he managed to regain control. He raised his elbow, intending to smash it into Hubert's face.

Again the abbot made a small turn of his body, reached up towards William's throat and, like one who knew the failings of a suit of armour, pushed his fingers in behind the gorget and grasped his assailant round the windpipe. Coughing and struggling for breath, the knight was driven back, only to trip over Hubert's outstretched foot. He stumbled backwards, sliding full length down the altar steps.

With a roar, he staggered to his feet but by the time he lunged at Hubert with the full force of his armed weight behind the thrust, the abbot had snatched up the mace from the altar and, wielding it like a sword, parried until he had forced William away from the frid-stool and held him hard against the railings round the shrine of St John.

The final blow knocked William's helmet from his head. As it spun away Hubert brought the mace to within inches of his opponent's snarling face. He could have killed him then with one hard blow but it was as if an unseen hand came down to restrain him. Jamming the mace across William's throat instead, he said, 'Don't die. I'll not be responsible for that. Just drop your sword.'

There was a pause. The note of menace in the abbot's voice made William falter.

'Yield,' repeated Hubert.

William let his sword clatter to the ground. Hubert picked it up. There was a cheer from the minster men and Hildegard let out a shuddering breath. This was Hubert de Courcy, back in control.

'The hounds,' whispered a clerk to Hildegard.

'Go, Duchess!' murmured Hildegard with a dry throat.

While the lymer and the kennet pinned Sir William against the railings the minster men swarmed back, overwhelming him with sheer force of numbers.

'Drag him into the sacristy,' Hubert ordered, 'and lock him in.'

They bundled him eagerly into the small, windowless chamber and returned carrying the key.

Just then there was a further clamour at the west door. A thunderous knocking could be heard.

In the lull that followed a voice outside shouted, 'Open up, on pain of death!'

There was a pause then the voice came again. 'I am the Archbishop of York and demand entry into my own church!'

'Damnation!' exclaimed one of the students under his breath. 'It's Neville himself. We'll have to let him in or we'll be hung out like crows!'

'Open the doors,' Hubert ordered. He glanced at Hildegard where she stood protectively in front of Pierrekyn. Still clasping William's sword with both hands, he held it point downwards in the stance of a knight at yield. Then he carried it over to the altar where he offered it, hilt first, then placed it in front of the cross. She saw him kneel and mutter a short prayer.

When he rose to his feet he positioned himself at the top of the steps to wait for the archbishop to appear.

As the great doors were flung open a splendid retinue flooded in, armed men, squires and retainers, with in their midst, magnificently attired in a sweeping velvet riding cloak, a jewelled cross on his chest, Archbishop Alexander Neville of York.

He strode down the middle of the nave, repossessing the entire building with a royal glare, and when he reached the place where

Hubert was standing he gave the abbot a long, considering glance before growling, 'Abbot de Courcy, I might have guessed you'd be somewhere in it. What's going on?'

'We should speak privately, your grace.' Hubert indicated the dean's office and the two men went in.

The minster men, subdued by the appearance of their master, hung around the door, muttering about what new sanctions the archbishop might now seek to impose on them. Most were defiant; only one or two kept silent while the archbishop's bodyguards observed everyone with narrowed eyes.

After a prolonged delay the two men emerged.

Hubert seemed his usual authoritative self. His glance, however, like that of the archbishop, slid past Hildegard as if she were no more than one of the statues along the wall.

Archbishop Neville was aware of the hostility of the canons, and of the support given them by the rest of the minster men, and he chose now to ignore them too, merely demanding that Sir William be brought forth. Eventually, taking William with them, the whole contingent departed as swiftly and as magnificently as they had arrived.

Pleased with themselves, the minster men returned to their beds, while Pierrekyn, assured that there would be no further attempts on the privilege of sanctuary, fell into a deep slumber on the frid-stool. Someone draped a cloak over him.

'We'll leave at first light,' Hubert told Hildegard when everyone had gone. He would not meet her eyes.

'What brought Neville here?' she asked.

'Apparently he was riding back from Swyne.' He waited for her to add something but she felt no obligation to do so. 'Whatever happened there put him in a foul mood.'

'That's not difficult. He's known for his choleric nature.' The prioress had stood against him then? Had he not obtained his cross after all?

'It made him decide to break his return to York at Meaux. My strict regimen may not have reached his ears, either that or he expected preferential treatment at my table.'

'Would he have got it?'

Hubert's sombre expression briefly lightened. 'You may see me as someone who capitulates too easily,' his voice thickened, 'but I can assure you, Hildegard, that's not the case in general.' He held her gaze. Scarcely moving his lips he said, 'You would be damned along with me.' He turned away.

'What happened when Archbishop Neville arrived at Meaux?' she asked with an effort.

'He found Sir William fuming over his lame horse and the hue and cry still out. William told him about a minstrel arraigned for spreading seditious texts and how he'd broken out of prison and made his escape. His grace ordered one of his men to dismount from his horse so William could set off in pursuit. He must have seen me start out in this direction.'

'The archbishop offered help to Sir William?'

'I've just given him a more accurate version of events so that he can reconsider his position. He finally agreed that Pierrekyn should have an opportunity to request the king's pardon.' He peered into her face. 'Does that surprise you?'

'Things have turned out other than I expected.' The prioress sending Neville away with a flea in his ear? Neville himself supporting Sir William then changing his mind? She glanced at the sleeping boy. 'At least he's going to have a chance.'

He caught her eye. 'He owes you something. As do I.' There was a moment of awkwardness. Hubert covered it by saying, 'Sir William has demonstrated his allegiance, should it have been in doubt. He must be the power behind Coppinhall, the maintainer who ordered Reynard's death.'

'My feeling is that William is the instrument and not the instrument maker. I believe,' she went on cautiously, 'we must look to the new constable at Scarborough Castle for the motivating power here.'

'Sir Ralph Standish?'

'Is it not more than coincidence that Escrick, lately in the service of Sir Ralph de Hutton, should have figured so prominently in this whole business? And where is Escrick's home territory? Scarborough. And who is Gaunt's man at Scarborough?'

'That same Standish,' Hubert supplied. His mouth set in a grim line. 'Say nothing more. I am bound to a different master. Discretion might save our necks.' He gave her a despairing glance.

'You say you owe me something?'

He seemed to struggle for a moment and then advised, 'Betray me to the pope if you choose.'

She dashed the idea away with a hand. 'Which one?'

'The schism won't last for ever. I should have held my tongue. What I told you has made matters worse. If you knew the truth you would despise me even more—'

'I have never despised you—'

'Then it's only because I've concealed the truth from you.'

Fearing that he was going to admit openly to involvement with those who wished to overthrow the king, she begged him not to go on but, with a resigned smile, he insisted. 'I must clear my conscience. I've lied about myself.' Observing her look of disbelief, he corrected himself. 'If not lied, I've allowed you to believe something about me that is not true.'

'How so?' she asked in alarm, convinced she was about to be tested further. His next question confused her, however.

'Remember a remark you once made about Lady Sibilla and Escrick? That you thought she might be drawn to him because he was so unlike her husband?'

Mystified, she agreed that she did remember.

'And do you also remember mentioning your own husband, a knight in arms, I believe?'

She nodded.

'And do you remember one particular afternoon in my garden at Meaux?'

Again she agreed she did, without having it described in more detail.

'I believe my feelings were just then beginning to become known to me, to torment me, and on that particular day you seemed to return them.'

'Yes,' she agreed, her heart missing a beat.

'But it was based on a lie, don't you see?'

'No, I don't see! And what does it matter where your allegiance lies in all this?'

'Allegiance?' He looked as if he had never heard the word before. Ignoring it, he said, 'I am not as different from your husband as you imagine. You saw me just now, giving a reasonable account of myself against Sir William?'

'Reasonable? You were magnificent! A monk to have such fearlessness in the face of a murderous and fully armed knight—'

'But, Hildegard, what I have to tell you is this: I have not always been a Cistercian.' He seemed unable to go on and instead gripped her convulsively by the sleeve. 'This is my confession. It will damn me in your eyes for ever: for many years I was a knight in arms, fighting in the hire of one of the dukes of France.'

His expression was bleak.

'I was paid to kill. I have killed men.'

There was a silence while Hildegard struggled to understand.

'I can never be other than what I am,' he continued. 'It has just been proved beyond doubt by my immediate recourse to violence. I should have bowed my head beneath his sword and trusted in God's divine will. But I had no faith. I was ready to kill again. It was maybe only your presence that stayed my hand. You wrongly believed that I was a true servant of God, different from your husband, worthy of your regard for that reason. But I am at fault for conniving in the misunderstanding and at fault for trying to drag you down into hell with me'.

Hildegard gave a stricken cry as he began to walk away.

'Hubert! You could not be more wrong.' She followed, putting a hand on his sleeve to detain him. 'I see no virtue in submitting to death in meekness.' She recalled the effigies in the church of Santi Apostoli, the glittering defiance of the martyrs. 'You have gained my love by everything you do. You are without fault.'

He turned to gaze into her face. His fine eyes smouldered. His lips were within inches of her own. They were so close she could feel the heat radiating from his skin. She breathed in the scent of him. A feeling of joy swept over her and with a final unlocking of her heart she realised she could not resist him.

'My better self,' he breathed. 'I have found you. There is no further purpose for me under heaven but to love you.'

As in a dream she felt him lift her fingers towards his lips. Her skin tingled but the distance between them remained.

'If angels exist anywhere but in our minds,' his voice roughened, 'then at this moment they are conjoined.'

It was the darkest hour before dawn. Even as his words died away the first light began to slip in through the coloured glass of the east window, gilding bright points on the shrine and draining the shadows in the arcades. Hubert's exhausted face was picked out in its glow, stains of blood visible on the edge of his robe.

'Your wounds are bleeding,' she observed. 'May I tend them?'

He shook his head. 'This blood is nothing to the blood of the men I have killed.'

He stepped backwards, his glance locked on hers as if to retain her image to the very last moment. Then, one hand lifting in farewell, he turned and – she understood too late – began to walk rapidly away towards his master.

She could only watch. Everything was lost.

Chapter Twenty-eight

TALL MAN, straight-backed, his face as white as powder, walked towards her across the corrodians' hall at St Mary's abbey in York. Although elderly, with silver hair trimmed to his scalp, Master Gyles moved with the supple stride of an acrobat.

Although pensioned off for the past year, his inactivity had not added girth to his spare frame. Heavy-lidded eyes alighted on her face, speculatively, as he approached. His features reminded her of her lymer, Duchess, a hound trained for the kill. When he was near enough he made his wide mouth turn up at the corners in a smile. Behind the white mask, his eyes were watchful.

'Follow, if you will,' he invited with a flourish. He led her out of the hall where other less agile corrodians dozed in front of the fire and grew fat and slow. Knowing something of his fame, she wondered how he survived this backwater.

They went out into the garth. Rain was falling, little more than a fine mist. A bell began to toll bringing the monks into the cloister but he led away from them towards a comfortable-looking house on the other side.

'This is where harmless old fellows like me spend the last of our life's profit,' he said with no sign of self-pity in his voice.

They were soon seated in his chamber with drinks brought by a servant. She saw now with surprise that he had been carrying a sparrow in his sleeve all the while. He produced it seemingly from nowhere. With the skilful fingers of a drawlatch he played with the creature while they talked, the bird, entranced, turning round and round in a kind of daze, following the movements of its master's fingers.

'I'm training him to do a jig,' he explained. 'It amuses the other corrodians, poor fellows, and keeps the bird from the hawks.'

The chamber they were in was like a cavern crammed with musical instruments. Made of walnut, lime and beech, they shone with use. Noticing her interest he carried the bird on one finger to a cage hanging from the beam above the window and snapped the door on it. Then he picked up one of the lutes. Even before he played a note his affinity with the instrument was obvious from the fluid way it seemed to become part of his body the moment he touched it.

His long fingers began to trail in a seemingly random manner over the strings, plucking out an effortless little tune while he observed her reaction.

She told him, 'Last time I heard that was in Tuscany.'

He raised his eyebrows in a comical mime of surprise, neither asking who had played it nor admitting what it was. Nor did he deny any favour towards its sentiments. Instead he waited, as if to invite her to say more.

A dangerous man, she decided, refusing to identify the anthem of the White Hart. Clearly he was adept at luring the innocent or the careless to confess more than was good for them.

She cut out any further preamble. 'I'm here to inform you that a musician you know has sought sanctuary at the shrine of St John of Beverley. He has, in addition, obtained the temporary protection of the Archbishop of York.'

The eyebrows could not rise any higher so he blew out his powdered cheeks instead. He did not ask who the sanctuary man was, she noticed, but she supplied the name without hesitation.

'It's John Haverel. You know him. He knows you.'

'Young Jack. Been up to no good, has he?' His eyes gave nothing away and there was no change in his blank, mime's face.

'His friend, Reynard, was murdered shortly after Epiphany. As of course you'll know. For a time, John was blamed and might have lost his life if the indictment had stuck. But it didn't.'

'So why is he in sanctuary?'

'Because he was accused of a further crime, that of passing on a seditious text known as *anomenalle*.'

'The silly lad.'

'Someone found out Reynard was making copies and distributing them. Whoever this was allowed it to become known in the wrong quarters. A spy,' she said, 'no doubt working for gain. The spy's master decided Reynard should be stopped. John as well, when it was feared he knew what was going on.'

'Careless talk. Dangerous talk. Whom can any of us trust?' He gazed out from behind his mask. 'So the lad's well and in Beverley?'

'He is. Sir William made an attempt to prise him forth but was resisted.'

'My gratitude for this gossip, Sister, but I hardly think it worth your ride over to York to tell *me*.'

'I think it well worth it.'

His eyes came alive now. They flickered over her face while waiting for her to explain but she rose to her feet.

'The identity of Reynard's murderer was proven beyond doubt. The identity of the man who maintained the murderer is also known. I believe the identity of the informant could become known too – if the circumstances are right.'

She was at the door and put her hand on the latch.

'Wait.' Master Gyles's face had disintegrated before abruptly rearranging itself with a look that could have been seen as kind. 'Does the boy need anything?'

'Patronage. Entry into the guild of musicians. Maybe, in time, a royal appointment. He certainly has enough talent. You yourself were minstrel for many years at the royal court.'

He nodded. 'A word in the right place can work wonders—'

'Or bring scandal and the death of innocent men?' She laughed as if merely finishing the thought.

Before she went out she had one more thing to say. 'I wonder, master, whether you know that Reynard renamed the boy? He called him Pierrekyn in homage to you – because he held you in such high esteem.'

The powdered face crumbled into a mixture of shock and remorse – unless it was an actor's trick or the slant of light.

She left with the pearl-embroidered turnshoe still in her possession. It belonged, not to Master Pierrekyn Gyles, spy and one-time minstrel at the English court, but to someone who knew its true significance: Pierrekyn Haverel, minstrel at Beverley.

Epilogue

The archers were practising in the orchard when she arrived. She had ridden directly back to the priory after a short delay while she attended to the abbey's horse and obtained another. She had spent some time praying in the little church of St Olave by the river.

The skills of her sisters had improved while she had been absent. She made her way towards them through the grass. A burst of cheering broke out as the latest scores were totted up.

Then someone noticed her and everyone swarmed round in welcome, bombarding her with questions about her travels – she had no sooner arrived from Tuscany than she had ridden off again on another errand – and now they wanted to know what it was like to travel so far and whether she was as exhausted as she looked. For sure, one of them said, she would be going off to her grange as soon as possible, the work on it having gone so well.

Hildegard heard it all as if from a distance.

The prioress materialised at her side. 'Our archers have improved while you've been away, haven't they?' She made shooing motions with her hands. 'Back to the butts, sisters!'

The nuns took up their bows and moved off under the avenue of trees back to where the butts were propped.

'You have something to say to me in private, Mother?'

'And you to me, no doubt,' the prioress replied. 'Come, let's walk a while in my garden.'

Hildegard followed her.

'So, Sister,' said the prioress when they were out of earshot of the others, 'I hear that Standish's men were routed in Beverley by a couple of Cistercians and two hounds?'

'With some help from the townsfolk too.' Hildegard smiled. 'But Standish, you say? So they were his colours?'

'We'll be seeing them around for some time to come.' The prioress frowned briefly. 'Unless something happens to him.' She brightened. 'I also hear Meaux still has its Talking Crucifix. But what has York got, may we ask?'

'Nothing, judging by his grace's temper after he left here.'

The prioress chuckled. 'Men. They hate it when they're thwarted. Neville especially so – after putting up the money for your escort to Tuscany. His grace, however, plays a close hand. Never trust a man who uses rage to force his way.' She gave Hildegard a sharp glance. 'You're probably thinking, never trust a man at all?'

Hildegard gazed off into the distance. 'What did the archbishop get – if anything?'

'The return of his bill of exchange, less a percentage for our trouble. He was lucky to get that, in my view. You weren't extravagant overseas.'

'But is Constantine's cross still here then?'

'You're wondering why I've kept it. The views of that sacristan, its guardian, appeal to me. I would have liked to have met him. I think we can acquit ourselves with a similar purity of purpose. Such a sacred relic should not be used to further worldly ambition.'

Hildegard felt her heart lift a little. There had been something askew about the archbishop's ambition to own it. Now that his allegiance was in doubt she wondered whether he would even have honoured the promise to return it when the period of its loan was up.

'You did well on behalf of that young musician,' the prioress told her.

'At first I didn't know whether to trust him or not. In fact I suspected everyone of double-dealing at some point until events brought all the pieces together – Roger because of his business with Ser Vitelli, and even the abbot—'

'Because of Avignon, yes.' In a casual tone the prioress remarked, 'It's well to remember we can always choose with whom to do business.' And as if on the same topic she added, 'I also hear that Abbot de Courcy's off on pilgrimage.'

'He is?' Hildegard had the sensation of falling from a high tower but pressed her fingernails into her palms to deaden the feeling.

The prioress looked at her with compassion. 'You'll have enough to occupy you when you move into the new grange. I believe it's almost ready.'

'I have only the promise of one lay sister so far.'

'I believe I can recommend a half-dozen nuns to get things started. You can choose your own women when you've established means of feeding and watering them all. I think some of your sisters could do with a holiday from this forsaken marsh country. Let them enjoy summer on the edge of the moors where they can keep their feet dry. I guarantee they'll be back here at harvest time to the harder life I offer them.'

'Harder yet more sociable?'

'I doubt whether you'll want for company up there. His lordship will keep an eye on you. He's full of gratitude for what you did.'

'He is?'

'Something you arranged with this Florentine moneylender, I understand.'

'I did hardly anything.'

'Even so, Roger was in my parlour discussing sopracorpo contracts the other day and rubbing his hands at the fat profit he's making. I gather we might benefit as well. His lady's *enceinte* by the way. A baby should test his mettle.'

The prioress pulled off a few leaves of *love-lies-bleeding*. The bright flowers of *heart's ease* grew beside it.

'Interesting planting,' she observed. 'We have my predecessor to thank for that.' She turned to Hildegard with a kind smile. 'Remember, Sister, heartsease outlasts everything else.'

As ever at peace with herself, the prioress gestured towards the archers in the orchard. 'Tell them they certainly scare me.' She left.

The sound of distant laughter floated through the trees.

He was off on pilgrimage then. And no word.

Hildegard took out the faded kerchief and fingered the embroidery of small blue flowers.

Courage.

It was all she had left.

The battlements were wreathed in a sea mist curling like smoke over the grey stones and shrouding the huddled rooves of Scarborough from sight. The visitor, wearing scarlet velvet and a ring with the crossed keys of St Peter embossed on it, had been riding hard from York. Now he strode into the hall, flinging his cloak to a waiting servant, and demanding, 'Where is he?'

At his voice a tall, languid knight emerged from a chamber off the main hall. 'Say nothing, your grace.' He made a perfunctory flourish. 'We shall continue to hunt these peasants with their seditious writings. Entertain no doubts.'

'You've made a poor showing of it so far,' the visitor observed mildly.

'Ever vigilant, your grace. The hounds of God never rest.'

Wine was brought. The two men settled down to discuss recent events in the county in greater detail. Outside came the incessant battering of the sea against the foundations of the castle rock.

Glossary

chaperon	fourteenth-century capuchon, a hood or cowl often of fantastic shape
char	covered passenger vehicle giving us the word char-a-banc
Cistercian	monastic order founded in 1098 in Citeaux, France (Roman town Cistercium). Established in England by twelfth-century and became successful international traders in English wool, especially in the Yorkshire abbeys of Fountains, Rievaulx, Jervaulx and Meaux
coif	close-fitting cap for men and women worn at all levels of society, usually ties under the chin
Conversi	lay brothers and sisters who worked the land and tended the animals
Corrodian	lay person living in a monastery in return for services
dagged	sleeves cut in patterns that often trail to the floor. Seen in many illuminated manuscripts
hauberk	shirt of interleaved steel rings
houppeland	long gown with sleeves either buttoned all the way down or just at the neck, has a high neck often with a pie-crust frill, worn by both men and women.
kennet	medieval breed of terrier
kirtle	loose gown or tunic
(k)naker	small drum worn on the belt
liripipe	long point on a hood that could hang down the back or be coiled up round the head like a turban
lymer	medieval stag hound bred to hunt in silence
mazer	hardwood drinking bowl, often ornately carved
palfrey	saddle horse, especially for women
rebec	stringed and bowed musical instrument
reliquary	container for holy relics
sacristan	church official with responsibility for movables such as sacred vessels and vestments
scrip	leather bag worn on the belt used for coins, herbal remedies and so forth
shawm	medieval woodwind instrument like an oboe
vair	squirrel fur, sometimes called miniver

Timeline

1338–1453	Hundred Years' War between England and France.
1348–9	Black Death kills nearly half the population of Europe.
1377	Richard of Bordeaux (son of the Black Prince and the Fair Maid of Kent) is crowned, aged 10, as King Richard II of England
1378	Papal Schism. Two rival popes, one in Rome, one in Avignon, divide Europe.
1381	Social upheaval and the imposition of the third poll tax leads to the Peoples' Revolt. It is brutally repressed.
1382	King Richard, now 15, marries Anne, 16, sister of the King of Bohemia. Wyclif's 'bible' appears in English.
1383	The Oxford free-thinkers are outlawed. The pope calls for excommunication. Flanders, essential for England's wool trade, falls under the control of the count of Mâle in alliance with the duke of Burgundy. The Flemish weavers are put to the sword.
1385	With his uncle, John of Gaunt, Richard leads an expedition into Scotland. In August his mother, Princes Joan of Kent, dies of a broken heart when Richard's half-brother is accused of murder and Richard is forced to banish him.